A BODY IN
BELMONT
HARBOR

A *PAUL WHELAN* MYSTERY

T0165727

MICHAEL
RALEIGH

DIVERSIONBOOKS

Also by Michael Raleigh

Paul Whelan Mysteries
Death in Uptown
The Maxwell Street Blues
Killer on Argyle Street
The Riverview Murders

Diversion Books
A Division of Diversion Publishing Corp.
443 Park Avenue South, Suite 1008
New York, New York 10016
www.DiversionBooks.com

For more information, email info@diversionbooks.com

First Diversion Books edition February 2015.
Print ISBN: 978-1-62681-764-7
eBook ISBN: 978-1-62681-620-6

For my wife, Katherine—this, and every line I write.

PROLOGUE

CHICAGO, SUMMER 1984

He looked nervously back in the direction of the parking lot behind the Belmont Yacht Club but couldn't see his car. The yacht club was dark and there was no moon, and the closest light, a few feet to his left, had gone out, so he found himself in nearly total darkness. He didn't like it, but this was where he'd been told to wait. The wind was beginning to pick up from across the vast, dark expanse of Lake Michigan, and the boats in Belmont Harbor rocked in the choppy water. He could just make out the white forest of masts swaying with the wave action. He could hear the gentle clanging noises of boats on moving water, rigging slapping against masts and hulls thudding dully against buoys and anchor cables. They were alien noises, a world outside his own, and he didn't like any of it. But these were the things you had to do to pull off a big one.

He craned back again to look for his car, the only car in the yacht club lot, but he couldn't see it. He was as worried about the car as anything else—a dream of a car, a yacht on wheels, actually, like these fat white things rocking and bobbing on the waves. *His* yacht. He smiled at the thought and walked a few feet to the south until he could see just the gleam of a distant street lamp on the gentle curve of his trunk. It was still there, his yacht, a cream-colored Lincoln Mark IV less than three months out of the showroom. And loaded, loaded with everything he'd ever wanted to put into a car. A "pimpmobile," somebody had called it. Okay, so what? He was in love with the car, thought more about the car than he thought about any woman or even any of his business dealings. The car told people things about him, told them who they were dealing with. He looked out on the water in what he presumed was the general direction of the boat he was waiting for. This guy on the boat, he had money, all right, all these guys had money, but not the street smarts to go with it, none of them did. The car told people like this that they were dealing with somebody now, somebody not to be jerked around.

Pleased with this knowledge, he lit a cigarette and continued to pace. Gradually his eyes grew accustomed to the darkness and he could make out individual boats, and then he thought he could see the one he was looking for. It was a big cabin cruiser, not the biggest boat in the harbor, because a couple of these other boats were really monsters, but he'd seen the boat by day, a big, sleek one with a bright blue hull and light blue superstructure. The boat was dark, as he had expected, and he smiled and took one last puff and then tossed his cigarette in a high arc out into the water.

Of course the boat was dark. There wouldn't be anyone out on the boat yet; getting here an hour before the appointment was a pain in the ass, but it would be worth it. He'd be here, in place and ready, and would be watching when the other man showed up. Then they were supposed to have a meeting out on the boat. Screw that, he thought.

The wind was beginning to chill him for the first time all day, and he wanted this guy to show up, wanted to get down to business. He reminded himself that there was a payoff to all this, a pretty sweet payoff. He was going to take this guy down, this guy with his fancy boat and his habit and his money. The woman had dropped the whole thing into his lap and he wasn't going to let it get away from him. He thought about the woman. A little bit of a woman, skinny, actually, but a lot of style. Money, too. Money and style. What a combination. He shivered slightly and decided to take another look at his car.

There was a slight noise, a rustling behind him, and as he turned to look he became aware of movement, movement toward him. He squinted and the man he had been waiting for stepped toward him and reached him in two quick steps. He noticed the man's raspy breathing, as if he'd exerted himself, and noted the high, bald dome of the man's head. The man was shirtless, he could see now, and he seemed to be...wet. He forced a smile and was about to say something when the man's arm moved up in a short, hard arc. The man's arm struck him in the middle of his stomach and drove the breath out of him. There was a sharp pain in his stomach and he heard himself gasp and then he seemed to be having difficulty breathing, and as his legs came out from under him he saw the look in the bald man's eyes. A nervous look. Nervous, yes, but on top of it.

ONE

There were two patrol cars, both on the sidewalk, an ambulance that would not be needed, and a dark, late-model car carrying a couple of park supervisors from the Chicago Park District. A bright, hot morning and the park was alive, so the commotion had already attracted a small crowd of joggers and fishermen and sunbathers and a handful of the people who spend their days sitting on park benches. A gray Caprice drove up the cinder bridle path from the direction of Belmont. From the other direction a pair of young women on horseback came trotting down the jogging path that had replaced the old black-cinder bridle path. The Caprice came to a rolling stop and the driver hit his horn. The girls reined their mounts in and one of them yelled something at the driver. He hit the horn again and thrust a heavy crewcut head out the window, flashing a badge. The girl made a gesture toward the path and said something more to the man in the car, and then the two riders let the Caprice drive between them. The car sped up for a few feet, made a sharp, sudden turn, crossed the sidewalk, and pulled up behind one of the squad cars.

A dark, young, good-looking man in a neon-yellow knit shirt emerged from the Caprice, unstuck the shirt from his back, ran a comb through his thick hair, and walked slowly toward the scene. A moment later the driver emerged, moving slowly and hitching up his pants as he walked. This man was tall and heavyset, with a florid complexion and a nose a shade darker. He wore a blue short-sleeved shirt over a crew-neck T-shirt and blue-and-green plaid pants. A few heads turned to watch him and a couple of young men smiled at his pants. The heavy man stopped, looked at his audience for a moment, and then blew his nose into a bandanna handkerchief. When he was done he rubbed his nose and approached the other squad cars.

A green cyclone fence ran around the harbor and he walked up to the fence and leaned on it. About six feet below him was a narrow expanse of sand, wet from the action of the waves and dotted with cans, discarded paper cups, an old tire, and what appeared to be a shirt. And on the sand lay a body, completely uncovered but with pockets of sand still clinging to the hollows, the eyes, the wrinkles and folds in skin and clothing, the hair. The younger man stood a few feet away looking down at the body, and between them, a short ladder had been set up against the fence from the little beach. There were four men down on the sand around the body and the heavyset man looked at them and then at his partner.

"I hate fucking ladders."

The younger man shrugged. "You want to wait up here till they bring him up?"

"That a joke?"

The younger man looked confused. "No, it's not a joke. I just thought, if you didn't…"

The heavyset man shook his head. "Body's down there, right? That's where we go. How you gonna find anything out if you wait till they bring him up, huh? You look at a corpse later, you miss a hundred things. You got to examine the body—"

"In situ."

The older man looked at him without saying anything.

"I wasn't trying to show you up, Al, I was just—"

"Finishing my sentence for me. Thanks. Yeah, we got to look at the body *in situ*." He shook his head irritably and put one foot up on the fence. As he boosted himself over onto the top rung of the ladder, his partner spoke again.

"Just thought you might want to wait up here."

The heavyset man grinned maliciously. "No, you just thought maybe I couldn't climb a fence." And with that, he pushed himself out from the fence and dropped down onto the sand.

Shaking his head, the younger man climbed onto the fence

and vaulted down alongside.

The big man nodded to the two uniformed officers, looked briefly at the park district workers leaning on shovels, and walked over to a gray-haired man in a white sergeant's shirt.

"Hello, Michaeleen."

"Hi, Al."

"Whatcha got here?"

"Dead person."

"That's exactly what I was gonna suggest." The heavyset man laughed and the sergeant cackled with him.

"So who's this young fella followin' you around? Bodyguard?"

"This is my new partner." He turned and looked at the younger man for a moment and his smile drooped. "This is Rick Landini. Landini, this is Sergeant Michael Shea, once the scourge of the city but now gone to fat, so they give 'im a white shirt and made him a sergeant."

Sergeant Shea laughed and Landini held out his hand. They shook and the older cop inclined his head toward the heavyset man.

"I bet they assigned you to Bauman to keep him out of trouble. Tough assignment, young fella. His last two partners had to be put out to pasture."

"That's what I heard, too." Landini tried not to smile.

"See, Al? He's been briefed. Everybody knows about you, 'bout how you gave your partner ulcers."

"Ah, bullshit. They gimme partners that're ready for the home. And Rooney was born with gastritis." Bauman looked at the other men standing around watching them. "Hey, all these young guys are gonna think we stand around pullin' on ourselves all day. Let's have a look at the deceased."

He went over to the corpse. Landini followed him and the others moved in closer.

Bauman got down onto his haunches and stared at the dead man for a long moment. The face was dark and sharp featured, high cheekboned and thin. The dead man had worn a thin mustache carefully trimmed and a tiny triangle of beard just below his lower lip. The detective held the dead man's sport coat open with two fingers and examined the torso. The shirtfront was stained brownish red, and after a moment the detective made little pointing motions toward the dead man's chest, lower abdomen, and right side.

"Three wounds?" Landini asked.

Bauman nodded. He looked at the dead man's face again, studied the body, shook his head. Then he touched the man's forehead with his fingertips, quickly but gently.

"What's…what was that, Al?"

Bauman shrugged and looked around at the little circle of faces watching him.

"Just something I do. Don't worry about it."

"What'd you do?"

"Somebody should always touch a dead man, that's all."

"Oh," Landini said, and his face showed confusion.

"Don't think about it, Landini, all right?" Bauman's face reddened. "It's a fucking personal…whaddyacallit? It's an idiosyncrasy. All right?"

Landini nodded. Sergeant Shea came closer.

"Got any ideas?"

Bauman nodded. "Yeah. I think this is that guy we're lookin' for, goes with the Lincoln we found in the parking lot Friday."

"Nothing on the car yet, right?" Shea asked.

"No. Registered to some guy that don't exist. Tell you something else. Somebody did a fucking sloppy job of sticking him."

"He's cut up pretty bad," Landini said.

Bauman ignored him. "Shit, look at this guy." He reached down inside the dead man's collar and pulled out a heavy gold chain. "Lookit this. You and me, we can't touch jewelry like this." He noticed the narrow gold chain gleaming from his partner's throat. "All right, I can't afford a chain like this. Probably got rings and shit, too." He turned the corpse's wrist slightly and a heavy emerald and gold ring turned up. He laughed. "I think we can rule out robbery." He reached under the man's body, then felt around inside the jacket. "No wallet, though."

"A hit?" Shea asked.

Bauman shook his head. "No. This is amateur night here. Somebody wasn't sure how you kill somebody with a knife, so he stuck him all over the place. Oops, what do we got here?" He leaned over and pried at the man's mouth with his fingers. A piece of plastic wrap came out, just the corner. There was something white wrapped in the plastic but Bauman didn't bother to pull the entire package out. He looked up at Landini.

"I think what we got here, my lad, is a business transaction that went sour. I think this here is a businessman and his customer had a complaint about the service or, from the looks of it, the product. That's what I think."

Sergeant Shea laughed and looked around at the other cops. "Ah, he's a good one, my pal Albert. What else can you tell us, Al? This is like TV."

Bauman shrugged. "I don't know for sure, but I'd say he's been dead a couple, three days. Face is startin' to bloat up. And he probably wasn't killed here. Dumped here."

"How can you tell that?" Landini asked.

"I can't, but it don't figure. What would he be doin' standin' around on this fucking little sandbar?"

Landini tilted his head up toward the sidewalk. "Got killed there, dropped over the railing, then the guy just hopped down here and covered him up."

"Not bad. But they found a pool of blood up there closer to the yacht club, remember? Lotta blood. That's where I think this guy got killed." He fingered the dead man's shirt. "And I can tell you I wouldn't like this guy. I don't like nobody that wears silk shirts." He shot a look at Landini and laughed when the younger man refused to meet his eyes.

Bauman winked at Shea. "You got silk shirts, Landini?"

"My chick bought me a couple. From France. She went there last year with her girlfriends." He looked around and attempted nonchalance.

Bauman raised an eyebrow. "Oh, they're from France. Well, that's different. Hey, Shea, I got a partner that wears silk shirts from France. I thought we were still at war with France, no?"

Shea shook his head. "No, no. Not a bad idea, though. Be a short war. Nobody'd get hurt."

Bauman looked at his partner and shook his head. "Silk shirts from France. I'm a dinosaur."

"That part's true, Al."

Bauman looked again at the corpse. The dead man's trousers were heavily wrinkled but expensive looking, cream colored and fashionably baggy. He looked down at the man's feet.

"See there? Ankles and feet are all swollen. Nice shoes, though." He looked up at Shea. "I'm gonna take the shoes, all right?"

Landini blinked. "Al, you can't—" He caught himself but it was too late.

Detective Albert Bauman looked at him and roared, a great, red-faced laugh, and Shea and the other cops joined him.

When he could get his breath again Bauman nodded toward the dead man.

"I know it's just my own prejudice here, the clothes and all, but I got a strong hunch this here was not a successful merchant, you know what I'm sayin'? This here was a hood. Either that or a rock star," he said and winked at Sergeant Shea.

Bauman studied the swollen features for a moment and then nodded.

"You're thinkin' again, Albert. Whatcha got?"

Bauman looked up at him with a slight smile. "I think I know who this guy is."

TWO

Paul Whelan sat down on his front porch, set a cup of coffee down on the top stair, and unrolled his newspaper. He'd be going off to work later, in time for a 9:30 appointment, but now he sat and watched others go off to work and took the time to read his paper.

It was Monday morning, and according to the *Sun-Times* the city was reeling under a massive invasion of pharmacists, thousands upon thousands of pharmacists, from all the states in the union and the wind's twelve quarters, all gathered ostensibly to review pharmaceutical research and developments, to listen to scholarly papers on pharmacy, and to offer their wisdom to their colleagues. In reality eleven thousand men in white smocks had descended upon an unsuspecting metropolis in the dog days of summer, overrunning the city's defenses, mobbing its restaurants and saloons, taxing its hotel capacity and the patience of its police, and annoying its women.

The *Sun-Times* carried an account of a Rush Street brawl involving a half dozen of these errant druggists, the arrest of an Ohio pharmacist in the women's room of the Drake Hotel, and the successful rescue by Engine Company No. 26 of a pharmacist from Boston who had been overserved by several taverns and found himself standing on the fifth-floor windowsill of a friend's hotel room.

"Oh, good," Whelan said. "A convention, life blood of the city."

He sipped his coffee and glanced at the box score of the Cubs game. Still in first place, against all the sportswriters' predictions, against all the laws of nature and the wisdom of fan tradition. Tomorrow night the amiable boys from Wrigley would

15

open a three-game series in Shea Stadium against the unholy Mets, the universally loathed Mets, the only team in all of sports whose name began with the word "hated." And if this were to be like other seasons, tomorrow night would be the beginning of the end, the start of the swoon. It was August 1 and the Cubs were about to play the Mets. To a true Cubs fan, it was always August and the opponent was always the Mets.

He heard a noise on the left, turned his head slightly, and saw the wrinkled, haggard face of Mrs. Cuehlo. The old woman stared at him for a moment, then slammed the door, and for the only time since he'd known her, Whelan felt sorry for her. Mrs. Cuehlo was in mourning for her cat, and suffused in every pore of her ancient being with hatred for Whelan, whom she believed somehow responsible for the animal's untimely death under the wheels of an ice-cream truck. And while it was true that Whelan had loathed the animal and been caught several times in the act of throwing stones at it to drive it from his garden, he hadn't yet stooped to killing animals. Not even that one.

The brown Chevy returned, slowed down when it reached the house across the street from Whelan's, then laid rubber and tore off toward Lawrence. Same four inside: an old guy driving, a heavyset one in the shotgun seat, two teenagers in the back. No license plate, muffler tied on with rope, rust holes everywhere you could have rust on a car, and a Confederate flag decal on the rear bumper.

They were interested in the new residents across the street, a married couple. The husband was black and the wife was white, and these four in the beater seemed to have a problem with that. They weren't local. Only outsiders would think anything of a mixed couple in Uptown, and there had been rumors when the couple moved in that they'd experienced racial harassment in another neighborhood. Whelan wondered if this was just a continuation of their earlier trouble. This was the fifth time in three days that the Chevy had visited Malden. Several times the car had appeared late at night, and Whelan saw trouble coming.

* * *

He walked east on Lawrence past the dark gray walls of St. Boniface Cemetery, grabbed a cup of coffee from the smoky little diner under the El tracks, and went to the door of his office building. He paused a moment to study the street—the storefront that had once housed his beloved Persian A & W was still vacant, the marquee of the Aragon Ballroom promised more boxing, and there was already a collection of men standing outside the pool hall on the corner.

He turned to go inside his office building and had to step over an old man sleeping, sitting up, against the doorjamb. The man didn't stir and Whelan quickly and deftly touched the man's throat. There was a pulse.

Well, that's a start, he told himself.

He trotted up the dark stairwell, opened his office door, and sucked in a lungful of stale, hot air. There was no mail yet. He walked across the room, opened both windows, and thought he felt a slight stirring in the air. Then he sat down to wait.

Twenty-five minutes later she arrived. She was late, and he would've bet the rent on it—it fit with the phone voice and the grammar and all the other baggage that went with them. She stood in his doorway as though deciding whether to come in. She was just like her voice, this woman, but prettier than he'd envisioned, quite a bit prettier, and he was conscious of the heat and the smallness of the office, of the exhaust and street noises coming in the window, and of his own clothes, for this was the type of woman who'd make you conscious of your clothes.

"Mr. Whelan," she said, and it wasn't a question.

"Morning. Have a seat, Mrs. Fairs."

He came around the desk to pull out a chair for her, and she looked down at it before sitting. He went back to his chair and sat. She gave a short shake of her head when he asked if she wanted coffee.

Janice Fairs was a short, slender woman in her early thirties, with frosted brown hair pulled back, very pale blue eyes, high, sharp cheekbones, and fair, almost translucent skin that gave her an ascetic look. She looked at him calmly and the bottom half of her face smiled. She wore a gray business suit and a cream-colored blouse and there wasn't a hair, not a molecule of her existence, that was out of place. In her world it probably wasn't even hot. She tilted her head slightly, looking at his loose cotton shirt.

"A *guayabera*, isn't it?"

"Right."

"Is that because of the location of your office?" Perfect eyebrows went up in question. "I mean because of the, ah, Latin population?"

"No. I just like cotton shirts. And if I wanted to look like my neighbors up here I'd have to wear something different every day. Something Vietnamese today, something Nigerian tomorrow, something from the Tennessee hills on Friday."

She nodded and looked around the room. "Are you aware that there is a man lying unconscious on your doorstep outside?"

"Sure," he said, and decided to let her run with it.

She decided not to. "You work in an interesting area, Mr. Whelan."

"I live not far from here. My parents' home. I didn't have the heart to sell it." He realized that that didn't explain an office in Uptown.

"You live up here?"

"Lot of folks do." She was about to comment but he hit her with, "The Governor is purchasing a large home two blocks from mine. Mr. Lobster Jim Thompson's going to rehab it, and then his whole block will be gentrified and my neighborhood will be respectable. And no shellfish on this side of town will be safe."

Mrs. Fairs seemed to be weighing several comments.

"Interesting," was all she said.

"You said on the phone that you'd gotten my name from a 'reputable source.' May I ask who referred you to me?"

She shrugged. "It wasn't a direct referral. A friend of my family is a police officer in Lake Forest. He has a summer home on Lake Geneva. Near mine."

"Police work must pay better in Lake Forest."

"He's the deputy chief. His name is Myers." She cocked

an eyebrow.

"And he was my watch commander in ancient times. We didn't much like each other."

She shrugged. "Your old war stories are irrelevant, Mr. Whelan. What matters is that he recommended you. He told me that you were honest and good at what you do."

"But I know Fred Myers, and that's not all he told you."

"No. He told me that you are stubborn and unnecessarily independent, a born lone wolf and proud of it, and that some of these qualities are unfortunate in a police officer. You couldn't, ah, 'work in harness' is the way he put it. He said you have a high opinion of your own intelligence and that you dress and think like a hippie."

"He thinks anybody who hasn't served in the marines is a hippie. He thinks Kennedy was a hippie, probably Nixon, too. So, with all these glowing references, you still came to see me."

"As I've already told you, these old conflicts have nothing to do with me, or with what I need you to do. He also said that you never, ever let anything go." She sat back and stared. He decided he wanted a cigarette but he wasn't going to light up yet. After a moment she made a little shrug and went digging around in her tiny gray handbag for a cigarette. When she came up with one, he leaned over and lit it with a Zippo, then took one out of his own pack.

They traded little gusts of smoke and he noticed that she puffed at hers a lot harder than he did. When the air had gone a comfortable cloudy gray he put his cigarette in the ashtray between them and sat back.

"So…would you like to tell me what you want done?"

"Of course." She blew smoke with a sharp upward jerk of her head. "It is in the nature of surveillance. I want you to perform surveillance on someone."

"Why?"

"I require…certain information on this person."

"Who?"

"The man I believe responsible for my husband's death."

"Are we…are you suggesting something here?"

She raised her eyebrows again and surprised him with a smile, a sincere one this time, and it made her look ten years younger and twelve times more attractive.

"'Suggesting,' Mr. Whelan? How charming. Yes, we most certainly are suggesting something." The smile went underground and she leaned forward, and the look in the blue eyes was the one that makes the servants jump. "We're suggesting that my husband was murdered by the person I want followed."

He thought for a moment about the various ways to couch the necessary and usually offensive questions. "There are a number of ways to…"

She made a hissing sound and waved irritably in the air, as if dispersing the smoke. "My husband's death was ruled a suicide. Were you going to refer me to 'normal channels'?" She let her voice go down low, in an imitation of a cop speaking the universal language of cops.

"There was a complete investigation of my husband's death, Mr. Whelan, but it was over before it started. He was killed on his boat. Someone covered it with gasoline and then torched it, with him on it. And it was determined that he did it. Phil was seen on the boat shortly before the accident. This happened exactly two years ago this weekend."

He nodded and waited. He could see the end of this one already, understood the motivation and the way a person could misread the evidence and refuse to see the proof.

She went into the little bag again and extracted a photograph. It wasn't a recent picture and it had been a lousy processing job, so that the color was garish, unnatural, but in it a pair of good-looking young men stood arm in arm in front of a twenty-five- or thirty-foot boat. The boat's name, *The High Pair*, was painted across the stern in bright blue lettering.

"The man on the right, the bigger one, is Phil. My husband. The other man is his friend and business partner, Rich Vosic. I think Rich had my husband killed."

He began to shake his head over the poor quality and the age of the picture. "Mrs. Fairs, this really wouldn't be much…"

She held up one hand and then took out another picture. It

had obviously been clipped from a larger picture, and showed a good-looking blond man sipping from a Styrofoam cup and smiling.

"The other one was taken when they were very young and thought they had the whole world figured out." She nodded as she handed Whelan the new picture. "That one's a little more recent. He's about five nine and he weighs about one hundred seventy pounds. It's a good likeness."

"Why?" He kept his face passive.

"Why what? Why did he do it, do you mean?"

"No. Motive doesn't concern me. Why do you suspect his partner, and why do you think it was murder when the police think it was suicide?"

She stiffened. "You really don't sound particularly interested in this, Mr. Whelan."

"What I'm not interested in is running around on a snipe hunt, Mrs. Fairs. I mean, have you discussed your ideas with the police?"

"Of course I have. Well, no, no, that's not true. There was no discussion. They had their preconceived notions of what happened and they didn't pay any attention to me whatsoever. Besides, Mr. Whelan, I was just a pampered suburban housewife—and after I'd identified the body, a hysterical suburban housewife—whose husband happened to die in Chicago waters. An inconvenience, I suppose. And they saw a convenient way to wrap it up, one more case solved in a very efficient day's work."

"I assume they found evidence that this was a suicide."

He could see her begin to shake her head and watched the visible struggle between impulses. Then she sighed and nodded. "There was a note, of sorts. I mean, they believed it was a note. It was…it could have been anything, it was just a scrap of paper with some words on it. It must have been part of something else. It was on his desk with some of his papers."

"And what did it say?"

"'It's all out of control.'" She shrugged. "That was it, the whole thing. The whole 'message.' 'It's all out of control.'"

"Any idea what it meant?"

"No. So they took that little scrap of paper and…and bits and pieces of things and came up with suicide."

"Couldn't it have been?"

"No. No, it couldn't have been," and she favored him with the look that she probably saved for clumsy waiters.

"Why not? All right, that's not a fair question. What factors in his life might lead someone to believe your husband would consider suicide?"

She made a shrug of pure stubbornness and a little wave of her hand. He noticed that the cigarette was a long, slim column of ash now. She caught his glance and tapped the ash into his ashtray.

"Excuse me. He was a businessman, so of course there would be money worries at times, and he was a little concerned over the stability of his business ventures."

"What business was he in?"

"My husband and Rich Vosic had a computer software company. That was the primary source of income, and there were other investments and interests. There was perhaps a bit of…of overextension."

"Such as?"

"You mean you want—"

"I mean I want it in English, Mrs. Fairs."

"They expanded their interests rapidly, bought property, too much property, and with so much of their assets tied up as collateral, there was bound to be some trouble."

"What kind of property?"

"All sorts of things. A couple of small commercial properties, a twenty-two-unit apartment building, and…other things. And there was concern that their investments weren't turning a profit as quickly as they'd hoped, but not overmuch. After all, Phil had been in debt before. But they had wonderful credit, Mr. Whelan, and mostly because of Phil's ability to win people over to his way of thinking. Although…I suppose it's only fair to give some of the credit to Rich Vosic. He was what I believe is known as a 'front man'—very charming, a marvelous way with people."

"Anyone in particular that they were into for a great deal of money?"

She hesitated. "They had a number of debtors, Mr. Whelan."

"Besides the usual bank loans—anybody who made large personal loans?"

She sighed. "They owed a large sum to a mortgage banker named Victor Tabor. The loan was secured, Mr. Whelan."

"All right. So what have we got? A lot of investments and more mortgage than most people are comfortable with."

She nodded. "They both spent freely, and I'm sure anyone would say too freely, but the money was there. Spending wasn't the problem. There were other things that didn't help, of course."

"He was a drinker?"

"No. But he gambled. He took risks with his...with our money."

"You mean on business, or real gambling?"

"Real gambling."

"He gambled heavily?"

"Yes. Sometimes he made a lot of money at it and other times he lost quite a lot. He didn't have a problem with it, though."

No, they never have a problem with it. He shook his head. "Well, Mrs. Fairs, problem or not, to gamble on that scale you have to come into contact with people that are best left in the holes they live in."

Mrs. Fairs seemed on the verge of saying something important and then caught herself. She shook her head. "But none of that would have damaged the company as severely as it was."

"No? Seems like enough to sink just about anybody's boat to me. Overspending, overextension of their resources, a good deal of borrowing, and large-scale gambling. Yeah, that would just about do it."

"But I'm telling you that it wasn't, Mr. Whelan. I know this for a fact." Spots of red appeared in her cheeks and Whelan thought she might be just a few seconds away from losing her temper.

"I was just telling you how it seemed to me. Go on, please."

"There were other things, Mr. Whelan. They made a major mistake—at least Phil did. Rich…I think Rich knew exactly what he was doing all along. It was a hiring mistake. They took on an accountant, a man Rich found, named George Brister. A very strange man."

"How so?"

"Oh, in many ways. A very unstable person. A very disquieting person as well. He was a big, hulking man, first of all—bigger than Phil, and my husband wasn't small. And he had very dark eyes, set close together and very piercing. He seemed to fix his eyes on you and keep them there, long after it was polite or even normal. I think he realized he was doing it and that it made people uncomfortable. And he said almost nothing, answered people with one-word answers when asked a question. The first time I met him I was very uncomfortable around him, and there was no reason for me to feel that way. I mean, he was just—"

Just the hired help, Whelan thought.

"—just another man working for High Pair Enterprises."

"That was the name of the company? Same as the boat?"

"Yes." She allowed herself a sad little smile. "It was how Phil always thought of himself and Rich, the High Pair. It also said that they were…equals, a team, and that Rich was just as responsible for their rapid growth as he himself was. He was a generous man, my husband, and quick to accept the ideas of others, and that is why he hired George Brister, in spite of everything."

"What 'everything' are we talking about here? A police record or something like that?"

"Brister was…unstable, as I said."

"So are the rest of us, more or less. What were his particular symptoms?"

"He was an alcoholic. You could tell it from his resume and references, even though nowadays they try to dress it up or camouflage it to avoid lawsuits. He was a drunk."

"But that's no reason…"

She leaned forward, eyes glittering. She looked ready to pounce. "There were rumors about him. About his instability, about the way he kept the books. He had been fired from several positions. Phil didn't like the whole situation but let Rich talk him into hiring Brister. Phil decided to give Brister a chance, Mr. Whelan, and inside of a year George Brister had embezzled hundreds of thousands of dollars from company accounts."

"Whoa, hold on a minute, Mrs. Fairs. How could an accountant working for a small company get away with something like this without a partner noticing?"

She seemed to sag. She looked out the window and shook her head and then decided to go fishing for another cigarette. When she seemed to be having trouble locating one, he leaned forward and shook one up from his pack, then lit it for her.

"They made it easy for him, Mr. Whelan. They had him making all kinds of…of dummy transactions. They even had a second ledger to use for audits when they went in for another loan. Brister got to play all the games he wanted with their numbers, and he had no trouble at all taking money out."

"I see."

She gave him a cynical smile. "Oh, you haven't heard anything yet." She nodded slowly. "He took out hundreds of thousands and then he left. Right about the time things were really beginning to come apart for the company. I think it's what put everything, you know…"

"Over the top? Yeah, I bet it did. But you implied a couple of minutes ago that Rich Vosic was involved in this, that he 'knew what he was doing' when he hired Brister."

"It was his idea. And the way it all turned out, I think it's obvious he was behind it." She took a puff on her cigarette.

Whelan thought for a moment and then said, "Do we know whether he really left town or did he go on a prolonged bender? Did he clear out his bank accounts, sublet his apartment, cut off his utilities?"

She gave him an odd look and the hint of a smile appeared around her lips. "You have experience in these things."

"It's what I do."

"Well, Brister did some of the things you mentioned, but not everything. The police did look into that but said there was no evidence that Brister had anything to do with my husband's 'suicide' other than being a factor in it. They said he closed his bank accounts and took the money out in cash."

"Large amounts or small, did they say?"

"Small. They said there was nothing out of the ordinary in his bank records, no large deposits or withdrawals."

"Could've had other accounts. What else?"

"Well, Phil told me he'd heard that Brister might be relocating to the coast. Seattle. That's where he was from originally."

"Is there any evidence that that's where he went?"

"Yes." The blue eyes took on a little color now and Mrs. Fairs nodded in satisfaction. "He bought a one-way ticket. First class," she added as though it was significant.

"And were the police able to track him down in Seattle?"

"Phil found out about the plane ticket himself. The police were never called in about the money. Rich never pressed any charges against Brister." She smiled slightly. "It was very nicely done; I'm sure Phil wouldn't have been able to do anything anyway. If he'd lived."

Whelan nodded. "I guess not. They had books they couldn't hold up to the light and they were saving a few bucks from Uncle." There was a certain justice to it, a perverse beauty—a pair of well-heeled high rollers conning dozens of underwriters and investors and then an accountant cleaning them out.

"But none of this really points very convincingly to Rich Vosic as the man behind the swindle."

She gave him a long look intended to work as a dramatic pause. "Two years after my husband's death, Rich Vosic has a small empire going, Mr. Whelan."

"So what? You've already told me what a bright guy he was, and he's had two years—careers are made and undone in ten minutes at the stock exchange, Mrs. Fairs. There's nothing surprising about him making it again."

"With what credit, Mr. Whelan? With what money? George

Brister left the company with almost nothing in the way of ready cash, and the firm had nothing that wasn't already tied up in collateral. No money, no credit, and not much of a reputation after word got out about Phil's alleged suicide and Brister's getaway."

"I don't claim to understand business, Mrs. Fairs."

She puffed at her cigarette and gave him the look of someone who hasn't played a hole card yet.

"Mr. Whelan, Rich Vosic owns another software company, he owns an enormous house in Lincoln Park, one in Melrose Park, a condominium on the Gold Coast, buildings in several neighborhoods undergoing gentrification, and a very large Rush Street bar. On paper he owns these things in partnership with his younger brother, but Rich Vosic is the owner of everything. *Everything*."

"So the banks went along with him."

"No. The banks don't wait for their money, Mr. Whelan. I don't know what he did, but he did something."

"All right, Mrs. Fairs, but if all this stuff is true and Rich Vosic is as dirty as last week's laundry, I'm still looking for a motive. Why would he kill your husband? It couldn't have been for money—doesn't sound like there was much, even before they hired this accountant. And your husband was the one with the connections. So—why?"

She made a noise of exasperation and gave her head a little shake. "Mr. Whelan, their relationship...deteriorated."

He began to shake his head and she leaned forward.

"They hated each other, Mr. Whelan. Do you need more than that? They were the most intense competitors, Mr. Whelan, always had been, even in better times. And when things began to come undone, each one blamed the other. Rich talked about getting out of the partnership and Phil threatened some sort of court action. Does that soothe your logical mind?"

"I'm sorry. It's the way I work. Hatred is a much more solid motive for a killing than financial difficulties. Still..." He thought for a moment. "Okay, then tell me this. Why now? After all this time, why come to me with your suspicions? What else has turned up that would make a difference now?"

She smiled; she'd been waiting for this one. "This." She pulled out a newspaper clipping, took a fast look at it, and then handed it to Whelan.

It was from the preceding Friday's *Tribune* and he recognized it immediately—it recapped an earlier story about the discovery of a body in the sand along the fringe of Belmont Harbor and added that the body had now been identified as that of Henry "Harry" Palm. The article went on to describe Palm as a gambler, drug dealer, and "reputed underworld figure." Whelan allowed himself a smile as he read the article again.

"What's so amusing, Mr. Whelan?"

"It has nothing to do with you, Mrs. Fairs. I was familiar with this gentleman. I busted him once, actually. All his life Harry Palm tried to get into the mob, first in Milwaukee, then here. He was nobody, a punk, a small-timer, and they had no use for him. And here he goes and gets himself killed and some stringer on the *Trib*, probably seeing his first dead body, decides Harry Palm was the genuine article and puts it in his story. All over the western suburbs where these creeps live they're laughing about this. Harry Palm, 'underworld figure.'"

"You knew this man?"

"No. I try not to *know* people like him. He was a runner, Mrs. Fairs. He had a little saloon on Irving and he was a small-time dealer and he ran a small book." He looked at her and smiled. "Ah. And that's how you know him. Phil's gambling. He was your husband's bookie."

She nodded.

"Phil even introduced us once. He had made a good deal of money on a football game, and later that week we were at a party at one of the hotels out by the airport, and this dark-haired man in a loud jacket came up to us, and Phil started laughing and he gave the man a big bear hug and introduced him to me as his bookie. I was so mortified, I could feel people's eyes boring into me."

"I bet it didn't bother Harry."

She smiled slightly. "No, that was surprising. He seemed to

like it. I would have thought…you know, since these people are involved in illegal things…"

"You're right. A genuine gambler or a hood worthy of the name would have taken Phil to the men's room and threatened to punch in his larynx if he didn't shut his mouth. But, as I said, Harry Palm was no big deal. He would have liked it if your husband had described him as a hoodlum. He would've offered his autograph. By the way, was he using the name 'Palm'?"

"No. It was Palmisa."

Whelan allowed himself a quiet chuckle. "He called himself a lot of things. For one thing, he could never decide what ethnic group he wanted to belong to. Called himself 'La Palma' when he wanted to do business with Latins, 'Palmisa' when he thought it would help to sound Italian, and 'Palm' or 'Palmer' when he wanted to be taken for an Anglo, which I believe he was."

"Well, we ran into him several other times. Once, at a Bulls game, he came to our box and he and Phil went off someplace, and when he came back he was absolutely giddy, all flushed and grinning and smelling of liquor, and dropped a roll of fifties into my lap. A little over two thousand dollars, from a bet Phil had placed on an earlier game."

Whelan nodded. Time to play devil's advocate again. "But this is Chicago, Mrs. Fairs, and a lot of people have bookies, and a lot of people are bookies, and there are thousands more waiting to become bookies after the other bookies go into stir or wind up in alleys. There are more bookies than detectives, and probably more bookies than computer software specialists. They're everywhere, you can get a bet down on anything—on when it's going to rain or who the next Pope is going to be, or when the giant pandas are going to mate. I've put a few bucks down here and there."

She leaned forward suddenly, like a hawk diving, and put her hand on his desk.

"Did they find your bookie buried in the sand with knife holes in his body?"

He shook his head slightly and scanned the clipping again. No suspects, no witnesses, and only robbery had been ruled out as a motive. The "motive" was probably the simplest one: Harry had finally pissed somebody off at the wrong moment, had pressed the proper button and gotten himself taken out.

"I can understand what you're thinking, given the association of your husband and Harry Palm, but…we're really talking about two deaths, two years apart, with nothing else to connect them. You must see the problems there are with that."

She shook her head quickly. "There's another connection."

"Show me."

She tapped the clipping. "This man was killed after talking to me." He watched her and waited to force her to come up with more. "I contacted him, Mr. Whelan."

"When?"

"About a month ago, and again about two weeks ago. I saw him in a downtown restaurant where I was attending a dinner party for a friend of my parents, and something made me…I just got up and walked across the room and tapped him on the shoulder. He couldn't place me at first, so he just gave me his, you know, his make-out smile and called me 'baby' a lot. My name meant nothing to him, but when I identified myself as Phil's wife, this little light went on in his eyes and I knew my instincts were right. I knew it. There was something there and that man knew about it. For a second there, Mr. Whelan, that man was afraid of me." She smiled coldly.

"Go ahead."

She made a visible effort at self-control and it was apparent that she thought this was the critical moment in the interview— this was game, set, and match.

"I arranged to talk to him on the phone the following day. He wanted to meet, kept suggesting that we get together for a drink at his, his tavern."

"The King's Palace. On Irving."

"Eventually I got him to talk to me over the phone. I told him what I suspected, and while he didn't come right out and say it, he knew something. He was coy with me. He said he knew Rich but he wouldn't say much else."

No, he wouldn't, Whelan thought. He'd hang onto the

phone for dear life and squeeze it till it turned into money. He'd tell this woman anything she wanted to hear and see if there was a dollar in it for Harry Palm.

"He knew something, Mr. Whelan. And he said Rich still owed him money."

"For what?"

"He didn't say. A gambling debt, I suppose."

Whelan nodded and said nothing. He was imagining this conversation and getting quite a different picture from the one Mrs. Fairs wanted him to have. He saw a cheap, gaudy little hood who knew nothing more about Rich Vosic except that someone wanted to make trouble for him. He would have told her anything to keep the scam going. If she'd told him Jesse James was living in Chicago, Palm would have said, "Yeah, I been thinking that way myself."

"So how did this develop, Mrs. Fairs?"

She stared at him for a moment and then gave her head a little shake. "Mr. Whelan, I know what I was dealing with. He was a nasty little man and he sat on the other end of that phone and fed me a solid line of bullshit. *That's* how it 'developed.' Are you satisfied? But he had something on Rich Vosic. He told me he'd get back to me in a week with something I'd be interested in. I told him I'd call him."

"And then?"

"I contacted him later that week and we met in a restaurant."

"Did he have anything?"

"He was somewhat evasive, as I expected him to be. He was also…he behaved very strangely, he may have been drunk. But he was giddy and his conversation was rather disjointed, and he kept interrupting himself to say things like, 'Lady, things are really getting freaky,' things like that."

He laughed. It was a very accurate rendering of Harry Palm and it took him by surprise. "That's just how he'd talk. Did he seem nervous?"

"Yes, but not frightened, if that's what you mean. He talked as though he'd fallen into something. That's the impression I got."

"A windfall."

"Yes. And he said he thought we could both make a lot of money if I went along with him. If I 'went with the program' was the way he put it."

"And what was Harry's program?"

"He wouldn't say. Just that he was going to 'take these dudes down.' That's what he said."

"'*These dudes*'?" Whelan asked. "Somebody besides Vosic?"

She made a little shake of her head. "I don't know what that meant. At any rate, he asked me what it would be worth to me. I told him it would depend on what he had."

She rooted around in her purse again and pulled out another cigarette. "He said it would cost me money up front but that in the long run I would get my money back five times over…but he needed cash. To grease a few palms."

"You didn't give this guy money, did you?"

"Mr. Whelan, I am accustomed to money and I don't need anyone like you to counsel me on how to spend it. No, I didn't give him anything. He didn't like it, but after hemming and hawing, he finally told me he thought he could prove Rich was a drug dealer. On a large scale." She put the unlit cigarette in her mouth and took it out immediately.

Whelan wanted to laugh at the image of Harry Palm turning in someone else as a pusher. "A dealer. This guy doesn't sound like the type."

She shook her head. "It didn't really seem right, but I decided that perhaps I'd go along with him and see what turned up. So I told him if he could furnish evidence of that, I'd come up with money. So he asked me to meet him and bring money."

"Where and how much?"

"To Antonio's on Rush Street. With ten thousand dollars."

"Let me guess. He called it 'ten K.'"

The ghost of a smile returned to her face. "Yes, he did. And when I told him I didn't have that kind of money, he laughed and said he'd been doing some research on me, too, and that he knew ten thousand would be no trouble for me."

"And is that true?"

She nodded casually. "My father died shortly after... after Phil. He left me a good deal of money and a substantial insurance policy. I have more money now than I did when my husband was alive."

Mrs. Fairs looked at her unlit cigarette again as though noticing it for the first time, and Whelan came up with his Zippo again.

She nodded, puffed at the flame, exhaled smoke, and nodded thanks. "We never had the meeting. I went to the restaurant and he never showed up. I heard nothing from him for almost two weeks and then I came across that." She nodded in the direction of the clipping, then sat back and looked for a reaction.

"Have you told any of this to the police?"

She rolled her eyes, took a hurried puff on the cigarette, and blew smoke without inhaling. "Are you telling me you don't see a connection, or at least a possible connection, between this man's death and my husband's?"

"I'm not saying that at all. I'm saying that there's an ongoing police investigation into this man's death and that any evidence of any kind should go to the police first."

"It went to the police first. I spoke with several people, including one officer whom I talked to after Phil died, and he noted all my information dutifully and said it would be looked into. And you know what that means."

"Probably means somebody will look into it, whether half-heartedly or not. But this is not something I can do for you, Mrs. Fairs. I don't get involved—"

"I'm not asking you to get involved in this man's murder or the police inquiry or whatever you call it, I'm asking you to provide a service. I'm asking you to investigate Rich Vosic, find out about him. And if you learn anything about the other man's death, you can take it to the police."

Whelan turned slightly in his chair and looked out the window to give himself time to think.

"Mr. Whelan?"

"I'm not ignoring you. I'm trying to see an angle of approach to this. I'd need—"

"What?" She'd caught the faint note of promise and leaned forward like a schoolgirl following her lesson.

"Divine guidance, for one thing. That and some luck, and more than anything else, some idea in plain English of what you expect me to do. Knowing, that is, that I won't get involved at all in this Harry Palm thing. Not while it's still an open case. What do you want me to find about Vosic?"

She smiled brightly, a smile for show. "His habits. His associates. His money. Anything that will send him to jail. Follow him for a few days, Mr. Whelan, and if you're as good as you're supposed to be, you'll see something, or you'll notice a pattern. If Rich is a drug dealer, as this man believed, I'm sure you'll be able to determine that. But he's guilty of something, Mr. Whelan, that I'm sure of."

"And if I don't? If there isn't anything?"

She made a little puffing noise. "Oh, I don't think you'll have trouble, Mr. Whelan."

"It's something you should think about."

"I'm not worried about it. Now—should we discuss your fees, Mr. Whelan?" She reached into the handbag again and came out with an elegant gray wallet.

He sighed. "My current rate is two hundred a day plus expenses."

She shook her head sharply. He thought the change that had suddenly come over her was remarkable—now that she was discussing money and service rates and terms, she was calm, relaxed, assured.

"I dislike the small print intensely, Mr. Whelan. I don't get involved in things like expenses and receipts." She looked off at the calendar on the wall, stuck her tongue into her cheek, nodded and looked at him.

"I'll give you three a day and you eat the expenses," she said, and her tone made it clear that this was not a negotiation but a statement of fact.

He shrugged and smiled. "Fine. And let's put a limit on it. Let's say two weeks. If I haven't come up with anything by the end of that time, we'll wrap it up."

"I'm not worried about money, Mr. Whelan."

"I wasn't implying that you were. But I'm sure you aren't in the habit of throwing money away. And you can always hire another investigator at the end of that time if you want."

She nodded and looked around, and it was clear that the prospect bothered her. She nodded again. "All right, Mr. Whelan, two weeks." She opened her wallet and took out a sheaf of crisp new bills, fifties, and laid them on his desk. "One thousand dollars, Mr. Whelan. Your retainer." She raised an eyebrow. "Will this be enough?"

"Of course." Whelan took out a cigarette of his own and lit it. In a fairly barren summer, a thousand bucks wasn't the worst way to start the workday. He told her the kind of information he'd need to go on. She gave him dates and names and numbers. Then she stood, did violence to one final cigarette in his ashtray, and held out her hand.

"Thank you, Mr. Whelan. I appreciate your assistance."

"I'll be in touch. You'll receive regular reports by phone and a written report upon completion. Can I get you a cab or give you a lift somewhere?"

She gave him an appraising look. "I got here under my own power. I should be able to manage."

She left the office and Whelan stood in the doorway and watched her walk toward the stairs. When he went back into the office he was asking himself what he'd gotten into.

THREE

At Area Six headquarters he got a desk sergeant who sounded like a bad tape. He could make out "hello" and "sergeant" and then something else that sounded like "anchovy."

"Hello. I'd like to speak to someone working on the Harry Palm killing."

"Thewhat? Thewhatsir?"

"The body found at Belmont Harbor about a week ago. Who are the detectives working on that one?"

"Whosisplease?"

"My name is Whelan, and I used to work out of Eighteen, and I was at Town Hall for a while, too. I came across some information and I wanted to run it by the guys working on that one."

"All right." The sergeant wheezed into the phone and seemed to slip into a lower gear. "Leave your name and number and I'll have the investigating officers get back to you."

"They're not in now?"

"If they were in, I'd put you through to them, wouldn't I, sir?"

No, he thought, but he said, "Guess so." He gave the sergeant his name again and his phone number and then, before the sergeant could cut him off, thought of something.

"And who's going to be calling me, Sergeant? Who are the officers involved?"

"Detectives Bauman and Landini," the cop said, exhaling.

"Who?"

"Detectives Bauman and Landini," and now sergeant Whateverhisnamewas was irritated.

"Must be getting on to lunchtime, huh, Sarge?"

36

"What?"

"So Bauman got another partner, huh? What, did he kill the last one? What was his name…Schmidt?"

"He went on disability," the sergeant mumbled.

"Just pulling your leg, Sergeant. Have a nice day."

He hung up and looked out onto Lawrence. He shook his head and sighed. "Bauman. And I was having such a nice morning."

It took three calls, but he finally got hold of Fred Myers, now Deputy Chief Myers. The chief wasted no time on pleasantries.

"You're calling about Jan Fairs, right, Whelan?"

"Right. What can you tell me about her husband's death?"

"Nothing to tell. He killed himself. She won't accept it. Same old shit, Whelan. You been there before."

"How solid is the evidence that it was suicide?"

Myers snorted into the phone. "About as solid as it gets, Whelan. The guy was seen torching his own boat."

"She told me he was seen on the boat, but—"

"No, not *on* the boat. *Torching* the boat. Pouring gasoline on the boat, all over it. He killed himself, Whelan, there's no question about that, except in her mind."

"So why did you refer her to a private detective?"

"Why not? Thought she might believe it coming from you. She thinks the police just don't give a shit. Besides which, she's got a hard-on about her husband's partner."

"So I gathered."

"That's what she really wants, Whelan. She wants a piece of that guy Vosic."

"Got any idea why?"

"Sure—he's alive and he's rich. And who knows, maybe he's a crook, but just between you and me, they were both dicking the system around for all it was worth. Her husband was certainly no better than his partner."

"Did you know both of them?"

"Sure. And I wouldn't buy a used car from either of them."

"Phil Fairs seem like the type to commit suicide?"

"He was a cokehead, Whelan. Pretty serious habit, too. Yeah, I think a guy like that, his brain's fried, his whole career starts coming apart, yeah—he might do it. Why not?"

"Well…thanks for the business, anyway."

"Don't mention it," Myers said without any emotion and hung up.

He called his service and Shelley answered, whiskey throat and all.

"Hi, baby. How's tricks?"

"Shelley, it's always a pleasure to hear your professional phone manner. Do you speak to all my clients this way?"

"Only you, babe. Hey, I made an appointment for you with that Ice Maiden, and she didn't complain, did she?"

"Mrs. Fairs? No, but people like that don't complain, Shel, they just rip out your page in the phone book. Listen, I'm ducking out for a while and I'm expecting a call from Detective Bauman."

"Oh, God."

"You remember him, huh? Well, I need to talk to him, so I hope he calls."

"Sure I remember him. 'Dese and dose' and phone manners like a mule skinner. Nice man. I know what he needs, honey."

"Yeah, but are you ready to make that sacrifice?"

"Anything for my country, baby," she laughed.

Whelan told her he'd check back with her later in the day.

"Okay, but you call after six and you'll get Abraham. He's on nights this week."

He sighed. Speaking with Abraham was one of the great burdens of his professional life.

"Okay, Shel. Thanks for the warning."

He walked back home and got his car. It started, and he was impressed—perhaps it was an omen. He drove to Irving and Sheridan and parked a few feet from the corner. Half a block down Irving was Byron's, where a hot dog was still an art form, and he couldn't think of any reason to skip lunch. He ordered two, with all of the wondrous additions and afterthoughts that marked a classic Chicago-style hot dog and consigned imitators to an eternity of mediocrity. When he was finished he thought about having a third but controlled himself with effort, settling instead for a quick cigarette. Then he went back to the corner. Up the street on Sheridan the great gray hulk of the Palacio stuck an empty marquee out at the traffic. Former synagogue, sometime church, occasional movie house, the place was as unpredictable as its neighborhood. Two blocks away in the other direction stood the Festival, another dead movie house, the place where, as a teenager, he'd watched his first strip show. In other neighborhoods the old theaters were snatched up and rehabbed and turned into night clubs and glorified dance halls; in Uptown they sat empty.

The King's Palace was still open for business, still surviving, still offering the same entertainment night after night, year after year, so that the marquee never needed changing: TONIGHT, TWO BIG SHOWS, THE KING'S PALACE PROUDLY PRESENTS, DIRECT FROM LAS VEGAS, THE HIGHTONES.

Whelan shook his head and smiled. When he'd gone off to Vietnam the Hightones had been the nightly act at the King's Palace; when he returned, the Hightones were still there. Through Johnson and Nixon and Ford and Carter and now Reagan, the Hightones came to the King's Palace six nights a week and strutted and sang and mauled the works of songwriters who deserved better, and Whelan had no doubt that ten years from now, after a nuclear holocaust or bombardment by asteroids, the Hightones still would be showing up at the King's to croon to the drunks and pick up a paycheck.

And like its entertainment, the King's Palace itself had now outlived four owners—five, if you counted Harry Palm. In a way it was a sad thing that Harry was dead, for in Harry the King's Palace had found its true soul mate—cheap, jaded, sleazy, and insincere. In the hands of Harry's partner, a former accountant named Hoban, the place might undergo a dangerous transformation, might clean its johns occasionally, get rid of its unique smells, change clientele, and, yes, maybe even hire musicians who could play and sing.

He walked back to the bar and pushed open the door, bracing himself for the smell. It did no good; you can hold your breath only so long, and the smell was waiting for him when he took his next breath. The smell came from the carpet, a dark brown layer of polyester that looked like the pelt of an otter caught in an oil slick and gave off all the odors that make a tavern—stale beer, spilled liquor, ashtrays and cigarette butts, rancid perfume, and vomit. The air conditioner hadn't had time to kick in yet and was doing little more than stir up the odors.

He nodded to the bartender, a young man with long hair worn in a ponytail, and sat down at the bar. The kid plucked at the ugly black tie he was forced to wear, wiped his hands on his pants, and walked over to Whelan.

"Nice and cool in here," Whelan said, checking out the bartender.

The kid nodded curtly and looked at him. The sullen, I'm-just-working-here-till-I-get-a-call-from-my-agent type. Okay. He looked at the kid and then at the other customers, both of them, a pair of guys in sport coats at the tail end of the bar. One was staring at his cigarette and the other seemed to be talking to himself.

"Got any coffee?"

The kid shook his head.

"You speak any English?"

The kid gave him a sarcastic look. "Yeah, I speak English. Is that supposed to be funny or what?"

"I just wondered. Most people speak when they're spoken to. I thought you were from, you know, Pakistan or someplace like that."

"I look like I'm from Pakistan, man?"

"I don't know what they look like, actually. How about a Coke?" The bartender gave him a nasty look and stalked down the bar to the soda gun. He came back with a short Coke, slammed it down on the bar so that some of it spilled over, and looked at Whelan.

"A dollar." He waited for Whelan to object.

Whelan put two singles on the bar. "All yours. Hoban around?"

The kid nodded his head toward the back of the bar and Whelan stifled an impulse to laugh. Just like in the movies. Okay, I'll play, too.

"Anybody with him?" he asked, straight-faced.

The kid shook his head and looked at the two singles. Whelan shoved them toward him.

"Put 'em in your pocket. Cokes ought to be free, anyhow. And listen." He leaned over the bar and looked around furtively. "Anybody comes in looking for me, you didn't see me, all right? Especially cops."

"Cops?" The kid licked his lips and some color crept into his sallow face. In an otherwise unpromising shift, an adventure had materialized.

"Yeah, especially cops. Most especially plainclothes, you understand what I'm saying?"

"Sure. No problem."

"They've probably been crawling out of the woodwork since Harry, right?"

The boy bartender held up two fingers and raised his eyebrows significantly.

Two what? he wondered. Two cops, two visits, two o'clock, two horse in the eighth race? "Two, huh?"

"Just on my shift," the bartender said. "Who knows how many times they been in on other shifts, you know?"

"They got anything yet?"

The kid shrugged. "You really think they give a shit?"

"You didn't like old Harry, huh?"

"I didn't give a shit one way or the other, long as I got paid, okay? He didn't bother me, I didn't bother him. I just gave him his messages. That's all I had to do with him."

"Hoban runs the bar, then?"

"Of course." The boy gave him a suspicious look.

Whelan smiled. "You know how it is, if a place has three owners, each one tells the world that he's the real deal, that it's his place and he's got junior partners. Harry told everybody it was his place, that Hoban was his, you know, his accountant."

The kid looked toward the back room. "No, it's his joint. Harry just had money in the place. Liked to come in here late at night…"

"And strut, right?"

The first smile appeared on the bartender's face. "Absolutely. He was just copping a stance, man. Showing off his chicks, doing a little business."

"Do a couple lines in the john, sell a little blow, am I right?" Whelan grinned, one streetwise guy to another.

"You got him down, man. Yeah. Spent half his time in the john or on the phone, wanted to look like a fucking major operator."

Whelan snorted. "Wasn't major when I did business with him."

"He always had somebody pissed off, like he was late with a delivery or he put out some bad shit or he changed the price or something like that."

Whelan nodded and took a sip of his Coke. "Know what I think? I think he pissed off somebody he was dealing with and they got tired of it. I think he got himself a disgruntled customer."

"Always. You couldn't get through a week without somebody coming in here with a hair up his ass looking for Harry."

Whelan nodded knowingly. "I probably know every one of them." Time to go fishing. "Let's see, you probably saw a little guy, wiry guy, about so high." Whelan held his hand out at about five and a half feet. "Right? Little guy?"

The bartender nodded slowly, looking off into the back. "Yeah, yeah, I think there was a little guy. Puerto Rican guy, I think."

"No," Whelan said confidently. "That's what he wants everybody to think. He's Greek. How about a good-looking blond guy, well dressed, about, oh, five nine?"

The kid shook his head briefly.

No Vosic. Okay, let's try again.

"And, let's see…a big guy, about…" He was trying to think

of a way to finish his imaginary description, but the bartender was already nodding.

"Oh, yeah, I know the big one. Weird dude. Real weird. A duster, right?"

"Well, wait a minute now. Who are we talking about? There was one guy, tall and real thin, but I don't think he was into angel dust. The other guy, he was real big…"

"The bald guy," the kid said. "The bald guy, real nervous, real…you know, always in a fucking hurry."

"Oh, oh, him. Yeah, yeah, yeah, but I don't think…no, he didn't do dust, not the guy I'm thinking of. That's just how he is. You're right, though. A strange one."

"Yeah, I couldn't deal with that guy, not at all. Made my fucking skin crawl. He'd come in looking for Harry and if Harry wasn't here he'd look at me like he wanted to take a piece out of me, like it was my fault, you know?"

"Don't fuck with him, though."

The kid held up both hands. "Hey, they don't pay me enough for that."

The door opened and three men walked in carrying music cases. Whelan's mouth opened and he wanted to laugh. I'm in a time warp, he thought.

If it was a time warp, the Hightones were in it with him, three middle-aged men in Beatles haircuts and Nehru jackets, three heads full of hair dyed shoe-polish black, three lined faces with sunlamp tans. Three men who couldn't sing and couldn't dance and couldn't play if their lives depended on it, eking out their existence in this dark little corner of Chicago, on the fringe of Uptown, on the lunatic fringe of life, DIRECT FROM LAS VEGAS the marquee said, but it had said that in 1967. Whelan wondered if there might not be a place for the Hightones in the *Guinness Book of World Records:* "Most sets played in the same sleazy tavern" or "Longest gig in one place." But more likely their place in music history was secure as "Most performances of the same material." Whelan smiled; he was in the presence of celebrity. These three men were the Musicians that Time Forgot.

He heard the kid whisper "Shit" and turned to smile at him.

"Let me guess—you were hoping they wouldn't show up."

The kid glared genuine hostility at the three Hightones and looked back at Whelan. "You don't have to listen to their shit music five nights a week, man."

"Little early for them, isn't it?"

The kid snorted. "Rehearsal. They actually rehearse the shit they do."

"They still do the Beatles medley?"

The kid winced. "People ask for it, man."

"How about the Temptations number, where they dance around in little white shoes, they still do that?"

The bartender nodded and stared as the musicians set their cases down and turned to face him.

"Hey, kid," one of them said. "What's shaking?"

He shrugged.

"Where's all the broads?" the drummer said, affecting surprise, and the others laughed.

"Time to go," Whelan said. He winked at the kid and made his way to the back as though he'd done it a hundred times. He knocked once, a voice said "Yeah?" and he opened the door.

Hoban looked up from the business at hand, which was apparently lunch. Spread out on the desk was the bloody aftermath of a rib dinner—a half-eaten salad, a sauce-soaked piece of white bread, a little plastic container of cole slaw, and, in the midst of it all, a mound of rib bones, gleaming and white like a paleontologist's dream, and on one or two Whelan thought he could actually see tooth marks. He stood staring at it for a moment; whole villages in Asia didn't eat this much in a day.

"Whaddya need?" Hoban asked, punctuating his question with a little gesture with a rib.

If I said I needed food this guy would jump out of his shorts, Whelan thought.

Hoban chewed a moment and then stopped. It was a small room and Hoban just about filled it, and Whelan felt as if he'd intruded on someone in the bathroom.

"Just a minute of your time," he said. "A few questions about Harry Palm, just one more time. You can go on with your lunch, sir."

"Oh, for crying out loud, I can't even have a bite in peace." He tossed the rib onto his desk and splattered sauce on his chest.

A bite? This was a bite? I'm watching Godzilla eat lunch.

"It will just take a minute, Mr. Hoban. You know how it is, we come up with something new, we have to run it by you." He pulled out a small spiral notebook and a ballpoint pen, clicked the pen nervously a few times, and looked at Hoban.

The huge accountant eyed him sullenly, a child deprived of his privileges.

"Detective Bauman spoke to you already, probably, but let me ask this: did Harry have any business dealings that you are aware of that were, ah, acrimonious? Anybody he dealt with that was angry with him, unusually angry?"

Hoban sighed. "What, I gotta go through this bullshit again? Yeah, everybody was pissed off at Harry. Okay?"

"Yes, sir, but was there anyone who was more than a little pissed off? Anybody who was pissed off for a long time? Any loud arguments that you remember? Altercations…"

Hoban picked up the rib again and bit meat off the end. "Yeah, for Chrissake, there were a half a dozen of 'em, they all wanted a piece of him. His ex-wife, for one, he wouldn't send her shit, never paid alimony, he was fucking proud of it."

Whelan looked at him calmly. "I'm talking about customers, sir. His customers, not the bar's."

Hoban held up both hands. "Hey, we don't run that kind of joint. This is a nice place, people come here for a couple of cocktails and some nice music—"

"Gimme a break, okay, Hoban? I'm not talking about your operation here, I'm talking about Harry's. I want to know if there's somebody who he had trouble with over his business."

Hoban looked down now and Whelan could tell what was coming.

"I donno nothing about what he was doing. I donno who he was dealing with or…"

"Anybody he was afraid of? Anybody ever come here looking for him, anybody that made him nervous?"

Hoban started to shake his head and Whelan held up one hand.

"I'm not a cop." Hoban looked at him and his mouth opened. There was sauce on his lips. "I'm private, but I have proof that Harry was dealing here—here, on your premises, and I'll turn it over to the cops if you stonewall me here. I want to know if there's anybody that ever came in here that made him nervous."

"I didn't want him dealing that shit here, I didn't want to have nothing to do with that. I tried not to get involved in that stuff, so I don't know who he might have had some trouble with. He had a couple problems. There was this black guy one night, another bookie. He wanted a piece of Harry. Said Harry wasn't gonna make him look like a fool in front of his people. Wanted to take Harry out back and kick the shit out of him. We called the cops and he left." Hoban shrugged.

"You give that to the cops?"

"Sure."

"Anybody else he had problems with?"

Hoban gave him a tired look, a look that said, You're not going to go away, are you? He sighed. "I know there was a guy that came in here one time asking for Harry, and when I told Harry about it, he got this look like he was gonna shit in his pants, said he had to do some fast dancin'."

"A big man, bald?"

He shook his head. "No. I think I know who you mean, but no, this was another guy. A guy with one arm. Little guy, dark hair, kind of good looking, but he looked like somebody not to fuck with, you know the look?"

"Yeah, I know the look. Our prisons are full of it. This guy have a name?"

"He didn't say, and Harry didn't tell me, he just looked like he fucked up and had to fix it real fast."

"What about the big man I mentioned. You said you knew who I was talking about."

Hoban belched, a long, low rumble. You make a nice first impression, Whelan thought. Hoban shrugged.

"If it's the same guy. Big, bald guy, completely bald. A little beard here," Hoban said, touching his chin and coating it with sauce.

"Ever see any trouble between him and Harry?"

"No. Harry wouldn't dick around with somebody like that guy, though. He looked like serious trouble."

"Anything else?"

"That's all I know about it. Like I said, I tried to stay out of it, you try to run a joint with that shit goin' on and you're dead in the water, you know?"

Dead in the water. "Yeah, you're right. Well, thanks for your time. I'll let you get back to your lunch." He got to his feet. "Looks good. Where do you order from?"

"Place up on Broadway. The Carnival."

"Really?" Whelan gave him a surprised look, looked down at the one-man picnic, and shook his head. "They're open again already? I thought, you know, when the city closed them down they'd be out of business for at least a little while."

"Closed them down?"

Whelan nodded. "Did that guy die? Probably not, but…" He shivered. "Salmonella, I had it once. Ever had that?" Hoban shook his head and looked owlishly at his ribs.

"Well, thanks for your time. Enjoy your lunch."

When he left, the Hightones were doing their unique rendering of "Eleanor Rigby." It wasn't exactly the way Lennon and McCartney had intended it, but they had probably never intended any of their tunes to be polkas. He waved at them from the door.

"Very nice," he yelled, and the lead singer winked at him.

From the King's Palace he went to the Hild Library on Lincoln and did a little homework. It took him a while to find the story, but it was there, in the *Sun-Times* from July 30, 1982. There wasn't much to it, just the account of a yacht going up in flames a half mile off the breakwater at Monroe. The initial story said a man had been seen on the boat before it finally went under and that police and coast guard vessels were searching for the body.

The papers for July 31 and August 1 mentioned only that the missing man was Philip Fairs, a wealthy Arlington Heights businessman and that foul play was not suspected. A newspaperman or a cop could read between the lines and tell that they were thinking suicide from the get-go, but the word wasn't mentioned till the body was found several days later. The paper for August 2 had an account of the discovery of the body, identified by his wife, and the first mention of the police theory that Fairs had set fire to the boat and taken his own life. There was a brief and sketchy summary of Fairs's moribund finances and the oblique suggestion that these financial woes had led to his suicide. That was all.

Whelan went back to the office and found his mail: a chain letter and the electric bill. He tossed the chain letter in the wastebasket and, after a moment's thought, tossed the electric bill as well. He'd pay when the electric company sent the warning notice, which was to say, about a day before they sent the turn-off notice.

He called his service and Shelley answered.

"One call, baby. Officer Charm School returned your call. That was his message, too."

"How long ago?"

"An hour, maybe."

"Oh. Well, won't do any good to call him now. Thanks, Shel." He hung up and sat at his desk for a moment, planning a general strategy for the next day—ask a few more questions about Harry Palm, see if he could get anything out of Bauman, then perhaps do a little legwork on Vosic. He thought again about the case Mrs. Fairs had presented him with and told himself there was nothing to it, no reason to get involved. He wasn't convinced yet that there was a connection between Phil Fairs and Harry Palm, but their paths had crossed and they were both dead. It would help him figure out whether he was spinning his wheels if he could just get Bauman to talk to him for a few minutes.

A year ago they had done their share of talking. Whelan

had been investigating the murder of his friend Artie Shears when he first met Bauman. After their reluctant partnership during that case, Whelan had been half convinced that the city's most belligerent detective had somehow accepted him as— what? Not a friend, actually, because as far as he knew, Bauman had no friends, a fact that would have surprised no one who actually knew the man. You didn't make friends with someone like Bauman, you became his acquaintance or you took him on as an assignment. There was never any question of getting close.

In the past year Whelan had seen Bauman perhaps a half dozen times, once in a bar—Bauman had bought him a drink, made some small talk, and then left a few minutes later, and Whelan was certain that the man was simply making a hasty exit because he didn't want company. For whatever reason, Bauman had thrown up a wall around himself again. The other times Bauman had been out in the gray Caprice with his partner, a rotund, pink-skinned man named Schmidt; Schmidt smiled all the time and seemed to be eternally in the midst of a snack, usually a Snickers bar. Whelan half suspected that assigning Schmidt to Bauman had been an inside joke.

He left the building and walked down Lawrence. In Sam Carlos's Carniceria, where price fluctuation was limited only by the boundaries of Sam's imagination, an argument was in progress. A short Latino woman leaned over the counter and put a stubby finger into Sam's face. Sam still masqueraded as a Puerto Rican, charged whatever he thought he could get away with, and lied to everyone about everything. Occasionally a customer, usually a woman, punched him out. Whelan believed that Sam would some day get around to selling road kill.

Half a block from his house a girl came backing out of a gangway and collided with him. She shot him a quick look and dismissed him immediately. She was a small woman, very young, thin, and sharp-featured, with dark brown skin, an Eartha Kitt type of woman. She wore a tight black skirt of a shiny material and a bright orange tube top. She took a few steps till she was closer to the curb, then looked back into the gangway. Her lip curled and she muttered something to herself.

A man emerged from the gangway, a big-bellied man with a broken leg. He was wearing light blue slacks and a short-sleeved white shirt and narrow tie. He had a cast on his right leg and the cast apparently went up over his knee, so he walked as though he were on stilts and hadn't quite gotten the feel for them. Over his shirt pocket there was a name tag: HELLO—MY NAME IS CAL. The man named Cal staggered out into the sunlight, a very busy man, for he was attempting to straighten his tie with one hand and zip up his fly with the other, and since he hadn't fastened his belt yet the zipper was proving to be an obstacle to his grooming. He glared at the thin black woman as though she were to blame for his unkempt condition.

"You come on back here, you," he said, and there was a cottony quality to his speech, a bad case of marbles in the mouth.

I see by your appearance that you're with the pharmacists' convention, Whelan thought. Five-forty on a hot August afternoon and this poor lost *turista* already had a load on, and his zipper was stuck and he couldn't dance anymore and his date wouldn't slow down so he could catch her.

"I say come on back here, you," he growled. He said "Bitch" to himself, then, as an afterthought, said, "You gimme my money back, you hear?"

The small woman stopped her retreat. He had her attention now, perhaps more of it than he'd really wanted. She wheeled around and came back till she was a few feet from him. She put her hands on her hips and leaned forward, putting her hard little face just an arm's length away.

"You wanted some, you got some, you paid for it. You don't get no money back, baby. This here," and she patted her hip, "this ain't nothing you can try out. You gimme some money, you get what you need, that's it."

Still fumbling with his pants, with the belt now, the man moved his broken leg toward her and shook his head.

"Wasn't worth no twenty dollars. Ain't no way that was worth no twenty dollars, no sir."

The woman's eyes narrowed. A drunk with a broken leg had just said she wasn't worth twenty dollars. For a second Whelan thought she'd whack him one. She took two more steps and put her face in the man's face. The conventioneer took a step back and put his weight on his good leg, unsure of himself now, in somebody else's neighborhood, in somebody else's town, aware of his broken leg and probably scared to death of black people anyhow.

"Mister, I gave you what you needed. Wasn't no time limit on it, wasn't nothing said it got to last an hour." She laughed. "You the only one can make it last long, baby. Ain't my fault it didn't take but half a minute."

"It didn't take no half minute," he said, defending his manhood. "Prob'ly more like a minute. Anyway, you coulda made it last longer, or you could—"

"That ain't how it works, honey. You paid your money, you got some. That's all there is. You ain't gonna get no more, baby. Next time, do it sober, maybe you last longer." She sniffed and turned to walk away, and he grabbed her.

He had his chubby hand on her upper arm and he pulled, yanking them both off balance. There was a look of alarm in her eyes and she tried to pull away, but he held on and grabbed her shoulder with his other hand.

"Get your hands off me, you mother f—"

"I get my money or we do it again."

He stumbled slightly as she attempted to wrest herself from his grip.

"You want to let go of that lady?" Whelan said.

They both looked at him simultaneously. The tourist gave him a quick once-over. He wasn't sure of himself but he wasn't terrified, either. He was Whelan's size, six one or so, but a good deal heavier, maybe two thirty and a lot of it fat. He looked Whelan in the eye.

"Mind your own goddam business."

"Let go of the lady. We don't do so much of that anymore. We don't grab our women and slap the shit out of them in public. Come on, friend, take your hands off the lady."

"She owes me money. Besides, this ain't no lady, mister, this here's a hooker."

"I don't owe him nothin." She was still defiant but he could see the alarm in her eyes—probably what every prostitute must fear every day she's on the street.

"Come on, pal. You don't want to make this serious."

"I just want my money, that's all. I didn't get what I wanted, no sir."

"That's your problem. But you can't slap a woman around. Let her go."

The man pointed a finger at him. "You think I'm afraid of you?"

"Buddy, nobody's afraid of me, but I'll tell you this, I don't think any guy with a cast on his leg is ever gonna take me. Not ever." Especially a fat guy, he thought.

The pharmacist thought it over and came back down to earth, but it was too late. People had gathered around them and a gray Caprice backed up Malden and stopped when it was even with them. A large shape in a bright orange knit shirt squeezed itself from the passenger side, hitched up its trousers, moved its shoulders uncomfortably, and plowed its way through the bystanders, and Whelan felt very sorry for the errant pharmacist, whose life had now gotten complicated.

Detective Albert Bauman of the Chicago Police Department pushed a couple of wide-eyed Vietnamese men out of his way and looked at the girl, the tourist, and Whelan.

"What's this, Whelan, a demonstration? You makin' a citizen's arrest?" There was a slight glimmer of amusement in Bauman's eyes.

"I was just helping these folks sort out a problem. They have what the TV people would call a business deal that went sour."

Bauman turned to the tourist. "Why do you have your hand on this woman? Get your hand off her."

"She owes me some money," the man said, "and I was just—"

"I don't give a shit about that—sir. Take your hand off her or your whole body's gonna be in a cast."

The man ran his free hand through his hair. "You can't threaten me," he said in a voice rich in doubt.

Bauman stepped closer to the man and just raised his eyebrows. The man let go.

"So what's the beef here?"

The man shrugged and tried to smile. "She just owes me a little money and—"

"For what, sir?"

The man looked around, mumbled something with his hand across his mouth, and looked down.

"For what? I didn't hear that. For what?"

"For a little, you know, a little, uh, fun. You know."

Bauman looked at him for a moment, then at the bystanders. He fished inside his jacket, came out with his shield, and waved it at the onlookers.

"All right, now. Get lost. Show's over. Police officer. Let's move it, g'wan." He glared sullenly at the audience till they began to shuffle off. When they were gone he addressed the tourist again.

"You gave this woman money for sex?"

"Well...yeah."

"Where you from?"

"Arthur, Nevada. I'm in town for the convention..."

Bauman squinted, looked at Whelan, shook his head. "Arthur, Nevada? That's a place?"

"Yes, sir," the pharmacist said. A good deal of his color was gone as his trip to Chicago had suddenly become a nightmare. Whelan could almost see the man picturing the reaction back home.

Bauman cleared his throat. "It is illegal in the city of Chicago to solicit sexual favors for the promise of money."

"Oh," the man said.

"And you paid this woman money?"

"Well, she's a prostitute."

Bauman shook his head. "Prostitution is illegal within these city limits, pal."

"But she is one, she said..."

"You gave her money, sir?"

The man started to nod and his eyes clouded. His entire

53

body seemed to sag as he viewed the prospect of spending a night or a week or who knew how long in a Chicago jail wearing a cast and a name tag that said HELLO: MY NAME IS CAL.

"So what were you gonna do here? They beat up their women in Arthur, Nevada?"

"No, sir. I wasn't gonna hurt nobody."

"What are you doing up here, anyway? This is Uptown, this ain't one of our tourist attractions."

"Taxi driver took me here."

"What for?"

The man shrugged. "Girls. You know…well, girls."

"No." Bauman shook his head. "There's nothin' like that up here."

"The cab driver said—"

"I don't give a shit what he said. We don't have that shit here."

The man gestured toward the girl, unable or unwilling to contradict Bauman verbally. Bauman dismissed her with a wave.

"Amateur night, pal. What you're looking for, they don't have it up here. This ain't, you know, Vegas or something like that. This cabdriver, probably a foreigner, right? Your foreigner, he wants to drive a cab, make a few bucks, be helpful. Can't even read the street names, most of 'em. Guy was probably from Nigeria. We got a lot of Nigerians driving cabs here."

"This was a white guy."

"There's a lot of white immigrants. Coulda been Yugoslavian or Polish or Greek."

"He didn't have no accent."

"Okay, fine, it was just a guy tryin' to deliver the goods, only we don't have the goods here. And I know. I'm the law here."

"Well, she's the one you oughtta be talking to, she's the one selling it. You oughtta arrest her."

Bauman shook his head and Whelan could see how much he was enjoying himself.

"Nope. I'd have to arrest you. It's illegal to buy it, pal. Besides, I'm not Vice. I'm Violent Crimes, which is what it looked like you were thinking about. You wanna put your hands on this woman, I'll be happy to take you in."

"I don't want no trouble. I'm just here for the convention."

Bauman seemed to notice the name tag for the first time. "The pharmacists' convention? That one?" He shook his head. "You guys are a civil disturbance. I feel like we're runnin' a day-care center. Tell you what, just get the hell out of here. Find another cab and go back to your hotel. And zip up your pants, for cryin' out loud."

The tourist stumped off, mumbling his thanks and his renewed intention to become a model visitor. The girl started to slip away between a couple of parked cars.

"Hey, darlin'. C'mere." Bauman held up a finger and beckoned. The girl stopped in mid-stride and came back sullenly.

"You free lance or what? Somebody's stable?"

She shrugged.

"C'mon, I don't have all day. So who's pimping?"

She looked up toward Lawrence. "Got an agent. That what you mean?"

"An agent, huh? Whatever. He around?" He saw her looking up the street. "Tell him to come out. Where's he at?"

She pointed up the street.

"Go on, tell him."

"Frankie? Hey, Frankie, the po-lice, he say to come out."

Whelan watched with interest and in a moment a man ducked his head out from around the corner of a building. Then the front of a bicycle wheel appeared and the man peeked out again.

"Hey, you. Out!" Bauman took a couple of steps toward the building and the man came out, bicycle and all. "Over here," Bauman said. "And bring your, uh, transportation."

The man coasted out on the bike and pedaled out as casually as anyone could under the circumstances. He looked around as he rode, a country squire taking the air in his neighborhood.

Whelan laughed. "This is style, Bauman. Take a lesson. I like this guy."

Bauman shot him a hostile look. "Style, my ass. This guy is an asshole."

He made an abrupt move of his hand and the pimp pedaled a little faster. He was young, about the same age as the girl, and white, with slicked-back hair and bushy eyebrows and heavy-lidded eyes. He was trying mightily to grow a mustache and the early crop was disappointing, so that it looked as if he'd just had a very dark milkshake. In spite of the heat he wore a black jacket of some shiny material and the entire outfit was crowned by the cigarette dangling from his mouth, because no one had ever told this one that nobody rides a bike with a cigarette dangling from his lip.

Bauman put his hands on his hips and made a show of looking him over. He glanced over at his car and shrugged, then looked at the young pimp again.

"So you're the newest talent on the street, huh? A pimp on a bicycle. Okay, I'll admit it's a new wrinkle. How old're you, Moe?"

"Twenty-four," the pimp said, looking nonchalantly from Bauman to Whelan. "And I'm not doing shit, you're just hasslin' me—"

"Shaddup. And how old is jailbait here?" He jerked a thumb at the girl.

"I'm nineteen," the girl said quickly.

"Your IQ is nineteen, lady." He looked at the pimp. "Frankie, that's your name, right? Frankie? Okay, Frankie, let me run it down for you, okay? You speak English, right? Or do I have to find an interpreter for you?"

Frankie sighed, rolled his eyes, and tossed the cigarette out onto the street with a deft flick of a thumb. "Yeah, I speak English."

"Good, good. You'll go far in the world. Can't do shit without English. Now, take this teenager out of here, and take you and your bicycle and your ass out of my line of vision. Find work, Frankie. Make something out of yourself. Get a man's job, kid. I see you up here again, I'll feed you one of your nuts."

Frankie turned his racer around and took off with the young woman trotting a few feet behind him, trying to talk to him. Bauman gave Whelan a blank look, walked over to the driver's side of the Caprice, said something to the man inside, and took the radio and made a call. Then he came back to Whelan.

"You having them picked up, Bauman?"

"I'm having a pimp on a bike picked up. The little hooker I don't care about. Some hookers aren't bad people, but pimps are all assholes and I know this guy will be on some other corner in fifteen minutes. That all right with you, Whelan?"

"Perfect. I assume you're returning my call in person."

Bauman gave him a slow look but said nothing.

"Now if I could just get about two minutes of your time."

"For what? I'm a busy guy." Bauman looked up the street, hitching up his pants. Whelan looked him over; up close A1 Bauman was showing some wear. Beneath the sheen of sweat his big, round face was red, skin blotchy, and the wrinkles at the corners of his eyes were more pronounced. His clothes were clean and the crewcut appeared to be newly minted, so he was still going through the motions, but Whelan could tell that Bauman was doing his health no favors. The indestructible Albert Bauman, detective extraordinaire and general loose cannon, wasn't going to have to worry about old age, simply because he didn't want to reach it.

He caught Whelan studying him.

"Whaddya looking at?"

"Your shirt. You look like a giant tangerine."

Bauman looked away again and Whelan thought the detective was suppressing a smile.

"I need a little background for something I'm working on."

"Good for you. I'm in a hurry, Whelan. My partner's waiting."

"Who's the lucky cowboy? And what did you do to Schmidt?"

Bauman gave him an irritated look. "I didn't do nothing to him. Guy was sick. They give me the two oldest, sickest detectives in the city as partners. First Rooney and then that guy." He shook his head.

"Got a new one now, huh?"

"Yeah, I got a new one," Bauman said tonelessly.

"So what's this one like?"

Bauman looked at him again. "You looking to meet somebody for your social life, Whelan? Go meet him yourself, okay? I'm busy."

"Fine, you're having your period again. Look, I need a little help."

"Got nothing to do with me, Whelan."

"Wouldn't kill you to return a favor, Bauman. Besides, you owe me lunch."

Bauman reached into his pocket, came up with a little roll of bills, and started to pull off a twenty.

"Okay, Bauman, save the theatrics. You don't owe me a lunch, you don't owe me any favors. That better?"

"Whaddya want?"

"Anything on Harry Palm."

Bauman's eyes widened and he gave Whelan an incredulous look. "No, no, we don't do that dance, uh-uh. That's an ongoing investigation. Nothing to do with you, Mister Private Dick." Bauman stressed and stretched the word *dick*.

Bauman stared at him, waiting for a reaction. Whelan simply looked at him, thinking. He took a shot in the dark.

"Let me guess, Bauman. There are still a few guys in Six that don't like me so much, and you'd shit in your pants if word ever got out that you were associating with a guy who was your social inferior. Ruin your image, wouldn't it?"

Bauman snorted. "I don't worry about my image."

"Yeah, you do. You think about it from the time you wake up in the morning till you toss back your last shot of Walker's DeLuxe. Fine. You don't owe me shit. But I have a genuine reason for asking about Harry Palm and maybe I'll come up with something while I'm working on this other thing. As a matter of fact, we both know I will, because we both know I'm pretty good. When I do, you'll have to ask me for it."

"I'm real worried about that, Whelan. I'm real worried that you're just a lot smarter than I am."

"Never said that. I just think I'll do a little better because I don't have your attitude."

Bauman gave him a malicious smile. "Nobody's got my attitude." He tapped his chest.

"Hitler did. Eventually nobody would invite him to parties."

"I'm my own party," Bauman said and walked over to his car.

"Have a nice day, Bauman." He watched the detective stuff his heavy form into the Caprice, and as the car pulled away it occurred to Whelan that some people, people unused to human contact, don't rush headlong toward it when it appears in their lives; they run from it, they fight it off, they beat it with sticks.

Four

Once inside the house he checked the mail and went back out, got into the rusting brown hulk that the Jet was fast becoming, and drove. At Wilson and Ashland it stalled, and as he wrestled with the ignition and pumped the gas pedal and cursed the old car he tried to calm himself with a mental picture, the picture of Paul Whelan behind the wheel of a red-and-white Chevy Blazer or a Jeep Cherokee or a Ford Bronco, something with size and an engine that didn't fall into a coma when you stopped for a light, something with pickup and four-wheel drive, something that would laugh at the Chicago snow and take potholes like bumps in the pavement, something with an air conditioner that did more than make noise and a radio that didn't turn itself off. A fight between two teenagers in front of his house a few weeks back had cost him his car antenna, and he could only be sure of getting WGN and one other AM station.

He found Vosic Enterprises with no trouble. It was a squat building on Greenview just off Diversey, a new red brick building with rounded corners and narrow windows with dark glass, and the double doors in front were shaded by a royal blue canopy that ran the width of the building. On it, in large white letters, was the name VOSIC and nothing else.

"Humility," Whelan said. He parked across the street from the building and watched. Vosic Enterprises was closing up shop. There were only three vehicles still in the parking lot, all of them up against the wall of the building: a blue Lincoln Town Car that looked as if it spent its life in a garage, a nondescript van, and, in parking space number one, a bright yellow sports car, low-slung and exotic. It dawned on him that he was looking at a Lotus. A Lotus convertible. He stared at it for a moment; there were cars whose existence was confined to the Auto Show and the pages of Ian Fleming novels, and this was one of them. Whelan smiled to himself. Gee, I wonder which one the boss drives.

As he waited and listened to the news on his car radio, two men came out the back of the building. One was tall and thin and wore a sweaty work shirt; he opened the rear door of the van and put a box inside. The second man was small and dark haired and the empty left sleeve of his shirt was pinned up; Whelan remembered Hoban's description of the man who'd come looking for Harry Palm. Both men then climbed into the van, with the tall one driving. A moment later a young blond man in a beige summer suit and dark glasses came out the front and got into the Lincoln and drove off.

Finally the front door opened and a security guard held it for a very tan blond man. He wore a powder blue summer sport coat and white slacks and shoes. He waved breezily at the guard without quite looking at him, walked around the corner to the lot, and hopped into the Lotus without opening the door. He burned rubber leaving the lot. Whelan decided he couldn't in good conscience let him go. There was, after all, nothing quite like tailing a rich man.

Surveillance of the rich, he had been told, is simple because they strive so mightily to be noticed. This was one of the many simple truths he'd inherited from Walter Meehan, the brilliant retired detective who had been his mentor when Whelan first set himself up as a private investigator. And like all of Walter's seemingly oversimplified advice, this piece was true. They wanted to be seen, these people, and even when they adopted some form of concealment or secrecy—dark glasses, say, or tinted windows in the limo—they still traveled in a Cadillac the size of an aircraft carrier and went home to a building with forty rooms and a sentry box out front. What was the point of being rich if no one noticed?

Whelan followed Rich Vosic to Diversey and then west to Ashland. When he was within a car length he could read Vosic's plate: I RUNIT. The Lotus went south on Ashland and pulled up in front of another building with a blue canopy, this one announcing VOSIC REALTY. He ran in and was out again in less than two minutes. Then Whelan found himself headed east on Diversey, three car lengths behind the Lotus. Vosic drove in a modest version of "the gangster lean," a pimp-inspired driving style that required the driver to slouch down in the front seat with one hand casually flung across the back of the seat and his eyes approximately level with the top of the steering wheel. At the stoplight at Lincoln and Diversey a carful of young Latin kids pulled up beside Whelan, the vibrations from their stereo rattling his doors. He turned to see four handsome grinning faces bobbing in time to the music. The driver waved to him and one of the faces in the back seat said, "Nice car, man."

Whelan laughed and hoped the light would change soon: the bass from their radio was bouncing off the fillings in his teeth. The light changed and they laid rubber pulling out ahead of him and around the car in front of them, heading toward the lake, where there were approximately a half million other people splashing in the unmercifully icy water of Lake Michigan or dancing in the sand. This was the changing of the shifts— the kids who had been at the beaches all day, at Fullerton and Montrose and Foster and North Avenue and Oak Street, were heading home in a long, dusty column like defeated bedouins, and they were being replaced by hundreds of cars full of kids who would spend most of the night at the lakefront.

Whelan followed Vosic up Lincoln Avenue through the heart of the Lincoln Park neighborhood with its maddening traffic. The yellow Lotus went from lane to lane, cut effortlessly between larger, slower cars, and pulled ahead, like a pat of butter sliding across a hot skillet. Half a block from the Biograph Theater, Vosic pulled up in front of a hydrant, put on his hazard lights, and ran inside a small restaurant calling itself the Hard Knox Cafe. Whelan drove a few yards past the restaurant and double-parked. From where he waited he could see into the alley where John Dillinger had been shot up by police and FBI agents some fifty years earlier. He remembered being taken to the movie house by his father many years before to see a pair of Joel McCrea movies. Across the street there had been a tiny, roach-infested theater showing different oldies three times a week, the Crest Theater. At the time they had been the high points of the neighborhood. Now it was as fashionable and expensive a place to live as there was in the city, a neighborhood overrun by single people, awash in eateries and taverns and places to see shows or hear music. He was never comfortable in the neighborhood; on a couple of occasions he'd accompanied Bobby Hansen up here to listen to jazz in the smaller clubs. Bobby, three times divorced and a self-proclaimed ladies' man, insisted that more than half the single women in Chicago lived within a mile of the Biograph Theater. Perhaps it was true, but it was Whelan's impression that all the single men in the city lived there, too.

He watched in the rearview mirror as Vosic came out of the cafe and got back into the Lotus. Whelan let the Lotus pass him and then followed.

Vosic took him on a tour of the North Side, up Lincoln to Wells, through Old Town and south to Division, and Whelan knew they were heading for Rush Street.

Rush Street, where somebody looking like Vosic would inevitably wind up, where conventioneers and self-styled playboys and old men in white belts and white shoes were drawn like lemmings to a cliff.

Some neighborhoods thrived on what they offered their residents, some on what they could promise the tourists, still others on what they could sell the city's gargantuan population of single males. There were a number of places young men could go to find women, but only Rush Street existed for this sole purpose. It promised women, encounters with women, all kinds of women.

He followed Vosic up Division and onto Rush and laughed as a cabbie ahead of him pulled up in front of a bar and burped up half a dozen grinning middle-aged men, all wearing name tags. Save yourselves, Chicago, the pharmacists have landed.

It was his theory that cabdrivers kept Rush alive. If you came to Chicago and wanted to go somewhere to drink, they took you to Rush Street. If you wanted to go to a nice restaurant, they brought you to Rush and you ate at a place with a name like Bernardo O'Callahan's or Uncle Charlie's. And if you wanted women, of course they took you to Rush Street. The customer said "Where's the action?" and cabbies ten weeks out of the mountains of Afghanistan smiled knowingly and headed for Rush Street. Nigerians still struggling with the street guide nodded curtly and took the customer to Rush Street. The taverns were no better than saloons in other neighborhoods and possibly a good deal worse, with prices a buck higher than anywhere else and all the sincerity of a guy selling carpeting on TV. The women were there—maybe one for every six men.

Rush Street was noisy, smoky, garish, crowded, expensive, and artificial, and that was on a good night, say on the night of a Papal Visit. Whelan nodded. Yes, this was where a guy in a yellow Lotus with I RUNIT license plates and white shoes would own a business.

Vosic turned up Elm and pulled up in front of a stately old brownstone that had been turned into a two-story tavern. A dark brown sign hanging from the second-floor balcony proclaimed this to be RICK'S ROOST. The old stone columns had been painted off-white and phony red shingles had been added to the facade, and the overall effect was that of a Taco Bell gone mad.

Tasteful, Whelan said to himself. Vosic hopped out of the two-seater and said something to a smiley dark-haired young man, who laughed. Whelan had the feeling this kid would laugh at anything Vosic said. Whelan drove around the block. When he made his second pass by Rick's Roost he saw Vosic standing in front of the tavern talking with a young woman. She was tall and model thin, with dark hair almost to her waist. A heavyset man in a business suit walked into a lamp post while craning to get a better look at her. This was a woman who could make you wear cologne, dress better, change your attitude, get rid of your vices, and lose weight. She was a woman who could cause fender benders, and she was having trouble getting old Rich to look at her as she spoke. She leaned forward as if to pierce his indifference and he pretended to be studying traffic. She made a little gesture of frustration with both hands and he affected to be checking the time.

This guy is not going to grow on me, Whelan thought. I just have a feeling.

Finally Vosic turned on his heels and walked into his roost, crooking a finger over his shoulder to the woman. Shaking her head, the woman followed.

Okay, Rich. My surveillance has revealed that you are a prick.

It was obvious that Vosic was going to stay in this place for a while, and Whelan decided to call it a day. There was a fight card at the Aragon tonight and he'd promised old Tom Cheney a ticket. What had seemed like a decent way to spend a Monday night with a friend was now looking like a stroke of genius, subliminal brilliance, because he was sure Sonny Riles would be at the fights.

There were landmarks and there were *landmarks*. To most people Chicago's genuine landmarks were places like the Water Tower, the John Hancock Building, the Sears Tower, the Art Institute, Wrigley Field, and Comiskey Park. To Whelan these were landmarks, but merely cosmetic ones. The true landmarks were stuck back in the shadows, thrust out of the limelight but there nonetheless, places that for better or worse gave a more honest view of Chicago, of what made the place tick: State Street, the Stadium, the old stockyards, the vast metal tangle of the railroad yards, the river, the slightly baroque old museums, the smelly and truncated remains of the great open-air garage sale that was Maxwell Street, the miles and miles of crowded beaches, and the Aragon Ballroom.

Forty years ago the Aragon had been a one-of-a-kind place, a place beyond description, where young couples crowded in to hear and dance to the great bands of the day, all of them— the Dorseys and Artie Shaw and Glenn Miller and Bunny Berrigan. It was a mixture of the fantastic and the grotesque, with imitation Moorish architecture, stucco walls, tiny balconies where lovers could get serious in the dark or pass the flask. And there was the ceiling, the Aragon ceiling, the brainchild of some now-forgotten decorator who should have been designing sets for DeMille. It was the only ceiling of its type that Whelan had ever seen, the only one he expected ever to see, unless they did strange things to their ceilings in the afterlife.

The ceiling of the Aragon was a living painting of the night sky, a high dome painted darkest blue, with tiny openings that showed flickering pinpoints of light to re-create the stars. The highlight of the ceiling, however, was the clouds, the passing wisps of cloud created by the clever use of projectors.

The last big-time show at the Aragon had been Lawrence Welk and his Champagne Merry-Makers in the late fifties. Now the paint was dull and flaking, there were cracks in the masonry and holes in the stucco; the young couples of the forties and fifties were now gone, the bizarre architect and the ceiling engineer probably long dead, like the men who made the famous music. The Aragon was home to salsa bands and entertainers from Latin America and deservedly obscure heavy metal bands, and to fight cards twice a month that drew five hundred people. All things had changed, except for the clouds on the ceiling.

From the corner of his eye he watched Tom Cheney study the ceiling. He made it a point to drop by Tom's house or take him out for a beer at least once a month. They'd become friends while Whelan was looking for Artie Shears's killer a year ago.

The old man chuckled and quietly said, "God damn." He looked at Whelan. "Now what in the hell makes those clouds?"

"Couldn't tell you. You never saw clouds in Wyoming?"

"Not inside our buildings, smartass. I like 'em, though."

"Me, too. My folks used to come here to dance, when they were going together. They saw Harry James here and Artie Shaw."

He looked around. There were a hundred or so people in the folding chairs on the main floor and a few dozen already firmly ensconced in the little balconies—best seats in the house unless you were looking for someone who'd be down on the main floor. It was warm and there was already a gray cloud of cigar and cigarette smoke hovering over the empty ring.

Ernie Terrell made his way down an aisle, tall and bulky

and smiling.

"There's your promoter."

Tom Cheney squinted. "Big one, ain't he?"

"Yeah, he is that. Ever see him fight?"

"Just the one time, the fight with Ali."

"Good fighter. Would've been a champion at another time."

A cluster of young men were gathered around a short black man with a gray mustache. Whelan nodded in his direction.

"See that stubby little guy there?"

"Yep."

"He fought Beau Jack, Bob Montgomery, all those guys. That's the man I have to see."

"He don't look that old."

Whelan shrugged. "Neither do you. Be back in a little bit." He got up and strolled up the aisle to ringside, nodded at a couple of men he knew, and approached Sonny Riles, who was standing behind the red corner of the ring and speaking earnestly to a young man in a plain blue boxing robe. Whelan stopped a few feet from Riles and waited for him to impart the wisdom of two hundred fights into the ear of the young fighter. Riles looked up for a moment, nodded to him, and finished his instructions, patting the young man on the behind and sending him into the ring. Riles watched the kid dance and strut and shadow box around the ring and then looked at Whelan.

"Hey, detective man."

"Who do you like tonight, Sonny?"

"I like this boy here, Westside boy. Six fights, ain't lost, ain't been down. Got one of my own boys going in the next one, got a pretty left hook, good chin, got some heart, too. And he listen." Riles laughed.

"Something different, huh?"

"Yeah, he listen. That mean if I tell him he ain't got it, if I tell him he got to quit, he gon' quit."

"Who else you got going tonight?"

"Couple boys. Light-heavyweight from Humboldt Park, white boy. And that crazy Indian boy."

"Alvin Thunder? Hot damn."

Riles laughed. "He worth the price of the ticket, huh?"

"No question. I get the feeling he'll be needing a new career soon, though. Am I right?"

Sonny Riles nodded slowly. "Yeah. Can't nobody get hit like that each time out and keep comin' back. He get hit like that in the gym, too. He say he gonna fight a little bit more an' then go to work in the lumber mill they got up there."

"Up where? The reservation?"

"Uh-huh."

"Well, I'll treasure each of these last fights, then." Riles laughed again and waved to a man Whelan recognized as a columnist for the *Sun-Times*. "I have to ask you about somebody, Sonny."

"So ask."

"Harry Palm."

Sonny Riles made a sour face and pretended to start walking away. "Don't be talking 'bout that boy around here. Bring bad luck."

"Well, he brought himself some of that."

"I heard. Didn't surprise me none." He frowned and looked at Whelan. "You lookin' into that?"

"No, not really. I'm—I'm checking out somebody with gambling habits. Serious gambling habits."

"Lots of folks got gambling habits."

"Did you see him around here lately? Past few weeks, maybe?"

"Oh, yeah. I saw him. He always here. He come to the fights to strut, you know. Wearin' them white suits and gold chains, look like that Camacho boy. He wear a suit coat and no shirt. Suit coat and no shirt and 'bout five pounds of gold chains." He slapped a heavy hand over his eyes and shook his head.

"Anybody with him?"

"Women. Old Harry Palm always had a woman with him. Some nights he be the only one here with a woman. He liked that, you know."

"Yeah. I never figured him for a fight man."

"He liked to make some money on a fight." Sonny

Riles raised his eyebrows and there was an edge to his voice. "Interested in fuckin' up some young boy so's he could make a dollar on a fight."

"Your boys?"

Riles nodded.

"What did he offer them, Sonny, the moon?"

"Didn't offer them nothin'. Offered me two hundred. Two hundred dollars to have one of my boys lay down. Didn't offer the boy shit. Said if I got a boy to go along with him, he'd work something out later. What'd he call it? Oh, yeah, said he need the kid to 'go along with the program.'" He shook his head and muttered, "Sheeeit."

Whelan looked at Sonny Riles and saw the little sparkle in the dark eyes.

"You hit him, Sonny?"

Riles nodded slowly. Whelan remembered watching films of Sonny Riles and Ike Williams, Sonny Riles and Beau Jack, and he smiled.

"More than once?"

"Didn't need to hit him but once. That boy didn't have no chin at all."

Another fighter now climbed into the ring from behind the blue corner, a Mexican boy in a brightly colored robe with LITTLE MANTEQUILLA across his back.

Riles laughed. "Lookit this little skinny boy callin' hisself 'Little Mantequilla.' The real Mantequilla be knocking this boy out with one hand."

"Harry Palm also liked to do his business in public places. Liked people to see him operating."

Riles nodded. "Prob'ly what got the man killed. All that showboat shit. Piss somebody off."

"That's what the police think. They think somebody took old Harry out because he pissed them off."

"What you think, detective man?"

"I think stupid people do stupid things. I think Harry did something stupid to somebody nasty and they killed him. I don't think it was anybody heavy, though."

"Anybody heavy, they wouldn't pay no never mind to Harry Palm."

"And if they did, we'd still be looking for parts of him."

Ben Bentley, the ageless boxing announcer, onetime promoter himself, climbed into the ring, took an enormous cigar out of his mouth, and reached up for the ring mike. He spoke into the microphone with the cadence of W. C. Fields and the vocabulary of a grand duke, called the evening "a night of pugilistic artistry," and thanked everyone for coming. The audience was "ladies and gentlemen" and the fighters were all "fine young men," and the bouts were going to be "memorable."

Whelan laughed and shook his head. "If you'd never been to a fight before, Ben Bentley'd have you thinking you were gonna see Zale and Graziano."

"Dempsey-Firpo," Riles said, laughing.

They sat down in a couple of second-row seats. "I got to be gettin back to the locker room," Riles said.

"Okay. Listen, ever see Harry Palm doing his other business here?"

"Shit, yes. All the time."

"Remember any of the people you saw him with?"

"Yeah. Couple of the brothers, couple young Mexicans. One white man. White man just like Harry." He puffed his chest out importantly.

"Another peacock, huh?"

"Yeah. Big man, look like a wrestler or something. Big body, look like his suit coat gonna bust. Had a shaved head like Marvin Hagler. Goatee and funny eyes. Stared at people like…he look like a bouncer, you know what I'm sayin'?"

"Like he was waiting for action?"

"Yeah."

"Any idea what kind of business they were doing?"

"What you think? Old Harry was wearin' his sport coat buttoned. They went downstairs to the men's room and when they came back, Harry was showin' his little hairless chest to the girls and the bald dude, he lef'. Three fights to go, and he lef'. He got his package."

Whelan nodded and got up to leave. "Thanks, Sonny. Always a pleasure to talk to you."

"Hey, come see me again. I got a new boy fighting next time, middleweight. That white man, that the man you looking for?"

"I really don't know yet. I know all this is about white men, though, and one of them was big and bald, and I think they all knew Harry Palm." He nodded and left.

The first fight was over by the time he got back to his seat. Tom Cheney gave him a sour look.

"Wasn't much of a fight, was it. That little Mexican boy didn't have a thing."

"No. But this is what a lot of it is like, club fights. Couple of kids dancing around because somebody told them to become fighters. A lot of them don't even really want to do this, and here is where they find out."

The next two fights were dull and one-sided: Sonny Riles's fighter won his fight easily and the third bout ended when a Mexican boy landed his first body punch of the evening and his opponent decided to go down and stay down. Whelan bought them beers and a box of popcorn and he made small talk with Tom Cheney, and eventually a murmur rose from the crowd, a murmur he'd heard before. He looked up to see Sonny Riles standing on the ring apron in the red corner and holding the ring rope up for Alvin Thunder.

"Here we go, Tom. The real main event of the evening. Forget about those dinosaurs listed on the program."

A muscular Latino climbed in through the ropes and began bouncing from foot to foot in the blue corner. His handlers took off his robe and Sonny did the same for the Indian, and there were hoots from the people in the audience who hadn't seen Alvin Thunder before. He was short and skinny with no visible muscle development, and when he strutted around the ring he listed to one side on a leg that was markedly thinner than his other.

Tom Cheney looked at the Indian, then at Whelan. "Sure looks like a mismatch. This is the boy you told me about."

"Yes. People think you need muscles to throw a punch."

"What happened to his leg?"

"Polio. When he was little."

Ben Bentley went through the pleasantries, the referee gave his instructions, and the bell sounded. The Puerto Rican fighter came out fast, confident, hands down almost to his belt, and Alvin Thunder came bounding out on his one good leg and floored him with a looping right hand that broke half a dozen rules of boxing. The Puerto Rican got up on the count of one, too pissed off to give himself a few seconds to clear his head. He gestured to the Indian boy to come and get him, and Alvin Thunder was all over him. They stood toe to toe for almost the entire round and neither gave way till Alvin ran out of gas with about half a minute left. Sensing his moment, the Puerto Rican boy threw three- and four-punch combinations and had the Indian covering up in a corner when the bell ended the round.

"Whooeee!" Tom Cheney shook his head.

"Told you," Whelan said.

"Think he's got anything left, that Indian boy?"

"Oh, I think he'll come up with something."

What he came up with was exactly what he'd started the fight with, a frontal assault and long, wild punches that did no real damage but took the taller boy by surprise and drove him back to his own corner. They put their heads on each other's shoulders and dug to the body and threw nasty little uppercuts and then Alvin was on his back from a short, sharp right. Unlike the other boy, Alvin Thunder took a count of eight on one knee, got to his feet, held out his gloves for the referee to wipe them, and then, to the delight of all present, grinned happily at the Puerto Rican fighter.

He charged across the ring, the Puerto Rican met him on the dead run, and they clashed in the center, throwing punches like windmills.

Whelan laughed. "This is how it was before they invented boxing."

The Puerto Rican boy was visibly angry, and he stood directly in front of the Indian and threw punches, his hands dropping lower and lower, and he never saw the hook that caught him just at the jawline. He went down heavily, got up at six, and fell over on his side again, and the referee waved his hands over him. Alvin Thunder limped across the ring with hands high in the air and Sonny Riles climbed in through the ring ropes and hugged him.

Tom Cheney watched the little celebration. "All his fights like this?"

"All of them. Except sometimes he runs into a smart fighter who doesn't get so carried away, and he gets knocked out. He's never been involved in a decision."

Tom Cheney shook his head. "Don't seem to be the kind of fighter that lasts long."

"No. He gets hit with everything. He'll be through soon. With another trainer he might get hurt. Luckily, Sonny Riles is his trainer and Alvin has no illusions about being the next Roberto Duran."

They settled back to watch the next bout, but Whelan was through for the evening. He kept his eyes on the ring, but his mind was on a bald, heavily built man with a goatee who had done business here with Harry Palm and come looking for him at the King's Palace.

Vosic's car was gone when Whelan returned to the Rush Street bar and he decided not to jeopardize his next move by going inside the place. Instead he went up the street to a tiny hamburger place that called itself Banquet on a Bun. There were three booths, two of them taken, and one waitress. She was having a hard night. One of the booths was filled with four teenagers, loud and liquored up and bent on jerking her chain. They ran her back and forth between the counter and the booth and laughed and giggled among themselves. Finally she came over to take Whelan's order.

She was somewhere in her late thirties, with brown hair pulled back in a ponytail and held with combs on either side. She had intelligent brown eyes and a sprinkling of freckles against very fair skin; she wore the time-honored black-and-white uniform of the greasy spoon waitress, and though she wouldn't have chosen it for herself, she was one of those women who look good in it. There was a hint of rueful humor in the eyes and laugh lines around them. At twenty she had probably been something special, and she still had some of it.

"Tough night, huh?"

She shrugged, shot a look at the booth full of adolescents, and smiled. "It could be worse. There could be more of them."

"Or they could be pharmacists."

She rolled her eyes and then laughed. "They've been here. They act like they've never seen women before."

He ordered a double cheeseburger and a chocolate malt and watched as she brought his order to the dark, hairy man presiding over the grill; as Whelan watched him, his little paper hat fell off his head and revealed vast quantities of black hair. A moment later she returned to the boothful of kids, and they seemed to be getting to her now. He saw her go red at something they said and then she dropped their check on the table.

"You're finished, guys. Go hassle your parents."

She walked back to the counter and one of the kids said something and she turned and pointed to the door.

"Pay your bill and leave."

One of them, a little bigger than the rest, leaned part of the way out of the booth.

"I don't need to take no orders from you, lady."

"Yeah, you do," she said.

"You can't make me do shit. Fat old broad."

"She looks just fine to me," Whelan said.

The waitress gave him a surprised look and the cook turned, carving knife in hand. "Whatsamatter, Pat?"

"Nothing," the waitress said.

The kid looked at the cook and at Whelan.

Whelan indicated the cook with a nod. "He killed a guy once. I'd say you're outnumbered."

The other kids started to mutter to the big one and gradually, grudgingly, they tossed money on the table and left.

When they had gone, the waitress brought Whelan's food.

"Thank you, sir," she said.

He noticed that she wore no ring. "My pleasure." He thought

of making a joke, making small talk, and found himself just a bit gun-shy. Another time—there was plenty of time, he thought.

He caught a couple of innings of the Sox game from Oakland and had a dark Beck's and more cigarettes than he needed. Time to quit, time to do something. Time to jettison some habits. He wasn't worried about drinking yet, but he was smoking more and was conscious now of the amount of time he spent alone. Some men could make a life out of being alone, seemed to prefer it. Not Paul Whelan, he said to himself. He thought about Liz, from whom his only communication had been a terse Christmas card, and felt old scars beginning to sting.

He thought of the waitress in the hamburger place and then tried to remember the last time he'd actually asked a woman out.

You don't know a damn thing about her…Yeah, I do. She has nice eyes. The eyes tell everything.

He recognized the car by the sounds of the dying muffler and got up to check. It was rounding the corner when he got to the window but he waited and it reappeared thirty seconds later, a beater full of men haunting the street, drawn by the promise of the trouble they could make for the black man who'd had the balls to move in with a white woman. All else was quiet and the car's wheezing engine could be heard pumping out its last few hours of life.

You drive exactly the car you belong in, he thought.

They drove by the black man's house a third time and someone yelled out "nigger," and then the car was gone. Whelan saw a face appear in the window of the house, a black face. The man looked out at the street, oblivious of Whelan looking at him, a worried man watching over his life.

FIVE

He called Area Six and was told that Bauman wasn't in yet. On a hunch he asked for Landini, but he wasn't in yet, either.

"Please leave a message for either of them to call Paul Whelan, okay?"

"Yes, sir," the sergeant said tonelessly.

He had no one else to call now—Jerry Kozel was no longer on the Chicago police force, having relocated and moved on to something presumably more lucrative and certainly a little easier, working for a north suburban police force whose most serious problem was teenagers cruising on Saturday nights. It was just as well; Jerry Kozel, his longtime partner, no longer had much to say to him. The last time they'd seen each other had been at a Cubs game, and Jerry had talked to him like an alderman running for reelection: "Hi, Paul, good to see you. You look great. How's everything? Great, great. Gotta run, Paul."

He stepped out onto the porch and looked around. It was cool and pleasant, with no warning of what it would be like later that day, when a south wind would carry hot air and dust like nature's scouring pad through the city and people would run for cover.

He walked up Malden to Wilson. Near the corner a pair of sheriffs deputies were going through the nasty steps of an eviction. A black woman in her sixties or seventies sat in the sun on a kitchen chair and watched as strangers emptied her apartment and deposited the belongings of her entire life on the gray soil of the front yard. Dull eyes stared from half a dozen windows in the apartment building, most of them on the woman, most of them probably wondering how they'd handle this. He stopped and watched the deputies; they did their work and didn't meet the old woman's eyes or his.

He shook his head. What the hell do we call this? The American Dream. In a country that congratulated itself daily on its quality of life, people were still put out on the streets with all their possessions. Some of them were young, people with families, but most of the ones Whelan had seen were old, people with no place to go, especially in Uptown. He remembered another eviction in Uptown, this one witnessed by a pair of elderly Russian Jews. They had stared at the grim procedure as if they were watching a killing.

Whelan looked at the old woman. There was something very wrong here, and he wondered how many other countries in the "civilized world" had such a process. He went over to the woman and stood beside her, fishing in his pants pocket. He came up with a little wad of money in an Indian money clip—a twenty, a ten, a five, and a couple of singles. He took out the twenty and folded it up small, then handed it to the woman without looking directly at her.

"This help you out any, ma'am?"

She said nothing for a while and eventually he was forced to face her, the only man here of this entire group who was looking at her. She stared at him and then her eyes moved to her possessions, lingering for just a moment on each of them, and slowly her head began to shake. She seemed to have no inclination to speak and he knew that this was no moment for false consolation. He stood there with the twenty in his outstretched hand and told himself he'd stand there till she took it. Eventually her dark, bony hand reached slowly and grasped the bill.

"Thank you, sir," she said in a low, soft voice, and then added, "God bless you."

"My pleasure, ma'am," he said and backed away. He turned to the nearest deputy. He was young and pale-skinned to begin with, but he looked positively sick to his soul, a tight-lipped young man with moist, dark eyes who quite clearly was getting more than he'd bargained for in this day's work.

"Human Services coming out, Deputy?"

"Yes, sir. They'll be out any minute now. They'll get her fixed up."

"You hope."

He turned and walked away, no longer needing coffee. I have a feeling, he said to himself, and I want to share it. He went back home and got into his decrepit, rusting car and decided to let the workday begin, and he found himself wishing, violently, that for just the duration of this morning he could be Bauman. Bauman would find something to hit.

There were seven or eight cars in the lot of Vosic Enterprises this time, and the Lotus was exactly where he would have expected it to be, in the slot marked NUMBER1. Number two was empty, and Whelan took it. He went around the front and swung the heavy glass door open, felt his body go limp in the wave of cold air, and found himself face to face with a young blond kid in a khaki uniform with a Harrison Security Agency shield on his shoulder.

He smiled at the kid, who had a clipboard and a facial expression that said he represented the forces of righteousness and order.

"Getting hot out already," Whelan said, smiling. The guard gave him a blank look.

"He likes this shit, the heat." Whelan shook his head.

"Who's that, sir?" The guard looked confused.

"Rich," Whelan said. "He likes it. Always has."

The kid nodded. "Oh, right." He looked up the hall and nodded again.

"He's in, right? I saw the pimpmobile out there."

The guard grinned now, one of the boys, in on everything, and Whelan patted him on the shoulder. He was by the guard in two steps. Then he stopped suddenly and turned.

"Hey, don't tell him I said that, all right? I'm trying to sell him something."

The guard laughed; he'd put it all together now. Another loudmouthed salesman. He shook his head and resumed his position with his clipboard. Whelan walked past a pair of large offices in which several people worked in cubicles under a bluish light. Piped-in music hung in the air everywhere and forced Andy Williams on defenseless ears. At the far end of the office the one-armed man was piling boxes on a two-wheeler as effortlessly as any man with two arms.

Whelan headed for an impressive double door with VOSIC stenciled on one side. As he pulled the door open he heard the Andy Williams song fade off, only to be replaced immediately by another Andy Williams song. Whelan asked himself if this could be punishment for the sins of these office workers.

The foyer inside was dominated by a desk, and the desk by a young woman who formed the final line of defense before one actually reached the inner citadel of Rich Vosic Enterprises. She was as predictable as the license plates and the car and the white shoes, and her desk had been placed so that she filled the room and the viewer's eyes. This young woman was a little darker than the one Whelan had seen Vosic meet the night before—younger, too, perhaps twenty-two, twenty-three. Whelan watched her beat the hell out of a computer keyboard, almost keeping time with the music that came out of her desktop radio—Smokey Robinson did battle with Andy Williams and sent him running, and it didn't seem to bother her at all that two songs assailed her at once. Across the room he saw a clouded glass door with the simple message, stenciled in a sort of italic script, RICH VOSIC, PRESIDENT.

Whelan let the door close behind him and waited there for the young woman to look up. She didn't. She hammered away at the keyboard for a minute or so, then stopped with her long, dark fingers poised just above the keys and said, "Yes? May I help you?"

"Yeah, turn off Andy Williams."

She looked up and lit up the room with a smile. Perfect white teeth and dimples, large brown eyes, and thick, dark eyebrows that had never been tweezed or plucked. She gave her head a little shake.

"I can't turn it off. It's everywhere. Even in the john. The ladies' room."

"Is he in?" Whelan nodded toward the door.

"Uh, yeah…" She gave him the quickest once-over he'd seen in years, took in the blue *guayabera* shirt, and decided he didn't quite fit in. "He's kind of busy."

"Me, too. And so are you, and you're talking to me. Just buzz him and tell him I need…oh, maybe five minutes of his time."

She pursed her lips and gave a little nod. "Who may I say is calling?"

"Paul Whelan. I'm an insurance investigator."

Something lively seemed to move in her eyes. She'd heard the term before. It didn't exactly make her jump out of the pale blue summer blouse, but it got her attention. She picked up the phone and hit a small white button. She waited, then said, "Hi. A Paul Whelan to see you." She listened for a moment, then said quietly, "Insurance investigator." Then, "Oh, I don't know," and another pause, then a laugh. "Okay."

She looked at Whelan, tilted her head to one side, and grinned about something she wasn't going to share.

"You can go in," she said, and her tone told him that insurance investigators were no match for Rich Vosic.

Vosic stood in front of his desk, facing the door. He was in quite a different color scheme this morning, wearing a kind of berry-colored shirt and pale pink slacks. The white belt had been replaced by a crimson one, the white shoes by gray suede loafers with dark red trim. Whelan had seen many men like this before, but they'd all been in clothing ads. He fought the urge to look around for a walk-in closet.

Vosic pushed himself off the desk, extended his tanned and manicured hand, and said, "Hi, I'm Rich Vosic."

Whelan shook the hand and said, "Paul Whelan."

"How you doing, Paul?" Vosic said, and Whelan instantly understood the man's particular brand of magic, knew instinctively what made Rich Vosic work. Vosic had what TV people called the "Q-quotient," a vague combination of characteristics supposed to account for a person's charisma.

Whelan had seen it before, particularly on the police force, in those officers who seemed to advance at an accelerated pace, the ones who wound up as lieutenants when their classmates from the academy were still street cops looking for sergeant's pay.

It helped that Vosic was handsome and that his looks held up close, but it was more than a good tan and blue eyes and a full head of blond hair. When Rich Vosic asked how you were, every pore and fiber and muscle and nerve of Rich Vosic radiated concern, the eyes wouldn't blink and wouldn't leave yours, the smile hung out there for the duration, and you believed that Rich Vosic really wanted to know how you were. This was the kind of person who studied you and made small talk and pumped you with selfless questions about your life and your work and your tastes and opinions as though you were the single most interesting person he'd ever encountered. Faces like this often made it into commercials and sold you things you didn't need and couldn't afford, and sometimes they wound up in the nation's penal institutions, but some of them stayed outside and made a lot of money. Whelan looked Rich Vosic over and thought that this one would be murder in negotiations, would make fortunes on the golf course or over lunch. Women would love this face, and they'd love it even if Rich were scarred and pockmarked.

"Come on, Paul, let's take a load off," Vosic said and walked around his desk to sit down.

It was a massive piece of mahogany, its top gleaming and uncluttered, an outward sign of a man in total control or one with nothing to do. Whelan admired the desk as he sat down. It was an aircraft carrier, obviously chosen as much for its size as its quality, for the width of this desk put space between the visitor and the man who owned it, and the space was obvious, impossible to overlook or misunderstand. Vosic might as well have been seated on a platform.

"Carmen said you're an insurance investigator."

Whelan took out the little vinyl wallet where he kept his cards and slid one across the desktop. Rich Vosic studied it for a moment and then frowned.

"You're…independent? She said you were with an insurance firm, I think."

"I do a lot of work for various companies—liability groups, general carriers, law firms—" He waved his hand in the air. "But, yeah, I'm independent."

Vosic nodded and continued to smile, but the smile no longer went all the way up.

"How can I help?" He made a little self-deprecating shrug: the ignorant country boy asked to perform beyond his gifts. Then he grinned. "I don't guess you're looking to buy some great software."

Whelan smiled and said, "No. But you can help, I'm sure of that. I've been asked to investigate a former associate of yours."

"Okay," he said slowly.

"This would be from your days with High Pair Enterprises." He paused here and took his cigarettes from his shirt pocket, noted the slight flush that spread across Vosic's face, and took out a smoke. He milked the moment, fished out his lighter, dropped it, held up the cigarette, and asked, "Mind?"

The easy smile returned. "Oh, no, not at all," Vosic said and opened his top drawer. He flipped an ashtray across the desktop, giving it a neat little spin with a flick of his wrist. It was tin, in the shape of a cartoonish face, and the open mouth formed the tray itself. Perfect, Whelan thought. He would have a gag ashtray. He took his time lighting up, took a puff, set the cigarette on the lip of the cartoon face, pretended to be admiring the ashtray, then leaned back and exhaled smoke.

Vosic leaned forward across the desk as if to remove the space barrier and folded his hands.

"Now, are you aware that this company has absolutely nothing to do with High Pair? I mean, I can put you in touch with my legal people if there are any questions about that. We're totally independent of what went on back then, totally independent of all that," and he made a little pushing gesture with one hand.

Whelan frowned and played dumb for a moment, then shook his head. "Oh, jeez, no, no, no, I'm giving you the wrong impression. I have no interest in the company, per se, but in one employee or…I'm not really certain what his status was— George Brister."

Vosic said "Oh" in the long, uncertain syllable of a man thinking on his feet. His eyes wandered around the room for a moment and then he collected himself. He said "George Brister" and raised his eyebrows comically. He gave Whelan a rueful smile.

"Oh, yes, George was with us, all right. Was he ever."

"Was he an actual partner?"

"No, no, Jesus, that's all we would have needed. If Brister had been my partner I wouldn't have anything." He made a little snorting sound. "Be cleaning out johns somewhere. No, he wasn't a partner. He was an accountant." He pronounced the word precisely, then repeated, "An accountant. Hell of an accountant. Boy, was he ever. I hired him, too." He gave Whelan a sheepish look.

"Something you lived to regret, I take it."

"Oh, yeah." Vosic laughed. "Oh, I learned to regret it, all right. We thought Brister was a pretty fair accountant, but you know, a drunk, a lush." He shrugged. "But I thought, what the hell, if the guy can make the numbers work, he's doing his thing, right? And we needed that, we needed a numbers guy, a real strong numbers guy. Well, old George turned out to be a lot of things. For one, he was an actor. Played dumb, put on this… whaddya call it, this act, this…"

"Persona?"

Vosic grinned. "There you go. That's it, that's nice, a persona. Exactly. He made himself out to be this kind of quiet guy, kind of sullen sometimes. We left him alone, thought it was just his daily hangover. And all the time he was milking the company in ways that were fucking dazzling. He took us for a mil and a half and almost all of it was borrowed money. Shot the shit out of my company. Killed my partner."

"What?" Whelan gave him a stunned look.

"You didn't know about that, huh?"

"No, like I said, I'm only interested in Brister, not in the companies he worked for."

"Yeah, my partner, Phil Fairs, he was the one who had the reputation, he was the front man, the one who had the credit, who borrowed all the money."

"Not you? I would have figured you for that part."

Vosic laughed. "Not if you'd met Phil, you wouldn't. No, he was the idea man and I was the administrator. He was the one who got hung out to dry. It was his name, you know? He borrowed the money, got us extensions, got us more money… so when we started to go under because this—" He leaned forward, a gentleman about to descend into ungentlemanly talk, "—this prick took us to school, Phil killed himself. He couldn't handle it, he killed himself."

"No kidding."

"Thirty-eight years old, nice house, nice wife. Killed himself." Vosic shook his head and looked at his tanned fingers for a moment. Then he looked up.

"So, ah, why are you looking into this guy?"

"Well, I can't go too deeply into that, but let's just say you weren't the first or the last victims of this man." He took a puff and nodded as Vosic waited for him to give up more.

Sorry pal, that's all you get.

"No, huh? We weren't the…we weren't the last ones?"

"No. Near as I can make out, this guy's got an income over the past ten years like the Shah. Spends it, too."

Vosic nodded, mouth open. For just a moment he looked dull, slow, unimaginative. Then he tilted his head slowly.

"And this is where? Here? Chicago?" He squinted.

Whelan shrugged. "Among other places. Seattle, for one, seems to like Seattle. Denver, Austin, San Diego," Whelan said. I'm cooking now, he thought as he watched Rich Vosic. Vosic was obviously waiting for more, so Whelan added, "Baton Rouge."

"No shit."

"No shit."

"And you're sure it's the same guy? I mean in all these places? Sounds like a movie." He worked at a smile but it didn't quite take.

Whelan nodded. It did sound like a movie. It sounded like *The Mask of Demetrios*—a manipulative scoundrel moving back and forth among unsuspecting businessmen and robbing them all blind, always leaving someone behind holding the bag. This had all the elements of the movie except the Balkan locations and Sidney Greenstreet.

"You're right. It's hard to believe one guy pulled all this stuff off, but…" He shrugged.

Vosic stared at him, waiting for more. He licked his lips. Then he got tired of waiting, made an irritated little shrug, and shook his head.

"Can you tell me any of the other companies he took down recently, Paul?"

"Sorry, Mr. Vosic—"

"Rich, Rich."

"Okay, Rich. No, I can't do that. I'm…" Whelan allowed himself to sink back into the chair; he blew out a long breath and shook his head. "I'm fairly certain they aren't telling me everything anyhow. There is some talk of a governmental investigation because there was an S & L involved. Federally insured funds are gone. So…so, this is all heavy shit and I think if I don't watch my ass, somebody's going to kick it. You see my position?"

Vosic nodded. "Oh, sure, sure. I understand perfectly. No problem. No problem." He continued to nod and Whelan waited.

Vosic looked around the room, his gaze flitting from object to object, and Whelan thought he could almost hear Vosic's heart sinking.

I hit your spot, my friend. I don't know what it is, or exactly what I hit it with, but I see it. He felt a little thrill. There was something here, the brittle Mrs. Fairs was right. He puffed on his cigarette, made a show of brushing ash off his shirt front, and put the cigarette out in the grinning ashtray.

When he looked up, Vosic was watching him and a slightly different look had come into his eyes. Round two.

"So what else can I tell you about this guy, Paul?"

"Well, my information, which is really based on very

85

scattered testimony, a lot of it contradictory, is that this guy Brister might still be here. No, more accurately, that he's back here, that he's got a thing about Chicago. Have you, in the time since he left your firm, heard anything about him, or heard from him, or had any word at all about him, no matter how questionable or unreliable?"

Vosic pushed out his lower lip and shook his head slowly. "No. No, as far as I was concerned, he vanished. He just disappeared. And I'll be straight with you, Paul, I'm not entirely surprised about what you've told me. I mean, I have enough evidence of my own that this guy was shrewd. He took us for a lot of money, in ways I never thought possible, and then he made it out of town and nobody found him. No dummy, this guy."

"So what's the last you ever heard from him?"

"About five days before my partner Phil killed himself. That's the last time I saw him. He went home after lunch, said he wasn't feeling well. That was nothing new for Brister, he came in hung over so often it was a miracle he could get through the day as often as he did. Never came back."

"Did you try to call him or anything?"

"Oh, sure. But—really, we figured he went on a bender. He was that kind, Paul. Then, the next thing we knew, he was gone. We found out that Brister had gone to Seattle."

"And that was how long ago?"

"Two years ago."

"Well, it sure looks like old George didn't stay in Seattle."

Vosic gave his head a little shake but said nothing.

"Did Brister have any friends or—you know, drinking partners?"

"None that we knew of."

"Women?"

"Nah. This was a pretty spooky-looking guy, Paul. Women didn't exactly throw themselves at him. No, he was a loner. No personal life that we knew about."

"Do you still have his personnel files? His personal data?"

The start of a frown, then a short nod. "I think I've got some of that stuff in a storage room. I didn't keep a lot of it but you're welcome to whatever we've got. I'll have Carmen give you a hand."

"I appreciate that. One more thing." Whelan did his best to look just a little sheepish. "If this guy is around, as he may be, is he dangerous?"

Vosic shrugged. "Brister? Never scared me. Guys like that, they don't have any balls, you know what I'm saying, Paul? Confront a guy like that, he's gonna back down every time."

"Just your typical little numbers guy, huh?"

"Well, he wasn't little. He was a big, hulking kind of a guy. A certain amount of muscle but he was carrying a lot of extra weight. Reminded me of a big old bear—he had a real thick beard. One of those guys that wears a lot of hair on his face to compensate for the fact that it's all gone on top, you know?"

He thought for a moment, shot a quick, ostentatious look at the Rolex on his wrist, and then got to his feet.

"I got an eleven o'clock in the Loop, Paul. Gotta sprint. I'll get Carmen to give you whatever you need."

Vosic ushered him to the door and walked him over to the young woman's desk.

"Carmen, I'd like you to help Mr. Whelan. He's going to need to see the old personnel files from High Pair. Those are the files we stored in those green cartons, back in the storage room?" He raised his eyebrows in question. She nodded. "Okay, so give him whatever he wants—" He winked at her. "—within reason." And he showed his perfect white teeth.

Carmen laughed, blushed beneath her tan, winked back, and looked up at Whelan, smiling.

Vosic patted him on the shoulder. "Nice to meet you, Paul." He held out his hand and they shook. Whelan looked him in the eye and saw Vosic looking right past him. A worried man. A second later he was out the door.

Carmen watched him leave, her eyes lingering on the door for a moment. Then she looked at Whelan again.

"I love women named Carmen," he said.

"So does he." She smiled till the dimples came back.

Carmen got up and crossed the room with short, light steps.

She was tan and bare-legged and wore sandals and an ankle bracelet, and Whelan thought it would be a fine thing to have an office with a Carmen in it. She opened a door and scanned a row of black file cabinets till she found the one she wanted. In a moment she came out with an armful of manila folders in green dividers. She lay the folders on her desk and shrugged.

"That's it. Small company, you know? So there's only a few personnel files."

"Good. Less to read that way."

"Sit anywhere you like. In a couple of minutes I'm going on break."

"Does that mean I have to answer the phones?"

She laughed and showed him the dimples again.

"Don't do that, Carmen."

"Do what?"

"Show me those dimples. I cave in when I see dimples."

She laughed and sat down at her desk again. Too young for me, he thought and picked up the folders. He found himself a work space at an empty desk. There were files on a dozen people plus partial information on a number of temporaries from three different agencies. He scanned it all briefly and then studied the file on George Brister. He read it twice, first quickly and then carefully, for it was in many ways a remarkable batch of documents. After the second reading he scanned it again, this time looking for something, anything, that would convince a serious businessman that George Brister was worth hiring. He couldn't find it.

Brister's file and resume broke every rule he'd ever heard—Brister had held too many jobs in too many places. There were gaps between some of the jobs, and several of the gaps were of uncommon duration, one of them almost a year and a half. There were jobs in Seattle and Portland and Denver, and then Brister was in St. Louis and Milwaukee and finally Chicago. The gaps and movement could have meant anything, but Whelan already had a pretty clear idea what they really said, and he confirmed it with a quick look at the "Internal Use Only" form that gave Brister's medical history. Brister had spent several months in Martha Washington Hospital and two months in Grant, for unspecified problems. Both hospitals specialized in the treatment of substance abuse, particularly alcohol abuse. He glanced at Brister's application and saw that the accountant had mentioned "depression" as the cause of some of his previous problems. There were no letters of recommendation, not even of the "To Whom It May Concern" variety that the client could furnish himself. There was a letter, written in confidence from Brister's supervisor in Portland. The letter gave reluctant endorsement of Brister's talents as an accountant and then added a paragraph of caution:

> George is a capable accountant and has at times performed competently for us. I feel, however, that it is incumbent upon us to inform future employers of certain personality disorders that will doubtless affect his performance. During his stay here, George exhibited a number of disquieting traits and gave strong evidence of emotional difficulties. For one thing, George has a serious alcohol problem. On at least two occasions, George reported to work in a state of intoxication, and on one of these occasions provoked a violent altercation with his supervisor.

In short, George Brister's presence in an office can become an extremely disruptive force.

Whelan looked over the rest of the file, particularly the application form. Much of it had been left blank, including questions about family, person to notify in case of accident, interests, and professional organizations. He jotted down the names and addresses of Brister's former employers and Brister's home address. He set the application down and thought for a moment. Except for the detailed work history it was the application of a man with no personal life, no life of any kind. It was certainly an alcoholic's application, but there was no profile of the man applying for the position and there was no reason that Whelan could see for any business to hire George Brister. You might hire a George Brister if you were desperate, but you'd give him the gate as soon as someone more reliable turned up. He shook his head. No, you only hired a George Brister if George Brister knew someone. Someone who had pull, perhaps, or called in a favor of some sort, but it would have to be a hell of a favor.

"Some favor," he said.

"Excuse me?" Carmen said, coming back from her break.

"Just thinking out loud, Carmen. I think I'm through with this stuff. Did you ever know Phil Fairs?"

"Before my time. That was the old company."

"Ever hear Rich talk about him?"

She made a little shrug. "Not much. I mean, his name comes up once in a while, but that's about it. I do know he was kind of a—what's the word—a boy wonder?"

"A *wunderkind?*"

"Yeah, that's it. A hothead, too. Real bad temper. Gambled a lot, too."

"Yeah, so Rich tells me. How about George Brister?"

She shook her head firmly. "No. Him I don't know."

One more try: "Did you know Harry Palm?"

She started to shake her head and he added, "Rich's bookie."

"Oh," she said and started to nod, then caught herself. "You have to ask him about that." She looked down, apparently fascinated by her computer keyboard. Her posture told him she had concluded the interview. He watched her tap a couple of keys and begin to study the screen.

"Okay, Carmen. Thanks for your help."

"Anytime," she said, and he wished mightily that she meant it, but he knew better.

As he left Vosic's office, the door to a smaller office opened and a taller, younger version of Vosic emerged. The man stopped, frowned slightly, then put on the family smile and nodded. "Hi," he said.

Whelan extended his hand. "Paul Whelan."

The young man shook it. "Ron Vosic. Meeting with Rich?"

"Yeah."

"What line of work are you in, Paul?"

"Insurance, more or less," Whelan said.

Ron Vosic tried to hold on to his smile but unconsciously took a step back.

"Nice meeting you," Whelan said and walked on.

As he was leaving he clapped the young guard on the shoulder. The clock on the wall said he'd been there for forty minutes. In forty minutes he'd learned a lot: George Brister had not been hired for his qualifications or his work record, which meant that he'd been hired for another reason; Vosic had known Harry Palm, and if Carmen knew him, the acquaintance had to be recent; and from the look on Rich Vosic's face it was clear that Whelan had spoiled the man's lunch.

I think I've caused as much chaos here as I could, he thought. Not a bad forty minutes' work.

Six

By one in the afternoon Whelan had hit three taverns where Harry Palm used to hang out, and he'd gotten nothing. People backed away as soon as he mentioned Harry's name, and by the time he left the third bar he had begun to feel like a plague carrier. He tried a pair of open-air restaurants where Harry had indulged in public strutting. In one of them a young waiter snorted at the mention of Harry's name.

"They found him in the lake, didn't they?"

"Yeah, and we think you killed him."

The waiter went white under his summer tan and almost dropped a dish.

No sense of humor, Whelan thought. "Only kidding. Did you know him?"

"I only waited on him."

"Let me guess: he always ordered something that wasn't on the menu, sent it back a couple of times, tipped heavy. How am I doing?"

The waiter tried on a small smile. "That's right on. You a friend of his?"

"No, and nobody's admitting to that these days, anyway. Did you ever see him meet people here?"

"A lot of times. I think he was dealing here. Everybody thought he was dealing here. That's so stupid—I mean, hundreds of people coming and going, and all the street traffic, it's no wonder somebody killed him."

"Well, there's a particular breed of guy that wants very badly to project that image, and Harry was a classic. You know what a 'wannabe' is, right?" The waiter nodded and smiled. "Well, old Harry was a hoodlum wannabe. It was what he lived for, near as I can make out. And it got him killed. There's a lesson there for us all, kid. Let me try a description on you. Young man, tan, handsome, blond, around five nine, drives a yellow Lotus."

The waiter chuckled. "A Lotus? No, man, I don't know anybody that drives a Lotus."

He tried again. "I've got descriptions of three more customers. A small, dark-haired guy with one arm." The waiter shook his head. "Skinny black guy with an attitude." Another shake of the head, but this time the waiter looked uneasy.

"I'm sorry. I wish I could help."

"Let me try one more. A big man, either heavyset or muscular, I'm not sure which. Bald or shaved head, green eyes. Funny green eyes, I'm told."

The waiter's eyes opened wide. Bingo.

"Oh, him I remember. Yes, he met Palm here a couple of times."

"Anything you remember about their meetings?"

The waiter made a little shrug.

"Overhear anything?"

"No."

"What do you think they were meeting about?"

The waiter made an exaggerated sniffing sound. "Oh, a little blow, I guess."

"Harry was selling to this man."

A shrug and a nod.

"What can you tell me about the man who met Palm?"

"I can tell you he was a nasty prick. He stared at everybody—waiters, customers, people walking by. Just stared at them with this little superior smile on his face, like he was just daring somebody to start some trouble with him. He acted like he was hip to something nobody else was."

"Did you ever speak to him yourself?"

"If you can call it that. You get people who won't look at a waiter or waitress when they order, like we're beneath them. People who love to look down on service staff."

"I know the type. They're everywhere. He was one of those?"

"Yes, he was. He'd order while looking around at the crowd." The waiter gave an imitation of a man watching the room. "It was fine with me, though. He wasn't someone you wanted looking at you, if you ask me."

"I've had several people describe this man. Why don't you take a shot at it."

"Well, big, like you say. Very muscular but not a bodybuilder type. There was a lot of fat there, he had a gut on him. This boy liked to eat, I'll tell you that. And his head was shaved, very clean job, like he did it every day, like he was fussy about it. And he had a reddish brown mustache and a little Van Dyck beard, just a little bit of a beard on the point of his chin. Green eyes, funny color, real bright. And he was dark, like a guy who spends all his time in the sun, every day on the golf course, you know?"

"He drink much?"

The waiter nodded. "Oh, yeah. Martini drinker, this guy."

"Anything else you can tell me? Has he been in lately, or did you ever see him here alone or with someone other than Harry Palm?"

"Nope. I only saw him with Palm. I guess that's all I can tell you."

"You've been very helpful." Whelan pulled a five out of his shirt pocket and flicked it on the table. "Why don't you give me a little more coffee and put that in your pocket."

The waiter brightened. "Thank you, sir."

"My pleasure." He waited while the young man poured him another cup of coffee and then lit up a cigarette and sat back, watching the traffic and the other diners. A strong breeze had come up off the lake, whisking napkins and menus off tables, and perfectly combed hair no longer preserved its intended shape. Dust and dirt blew in off the street and hung over the tables, settling onto people's hamburgers and omelets. Flies hovered at every table.

Some fun, he thought and finished his coffee. He was on the verge of ordering another cup when a cab pulled up in front of the restaurant and deposited a full load of middle-aged men in dark suits and name tags. Pharmacists. Red-faced and laughing and chortling over a joke, the conventioneers haggled with the cabdriver for a moment and eventually paid what they seemed to think was an unspeakable fare, then turned toward the restaurant. It was just past two and they were sweaty and giddy and probably hammered already. Whelan predicted that by eight or nine this evening they would be passed out in a bar somewhere. And if they could remember any of this day, or any of this convention, for that matter, it would become part of a legend that they'd talk about for years to come, embellishing and amending and editing and interweaving till things they'd heard about or seen on TV became events they actually thought they had witnessed or taken part in.

Time to go.

He'd left the window open in the office and the room smelled of tar from the roofing job next door. High summer and the whole world smells of hot tar, he thought. Could be worse, though—I could be a roofer. He sat down at his desk and pulled out the Yellow Pages. The name of the mortgage banker Mrs. Fairs had mentioned was Victor Tabor. He found Tabor listed under "Mortgages." He had an office on Wabash, in the Loop. He called and made an appointment to see Tabor on Wednesday afternoon. Then he called his service.

"Hello, good morning," chirped the male voice on the other end, a voice unmistakably foreign, exotic, a melodious voice, a voice that would be in its element if lifted in song with dozens of other voices just like it. Whelan had never seen the owner of this voice but had talked to him many times: Abraham Chacko, recently of India and currently working for Whelan's answering service.

"Hello, Abraham." You're supposed to be working evenings, he thought.

"Hello, sir. Good morning."

"It's not morning anymore."

There was a pause, rich in doubt, and Whelan knew exactly how Abraham would fill it.

"Hello, good morning, Mr. Paul Whelan's offices."

"And this is Paul Whelan."

"No, this is answering sarvice."

Whelan sighed, outflanked. "Abraham, my name is Paul Whelan. I am in. Do I have any calls?"

There was another pause and now heavy breathing. Great, I've overloaded his circuits.

"Mr. Whelan is not…Mr. Whelan has two calls."

"What calls, Abraham?"

Pause.

"Two calls, sir," Abraham said confidently.

Whelan waited, listening to the excited breathing on the other end. "Are you going to tell me who called, Abraham?"

"Sar-tainly, sir. Mrs. Janice Fairs, she called at 9:14. And the second caller, he is a policeman, a Constable Bowman. He is calling at 10:41."

"Any messages from either of them?"

"Mrs. Fairs would like Mr. Whelan to call her. Constable Bowman…" Abraham paused and made gurgling sounds.

"What did he say, Abraham?"

"I am not understanding all of his English. He is speaking very fast, he is in a big hurry."

"Was your conversation with the constable…uh, a pleasant one, Abraham?"

Abraham Chacko giggled. "No, sir, he is a very angry policeman. His language is not so nice, that one."

"Don't worry about it. He's like that with everybody. Did he leave a number?"

"No, sir, he is telling you not to call him anymore."

Whelan laughed softly. "Abraham, you've done a fine job. Your English is improving."

"I am studying English at the Truman College."

"Glad to hear it," he said.

"I am studying English composition."

"What are you learning this week?"

"We are studying the adverbial clauses."

"Excellent. I use adverbial clauses constantly, Abraham.

Adverbial clauses are your friend. Take it easy, Abraham."

He called the number Janice Fairs had given him. She answered on the third ring.

"Hello?" Her voice was low, tentative.

"Paul Whelan returning your call, Mrs. Fairs."

"Thank you for getting back to me so quickly, Mr. Whelan. I was wondering if you had learned anything yet. I realize you have only been working a couple of days…" She let her voice trail off.

He restrained himself from laughing into the phone. No, I don't think that's why you called at all, lady.

"I haven't uncovered anything major but I'm working on a couple of angles that may turn something up." He heard a low sucking sound and realized she was puffing away at the other end. He heard her exhale smoke.

"Mr. Whelan, you are being evasive."

"It's what I'm best at."

There was silence on the other end and then he thought he heard a faint sigh.

"Mrs. Fairs…was there another reason you called? Is there anything else I can do for you?"

"Have you had an occasion to interview…have you met Rich Vosic, Mr. Whelan?"

"Yes, I certainly have. And isn't he a package."

"Do you like him, Mr. Whelan?"

"No, ma'am, I'm kind of choosy that way. No, I haven't found much to like about Rich Vosic."

"Interesting."

"Why is it interesting?"

"Men usually like Rich. He's handsome and personable and he oozes that aggressive sincerity."

"He oozes a lot of other things, too."

"I'm gratified to hear you say that."

Whelan was silent for a moment and then he saw. "So you're worried that I'll fall under his spell, huh?"

She gave an embarrassed laugh. "Most people do, Mr. Whelan. I know Phil did, and he was always a very shrewd judge of character. It's just that…you can't accept anything he says at face value, Mr. Whelan. He's a very deceitful man, a very manipulative man. Please weigh anything he tells you carefully."

"Mrs. Fairs, I've been in the business of weighing what people tell me for many years now and I haven't fallen under the spell of too many men. I've had a few difficult moments with women, however."

"What do you mean by that, Mr. Whelan?" Her voice was sharper, suspicious, and it took him by surprise.

"Nothing. It was a simple statement of fact. I was half joking, anyway."

Mrs. Fairs waited for more, then gave up. "Very well. Call me at my home when you have anything to report."

"Will do. It might be a while."

"That's fine. Just remember what I said about Rich Vosic."

"I'll do that."

Mrs. Fairs thanked him in a voice like an answering machine and hung up. Whelan leaned back in his chair and wondered what Janice Fairs was afraid Vosic would tell him. Something about her husband, obviously. No, that wasn't it, or she would have warned him of that first. No, she was afraid Vosic would tell him something about her.

Nervous bunch of people, he thought.

He drove to the Southport address he'd taken from Brister's personnel file. The building was an old frame house, three stories and a basement apartment—"garden apartment" in realtor parlance. It had a dull tan tar paper siding intended to convey the impression of brick solidity and the banister was missing on one side of the front porch. In the third-floor windows he could see sun-stained shades; on the second floor all the windows were thrown open in concession to the heat, the curtains knotted to keep them back. A fan turned in the middle window on the first floor.

He got out of the car and looked around. There were a number of similar houses on both sides of Southport, and at the north end of the block there was a bricked-up gas station.

Gentrification was on its way here, but the new money and walking papers hadn't reached this little pocket of what had once been a solid German neighborhood. Now a mixture of working-class whites and Latinos, the neighborhood was living on borrowed time, and the faces that stared at him from the windows seemed to know it. The great Gothic monument of St. Alphonsus Church dominated the south end of the neighborhood, and told passersby that, like many other dog-eared Chicago neighborhoods, this one had once known prosperity.

A thin, gray-haired man watched him from the first-floor window as Whelan walked slowly up the stairs and rang the bell marked "Majewski." Whelan rang the bell again and saw the man turn his head and say something to someone else. In a moment Whelan heard footsteps and then the door swung open. A frank-faced woman as thin as the man in the window stood there for a moment, looking Whelan up and down.

"Can I help you?"

"I hope so. Are you the landlady?" She nodded.

He took out a business card and handed it to her. "I'm a private investigator and I'm looking into some things involving a man who lived here a couple of years ago. George Brister. Remember him?"

"Sure I remember him. He's another one owed us money and just took off."

"Well, who's there?" came a complaining voice from within. Whelan turned and looked at the man in the living room window. The man stared back but didn't smile or blink or show other signs of life.

"You shut up," the woman snapped, still peering at Whelan.

"I wanna know who's there," the man snarled. "Who's he?" The man nodded toward Whelan through the window.

"And I said shut up, you!"

She lifted her chin toward Whelan and then made a little shake of her head, and the man in the living room was dismissed. "Don't pay no attention to that one," she said. "Gotta have his nose in everybody's business 'cause he's got nothing to do all day."

"Retirement can be tough on people."

She snorted. "He ain't retired. He's on disability. Been on disability half the time we been married. If we didn't have this building we'd be on the streets." She handed Whelan his card back. "You're a private detective? I only seen them on TV." A faint smile tried to take hold on her long face. She watched him openmouthed and one hand absently brushed a tuft of gray hair back from her face. Something different had come into her life, something had broken up the routine of her house and the man in the living room window, who looked as if he'd be a millstone in any life.

"Nobody like that ever came to talk to me," she said.

He smiled at her. "You're exactly the kind of person a detective needs to talk to. Most people wouldn't remember George Brister right away, and you did. I'm trying to find whatever information I can about him." She nodded.

"Come in and have a cup of coffee or something." She stepped aside and held the door for him. Whelan entered and shot a fast glance at the sour old man in the living room. The old man sat in a gray cloud of cigarette smoke, watching Whelan through a squint.

"Come on, mister." The woman led him out through a dining room filled with furniture beneath plastic covers and into the kitchen. The living room was dark and stale, the dining room looked as though it had been retired forever, but the kitchen was obviously where Mrs. Majewski lived, her refuge. It was a bright, cluttered room, spotlessly clean and actually cool. Back and side windows were open wide and the pale yellow curtains flicked in the cross breeze.

"Coffee?" she asked.

"I'd love some," he said.

She pulled out a chair and then bustled about and came back with a cup and saucer for him. Bone china, so old that the floral pattern on the saucer had faded and the border on the cup was gone in places. She poured him coffee from a tall, green plastic electric pot, refilled the cup sitting on the other side of the table, and took her seat. Perhaps it was the brighter light in her crowded little kitchen, but Mrs. Majewski no longer looked quite as pale and even looked a little younger than Whelan had taken her for. She sipped her coffee and gave him a shy smile. He wondered when the last time had been that this woman had had company.

Whelan sipped at his coffee. It wasn't particularly strong, but it was fresh.

"Coffee okay?"

"Yeah, it's good."

"What do you want to know about that one, that Brister?"

"Well, for starters, was there anything unusual about him? Did you notice anything odd about his habits or his hours? Anything like that?"

She made a sour face. "I rented to him because we needed the money, but I didn't like him, not a bit. He was a strange one."

"In what way?"

"Always smelled of liquor, for one. Even in the morning. And I don't mean like from the night before, I mean he smelled like he just had a drink with his breakfast."

"From what I've heard about him, it's just possible he did have a cocktail with his cornflakes."

She smiled a little at that. For a moment she sat looking into her cup, frowning with concentration. Then she shrugged. "I don't know how to explain it, but he was…he had strange eyes, you could tell he was odd. He had…dead eyes." She looked at Whelan to see if he was following and he nodded to encourage her. "He wouldn't even look at you when you talked to him, just looked around like he wasn't all there, like he was thinking about something else. Sometimes I'd say something to him and he wouldn't even answer me, like I wasn't speaking English to him."

"Ever see him with anybody?"

She shook her head, then stopped. "Couple times. A man come looking for him, couldn't find the apartment, 'cause it was the one in back on the second floor—the second and third floors is divided into two flats, you see. Nice lookin' man, you could tell he was money. Tall young man in a nice car, curly hair and nice eyes, nice suit." She reflected on the memory and shook her head. "I think it was that one's boss, that's what I think. I think that one was drunk and didn't show up for work and the boss had to come looking for him." She pursed her lips.

Whelan thought for a moment. She was probably right: it sounded like Phil Fairs. And it sounded exactly like a supervisor looking for a wayward employee who had a habit of not showing up for work when he was on a bender.

"Ever see a shorter man, also a prosperous-looking guy, blond, about the same age as the big one with curly hair?"

She shook her head.

"Describe Brister for me."

"He was big and kinda fat around the middle. People like that don't take care of themselves." She shot a glance toward the man in the living room and wrinkled her nose. "Big and heavyset, and bald, just a little hair left on the sides. Didn't take care of his hair, neither."

He suppressed an urge to laugh. Brister's lifestyle was even responsible for his baldness.

"And nobody else ever came to look for Brister."

"Not while he was here. That nice young fella, he come back one time, just before that one left without paying his rent."

"He did? Did he say anything?"

"Just asked me did I know where George Brister was, and I told him no. The rent was past due already and I was thinking that one was gonna try something funny, and I was right."

"But Brister wasn't gone yet?"

"No. I heard him up there that night, walking around with those big feet of his, stomping around. I think he was clearing out his stuff. That's what I think. Running out on his rent."

"Did he take everything?"

"Just about. Left a couple of odds and ends in the bathroom. Toothpaste and a razor. You know what else? He left his dirty clothes in the hamper." She raised her eyebrows and then shrugged in amazement at the depravity that this suggested to her.

Whelan thought for a moment. "Did he leave the utilities on?"

"The gas was shut off. Turned off the electric, too."

"Phone?"

She snorted. "Never had one. Who'd call him? Didn't have no friends that I ever heard of." She leaned forward. "So, can you tell me what he did that you're lookin' for him? Or is that, uh, confidential?"

"There's evidence that he defrauded the company he worked for. He seems to have left town in a big hurry, and some people are very interested in finding him. That's all I'm at liberty to tell you."

Apparently it was enough. She nodded slowly and gave Whelan a knowing smile. Her life had been filled with deadbeats—she could tell them a mile off. Whelan sipped at his coffee and then, just as Mrs. Majewski opened her mouth to ask another question, he said, "I'd like to see that apartment. Is that possible?"

She paused with her mouth open, considered, then nodded. "I don't see why not. Come on. They're not home now."

Whelan followed her out her back door and up a narrow wooden stairway in need of paint. She took him to the back door of a second-floor apartment, knocked briefly, listened, then opened the door with her key. She entered, flicked on a light, and beckoned him in.

"Here you are," she said. "This is your kitchen, you got a small living room just through that hall, and this room here's your bedroom. Bathroom's in the hall there." He watched her and realized that this was the sales speech she gave each time she showed one of these little carved-up apartments. And little it was. The linoleum was yellowed, the kitchen wallpaper stained in places, and both paint and plaster were coming undone on the ceiling. The whole place smelled of rotted wood and ancient plumbing. He crossed the room and peeked into the bedroom, where the tenants had left the bed unmade and had piled dirty clothes on chairs and in corners. The bedroom walls were painted dark brown and posters were taped on two of the walls.

He smiled at Mrs. Majewski. "Let me guess: you rent this

one to a young couple, early twenties. Casual dressers, maybe odd hairstyles."

She looked at him with eyes wide and let out a little chuckle. "That's right. Young couple. He wears his hair with a little kinda tail in back and she dyes hers red like a fire engine. They both wear black all the time. They told me they're married, but I don't think so. None of my business, though. Least they pay the rent. The two in front, they're always late."

Whelan nodded distractedly. "Well, thanks a lot."

She gave him a doubtful look. "Did you find out...did this help any?"

"Oh, sure. You've been very helpful, and I appreciate the time you took. The coffee was good, too." She gave him a little smile and they went back downstairs. She led him out through her apartment to the front door.

"You come back if you need to ask any more questions," she said.

"I'll do that," Whelan said. He went to his car, got in, and lit up a cigarette. Each place he visited seemed to raise more questions than it answered. He turned on the ignition, then the radio. It seemed to be working better. He hit a couple of buttons till a jazz station came on and his car filled with Jimmy Smith running his magic fingers over an organ keyboard. He listened for a while and then drove off.

As he drove he found himself wondering several things, like why a man skipping out on his rent would turn off his utilities, and why a man who apparently embezzled hundreds of thousands of dollars wouldn't just pay the rent and be done with it. And he was puzzled by one more thing. Why would an accountant who was making a pretty good buck with a firm like High Pair live in a dump like Mrs. Majewski's rear apartment?

The Caprice was parked in front of his office building, in the bus stop.

He went quickly up the stairs and laughed when he saw the door to his office open. He went in and slammed the door behind him. A good-looking young man in a lavender sport shirt was standing at the window watching traffic and turned to look at him. Bauman sat on the edge of Whelan's desk, tearing the paper off a long, thin cigar. He had dug into his bottomless store of ugly sport coats, this one being a bright red-and-white plaid with some sort of piping along the lapels.

"A little late summer breaking-and-entering, Bauman?"

The young one looked at Bauman. "This him?"

Bauman looked up, lit his little cigar, puffed at it, and said, "Detective Rick Landini, meet Paul Whelan."

Whelan nodded at Landini and the young cop gave the faintest movement of his head, as though worried that his unutterably perfect head of hair would come undone. Bauman grinned.

"You guys should get along great, you got a lot in common—you both think you're hot shit."

Whelan crossed the room and sank into his chair and spoke to Bauman's broad back. "I just try to be like you, Bauman. I walk around in bright-colored jackets and stick my belly out and put the arm on people."

He heard a snicker from Landini.

"And our boy Whelan's got a smart mouth on him, too. Don't make fun of me in front of my high-class new partner, Whelan. He already thinks I'm nuts." He turned to face Whelan, then nodded toward Landini.

"This here is the new police detective, Whelan. He's not like me, he's real smart. This guy here was valedictorian of his high school class, and he went to college. Whelan here's a college man, Landini." He indicated the shabby little office with a sweep of one beefy arm. "See what that sheepskin can do for you, Landini? Got his own car, too, right, Whelan?"

"I hate to interrupt you when you're having a good time, Bauman, but believe it or not, someone's paying for my time, so why don't you let me in on the purpose of your visit. Or did you just come up here to introduce me to your newest partner?" He looked at Landini. "Careful, Detective, this guy runs through partners like Zsa Zsa Gabor goes through false eyelashes. Boot hill's full of guys that used to run around with old Albert here."

Landini's eyes widened and he laughed. "He calls you Albert and he's still alive? I'm impressed." Bauman looked at Landini for a long moment and said nothing. Then he shifted slightly on the desktop.

"Easy there, Bauman, this desk isn't used to having that kind of weight on it."

Bauman stared at him, heavy-lidded, then nodded. He took a puff on his little cigar and exhaled, and the room was rich with the smells of cheap tobacco and Right Guard.

"You're your own good time, right, Whelan?"

"I'm just having a little fun with you, because I know you didn't come up here to do me any good. Fair is fair. What do you want?"

"No, babe, what do *you* want? All over the North Side, I'm working on something and everybody tells me I got a helper I don't know about, I got another guy asking questions about Harry Palm. Why is that, Whelan? Why would you be dicking around with an ongoing police investigation, huh? Will you tell me that?"

"I'm not working on the same thing you're working on, Bauman. I'm doing something else."

"I thought you and I straightened all this out. But no, you're asking around about who Harry Palm did business with, asking who he pissed off, asking who people seen him with, and like that. I don't hear anything about you working on something else, Whelan."

"I am, though. I'm looking into the circumstances around the death of a businessman who allegedly killed himself a couple of years ago. This guy did business with Harry Palm, and I—"

"So what? If he was a businessman he probably did business with a hundred other people. You investigating everybody he did business with, Whelan?"

"No, but nobody found any of his other business acquaintances buried in the sand in Belmont Harbor."

Landini turned from the window. "Was this guy Outfit or was he really a businessman?"

"Far as I know, he was just a guy making a lot of money on computer software and gambling large amounts of it away with Harry Palm."

Bauman took a final puff of his cigar and tossed it across the room into a wastebasket, still lit.

"Thanks, Bauman. Maybe someday you'll have an office and I'll come and torch it for you." There were ashes all over the desktop. Whelan took out a tin ashtray and slammed it on the desk.

Bauman shrugged. "You didn't offer me an ashtray, Whelan. You're a lousy host. But let's stay on the subject at hand, okay? You got anything at all, anything remotely related to this Harry Palm thing, you give it to me, you hear? This is mine, and anything anybody finds out is mine, all mine." He leaned forward and put his face close to Whelan's. Whelan could smell whiskey through the tobacco on his breath.

"Am I reaching you, Whelan? Anybody home in there?"

Whelan sat back in his chair and said nothing.

Landini moved away from the window. "I'm going down to the car and sit in air-conditioning."

"You do that," Bauman said. "I'll be finished with the private investigator in a minute."

Bauman took out another cigar and lit it, puffed at it, and waited till Landini was gone.

"You can say all the cutesy things you want in front of this fucking teenager they give me for a partner, Whelan, but don't get too carried away. Don't fuck with me, Whelan. You know me."

"I don't have any secrets, Bauman. But maybe you've got a few I should know. Tell you what—let's talk. I'll tell you what I have and you tell me what you have—" He held up a hand to intercept Bauman's protest. "—if it has anything to do with this other thing I'm working on. Come on, Bauman, I'll buy you dinner."

Bauman shrugged and looked around the room. A seam was coming apart in the shoulder of the jacket, and Whelan wondered how Bauman's clothes stood the stress. Then

Bauman nodded.

"Arright. Where?"

"We'll go to Raul's."

"I give a shit," Bauman said.

SEVEN

The Caprice was parked in front of a hydrant just up the street from Raul's when Whelan pulled up. Whelan parked under the El tracks between Raul's and Kelly's Pub and got out. So far the evening was airless and didn't promise to get a lot better. He peered into Kelly's. The saloon looked cool and dark. It was also empty—the bartender, a moonlighting firefighter Whelan knew casually, leaned into the window and watched the street. He nodded when Whelan waved.

He walked over to the Caprice. Bauman sat at the steering wheel, staring straight ahead and smoking with the windows rolled up. Whelan knocked on the window.

Bauman rolled it down, releasing a little cloud of cigar smoke. "Whelan," he said.

"Well, you going to come out and have din-din, or are you pretending to be on stakeout?"

"Just waitin' on you, Shamus."

Bauman pulled his heavy body out of the car, gripping the frame and the door. He was in his lime ensemble—a light green sport coat over a bright green knit shirt.

"Does that shirt glow in the dark?"

Bauman took the little cigar out of his mouth and looked at Whelan's yellow *guayabera*. "You should talk. You look like a Mexican Christmas." He brushed imaginary wrinkles from his jacket.

Bauman gave off his familiar odor of cigar smoke and Right Guard. Whelan wondered if Right Guard had come out with a cologne.

He indicated Bauman's car with a nod. "Your car's gonna smell like a hamster died in it from you smoking with the windows rolled up."

Bauman smiled and hitched up his dark green pants. "I know."

"Let me guess: Landini hates the cigars."

Bauman winked.

"And you hate Landini."

Bauman shrugged. "I don't hate nobody, Whelan. You know me, I treat everybody the same," and he laughed, a wheezy, hoarse whisper of a laugh. He looked at Whelan. "He's a smart kid, real smart. Good cop, too, least he's gonna be when he fucking figures out he don't have all the answers. Let's go, Whelan, I'm hungry."

Whelan pushed open the door and was hit by the archetypal smells of a Mexican restaurant, the odors of corn tortillas and chilies and pork stewing in its own juices and beef frying in lard. Raul stood at his cash register, staring across the street and working at his huge *bandito* mustache with loving strokes. Pale and pouch eyed, he nodded at Whelan from the depths of his hangover.

"Hello, Pablo. How you today?"

"I'm doing better than you, I think, Raul. Been partying too hard?"

Raul shrugged. "A little cognac, you know? But I gonna be all right. Couple doubles, I gonna be all right."

Whelan looked at Bauman. "That's his remedy for a hangover. Ancient remedy from the hills of his beloved Mexico. Two doubles and then some breakfast." Whelan jerked a thumb toward Bauman.

"This is Albert, Raul. He's my date."

Raul laughed and stopped fondling his mustache long enough to extend a hand. "Hello, Albert. You Pablo's date, eh?" He shut his eyes and laughed again and shook his head. "Hey, Pablo, your date's bigger than you are. You like 'em big, huh?"

Bauman shook Raul's hand briefly but kept his eyes on Whelan. "Enjoy yourself while you can, Whelan."

Raul indicated the tavern across the street, a worn-out place that called itself the Friendly Tavern.

"That gonna be my new cantina. Raul's Cantina. Make this one look like…" His vocabulary gave out and he shook his head.

"Looks the same size to me," Bauman said.

"He bought that cleaners right next to it and he's gonna knock the walls out."

"Gonna knock the walls out," Raul agreed. Then he seemed to rouse himself. He came out from behind his little Formica bar with a pair of ornate, laminated menus and took Whelan and Bauman to a little table in the very center of his little one-room restaurant.

There were four other patrons in the restaurant. A young couple ate quietly at a table along the far wall and occasionally shot nervous glances at the other two patrons, though Whelan could see no reason to be nervous about these two, for they were the notorious Jack and Jamie, disc jockeys for a local radio station about to go out of business and self-proclaimed "party animals." Loud, pushy, and obnoxious, both nearing fifty and fighting it tooth and nail. Raul's was their favorite restaurant, and fans often came up to the North Side looking for them here. Jamie was hunched on a stool at Raul's bar, face down in what appeared to be a plate of enchiladas suizas. Jack wasn't immediately apparent, but Whelan used his detective skills and located him—on the floor, a pair of legs protruding from the restroom. Raul had only one restroom, with a single wet terry cloth towel and a primeval-looking condom dispenser. Jack's legs moved slightly and Whelan saw that he'd lost a shoe.

Bauman looked at the two drunks and raised his eyebrows. "Nice place. You got your style, Whelan. Gotta give you that."

"This is just the floor show. Wait till you try the food."

Bauman nodded toward the unconscious man at the bar. "Looks like he tried the food."

"That's just his drinking style. The food's good, Bauman. Best Mexican food I've ever had, and I eat everywhere."

Raul came back over. He looked fondly at Jamie and then at Jack. "Too many of Raul's margaritas, eh?" He laughed and shook his head. "Crazy fuckers. They're famous guys. They eat here all the time. Lot of famous people eat here. Look, you see?" He indicated a framed photograph of himself with the late mayor Richard Daley. Hizzoner wore a huge black *charro* hat.

"That's Mayor Daley," Raul said. "He used to eat here all the time before he died."

"How many times, Raul?"

Raul shrugged. "Ah, I don't know. Once. His kid don't eat here yet. It's okay; he ain't important yet. So, what you gonna have, guys?"

Whelan suggested the enchiladas suizas and a burrito. "To say this burrito is the greatest burrito in the world is to do it an injustice. Greatest burrito of all time, maybe." Bauman shrugged and said he'd have what Whelan was having. They ordered a couple of Dos Equis and Bauman also asked for a shot of Walker's DeLuxe.

Raul brought the drinks and a basket of tortilla chips and Bauman took the bourbon at one swallow, then half the beer straight from the bottle. The young couple across the room got up to leave and the young man crossed the room to use the restroom, only to find Jack still comatose on the john floor.

He looked down at Jack, then over at Raul. "Excuse me, sir? This man—"

"Ah, he's okay, just walk over him. You can move him if you want, he won't wake up till later."

"Is he all right?"

"Oh, sure."

"Maybe somebody should…I don't know if he's breathing. And his pants are…you know, down."

Bauman looked at Whelan. "You bring all your women here, Whelan?"

"I don't have any women these days."

"Can't figure out why." Bauman put his cigar in the ashtray and got to his feet. Hitching up his pants over the solid, lime green dome of his stomach, he strode over to the bathroom, looked down at Jack, and then up at the young man.

"This guy's a smooth act, huh? Pants down to his ankles and he's out cold."

He bent down and shook Jack by the shoulder, then

grabbed a large pinch of cheek and shook his face. "Yoo-hoo, anybody home? Come on, Sunshine, wake up. People got to use this facility." Bauman stepped over Jack and turned on the cold water, then splashed it liberally on the sleeping drunk.

The young man moved back a few steps and looked uneasily at his companion.

"He's a police officer," Whelan called out. "He won't hurt the guy. I don't think."

Jack moved slightly and made the sound a horse makes after a good run, then rolled over on his side.

"Hey, no, no, no. Nappy's over, guy. Time to get up." He poked Jack with his shoe. "Up, Oscar."

An eyelid fluttered and Jack attempted speech. He said, "Wha?"

Bauman splashed more water on him. Jack opened one eye completely and was working on the other. He began to focus on the crew cut apparition throwing water on him and Whelan began to feel sorry for him—coming out of an alcoholic stupor in a strange men's room with Bauman standing over him.

"Come on, babe, you're almost there."

Jack sat up on one elbow and tried to manage indignation. His face wouldn't form the necessary scowl, so he settled for confusion. "What?"

"You're in a place called Raul's. You're on the floor of the can with your pants down to your ankles and the door's open and there's a woman present."

"Who the fuck're you?" Jack sat up and tried to work up belligerence, but the left eye wouldn't focus. Whelan shook his head and laughed.

"I'm the law, dimwit, and it's time to pull our pants up and get off the floor. Come on. What would your ma say if she saw you laying on the floor of a public toilet with your schwantz hanging out?"

Jack looked down and squinted at himself, then began to wrestle with his pants without actually getting up. "Where's Jamie?"

"That the guy in the red shirt? At the bar?"

"Yeah."

"He's dead."

"What?" Jack stopped pulling on his pants and stared slack jawed at him.

"Fell asleep in his food. Suffocated." Bauman winked at the young man and grinned over at Whelan. "Naw, he's okay. Least we think he is. Got his pants on, anyway. Come on, now, you get yourself together so this gentleman can use the john." He then lifted Jack by one arm and swung the deejay around like a child. When Jack had his pants up and almost fastened, Bauman escorted him to a table in the farthest corner of the room, dropped him into a chair, and said, "Sit there till I tell you to get up." Then he went to the bar to Jamie. He put his fat fingers alongside Jamie's neck, seemed to listen, then nodded. "Not much, but it's a pulse."

He came back to his table just as Raul emerged from the kitchen with the food.

"Nice place, Whelan."

"You belong here."

They fell to their food and Bauman tried a little of everything set before him. He chewed and nodded, chewed some more. "Good. It's good. Real good. I like this place, Whelan."

"I kind of figured you'd fit in."

Bauman nodded. "So. You wanted to talk. Here we are. You first." He picked up the burrito and bit into it, then made little moaning sounds.

"I have a client. Her husband was killed two years ago in a boating accident. There is almost overwhelming evidence that it was suicide, but she refuses to believe it. She's convinced the guy's business partner is somehow responsible. Had him taken out or something, she's not sure."

Bauman stopped chewing and gave Whelan a funny look. He sat there for a moment, head tilted to one side, then shook his head.

"What was the guy's name?"

"Fairs. He died in a fire on his boat."

"So what are you doin' with that? That's no case, Whelan.

That's runnin' around chasing your tail. I remember that one, Whelan. I did a little pokin' around on it. We got a tip; there was nothing to it, though. We figure it came from the broad." He shrugged, then gave Whelan a puzzled look. "So what makes her bring it up now? I mean, after two years?"

"Mrs. Fairs remains convinced that her husband's partner had something to do with it, and her husband's bookie led her to believe there was something to the story."

Bauman resumed chewing, then took a pull at the beer. "Lemme guess: his bookie was Harry Palm."

"Right."

"That asshole. He was just taking her money, Whelan. He was just telling her what she wanted to hear. But why now, is what I'm wondering?"

"She ran into Palm a couple of weeks ago, and she talked with him recently. She was supposed to meet him one night around the time he disappeared."

Bauman cut into an enchilada with his fork, ate some, nodded. "This fucker can cook, Whelan. What were they supposed to meet about?"

"Harry Palm told her he had something on the partner. She says he was excited and acting very nervous, but that he seemed confident he had something special. He told her he was getting ready to take the partner down."

"That's the whole thing?"

"No, there's more. I'm fairly sure the partner, whose name is Vosic, made book with Harry Palm, too."

"Well, it figures if his partner did…"

"Recently. Since his partner died. I've been nosing around his place of business and I know his staff is familiar with the late Harry Palm."

"Don't mean he killed him."

"No, but it's a start."

Bauman shrugged, took a bite of enchilada, shook his head. "This don't sound like something for you, Whelan. How'd you get into this one? This babe something special?" He chewed and tilted his head slightly. "You're not goin' that route again, are you?"

Whelan squirmed. The question was genuinely embarrassing. "No. She's nothing to me. Just a client. Not my type at all. She's used to money and she probably thinks of me as somebody from the peasant class."

"What then? Money? She paying you a lot of money?"

"She's paying me, and right now any money is a lot of money."

Bauman nodded as though this made more sense.

"Mostly, though, she made me curious. Her husband didn't sound like the type to commit suicide, and she half convinced me that there was a connection between her husband and old Harry. And now that I'm in it, there are a couple of people in it that have…captured my imagination, I guess you'd say."

"The partner and who else?"

"Their accountant. A guy they hired who took off just before Fairs is supposed to have committed suicide. A guy everybody took to be a harmless drunk and who seems to have taken them all to the cleaners, to the tune of hundreds of thousands."

"Where's he?"

"Don't know. Everybody tells me he disappeared four or five days before this guy, Philip Fairs, was killed on his boat."

Bauman shrugged. "Always fascinates me when one of these button-down types with a lot of money punches his own ticket."

"What do you remember about it?"

"Not much to remember, except there was nothing to make it homicide, no evidence of any kind of violence. There was, you know, a bunch of witnesses—"

"A *bunch?* News to me."

"Yeah. Bunch of other richies on a boat off the breakwater. They recognized the boat, they knew this guy, they saw him pouring gasoline all over the boat. Then, boom. Pieces of boat all over the lake. Found the body about a week later in Monroe Harbor, kinda caught up in the anchor lines of one of the big sailboats." Bauman laughed. "Imagine you're some poor slob wants to go out on his sailboat and play sea captain, and here's this thing caught up in your ropes, looks like a man only it's kind of puffy and slimy and all white. You ever see a floater, Whelan?"

"Once, but he was only in the water a day or so."

"You don't wanta see 'em when they been in there a while, 'specially when the lake's warmed up a little."

Whelan thought for a moment. "Maybe these people on the other boat didn't see what they thought they were seeing. Maybe Fairs was already dead and they saw somebody else."

Bauman smiled. "Come on, Whelan. Where's the evidence of anything like that? The explosion would've killed whoever was on board."

Whelan shrugged.

"So what's your idea, that this accountant and the partner took this guy out for his money?"

"In a general sort of way, I guess I think the accountant wasn't who he was supposed to be—at least he wasn't the dumb drunk everybody took him for. And I think the partner smells funny. I don't know if he had anything to do with the death of Fairs, but he knows things he's not telling, and it was clear that I bothered him. I let a few things drop about the accountant being around town again, about him bleeding some other companies, and this guy turned green. He knows something I don't, and he's worried about something."

"*Is* the accountant back in town?"

Whelan sat back and thought for a moment. "I have no idea. He's a complete mystery to me; the pieces of him that people have given me just don't fit together. This Vosic said they tried to find him and that he seems to have gone back to Seattle, where he was from."

"And did he?"

"Don't know. I got somebody there I could call, but by now I can't believe there'd be any trail. And even if he went to Seattle, who says he's still there?"

"You think he came back," Bauman said, pointing with his fork.

"Yeah, I guess I do." He thought for a moment and then

added, "If he ever really left."

"But nobody knows nothing, right?"

"No."

"And did this guy know Harry Palm?"

Whelan smiled. "Such a smart cop, Bauman. That's what I'm working on now."

"Well, it ain't your case to be working on, so you got something ties this guy with Palm, I want it." A hard little glint came into Bauman's eyes.

"I don't really have anything. I thought you might. That's why I decided to buy you din-din. I've got descriptions of several guys who were doing business with Harry Palm—a skinny black guy, a little white guy with one arm, a big guy with no hair and a bad attitude. So what do you have?"

"Never mind what I got—skinny black guy, huh?"

"Yeah. Why?"

"No reason." Bauman looked around casually. "These three guys connected?"

"I doubt it. Maybe the big guy and the guy with the one arm, I don't know. Don't know a thing about the black guy."

"No, huh? So which one you really interested in? The big one?"

"Maybe, but he doesn't really sound like the guy I'm looking for. Got another question for you. How hard are you looking for Harry's killer?"

Bauman shrugged. He finished the last of the enchiladas and was scraping his plate with his fork.

"Easy on the plate, Bauman. I'll buy you another dinner if you're still hungry."

Bauman paused and looked at Whelan from up under his eyebrows for a long moment and said simply, "I'll live. And as for Harry Palm, it's none of your business. How many ways I got to tell you that?"

"Tell me this, then: do you give a shit who killed him?"

"No. He was a scumbag and I think another scumbag whacked him. But I'm looking. It's not the only thing I got on my hands, though."

"It never is, is it?"

Bauman smiled. "No. I'm looking for half a dozen people at the same time, Whelan, and I figure I'm gonna get a couple of 'em, at least a couple."

"And one of 'em's special."

Bauman nodded. "That's right. And if I have time, I'll maybe get serious about this asshole."

Whelan decided not to ask Bauman about his "special" case. "Your partner mentioned the Outfit."

"I didn't," Bauman said.

"You think it was amateur night." Bauman nodded. "That's how it sounded to me."

"That's how it looked, too. But maybe it was somebody small time. Everybody Harry Palm knew was small time. A genuine hood wouldn't work up a sweat killing a sleaze like Harry Palm. Another player just up from the minors, though, he'd do it."

"That what you think it is, a guy from triple A?"

Bauman shrugged. "Couldn't tell you."

"Yeah, you could, Bauman. The wheels are always turning."

"I don't know shit, Whelan. But if I had to place a bet, that's what it would be. Somebody small time, wants to be big shit, wants to send out his message, leave his, you know, his calling card. And if that's what we got here, you know what's gonna happen to this new kid on the block?"

"He's going to have a short life."

Bauman pointed at Whelan with his fork. "There you go. If this is new talent, Whelan, I don't really have to do much, you know? They're gonna find pieces of him twenty years from now, they're gonna find his teeth in the forest preserves. Which is what I think would've happened if somebody that was Outfit decided to do old Harry."

"So tell me, Bauman, if you think this Harry Palm thing isn't important, if you think it's gonna clean itself up eventually, why do you care if I dig around a little? It's not hurting you and it could help me."

Bauman shrugged. "'Cause it's mine, Whelan. That's all you

need to know. It's my case, and whether I'm workin' hard on it or lettin' it go for a while, you got nothing to do with it. And who says it ain't gonna hurt me? Who says you ain't gonna screw something up?"

"I gave you a collar last time I 'screwed one up.' You suffering from memory loss, Bauman?"

Bauman went red and dropped the fork. He leaned forward, giving Whelan a better look at the burst capillaries all over his face. "No, I don't suffer from no memory loss, Whelan. I remember everything. I remember you found who you had to find, I remember you found a couple guys just after they got whacked and you eventually put it all together and it was a nice piece of work, and I also remember I saved your ass 'cause you decided to play the masked avenger, take it all by yourself."

"I don't remember you having any major problems with it when it was all over."

"Maybe I changed my mind," Bauman said. He turned suddenly and held up his glass and Raul hurried over.

"How about another beer—a shot, too. And give Whelan what he wants," Bauman said.

"Okay, Albert," Raul said and hurried back to his bar. Whelan watched him and then looked for a moment at the two drunks—Jack was bent over his partner, trying vainly to wake him. Jack apparently hadn't yet noticed that he'd lost a shoe.

Bauman glared at Whelan. "This guy calls me Albert one more time and I think I'm gonna put a plate down your throat."

Raul came back with two beers and Bauman's shot.

"Take it easy, Bauman. Just nurse your cocktail." Whelan watched Bauman down the shot and then take a pull at the beer. Bauman let out a soft belch.

"Let me tell you what I think, Detective Bauman. I think you're getting nervous that a private investigator is going to start following you around like your pet monkey and it's gonna ruin your image. That's one. Two, I think you've got an idea about who did Harry and for some reason it makes a difference to you, you want this one all to yourself; you're afraid I'll come up with something. Three, I think you probably put down more liquor in one day than any three guys in the Chicago Police Department."

Bauman stared at him. "What are you, my ma? What do you care if I drink?"

Whelan shrugged. "Look, I'm not going to follow you around and I'll give you whatever I come up with. And I don't care if you kill yourself with that shit, actually. It's a free country—man's got a right to turn himself into a derelict if that's his taste. But I think I'm going to need help and I don't know where else to get it." He was about to say more, then stopped. There was nothing more to say.

Bauman looked at him for a second, then laughed quietly. "You got a mouth on you, Whelan. Some day I'm gonna read in the paper that they found you in the trunk of some car and I'm gonna say 'He got whacked 'cause of his mouth.'" He sipped at his beer, looked at his empty shot glass, and shot a quick look back at Raul, obviously trying to decide whether to have another one.

"So Mother Whelan thinks I drink too much, huh? All right, Whelan. Let's do this: you keep out of my way as much as possible, you go ahead and ask your questions and snoop around, and anything you hear, you come right back to me with it, is that clear?" Whelan nodded. "Okay. You be careful not to muddy up the waters and let me know what you got, and we won't have a problem."

"And what will I get out of this?"

Bauman grinned now. "The goodwill of the Chicago Police Department, particularly Area Six, Violent Crimes. And you'll have your health. That's gotta count for something, Whelan, right? You'll have your health." He chuckled and sipped at his beer. "No, I'm just jerking you around here, Shamus. You gimme what you got and I'll let you know if this guy Vosic's name comes up, or this other guy, the floater—Fairs? They come up in the course of my investigation, I'll let you know. And about my drinking, Whelan…fuck you."

Whelan smiled and sat back. Bauman finished his beer, wiped his lips, balled up his napkin, and took a hook shot for the trash container at the near end of the bar. It fell three feet short.

"Got your party manners tonight, huh?"

"This guy's got a guy in a coma at his bar, you think he cares if I drop a napkin on his floor?" He waved to Raul, who was pouring water from a glass into a potted palm in the window.

"As long as you're having a good time, Bauman, that's all I care about."

Bauman looked down at the wreckage of his dinner. "I did have a good time. Best Mexican I've had in a long time. And hey, you're buying, what a deal."

Raul came over.

"We'll take the check, Raul."

Raul stared at the table for a moment, did his impression of a man performing the lower math functions, and said, "Twenty bucks."

Whelan laughed. "The man has a mind like a calculator. Funny thing, it always comes out even like that."

"Even the tax, huh?" Bauman asked.

"Don't get Raul started on taxes, Bauman." He handed Raul twenty-five dollars.

"I pay taxes," Raul said, warming up, "I pay lots of goddam taxes—licenses, too, all these fucking licenses. Gotta have a license for the jukebox and the cigarette machine, gotta have a liquor license and a goddam food license…"

"It's a complicated world, Raul," Bauman said and laughed.

Raul took his money and walked away, still muttering about his burden from the government.

Bauman patted his stomach. "How about an after-dinner mint, Whelan? We can go to this joint next door."

"Fine with me."

The "joint next door" was Kelly's, and after the greenhouse humidity of Raul's, Kelly's air conditioner was a shock to the system. There were a dozen or so customers now and the bartender held up a finger to Whelan.

They took a pair of stools at the street end. At the far end of the bar the Cubs game was in progress and half a dozen upturned faces watched. Whelan looked at the screen and saw that the Mets were batting and that there seemed to be a great deal of screaming and cheering from the Shea fans. The batter was tall, slender Darryl Strawberry, and he was smiling. Better not to watch, Whelan thought.

Bauman looked around. "Nobody I know here."

"What did you expect? It's been a long time since you were a street cop up here."

Bauman shrugged. "I used to come here a lot, though. Used to play horseshoes here. There was a couple old guys could throw shoes with anybody. One of 'em didn't even have a home, lived in a car under the tracks out here. This was an okay place. Weren't any of these fern bars yet, so there was…you know…"

"All kinds of people," Whelan said. "I remember. I used to drink here once in a while. Every kind of person drank here—De Paul kids and tin-knockers and half the police on the North Side and lawyers and whatever." He looked around as the bartender came over.

"Beck's is okay, Whelan, right? A dark?"

Whelan nodded and Bauman ordered two beers and a shot for himself.

Whelan looked around at the red-flocked wallpaper and studied the wondrous back bar, a relic from a bygone age when people built things slowly and with the best available.

The bartender brought the drinks and Bauman paid. He was sipping at his Beck's when the back door opened. Bauman looked and then groaned.

"What's the matter, Bauman?"

"Old guy that just came in. Used to work out of Town Hall. I don't need to talk no cop talk. Wanna go to the joint across the street?"

Whelan looked out the front window at the saloon that would eventually become Raul's Cantina. "The Friendly Tavern? Yeah, that would be about your style."

"Cut 'n shoot bar?"

"They haven't had a shooting yet, but it's not a place to bring your best girl on a Saturday night."

"Remember the Harvest Moon over on Lincoln?" Bauman asked.

"Sure. I never did find out if that story was true, about the guy bringing in the head. Do you know?"

"Nah," Bauman said. "Always sounded like fairy stories to me."

"Well, this gin mill across the street isn't quite in that class, but they can't get through a weekend without a good-size beef."

Bauman studied the tavern with a look that was almost wistful. "Gotta check it out sometime. So. You got a theory about why this Vosic guy might have anything to do with Harry Palm's, uh, untimely death?"

"Nothing I'd put in writing."

"You got something, Whelan, I know you. You got an idea, anyway."

"From something Harry Palm allegedly said to my client, I wouldn't be surprised if Vosic was a dealer himself. If he was, and we know Harry was, that would be a source of some friction. I don't know. That's all I've got so far. He could be a dealer."

"Or he could be an asshole businessman that never broke a law in his life."

Whelan remembered Vosic's eyes as he'd listened to Whelan's fabricated biography of George Brister. He knew the look, could tell when somebody was feeling his collar go tight. "Maybe so, Bauman, but I don't think so. This guy's dirty, you'd know it as soon as you saw him."

Bauman was about to say something and then stopped with his mouth open. A slight smile came to his lips. "Oh, here we go," he said.

Whelan followed Bauman's gaze through the window. Across the street a cluster of bodies was jammed into the door of the Friendly Tavern, half a dozen bodies, and they spilled out onto the sidewalk, three on three. There were arms waving and punches being thrown and Whelan saw a pool cue swinging, and Bauman was off his stool and to the door before Whelan could speak.

"C'mon, Whelan," Bauman said over his shoulder. "You're deputized."

"Just what I wanted."

Outside Kelly's the sport coat dropped to the sidewalk and Bauman slipped his watch into a pants pocket, then turned to Whelan.

"What we got here, Whelan, is civil unrest." Then, grinning and flushed and sweating from whiskey and Raul's hot sauce and an August night in Chicago, he stalked off into the street. A cabbie hit his brakes and screamed at Bauman, and the detective whipped out his shield, flashed it, banged his big fist on the hood of the cab, and stormed on. Whelan walked in front of the cab. The hood was dented.

The cabbie hit his horn. "I'm with the stocky gentleman," Whelan said and followed Bauman.

The six aspiring combatants had drawn up loose battle lines and every one of them had something in his hand—a couple of bottles, a bicycle chain, a car antenna, a pool cue, a pair of chukka sticks. The pool cue made it a beef over money and a game of eight ball, Whelan thought, but more likely it was about something else—summer in the city, heat and liquor and somebody with woman trouble or somebody out of a job. It had just begun to go dark and there would be fights like this in taverns all over the city. This one was shaping up to be a dandy.

Bauman hit the sidewalk on the far side of the street and grinned at Whelan over his shoulder.

"These guys brought all their equipment, huh?"

The guy with the chukka sticks was the biggest of all of the fighters, and the chukka sticks said he'd been looking for it; he put his back to the wall of the tavern and dared the others to come after him. His teammates, the ones with the antenna and the chain, and both small, skinny men, took a few feverish swings at the three brawlers facing them and then took off running.

"Arright, break it up. Police officer," Bauman yelled, and no one seemed to care.

One came sprinting past Bauman with a bigger man in pursuit, and Bauman took the second one out with a forearm. The little one with the antenna took the opportunity to swipe at Bauman with his weapon. He missed with his first swing and was bringing his arm back for another shot when Whelan caught his arm from behind, grabbed him by his hair, and ran his head into a parked car.

"Hostile little shit, aren't you?"

He let the man drop to the ground and followed the beefy form of Chicago's finest. Bauman waded in, bellowing orders, identifying himself as a police officer and clubbing at everything in his path.

The guy with the chukka sticks opened the forehead of one of his assailants and Bauman pulled a second one off and threw him through the front window of the dry cleaners next door. Glass rained on the sidewalk and a crowd began to form on both sides of the street. Another man appeared in the doorway, a new contestant, holding a Budweiser bottle over his head and yelling some sort of personal war cry. He came pounding out of the tavern and Bauman took him out with a straight right.

Two more came out of the saloon. One had a beer belly that hung far over his belt and threatened one day to touch the ground, and the other was muscular and wore a dago T to show it off. He was grinning and Whelan knew this one was an asshole. They both ran for Bauman. Whelan came up from behind and caught the fat one by the back of his hair, pulled him around, and buried a hook in the epicenter of all that flesh. His arm went in so deeply he feared it would be sucked in, never to be seen again, and then the fat man went down and began to make retching sounds at the edge of the sidewalk.

A squad car pulled up and the youngest street cop ever to leave the academy emerged from the driver's side. No one came out the shotgun side and Whelan cursed one-man squad cars. The boy cop put on his hat, pulled out his stick, swallowed, and advanced on the roiling mass of street fighters.

The guy with the bicycle chain came up off the sidewalk where Bauman had planted him. He looked at Bauman, saw Whelan watching him, and decided to take a swing at Whelan instead. The chain caught Whelan on the forearm and then, on the backswing, grazed the side of his head. Whelan stepped inside on him, hit him once in the ribs and then with a kidney punch, and bounced a straight right off his jaw. The fighter went down on all fours.

The young cop yelled for everyone to stop and Whelan laughed. The fat guy was up on one knee and muttering death threats and Whelan kicked his hand out from under him and then sat on him. He looked up at the kid.

"Yeah, I know. You're a police officer. So's he." He nodded in the direction of Bauman, who was standing amid three prostrate forms and trading punches with the one with the chukka sticks. The guy in the dago T was sitting on the sidewalk, shaking his head.

The chukka warrior made karatelike lunges and grunted and postured. Bauman's hands flashed out faster than Whelan would have believed possible, and the man was no longer holding his beloved sticks. Bauman threw the sticks over his shoulder and took the guy out with a long, looping right as two late entries came at him from the tavern.

The young cop moved to assist him and Whelan just shook his head. "Nah, let him do it. He likes it."

The kid looked at him uncertainly, watched Bauman throw hands at his two newest opponents, and then said, "Who *is* that guy?"

"Errol Flynn's ghost," Whelan said, and when the boy looked at him in confusion, added, "That is Detective Albert Bauman of Her Majesty's Berserkers."

The kid nodded once, then a second time, eyes wide. He looked at Whelan and grinned, a small boy meeting Babe Ruth.

"That's Bauman? No shit. Bauman," he said, and nodded to himself. "Got to give him a hand."

"No. Just give him room."

The bodybuilder in the dago T came up off the canvas one more time and bounced a hook off the back of Bauman's head. Bauman yelped, shoved the man he was fighting into a wall, and turned on the bodybuilder.

The muscle man bounced on the balls of his feet, grinned, posed, nodded, and threw jabs at the air.

"C'mon, fat boy, show me something," he said.

Bauman advanced with his right up under his chin and his

left out and looked about as difficult to hit as the Water Tower. The bodybuilder threw a sharp little combination. Bauman's head moved six inches each way and the punches caught nothing, and then he waded in with a few of his own.

Whelan watched in wonder as Mother Bauman's favorite son worked out. He glanced over at the young cop, whose facial expression said he was experiencing the afterlife.

"Take a long look, kid. You're watching a master. You'll never see a fat man move like that again in your life."

And then it was over. Whelan was still sitting on the fat man. The bodybuilder was leaning up against a parked car. His nose was broken and his left eye looked like a diseased plum, his career on magazine covers over before it began. A crowd from Kelly's and Raul's and the grocery store on the corner now pressed around the scene. Half a dozen men lay in various stages of unconsciousness on the sidewalk. The proprietor of the cleaners came out to inspect the damage to his front window; a pair of legs still protruded from inside his establishment. Traffic on Webster had come to a halt as the number 37 bus had stopped in the middle of the street to allow its passengers to have a look.

Summer in the city, Whelan thought.

Two more squad cars pulled up at right angles to the sidewalk and four cops were now moving toward the scene.

And in the middle of it all, legs spread apart and his right still cocked, Bauman breathed through his mouth and waited for the rematch. Gradually he focused on the uniformed officers and nodded.

"Hello, Al," one of them said.

Bauman nodded and wheezed.

"Been having a workout, have you?" asked the oldest of the cops, a heavyset man with sweat stains on the back of his shirt.

"There's been a disturbance of the peace, Bernie. I want all of these fuckers arrested." Then, as an afterthought, he pointed to Whelan. "Except this guy."

The sergeant looked at Whelan. "And who are you, to merit such special treatment?"

"I'm his kid," Whelan said and got up off the spongy body

of the fat man.

The young cop was telling one of the others that the big man was Bauman, Al Bauman, and somewhere across the street, somebody from the Kelly's crowd was applauding. Whelan walked over to Bauman.

"You all right?"

"I look hurt to you?" Bauman said, still panting.

"No, you look like a guy that's going into cardiac arrest."

Bauman tucked in his shirt. "From a bunch of slugs like this? That'll be the day, Whelan." He started across the street to retrieve his Day-Glo jacket and then stopped in the middle. He nodded to Whelan. "Hey, Whelan, I had a real nice time. We gotta do this again." And he grinned. Then he was shouldering people out of his way.

Oh, not if I have a choice, Whelan said to himself.

EIGHT

He sat in the Jet and listened to the last few innings of the Cubs game. It was the quietest baseball crowd he had ever heard at Shea Stadium, and he knew they weren't smiling anymore. The Cubs were leading six to three, Lee Smith was blowing fastballs by overanxious Mets hitters, and the Cubs didn't seem particularly impressed by the Mets jinx. Four strikeouts and a groundout in the final two innings and Lee Smith had a save and the Cubs, the amazing Cubs, were still in first place with no sign of letting go. On the radio the announcers were coming slightly unglued and Whelan could just imagine Harry Caray singing one of his homemade ditties about the local heroes.

Who says there's no God? Whelan said to himself.

The knuckles on his right hand were swollen and the middle one on his left was skinned. His head stung a bit where the bicycle chain had struck him but there was no blood, just a slight lump. It was cooling off a bit and there was a lake smell in the air as a breeze from the east pushed its way through the exhaust smells of the crowded North Side.

Let's see what the boys are up to, he thought, and pulled out onto Webster.

Rush Street glowed several million watts brighter than the rest of the city, and it seemed that half the population and all the cabs were there, spilling out their loads of tourists and swingers and drunks and playing bumper cars with the rest of the traffic. Neon flashed in a hundred colors and rock music blew out onto the street from the open doors of taverns.

Vosic's car was gone from the space in front of his tavern. On a hunch he turned up a side street and into the alley that ran behind Rick's Roost. He cruised past and saw a pair of cars parked in the half lot just outside what seemed to pass for a beer garden. The Lotus was there. The "beer garden" had room for half a dozen tables and they all seemed to be full, for the young folk, Whelan knew, loved to share their food and drink with the insects that ruled the night. He drove through the alley and back onto Rush, then parked up the street from the tavern in a no-parking zone and watched through the rearview mirror. Right in front of his car a pair of rumpled, sweaty middle-aged men stopped two slinky young women and apparently attempted to sweep them off their feet. The women shoved them lightly out of the way and walked on without looking back.

Twenty yards up the street a pair of tiny black boys break danced to the music from one of the bars, and they were drawing quite a crowd. They were good, these little boys miles from their homes, and they didn't miss a beat or a step. As Whelan watched they were joined by a drunk with a name tag. The man, gray haired and bulging through his blue shirt, insinuated himself between the boys and attempted to match their steps, to the delight of the onlookers. When they hit the pavement and began twirling around on their backs, he hunkered down and pushed himself in a half circle, succeeding only in ripping the back of his shirt. And when the boys stood on their heads and defied gravity, the pharmacist bravely got into a sort of primitive handstand and then fell back, rolling off the sidewalk and falling between a couple of parked cars. A pair of chunky men with name tags came out of the crowd and helped him to his feet, then gave him a handkerchief. He appeared to be bleeding from a cut over one eye.

A police car stopped alongside the Jet and the cop inside told Whelan to move. Whelan pulled out and drove around for a couple of minutes, eventually returning to the same block. This time luck was with him as a long, dark blue Buick pulled out and handed him a parking space. Rick's Roost was across the street and two doors down, and Whelan had a perfect view of the front door and all its comings and goings. There was, at first glance, nothing to separate Vosic's tavern from forty or fifty other places within a quarter mile—the same unending file of single men, alone or in groups, and same steady influx of young women, always in pairs or groups. A bouncer at the door, young, very tan, tall, and muscular and wearing the obligatory knit shirt to show off the result of his thousands of sit-ups and push-ups and all the miles of roadwork. This one was a smiler; some bouncers believed they were Wyatt Earp, others smiled at the world in confidence of their physical ability to meet all situations. At some of the taverns in the area the bouncers screened their customers. Drunks were turned away, of course, but people who weren't particularly well dressed, people who looked like they didn't have a lot of money, people who were the wrong ethnic persuasion, and even people who weren't particularly attractive, all were told by a large man at the door that the tavern premises were filled to overflowing and could not accommodate any more customers. On his first night in town a new center for the Chicago Bulls had been turned away by a singles bar down the street on Division, ostensibly because the saloon was too crowded but in reality because he was black and seven feet tall.

Whelan watched the door of the tavern and listened to a jazz station. Twice cars pulled up alongside to wait for his parking space and he had to wave them off. He sat in his car with the window rolled down and listened to music and savored the slightly acrid smells of summer in the city and now and then caught a trace of perfume from the young women passing by, and he remembered times when he'd come down with friends and wasted his time and money in hot, dark rooms athrob with loud music and tried to pick up women. He looked at these young—very young, half-his-age young—women passing by and told himself he was retired from the bar scene.

He had been at his post for forty-five minutes when he saw him—on the crowded sidewalks of Rush Street, among the hundreds of strutting, preening males stepping out to show the female world their stuff, this man stood out. He was bigger than most, maybe six three, and heavy, with a pronounced stomach and big shoulders and thick arms. He wore a dark blue knit shirt that hung loose over a pair of white deck pants and dirty white tennis shoes without socks. He was big, all right, and dark and his shaved head caught the glints of the street lights, and Whelan could see the dark point of the beard.

Half the people on the street were tanned, but his was different, a reddish color obvious even in the mixture of artificial lighting of the street, the color of a man who lives in the sun. There was a cocky roll to his walk and he kept his hands loose at his sides, and he had *the look*—it was the same everywhere, universal, and on this night there were thousands of men in Chicago wearing the look that said they were here for a fight. And Whelan could see that with this man the look was a way of life. It was there in his posture, in the way he kept his hands, in the way he stared at other men passing by.

Whelan watched him walking toward Vosic's tavern. The bald man stopped at the door and lit a cigarette, surveying the street as he held lighter to tobacco. Whelan watched how this man took in each face around him, and for a fraction of a second he thought he saw this man's eyes rest on him. Then the bald man turned, looked the young bouncer in the eye, and walked past him without speaking. The bouncer stepped aside to let him in and Whelan saw the smile fade for a moment.

I'd get out of his way, too, kid, Whelan thought.

He continued to watch the door, saw the bouncer turn away a trio of staggering middle-aged men in Cubs hats, and then decided to call it a night. He thought of the bald man again and sighed.

Somehow, he thought, somehow I was hoping for somebody a little softer.

He started the Jet and then changed his mind, turned it off again, listened to the engine make strange gurgling sounds, and then got out. He walked the two blocks to the tiny hamburger place, pushed open the door, and let the cold air envelop him. The place smelled of grilling onions and potatoes turning gold in the deep fryer, and he wondered what he was doing there.

She was there again, taking an order from an elderly man in a sport coat and open-collar shirt. The same short, dark, dangerous-looking man was working the grill, his hair still jutting out from underneath the white paper cap at right angles to his head. Set this guy down in a playground and you could guarantee nightmares in small children.

The cook turned and gave Whelan a wild-eyed glance, then scratched at his chest and turned back to the omelets and burgers that lay in little crackling, spitting mounds on his grill. Whelan took the last booth and the woman came over.

"Hello again," she said and tried on a half smile.

"Hi," he said. He felt himself grinning. Good, Whelan, let her think you've never talked to a woman before. Make a nice first impression, like your ma told you.

She clicked her pen and folded over a page of her ticket pad.

"Just getting off work?" she asked.

"Uh, yeah, I am."

She nodded slightly to the west. "You work out of Chicago Avenue?"

He laughed. "Not in a long time. Do I look like a police officer?"

She shrugged and laughed a little. "Well…more or less."

He looked down at his tropical shirt and painter's jeans. "I know it's not the way I dress. So do I have that cop strut? I thought I got rid of that. They sent me to finishing school to learn posture."

"It's the way you scan a place when you come in. And the way you were watching those kids last night. Like it was routine to you, nothing special."

"It's probably routine to every bartender on earth."

"The bartenders I get in here don't watch the room the way you do. And they're usually not quiet, they're kind of…they're unwinding, you know?" She shrugged and watched him and he realized he was in the process of lighting a cigarette he couldn't remember taking out. He could see that she was letting him take his time. The laugh lines at the corners of her eyes were a little deeper and darker and he knew she was reading him like a book. Take a shot at it, Whelan.

"Your name's Pat, right?"

She nodded, hesitated for a second just to keep him honest,

and then smiled. "What's yours?"

"My name's Paul. And I'm not a cop."

"Hi, Paul. I bet you're hungry after all this talk, huh?" And she laughed, a young girl's laugh that brought a touch of red to her cheeks, and he couldn't help joining her.

"No, I ate already. Actually, eating's kind of a late-night hobby with me. I don't really have to be hungry." He realized that he was babbling and took a puff of his cigarette.

"I can think of a lot of worse habits you could have." She clicked her pen again and put it to the pad. He ordered a cup of coffee and a chocolate malt. She wrote and nodded and started to say something as she walked backward toward the counter.

He looked at her and caught her taking a quick glance at him. He shrugged. "You have time for a quick cup of coffee or something?" He started to shrug again and felt self-conscious. No, I'm not good at this anymore.

"Sure," she said quickly but stared at her pad as though unable to read her own writing. She went back around the counter and stuck the bill in a little clamp that hung over the grill. The cook looked up briefly and nodded, then went back to the little mounds of eggs and hash browns sizzling on his grill. Whelan watched the woman pour coffee refills for the three customers sitting apart from one another at the counter. She grabbed two mugs and a pot of coffee, then made a wide swing around the counter to the occupants of the other two booths, refreshed their coffee, spoke to the older man, and then joined Whelan. She smiled and set down her cup.

"Is this…does the boss mind?"

She looked over at the cook. "Nick? No, he doesn't care. People come in all night and we only have one waitress on, so I don't get a real break."

"And he's not the jealous type?"

She laughed and looked at him for a second before answering, and he was slightly embarrassed. She leaned forward and spoke in a low voice. "He just got married. He doesn't even know there are other women in the world. You should see his wife—he went back to Greece for four months just to find a bride. Came back with an eighteen year old with eyes the size of headlights; she thinks he's Alexander the Great and he's not telling her any different. Says he's gonna have ten sons."

"Oh, yeah? Wait till she has the first two or three: we'll see if she still thinks he's Alexander."

She tilted her head to one side. "Are you married, Paul?" She took a sip of her coffee.

"No. Never been married. I'm just talking about married couples I've known. How about you, Pat?"

"I'm not married. I'm divorced."

"Were you married a long time?"

She sipped her coffee and studied him over the rim.

"I'm thirty-nine and I've got a daughter in college."

He smiled. "I wasn't asking about your age. And I'm forty, so you're a mere toddler. A daughter in college, huh? You married young."

"That's when most of our mistakes happen, isn't it?"

"Oh, I don't know. I still manage to make a lot."

She smiled and was about to say something when the cook rang a little bell to tell her an order was ready. She went back to the counter and brought food out for the older man and came back to Whelan.

"Your malt is almost up, Paul. Where were we?"

"I'm not sure. What do you like, Pat?"

"What do I like? You mean like hobbies or something like that?"

"I was never much good at this. I think you find out more about a person by asking what they do for fun than if you go through the whole twenty-questions routine. So I won't ask you your sign or where you went to school or how you vote or how business is or how much you like working here."

"How about a cigarette, Paul? Save me the steps from here to my purse."

"Oh, sure." He shook a cigarette up from the pack and held it out to her, then flicked his lighter.

She blew smoke up and away from him, in the way that women always seem to. "Let's see. That's a nice question, what do I do for fun. I like to read, for one. I like mysteries set in big old English houses. And I like the beach. And I like old music and I like to dance to it, but I don't get much chance to do that. And I like old movies. And I like Chinese food. Any kind of Chinese food—Cantonese or Hunan or any of them."

"Ah, my favorite subject."

"Chinese food?"

"No, restaurants. Any kind."

"You got a favorite?"

"I'm pretty far gone on Korean. And I like Thai food."

"You like spicy food, then."

"Yes. If it hurts me, it's good."

She laughed and then left the booth to get his malt. The cook hit the bell and she made a wry face.

"Back to work, huh?"

"Has to happen eventually. I'll talk to you later."

"Okay." He watched her walk away and told himself again that there were few women in the world who could wear those unpretentious little black uniforms, and that this was one of the better-looking thirty-nine-year-old women he was likely to run into.

A pair of street cops came in and sat at the counter, and Pat was immediately involved in a conversation with both of them. The conversation was animated and friendly and one of the cops was good at making her laugh. Whelan sipped at the malt and looked out the window at the foot traffic on Rush and tried not to listen to the laughter from the counter.

Oh, well, he thought, did you think it would be that easy?

He finished the malt and had a cigarette and took his time over it, and when he was finished he looked around for her. She was pouring coffee refills for the people in the other booths and gave him a little smile.

She came over immediately. "Anything else, Paul? More coffee?"

"No, thanks. I think I'm done for the night. How about my check."

She nodded and set down her coffeepot, then leafed

through the checks on her pad till she found his. She tore it off and lay it on the table, face down.

"Thanks for the coffee and the conversation," she said.

"You're welcome. Thanks for sitting down."

The bell rang and she shot the cook a look over her shoulder. "Sorry I didn't have more time. Maybe…another time."

"That would be nice." He was about to ask her what nights she worked but she sprinted off to pick up her orders. Like her laugh, it was a young woman's run, exactly the way Liz used to run in her tight black uniform and white shoes.

Waitresses, he told himself, I'm a sucker for waitresses. He put out the cigarette, put money on the table for his bill, and tipped her, not ostentatiously but well enough so that it would be noted. Then he got up and left, pausing to give her a short wave as he pulled the door open. She was bringing the cops their food. She set the plates down hurriedly and waved.

"Good night, Paul."

"See you, Pat."

Whelan parked in front of his house and was about to go inside when he noticed the lettering on the porch across the street. It was done in black or dark blue and sprayed in letters a foot high and said NIGGER YOUR DEAD. This wasn't something that was going to wear itself out. It was going to get worse, perhaps very ugly, and he wondered if it would eventually involve him. It probably would, and he felt very tired of other people's troubles.

He sat down at the top step and had a cigarette. He thought for a moment about Pat, had a brief moment of jealousy about the two cops, and then was aware of the discomfort, a reluctance to start something, to go through all this again. Whelan wondered if he could compete for a woman again, go calling with hat in hand and try all the old dance steps and sell someone on the virtues of Paul Whelan. Perhaps there came a time when you refused to try to start relationships, when you simply put up little walls and clung to your routines and protected yourself.

Whelan looked at the house across the street and shook

his head.

Come on, Whelan, he told himself. This guy across the street, now *he's* got troubles. You've just got cold feet.

His knuckles were stiffening up and the welt on the side of his head was beginning to sting again, and he wondered if he'd feel any better in the morning.

I'm keeping the wrong company.

NINE

His head was fine but the knuckles ached. Whelan showered and had a cup of coffee and rye toast and listened to the news on the radio.

When he went out the black man was standing on the grass in front of his house, staring at the painted message, arms folded across his chest. He turned at the sound of Whelan's door closing and watched Whelan descend the stairs. Whelan looked at him and nodded briefly and the black man did nothing but stare, and Whelan knew this man would be staring at every white face in the neighborhood, searching for some clue, some evasiveness in the eyes that would tell him who wrote this on his home. Whelan got into his car and drove to Rich Vosic's office.

He parked around the corner from the building with the blue awning. The van and the Lotus and the Town Car were all there, as well as a station wagon he hadn't seen before and half a dozen other cars. He watched and listened to music and when it became clear he was wasting his time, he went for coffee.

When he returned forty minutes later the Lotus was gone and it was time to go to work. He parked in the little lot and went in the front door. The boy security guard was there again and nodded.

Whelan stopped in front of him and pointed to the door. "Rich's car's not here. He didn't come in yet?"

"He was here but he left. He'll be back at eleven or so."

"Eleven?" Whelan made a pained expression and looked up at the wall clock. He sighed and pointed to his bare wrist.

"Know why I don't wear a watch? Because nobody pays attention to time anymore. Damn." He shook his head, the irritated businessman. "Carmen back there?"

"Sure."

"All right. I'll leave a message with her and get back on the road." He gave the guard a friendly pat on the shoulder and then walked down the hall toward the double doors. Carmen was at her post.

Whelan found himself admiring the layout of the office. There were several people just barely visible in the smaller offices to the sides but the scene was dominated by Carmen's desk, the visitor's eye encountered Carmen. She looked up from her keyboard as Whelan entered and he was struck by how much Carmen did for an office. She was in yellow today, a sleeveless cotton dress, bright and tight and made for Carmen.

"Hi," she said, but she didn't smile, and he knew Vosic had said something to her.

"Morning. Your security force out there tells me I missed Rich."

She gave him a tight smile. "That's right. He'll be back in an hour or so."

Whelan nodded and pretended to be wrestling with scheduling problems. He glanced at the clock on her desk, bit his lip, shook his head, and shrugged.

"All right…just tell him I was here. I'll call him later." Then, as an afterthought, "While I'm here, can I take a look at those same files?"

She thought it over and then nodded. "I'll be right back." She disappeared into the little back room and came out with the personnel files again. Whelan took them from her and sat down at a desk a few feet away and began paging through the files again.

"Who's the woman I saw him with, Carmen?" She looked up and he saw that he had her attention. "I saw him with her yesterday. I think it was yesterday."

Carmen wrinkled her nose. "Probably his wife. Soon to be ex-wife."

"Oh. He likes 'em tall, I guess. She looked to be about five eleven."

Carmen looked up again quickly. "No, she's real little."

Carmen stared at him and he thought he saw hurt there. He looked back at the files and when he stole another glance at her she was staring off across the room and her face was flushed. Whelan thought he had the story of this particular office pretty well figured out.

"Probably business, then," he said and nodded as though that were the most logical explanation, but he could see that Carmen had other ideas. Time to ask things. "Listen, Carmen, what's the guy's name, the big guy that I see with Rich?"

"What big guy?" she said irritably.

"The one with the shaved head and the goatee. Big, heavy guy, looks like a wrestler or something."

"Oh, him." She curled her lip faintly and shook her head.

"He works with Rich, I think," Whelan said.

"No. That's Henley." She made an expression of complete distaste. "*He* doesn't work here."

"Well, no, I knew that, but I thought maybe at the bar…"

"No. He drinks at the bar. Drinks and fights. He's really a jerk."

"No, maybe I'm confusing him with someone else. First name's Jim—"

She gave her head an irritated little shake. "His first name is Frank." She looked away again and he paged through the files, leaving her to her hurt feelings.

He wasn't looking for anything in particular, just scanning the same pages to see if anything struck him the second time around. It came no clearer this time. If anything the picture of George Brister was muddier, the general impression of High Pair was more shadowy, and he wondered how much these files left out. He scanned Brister's personnel file, wrote down the three firms in Oregon and Washington that Brister had listed as former employers, and came away with the same impression, that there was no reason any employer in his right mind would hire this man.

He looked at the little stack of green folders and spread them out on the desktop like a poker hand. There were fourteen or fifteen of them, including a folder each for Vosic and Phil

Fairs. He pulled them out and spent a moment looking at Vosic's. It told him nothing of importance; if anything it was too clean to match the slick young high roller who currently ran things. Born in Racine, Wisconsin, graduate of Michigan State University, and in every way the all-American boy, two years on the baseball team and a degree in business. Military service in Germany with an honorable discharge.

Phil Fairs was apparently more of a wanderer. He was from La Crosse, Wisconsin, and had attended Michigan State at the same time as Vosic—probably where they met; he could envision a couple of Wisconsin boys starting up a conversation on the long train ride back home. Fairs had graduated with a degree in management and he, too, had enlisted and served in Germany. Whelan nodded to himself—if you enlisted in the early seventies you didn't have to go to Nam, and these two guys had decided they wanted to see Europe, not Vietnam.

From that point on they seemed to have gone their own ways with little obvious contact, though Whelan knew that an executive starting his own company doesn't have to put together a personnel file for himself that dots all the i's and crosses the t's. But Vosic seemed to have stayed in the Midwest and become something of a young hotshot in the rapidly expanding computer industry while Fairs got himself jobs with several importing firms in the Midwest, then abruptly showed up in California and then in Oregon, where he served as vice president of a small computer firm. There was a short stint in Oklahoma where he listed himself as a "developer" and then several positions in short order back home in the Midwest, now with computer firms, the last one a software company. A year after that job he and Vosic started a company.

He scanned the personnel sheet again; Oregon stood out clearly, but he'd lived and worked in Eugene, while Brister had lived and worked in Portland. Whelan looked at the two personnel files again and then at Vosic's. It was Fairs who had worked in Oregon, yet Vosic had apparently brought Brister into the firm. He looked at the personnel sheet for Brister again and saw Vosic's name listed as his reference. Where did they know each other from?

Yeah, Rich old boy, you got something over on your partner here. I just wish I knew what.

He closed the files, lay them on the desk, and nodded at Carmen. "Thanks again, Carmen. Have a nice day."

"Yeah. You too," she said without feeling.

If I keep coming back here, he wondered, will I get more confused each time?

Back at the office, he called Roy Swenson in Seattle.

"Hello, Roy. Paul Whelan."

"Do I owe you money?"

"Not yet. I might owe you some, though. I need a little help and my arms aren't long enough."

"All right. How's your life?"

"My life is all right, but it's dull. Business is a little slow, too. How's yours?"

Swenson started to say something and then began coughing. He laughed. "Pretty hectic. So I'm smoking more, as you can tell. We're working on a couple of industrial espionage things out here, Paul. They're keeping me pretty busy, actually busier than I'd like to be, but the company that's paying the bills is rolling in money and I can't say no."

Whelan laughed. "I guess you don't want any more work at the moment."

"Well, for an old friend…what's the job?"

"I'm trying to find somebody who worked here for a while and originally came from Seattle. I've got the names of three companies he worked for and an address he gave as his last residence in Seattle. I wonder if you could check them out for me."

"What do you really want to know, Paul? Since I know you could make some calls yourself and run up your phone bill."

"I want to know if anybody has seen or heard from this man in the last two years. That's what I really want to know. I think he might have come back to Seattle after…after some trouble he was involved in back here."

"Okay," Swenson said, and Whelan gave him the particulars.

"This'll take at least a day, Paul. Is that all right?"

"You're doing me a favor, Roy. You do what you can. I'll pay you for this one."

"No. I'd much rather you owe me a favor," Swenson said, and he laughed. A former FBI agent and an old friend, Swenson occasionally went cross-country on his cases.

Whelan smiled. "I think I'd rather pay you—I know you'll collect on a favor and it'll cost me dearly," and he laughed.

He sat at his desk and thought for a few minutes and made notes to himself, then spent almost forty minutes on the phone. He called old contacts at People's Gas, at Illinois Bell, at Commonwealth Edison, and at the secretary of state's office. He did not really expect any of the calls to turn up anything, and they didn't, but simply confirmed what he had expected— there was no record anywhere in Chicago of a George Brister, he wasn't receiving service from any of the utilities, and as far as the state's computer was concerned, he wasn't driving, either. There was no automobile license issued to George Brister and there was no driver's license. He got exactly the same answers on Frank Henley.

He called Janice Fairs.

"Yes, Mr. Whelan, something interesting?"

"I'm not sure. I wanted to run something by you."

"Run, by all means."

"You said Vosic had brought George Brister into the firm, correct?"

"Yes."

"Where did they meet?"

"Brister worked for him. I thought I told you that, Mr. Whelan." There was impatience in her voice, a tired teacher with a stupid pupil.

"So you did, but the personnel files of High Pair don't really spell that out. On Brister's application Rich Vosic is given as the only local reference. He lists a number of places, primarily in the Northwest, but no company that had anything at all to do with Vosic. Where would they have known each other from?"

There was silence at the other end. Then he could hear her lighting up a cigarette. "I have no idea, but…how important can that be? He probably put down all kinds of inaccurate information on that application. We've already established that the man was a hopeless alcoholic."

"With all due respect, Mrs. Fairs, the only thing I've established to my satisfaction is that Brister was a genius at covering his tracks."

He heard her exhaling smoke. "I don't know, Mr. Whelan. It's very hard for me to imagine that slovenly drunk as anything but a derelict. And a…a hireling."

"Well, maybe he's a derelict now. I have a little experience with derelicts, and they're not easy to find, but I'll tell you one thing: when George Brister worked at High Pair, he was no derelict."

"He was a drunk, Mr. Whelan, no matter how we romanticize him."

"So was Grant. Maybe Churchill."

"Well…"

He cut her off. "I have another question to ask you: did you ever hear the name Frank Henley? Or meet anyone by that name?"

He heard a little intake of breath and then what sounded like the beginnings of laughter, then she caught herself.

"Frank Henley? Ah, someone connected with Rich, Mr. Whelan?"

He hesitated before answering, wondering what he was hearing in her voice. Then he said, "I believe so. And maybe connected with Harry Palm."

"I see," she said, and now he knew she was acting.

"You know him," he said.

"Oh—I couldn't say that—I've heard the name, Mr. Whelan."

"From whom? Your husband? Or Harry Palm?"

She hesitated again and he could hear her puffing away to buy time. "Not from my husband, Mr. Whelan. But maybe it was from Palm."

He shook his head at the phone; you know the case has gone bad when the client starts lying.

"All right, Mrs. Fairs. I just thought I'd ask."

"Certainly. What will you do next, Mr. Whelan?"

"Have lunch."

She laughed without mirth. "You are an unusual man."

"Not as unusual as the people you have me talking to, Mrs. Fairs," and this time she laughed genuinely. There was a pause and he knew she was waiting for more. He wasn't going to give it to her. Not now. He told her he'd be in touch and she said good-bye with reluctance.

He sat back and swiveled around in his chair so that he could watch street traffic. Across the street, just in front of the Aragon, a young white guy with neat creases in his jeans was panhandling and getting nowhere.

Serves you right, kid, Whelan thought.

He watched the clean-cut panhandler and told himself that the whole world was overrun by con artists, millions of con artists, selling fake watches and hot radios and plastic jewelry and repro antiques, and bogus stocks, everyone in a mad scramble to make a dollar. He thought of Janice Fairs and wondered what her scam was. It was when you didn't know what you were being conned out of that you were in trouble.

He had lunch at the Cafe in the Park. The cost was high—he had to eat outside—but the overall effect on a bruised psyche was worth the sacrifice. Other folks all over the city were sitting in crowded beer gardens, inhaling exhaust fumes and pigeon guano, but Whelan was here, at the north end of the Lincoln Park Lagoon, at one of the city's little-known treasures, watching a handful of rowboats and the reflection of the first clouds he'd seen in days. There was a faint breeze from off the lake and he could hear gulls not far off.

He had a burger and an iced tea and then took a walk, first east to the lake and then north along the rocks and bicycle path past the Belmont Gun Club, where a half dozen men with grim facial expressions shouted "Pull!" and then blasted away with shotguns at little black disks made of clay.

The nation's last line of defense, Whelan told himself. After the Commies overrun our defenses and defeat our armies they'll have to reckon with these guys with the pump shotguns, and then they'll be in deep shit, and if the Reds come at us with little black clay disks, it'll be all over in a matter of seconds.

His walk took him past the crowded little patch of park where the gay men came down to the water and sunned themselves. Hundreds of gay men sat on blankets and towels or tossed Frisbees and bought hot dogs from the enterprising young vendor who brought his pushcart there every day. As long as Whelan could remember, gay men had collected at this place in summer. In the old days there had been only a handful, but the times had changed and now there was a crowd, and people left them alone.

He found himself walking past the squat cream-colored building that housed the Belmont Harbor branch of the Chicago Yacht Club and realized that he was near the place where the late Harry Palm had been found. He stopped a few yards farther and looked at the boats—hundreds of boats, literally hundreds, and this was just the iceberg's tip of Chicago's summer flotilla. All along the harbor, from Addison to Belmont, they were moored, sailboats and big twin-engine cabin cruisers and little, brightly colored speedboats, and there were hundreds more of them at anchor at Diversey Harbor and many, many more downtown off Grant Park in Monroe Harbor, the boats of the rich man and the social climber and the fisherman and the guy who just wanted to crack open a sixpack and waste gas.

If you stood there quietly and made an honest attempt to block out the city noises behind you, there was a different sound here—not a city sound but the gentle tolling of boats at anchor, of lines striking melodically against steel and aluminum masts, of chains rubbing against hulls of wood and fiberglass. There were people in Chicago who lived on the water for half the year, people who actually lived only for these times, people who became dark and wind burned and took on water smells that were so deep in their pores and hair that they couldn't be washed away. For a long time, as a young man, Whelan had wanted to be one of them. A man he knew, a news anchor for one of the local stations, had actually pulled it off, buying a yacht and quitting his job and living now as a sailor in an existence that Whelan couldn't fathom. His fascination with the idea of a life on the water had passed, but there were times like these when the water seemed a friendlier world.

He walked along the fence lining the harbor and looked at the fanciful and self-congratulatory names—*Papa's Dream, Bad Girl, Who's on Top, Hot Stuff, Weekend Warrior II, Top Dog, Harlan's Holiday, Mama's Hideout.*

A block farther on there was a spot where the harbor wall curved, and the gradual lowering of the lake's level in recent years had revealed the little beach, more of a sandbar, where they'd dug up Harry Palm. Whelan walked over and looked at it. The constant action of the lake tides had smoothed it over and deposited a new collection of seaweed and floating trash and there was nothing to indicate that a man had been buried here. Whelan tried to form a mental image of the killing, tried to picture where a killer would have had to hide to surprise Harry Palm—if the killing had taken place here. Finding Harry's car in the lot a short distance away made it likely. Harry Palm's obsession with his car was legendary—he wouldn't have let it out of his sight for more than a few minutes unless there was someone to watch it for him.

Whelan leaned against the fence and looked at the sand, then at the water; the lake was getting a little cleaner every year, they said, but you'd never know it by looking at the harbor water—it was discolored, fouled by gas and emissions from the boat engines, and paper cups and fast-food containers floated here and there, tossed carelessly from boats ten miles out and inevitably brought back to the city by the action of waves and tides. Between a pair of small sailboats moored close to the shore he could see a chunk of watermelon rind bobbing like a green buoy.

A small dinghy left the shadow of the yacht club and carried a pair of white-haired men out to a boat moored in the center of the harbor. They were both dressed entirely in white, as though they had the next court at Wimbledon. Whelan looked at the yacht club building again and decided to play a hunch.

He got through the black steel gate to the yacht club and was no more than three feet inside when he was met by a sign that read MEMBERS ONLY and a guard whose eyes said the same thing.

"Can I help you, sir?" the guard said.

"Uh, yeah. I'm looking for Rich Vosic."

"I haven't seen him yet today, sir."

"I was supposed to meet him at the office. He told me if we missed each other he might be down here having a late lunch."

The guard shook his head. "Hasn't been here yet, sir."

"We used to run around together on this little bitty boat he had. Little white thing—*The High Pair*, he called it. I don't even know if he still has it. I've been on the coast for a couple of years."

The guard grinned. "Oh, he's got a boat, all right. It's not little and it's not white." He nodded back in the direction of the water. "Fifty footer, sky blue. That's a boat. Twin Mercs, lotta chrome, built-in bar, sleeps six. You name it, he's got it on that boat. Top of the line."

"Like everything else he buys," Whelan said.

"You got that right," the guard said.

"Hey, listen, he was telling me the cops found a stiff here a couple of weeks ago."

"Not here," the guard said, laughing. "Down at the other end of the harbor. In the sand."

"Who was he, a member that didn't want to pay his dues?" The guard smiled. "Nobody around here knew him. He was some kind of small-time gangster."

"A gangster? Good old Chicago, just like the movies."

The guard indicated the club with a nod. "You want to wait in the bar, sir?"

"No, no. If I start drinking now I'll need a nap." He waved

and went out again.

Rich Vosic's boat wasn't the biggest of the cabin cruisers but Whelan found it with no trouble, for it was the newest and the most colorful and it was easy to picture Vosic on this boat, of all the boats in Belmont Harbor. It was a gleaming seagoing dream, capable of taking a man anywhere he could go on the water and for about as long as he needed to be there; a torpedo might take it out, but it wouldn't even notice bad weather. It was glossy and ostentatious and exactly the kind of boat that would appeal to a man like Rich Vosic, and it was called *The Score*.

Something was changing in the lighting. Rain clouds were forming to the west and had just begun to cover the sun as it began its slow descent. A storm was coming.

Rain might not make it any cooler, but a storm, a nice summer storm, might clean it up a little and bring some relief from the humidity.

He took the El to the Loop and it almost cost him his appointment with Victor Tabor. All the trains into and out of the Loop were frozen in time because the bridges were up. One after another the huge gray trestles swung slowly up into the air to allow a single high-masted sailboat to pass up the Chicago River to the locks leading into Lake Michigan.

He got a look at the boat as it passed the Merchandise Mart on its way east. It was a twenty-five footer and there was one gnarly looking old man on it. As far as Whelan could tell, the man never once looked up to see all the traffic that hung in suspended animation overhead.

Victor Tabor's office was in the Pittsfield Building, a relic of a more genteel time, when office buildings were expected to have a little brass-and-marble to tell visitors they were going someplace special. He found Tabor's business on the eighth floor, a small suite of offices with clouded glass door and windows. The sign on the door said RELIABLE FINANCE COMPANY.

A good-looking woman in her forties led him immediately into the inner sanctum and closed the door behind him as though she were late for lunch.

Victor Tabor looked up at him briefly over dark-rimmed reading glasses. "Right with you, sir."

He was a small, tidy-looking man with red cheeks, a drinker's nose gone swollen and purple, a thick shock of silver hair, and the most amazing mass of eyebrows Whelan had ever seen.

He scribbled a few notes in the margin of the document he was studying, shook his head briefly, and shut the manila folder. "Everybody needs a dollar these days, sir."

"That's a fact."

"But they all want you to make it easy on them. Perfect strangers come to me for the cash to underwrite major business ventures and expect favors from me. People I've never even heard of, people that got our name from the Yellow Pages. And they want to borrow for the damnedest things. This guy plans to open up a video game parlor in a ritzy neighborhood—'for the youth of the community,' he says here. The place he's picked out isn't even zoned for commercial properties. Neighbors'll kill this guy." He laughed a brittle, high-pitched laugh and his face was transformed. He looked like a bad boy in a nice suit.

"You're looking into some companies that we made loans to a few years back, or so I'm told by my secretary. She's not too free with the information, my girl Estelle. So who you with?" The joviality disappeared and the reading glasses came off and Whelan knew he wouldn't want to be the one to tell this man he couldn't pay back a loan.

"I'm not with anyone." He took out a card and tossed it on the desk. "I've been hired by a party interested in starting legal proceedings against a firm that I believe did some business with you and a number of other lending institutions over the past five or six years."

Tabor studied the card, turned it over as if to find some explanation on the back, then handed it back to Whelan.

"Who is it you're interested in?"

"A firm that was called High Pair and run by a Richard Vosic and a Philip Fairs. You remember the company?"

The red cheeks went a shade darker and Victor Tabor

blinked several times. "Do I remember? Is this the first time you've dealt with a private lending organization? I lend money to people, mister, I don't ever forget them. I remember who I lent money to and how much and what happened when it was time to pay it back, and some people I remember a little more, uh, vividly than others. And I remember High Pair Enterprises because they almost put me out of business."

"I'm sorry. It was just a figure of speech. What can you tell me about them?"

"I can tell you one of them is dead. And I can tell you they were a couple of punks, they were bad people."

"In what way?"

"The simplest way. They were crooks. They borrowed money they never intended to pay back. They used the same properties as collateral for different loans—yeah, I know, that's just the stupidity of the lending institutions—and they lied about the purposes to which they would put the money they borrowed. In my case they took out a note for a sum of money to be used in an ongoing project in the North Loop. They were renovating an old tavern and turning it into a small nightclub. What they really did was to use my money to pay off a pack of other creditors, particularly a couple of the big banks."

"Did you ever get any of your money back?"

"No. Not one penny. Less than four months after I made the loan to them, they were out of business. Their money was gone, their company was defunct. And then I got the news that the guy Fairs had killed himself." Tabor made a little shrug of helplessness.

"And whatever they pledged as security was already gone?"

"No, I didn't do anything like that. I made them a special little, ah, package. I lent them a lot of money and took a couple of their newer company cars as security." He shrugged again and laughed. "A Buick and a Lincoln, for a hundred and a half. And the Lincoln was already collateral in a previous loan."

He smiled and looked almost embarrassed. Whelan realized that he was waiting for the inevitable question.

"Why did you lend them so much for such small collateral?"

"They played me for an old sucker, that's why. Couple of earnest young guys with a lot of ideas and what seemed like a lot of money. This was to be a very short-term note. They were going places and they needed a little help, very temporary, it was. And they mentioned a project they were going to be starting in a year or so. Big one. And I knew they'd be needing help with that."

"Or a partner."

"No, but a rich uncle. They were going to need a rich uncle. There's money to be made over there in that River North area. You've got all kinds of celebrities putting their money in and they're going to be rolling in it soon. And I was looking for a vehicle, I was looking to provide capital in something like that. These two, they seemed to be what I was looking for, so I lent them the hundred and a half, thought I was dealing with genuine people."

Tabor looked away for a moment and Whelan could see the wrinkles around his eyes more clearly. He seemed older, smaller, deflated.

"Too bad about that boat going down, huh? Too bad they weren't both on it." He looked away, then back at Whelan. "I know what you're thinking. But it's not the money. I have plenty of money." Tabor stared as though daring Whelan to contradict him. When Whelan said nothing, Tabor said, "Tell your client I'll be rooting for him."

"Thanks. I will."

"I'm afraid I have nothing that you could use in a court of law, Mr. Whelan."

"Maybe not, but you've been helpful."

He got up and Tabor showed him to the door. When he had gone through the outer office he turned to say thank you to the secretary. Victor Tabor was behind the half-closed door, staring at him.

It was almost six when he got back to the office. The humidity sucked the oxygen out of the air. His feet burned and his shirt stuck to his body in a dozen places, and as he walked up the stairs to his office he didn't see the man in the hall till he was almost on top of him.

The visitor was black. He was a little over six feet tall, thin and long limbed, and wore a loose-fitting striped shirt that was vaguely African. He had very large eyes, a little wispy goatee shot with silver, and a smile that made him look positively jovial.

"Mister Whelan?" The accent was heavy—Nigeria or Ghana, Whelan thought. He nodded to Whelan and made a little half bow.

"Yes. Can I help you?"

The man made a shy shrug and inclined his head to one side.

"I don't know, sah. I was going to ask you the same question." The big eyes narrowed and put a new color on the smile, and Whelan began to understand who his visitor was.

"We don't know each other."

"No, we sure don't." The accent left town and the voice took on an edge to match the look in the eyes.

"So you tell me why I keep hearing about a white man asking about me up and down the street. Asking about my business."

"I wasn't asking about you."

The black man stared at him for a moment. "I have other information, sir."

"I was asking about people who had been doing business with Harry Palm. Several people mentioned you. I didn't even get a name, didn't ask for one; you weren't the one I was after."

"And who are you after?"

"A white man. A big white man with a shaved head. Green eyes."

"And this man is supposed to be...an associate of mine?"

"No. He was an associate of Harry Palm. I got the notion that he might know what happened to old Harry."

The black man brought up a long, slender index finger and pointed it in Whelan's face. "But you were asking about me. About a black man. Why was that?"

"At the beginning I wasn't sure who I was looking for, so I asked for information about people who Harry Palm had had business dealings with—"

The man wrinkled his face with distaste. "I didn't do business with Palm."

"—and people who might have reason to wish old Harry some harm. Shoe fit?"

"If I did Palm, they'd still be looking for him." He moved a step closer to Whelan. "You've caused me some trouble, Mr. Whelan. I don't need trouble. I am a businessman. I go into places where I am known and I hear that a private detective has been asking questions about me."

The man moved still closer and Whelan held his ground.

"How can I convince you not to make more trouble for me?"

"You keep coming at me, you're going to have more."

The visitor smiled. "I could kill you with my hands."

Whelan let his hands hang loose at his sides. "Maybe so, but I'd mark you up for life. All your friends would laugh at you."

For a moment the visitor studied him, then he shrugged. "It's not worth my time. And I think you understand me now."

"I wasn't looking for you before, and I'm not interested in you now. You want to complicate your life, it's your decision."

"You just better hope I don't hear any more about you, Mr. Whelan." He nodded once and then walked past Whelan.

Whelan opened his office door and went inside. From his window he watched the black man walk west on Lawrence.

He sat down and took a notebook from the desk and began to jot down what he knew about George Brister. When he had listed all the known facts, he sat for a long time looking at them. The shadowy profile of George Brister was unlike any resume he'd ever seen. There was something more there, something he wasn't seeing, and no matter how long he looked at it, he couldn't find whatever it was.

It was dark when he came out again two and a half hours later. There was rain in the air now, a heavy, imminent presence, and the steady breeze had become a wind, a cooling wind that seemed to be getting stronger. Leaves and paper and street grit swirled down Lawrence toward the lake and the dry dust of summer in the city was in his eyes as he made his way home.

Just beyond the El tracks he stopped in a doorway to light a cigarette out of the wind, and when he turned, the one-armed man stepped back into a gangway across the street just a beat too late.

Whelan crossed Lawrence but the man was gone, as Whelan had known he would be. He stood near the curb and smoked his cigarette and looked around, half watching, half listening. A visitor to the office and now his very own tail. Life was becoming interesting.

He was sitting in his darkened living room and the Cubs were leading the Mets again when the storm broke. He crossed the living room quickly and threw open all three windows, then went to the back of the house and opened the kitchen window to create a cross-draft. The wet-smelling air filled his house and scoured it, and the heavy rushing noise of the rain drowned out the sound of the baseball game. The rain fell in a dark, slanting wall and danced loudly on the car tops and drove all of the urban life forms inside.

He realized that there were people cursing the rain right now, men and women who lived in the streets and couldn't get to a doorway in time. He went to his window and looked out at the street. The men in the beater wouldn't be out tormenting his black neighbor tonight and he was certain that nobody was watching the Whelan household, either.

He was thankful for a little rain.

Ten

When he woke in the morning there was a fresh coolness in the air and the birds were going crazy with the morning's worm crop. The air in his house was filled with the rich, rank smell of the aging cottonwoods that lined his street.

He had scrambled eggs and a cup of coffee at the Subway Donut Shop on Broadway, then walked to his office and called his service. To his relief, Shelley answered.

"Nice to hear your voice, Shel."

"Nice to hear yours, doll. I been trying to get ahold of you."

"I was out for my constitutional. Any calls?"

"Two. Your friend Mr. Personality."

"Bauman? What did he want?"

"He didn't leave a message, hon. He just grunted when I said you were out. Tried his rap on me, though."

"Does he have a rap, Shel?"

"Yeah, very low-key and, you know, restrained, kinda like Robert De Niro in *Raging Bull*. And he wheezes into the phone. Also, you had a call from the Ice Maiden, Mrs. Janice Fairs."

"I bet you like her, Shel."

"Yeah. She wasn't pleased, either, about not getting ahold of you. Gave me the impression she thought I should come over and do her floors. These people all think it's my fault you don't stay in one place for more than ten minutes."

"She leave a message?"

"She said she'd catch up with you later. At the office."

"Well. That's probably not such a good idea. I'll call her at home."

"She have servants?"

"I don't know."

"She should have servants. An attitude like that, it's a waste if she doesn't have servants."

"I'm running into a lot of people like that lately, Shel."

Bauman breathed into the phone. "So where you been, Snoop?"

"Out taking the air. You called before?"

"Yeah. I called. So you feelin' all right today, Whelan? You didn't, uh, sustain any permanent damage in that little disturbance there, did you?"

"I'm contemplating retirement; boxing's not for me."

Bauman laughed into the phone and then sniffed. "Listen, you ain't been runnin' a con on me, Shamus, have you?"

"Not knowingly."

"You're looking for a bald guy, a fat guy, you said."

"Yeah."

"And he's, uh, Caucasian."

"Uh-oh, you just slipped into that cop talk. We're on official business, huh?"

"Aw, I don't know if you'd call it that, Whelan. It's just that I come by some information and it don't, you know, it don't jibe with what you and I talked about the other night. Least it don't jibe with what *you* said."

"What do you have?"

"Let's just say I got some information that maybe you aren't really looking for a white guy that killed Harry Palm."

Whelan could see what was coming. He smiled into the phone. "What did you hear? Or don't you want to share it?"

"I don't share, Whelan. I wasn't brought up right. Do you share, Whelan?"

"Not all the time, but I gave you what I had the other night, or what I thought I had." He listened to Bauman wheezing into the phone for a long moment.

"You know, Whelan, the thought has occurred to me that maybe you were, you know, fishing the other night. Feeding me burritos to see what I knew about the guy you were really after. You wouldn't do that, would you, Whelan? That would, you know, shake my faith in human nature."

"Why don't we cut to English and you tell me what you really want."

"Whelan, I want you out of this Harry Palm deal. You tell me you're looking into this fair-haired yuppie type and what do I hear on the street? I hear you're meeting with an acquaintance of mine, a guy of the African persuasion."

"Oh, you *heard* that, huh?"

"That's right. I heard you had a meeting with this gentleman. At your office."

"I don't think you heard that. I think you were watching. Maybe you were watching him, maybe you were watching me. Hell, it wouldn't be the first time you followed me around, Bauman."

"But you met with this soul brother, am I right?"

"No. I didn't *meet* with him. He was waiting for me in the hall outside my office. Told me he'd been hearing that a white private investigator was asking about him. He seemed unhappy about that. He told me not to do that anymore. I believe he made threats to my person. Want me to fill out a report?"

"Yeah, you do that. Fill out a report. Can't have people threatening you. Especially since you don't even know this guy, right? This guy you didn't meet with."

Whelan cupped his hand over the phone and looked out the window. He knew how it looked. There wasn't much he could say.

"Whatsamatter, Whelan? Got nothing to say for once?"

"I'm still looking at the same guy I told you about. And I'd like to find out a little more about the big, bald guy that did some business with Harry Palm. But I'm not interested in this black guy."

"So this meeting you had with him, this was all just a misunderstanding, huh?"

"Yep."

"And it was a coincidence that you were asking around about him, right?"

"Not exactly, but I didn't know who I was after, so I was—"

"I'm glad it wasn't a coincidence, Whelan. I think I told you once that I don't believe in coincidences."

Whelan said nothing.

"And when were you going to tell me that this guy came around to visit?"

"I would have told you." Eventually, he thought.

"Tell you what, Whelan. You go ahead and look into this guy you're investigating, and let's say you come see me with anything that comes up that's even remotely related to Harry Palm. That okay with you?"

"Do you care if it's okay with me?"

"No." Bauman laughed and sniffed into the phone. "Hey listen, Whelan? This broad that answers your phone—what's she look like?"

"Shelley?" He laughed.

"What's funny, Whelan?"

"Nothing. I just don't know how to answer. I've never seen her. She's just a voice to me."

"Nice voice."

"Yeah, like a big Lauren Bacall."

"No idea what she looks like, though, huh?"

"None at all."

"I'll be in touch, Whelan. But you knew that, right?" And Bauman hung up, laughing.

He was coming back from the restroom when he heard the phone. He assumed it would be Vosic, but it was Roy Swenson.

"Hello, Roy."

"Hi, Paul. I've got what you wanted. At least I hope I do."

"Fast work. Let's hear it."

"Well, first of all, there is no trace anywhere of anybody named George Brister. As a matter of fact, there are no Bristers in Seattle at all. Couple in Olympia, but none in Seattle. Surprised?"

"No. I've got a hunch that he never went back at all, that he just bought a plane ticket."

"Oh, that old scam. Well, whatever works. Okay, so there's

no trace of him, and I checked the employers you gave me. Here's the deal: he worked for one of them, but the other two never heard of him. The hospital he listed, St. Anne's, they knew him and they apparently fired him."

"Drinking."

"Right. But the other two acted like this was some kind of practical joke. I gave them the dates you told me and, just to play it safe, I had them go back a few years, in case he doctored his work record. Nothing. Sorry, Paul."

"No, Roy. I'd have been surprised if you'd found him, and almost nothing else that I've been told about this guy makes sense, so why should his work record jibe with the facts? Thanks, Roy."

"I'm gonna be in your neck of the woods in October, Paul."

"Let me know when and I'll block off some time. Sure I can't send you a few bucks for your trouble?"

Roy Swenson indulged in malicious laughter. "No, buddy, you knew it wouldn't be that simple."

The phone rang again and he smiled. This is the busiest I've ever been, and I've got a hunch I know who this is.

"Paul? Rich Vosic here."

"Hello, Rich. What can I do for you?"

"I was going to ask you the same thing. Seems you've been here and gone. Anything I can do for you?"

"No, I guess I got pretty much everything I need."

"You did, huh? Hmmm. Look, Paul. We should talk."

"Does this mean you like me? Are we gonna be buddies, Rich?"

Vosic laughed and Whelan was impressed at how sincere he sounded.

"Yeah, right, we're gonna get emotionally involved. Look, Paul, I know you're a busy guy and I know I'm a busy guy, so I won't beat around the bush. But I think I can be of some help to you with this…ah…this thing. I can save you some time and trouble."

"Sounds good to me."

"So what say we have lunch together tomorrow, Pablo."

"It just happens that I'm free tomorrow."

"Fine. Want me to pick you up?"

"No. I'll meet you at your office."

"Okay. Twelve thirty all right?"

"Perfect."

"See you then, Paul."

"See you," he said and hung up.

I hate it when assholes call me by my first name, he thought.

She was waiting in his dark, airless hallway when he returned, and the look she gave the Burger King bag in his hand withered his french fries. She stared at it for several seconds and he could tell she was keeping the disgust out of her face only with the greatest effort. He knew there were people all over the country who had never eaten at a fast-food restaurant, but up to now their existence had been merely a rumor. Here was a woman who would never set foot inside a Burger King. He decided it was his hallway and she could speak first or there would be no conversation. Janice Fairs collected herself and reverted to her icy politeness.

"Mr. Whelan. I see that I'm interrupting your lunch. I'm sorry."

"It doesn't bother me if it doesn't bother you. Come in."

He opened the door and held it for her, then followed and pulled the door shut. She stopped just inside the office and looked around.

"Take a load off, Mrs. Fairs." He indicated the chair and then took his own seat behind the desk. He started to open his bag and decided he couldn't eat a Whopper with cheese and an order of fries in front of this woman. But when she shot another look of distaste at his lunch he decided the hell with it and opened the bag.

"Be with you in a second," he said as he spread open the paper to reveal the big, flat burger flapping out of its bun and dripping ketchup, mustard, and mayo on all sides. People could say what they wanted about Burger King; he'd always be in their debt, for they had taught him what mayonnaise could do for a hamburger. His own mother hadn't been able to impart such knowledge. He grabbed the burger in both hands and took a large bite and concentrated on it. He looked up at Janice Fairs, who was watching him with the same expression she might use on a man eating garbage from her trash disposal. He wiggled his eyebrows. Bet there's no Burger King on your block, lady, he thought. He chewed, swallowed, popped a couple of fries in his mouth, took a pull at his Pepsi, and felt that now he could face responsibility.

Her eyes moved around his office again. She took out a cigarette and was about to light up when she looked at his food. "Oh, I beg your pardon. You're eating…"

She must be impressed, he thought. She now recognizes that I have rights.

"Go ahead and smoke. It doesn't bother me."

She lit her cigarette and took a puff and blew smoke away from him and nodded, looking once more around the room.

"Mrs. Fairs, I don't want to seem impolite, but I don't think you should be coming to see me at the office. I recommend that you call me and set up a different meeting place next time. I think there is reason to be concerned for your safety."

She blew smoke and gave him a surprised look. "*My* safety, Mr. Whelan? Oh, I don't think there is any cause for concern on that score. They wouldn't dare—"

"They? Who, Mrs. Fairs?"

"Well, Rich Vosic's people. And I'll tell you something, Mr. Whelan: Rich Vosic…I know Rich Vosic, Mr. Whelan. He wouldn't have the nerve."

"I don't understand. You have me investigating a pair of killings that you believe Vosic instigated, and he wouldn't 'dare' harm you? Am I misunderstanding something?"

She smiled but it wouldn't hold. She shook her head and took nervous puffs at her cigarette and he could almost hear her thinking.

"If he had your husband killed, or Harry Palm, what's to

stop him from having you killed?"

She opened her mouth and made a little shrug. "Well, I just think the whole idea is…ridiculous. It's just beyond the realm of possibility."

"If even half of what you suspect is true, Mrs. Fairs, then nothing is beyond the realm of possibility. Next time call me and we'll set up a meeting. Now, what brought you out today?"

"I'm staying in town for a while, Mr. Whelan, and I thought I'd come by and see if you had learned anything more."

"In half a day's work? No, Mrs. Fairs, I'm not a miracle worker." She seemed to be holding something back, and he had a vague impression that she was waiting for him to give her something, something that she wasn't going to ask for. "I met Victor Tabor."

She frowned and gave a little shake of her head. "Whatever for?"

"I wanted to talk with someone who had actual dealings with your husband and Rich Vosic. He has a somewhat darker view of High Pair and its financial maneuverings."

"He still harbors some resentment over the loan."

"Oh, I think it's something a little stronger than resentment. He thinks they took advantage of him and that they knew what they were doing before they went in. Both of them."

"He is a bitter old man. My husband was not a crook."

Whelan decided to try the one he had really been waiting for. "Mrs. Fairs, have you thought any further about the name I mentioned?"

"The name? Oh, yes. Henley." A new life came into her eyes and she reddened slightly, as though excited.

No, not so hot, lady. Playing dumb is not your strong suit. "Yes, Henley. You said you thought you knew the name."

She frowned now and her acting wasn't getting any better. "I'm sure I've heard that name before, Mr. Whelan, but it's impossible for me to tell you where or when. Someone I heard Phil mention, perhaps, or as I said, a name I heard Mr. Palm mention." She shrugged and smiled a saleswoman's smile. "I wish I could be more helpful, Mr. Whelan."

"Well, if it should come to you, please give me a call. It may be important, and I can use any help that comes my way."

She put out her cigarette and there was something like humor in her eyes. "Oh, Mr. Whelan, I think you're doing just fine the way you're working. Just fine. I'm quite satisfied. As a matter of fact—" She dug inside the little purse again and came out with her wallet. "—I have something for you. Here." She lay a small, neat sheaf of bills on his desk. She didn't spread them out for effect, just set them down in a perfect pile. The top one was a hundred and there was no reason to believe that the ones below were anything else.

"Pictures of President McKinley. My favorite. But what's this for?"

She gave him a tight smile. "Call it a bonus, Mr. Whelan. I still intend for you to bill me when all this is…concluded. But for now I'd like to give you this."

"That's very generous," he said.

She was getting up and straightening her skirt. She made an unconscious attempt to brush the imaginary dirt of Whelan's office from her skirt, and he smiled. "I'll be in touch, Mr. Whelan. By the way, I'm staying at the Harrison-Stratford. You can reach me there."

"Just as long as it's not the Estes."

She frowned. "I don't know the Estes."

"Just as well. One quick question: I'd like to know more about Vosic. I know he's married and that his marriage is unstable."

She laughed again, a laugh with an edge to it. "Unstable. What a delightful piece of understatement, Mr. Whelan. His marriage is a shambles. His wife hates him, Mr. Whelan. She is rumored to be planning to take him to the cleaners, but no one takes her very seriously. Susan Vosic is what you'd call a lightweight, Mr. Whelan. She has no idea what he has or owns; she'll do all the damage of a fruit fly."

"Do they still live together?"

"Ostensibly. His name is on the mailbox, but he hasn't set foot inside that house in months. He uses the brownstone in

Lincoln Park and the condominium on the Gold Coast. She has the house in Melrose Park." She gave him an amused look. "Why? Are you thinking of calling on Susan Vosic, Mr. Whelan?"

"Maybe. I'm not shy, Mrs. Fairs."

She nodded and a smile spread across her face. "What a wonderful idea, Mr. Whelan. And one that would never have occurred to me. I know Susan will talk to you, Mr. Whelan."

"You're sure about that?"

"Oh, there is no doubt in my mind. She'll talk to anyone about her situation. But don't tell her you're looking into my husband's death. The rest of the world believes it was a suicide, and Susan is a follower, not a leader. Tell her you're trying to find out about—"

He held up a hand. "No offense, but I think I can manage."

"Of course you can. You are a very capable man, Mr. Whelan. I don't mean to tell you your business. There is one thing you should know, though: it would not be helpful to your cause to let Susan know you're working for me."

"You don't get along."

She smiled tightly. "Another of your understatements, Mr. Whelan." She nodded once more and turned toward the door.

He got up and showed her out. Then he went back to his desk, picked up the stiff little packet of new bills, and looked at it. Ten hundreds. Some bonus. He took a quick look out the window just in time to see her crossing the street toward a gray Lincoln. These people liked Lincolns. Hers was parked in a loading zone and there was a ticket under her wiper. She glanced at it briefly and then ripped it in pieces, small pieces, many of them. Then she got in, made a U-turn on Lawrence that earned her the hostility and the horns of half a dozen drivers, and she was gone, this woman who drove into run-down neighborhoods and called on private detectives for the sole purpose of giving them handfuls of cash. Now why don't I believe that? he wondered. He looked at the bills again. The bonus was for coming up with the name.

Whelan sat staring out at the street traffic and wondering when the last time was that someone had told him the truth.

Eleven

Susan Vosic answered the phone on the second ring, a youthful-sounding woman with a nervous phone manner and a habit of hesitating before speaking.

Whelan explained who he was. She wasn't impressed, but when he told her that he was investigating a connection between her estranged husband and his former accountant she gave him her longest silence.

"I don't see why that should concern me. I was never involved in the business. I don't think I said six words to that man Brister."

"Of course not. But you might have information I can use about the company's financial picture. It's pretty nebulous. The companies I'm working for…my clients have some question as to where High Pair's money actually went. And there is a lot of money involved. A great deal of money."

There was a long hesitation and then she told him she'd see him in the evening.

It wasn't a castle but it was easily the largest house on a street of modest but perfectly maintained houses—by Melrose Park standards, a mansion. Whelan had no idea what a guy with a name like Vosic would be doing here in an Italian neighborhood and assumed that Mrs. Vosic was a local girl.

On a summer night in Melrose Park you were never alone. People sat on their front porches or set up folding chairs on the sidewalk in front of the house and watched newcomers with interest and occasional suspicion.

They knew how to throw a party, these people, and once a year for many years, usually in the company of Liz, Whelan had come to Melrose Park for the Feast of Our Lady of Mount

Carmel, known more commonly as the Feast, a weeklong carnival and food binge that brought thousands of people to the church grounds and death to half the clams on God's earth.

A fun neighborhood to visit, so long as you remembered not to park where someone had staked out his space with a kitchen chair. Better to park in front of a hydrant than take somebody's space.

He walked back up the street to the Vosic house and when he rang the bell, a woman answered. She was young and sharp featured and there was a washed-out quality to her looks, as though she had just recovered from an illness. She was also, as Carmen had said, small, with slender arms and legs that gave an air of frailty. This fragile quality evaporated as soon as you noticed her eyes—they were large and very dark, not the eyes of a woman whom people walked all over. She had shoulder-length dark brown hair and she had put on some makeup to combat the paleness.

"Mr. Whelan?"

"Right. Hi."

"Come in."

She led him into a large, luminous living room, a room contrived for light. There were windows on three sides of the room. The carpet and draperies were off-white and the furniture was a mixture of blond wood and beige fabric—modern, every stick of it. A bookcase took up one wall, its shelves lined with hard covers still in perfect dust jackets, and he saw a set of the *Encyclopedia Brittanica* that looked as though someone had polished it. The light from the setting sun made gold of her glass tabletops, one of which supported an enormous book on Greek and Roman art. It wasn't a living room so much as a showroom for furniture and beautiful things, and when she asked him to make himself comfortable, he wasn't sure he could.

She smiled. "Anywhere, Mr. Whelan. It's all for sitting. Can I get you something to drink?"

"No, thanks." He took a large armchair facing the sofa, where she sat back, folded her arms, and looked at him with a half smile.

"What is it exactly that you want to know, Mr. Whelan?"

"A number of things. I'm just not sure you're the person I should be asking. Some of my questions may prove to be quite offensive to you—prying, at the very least, and perhaps insulting to your husband."

A look of amusement passed quickly over her face and she shook her head. "I doubt that you'll say anything about Rich that *I'll* find insulting. Have you ever met my husband, Mr. Whelan?"

"Uh…yes, I have."

"Did you like him?"

"I try not to form judgments too quickly. You wind up taking a lot of those back."

She smiled. "What a diplomat. So you didn't like him much."

He laughed. "No, ma'am, but it's all right. I don't think he cared much for me, either."

"Then let's drop all the pretense, all right? You can't offend me by anything you ask about Rich. He's a crook. He's an operator, Mr. Whelan. He uses everybody. He used me." She held up one hand. "No, wait. I know what you think I'm going to say. I'm talking business now. He married me because I had money." She gave him a sardonic grin. "Just like his partner."

Whelan shook his head. "His partner?"

"Phil Fairs. The one who killed himself."

"Oh, right."

"Phil married a richie girl, too, Mr. Whelan, only her father didn't trust him and would never give them more than a few dollars, nothing like the big money Phil and Rich thought they'd get from the Anders family." She thought for a moment and then smiled. "Phil got more than he bargained for there."

"Where? You mean his marriage? His in-laws?"

"His wife. There's a princess for you, Mr. Whelan. I don't know, maybe I seem like a bitch to you." She shrugged. "Maybe I am."

"Maybe you are. That's not really the impression I'm getting."

She smiled. "Thanks. I like to think I'm just a tough *paisan*. Anyway, you should meet Janice Fairs sometime. She's an experience. She might not talk to you, though. You don't wear a suit. She's one of those people you read about. Somebody on her ma's side came over on the *Mayflower*."

"If everybody who makes that claim is telling the truth, the *Mayflower* was an aircraft carrier."

She laughed. "Anyhow, you might want to look her up sometime, just to get her side of this stuff. Wear a nice suit, though, and rent a Porsche."

Whelan gave a little shake of his head. "Look, Mrs. Vosic…I don't really know a lot about the early days of High Pair and I know even less about Fairs, and I'm not sure any of it has anything to do with what I'm looking into. Your husband's partner killed himself but two other people came out alive, and I'm trying to find out more about them. Your husband is doing just fine and the accountant, the mystery man of the whole business, he's nowhere to be found. Cleaned out his bank accounts and made himself disappear."

She watched him for a moment and then shrugged. "I assumed you wanted information about my husband. Did I misunderstand you?"

"No. I'm interested in anything you can tell me about your husband's finances. I wasn't sure I could expect you to be too frank about him, given the fact that what's his is a matter of contention between you."

"That's true, but don't overestimate the significance, Mr. Whelan. I'm not going to starve." She indicated the room around her. "This is mine. All of it. There was never any question of that. We bought this house with my money, at a time when Rich and Phil didn't have two nickels to rub together. You marry a nice Italian girl, Mr. Whelan, you can leave her, but you can't take her house. It's my house. I have a car, too, and a private bank account and a good lawyer. Don't cry for me, Argentina." She smiled.

"Okay. I appreciate your frankness."

"My pleasure. Maybe you'll tell me something I can use."

"Maybe I will. First, I'd like to know anything you can tell me about George Brister."

She frowned. "What's to tell? I…it seems to me, Mr.

Whelan, that you're barking up the wrong tree. You want to know the truth? High Pair was run by a couple of good-looking, cocky, self-indulgent young crooks who both had gambling habits and both did a lot of coke and both drank like fish. They lied to people to get backing and took advantage of people who helped them. And when things got too heavy, one killed himself and the other one took a beating."

She looked around the room and he wondered if she were reliving painful moments from that time, perhaps in this room.

"For a while," she added a moment later.

"But not for long, it seems."

She smiled. "If you knew him better it wouldn't surprise you at all. He's one of those people who always land on their feet. They always come out on top and no one seems to understand why. He has amazing luck, Mr. Whelan, just amazing." She leaned forward on the couch as if to close the space between them, and she touched her temple with a long, pale finger. "And he's very smart, a lot smarter than he seems. I think Phil found that out the hard way."

"What do you mean?"

She shrugged again. "Nothing dramatic, Mr. Whelan. I just think…there was a certain relationship between them, all along, I think, even when they were college boys. It was Phil the leader and Rich the follower. The general and the soldier. And it was that way when they began High Pair—Phil had all the ideas and Rich bought it all, everything Phil said sounded brilliant to him, and for a while everything was that way, they made money hand over fist and it seemed they couldn't make a mistake. They went into software and it exploded into money overnight. They went into real estate and the sky was filled with dollar bills. A couple of fair-haired boys with a golden touch."

"The American Dream," Whelan said.

She made a sniffing sound. "Yeah. That's exactly what I thought it was. And that's how we—" And she caught herself. She looked at him suddenly, then made a little fluttering motion with her hand as if to sweep away the thought. No, there would be no tearful recounting of the dissolution of her marriage. She was tougher than she looked, this woman, and no fool.

"Anyway, it all came undone eventually. They overextended themselves and gambled their money and spent incredible amounts on drugs and partying. And maybe that accountant took off with…who knows what, and they woke up one morning and found that they were in the deepest shit they could imagine. And Rich handled it and Phil couldn't."

"You implied a moment ago that their relationship changed at some time during the years at High Pair."

"Yes. It didn't really surprise me, Mr. Whelan. I had always known that Rich was a very strong person, stronger than people were willing to take him for. And it didn't really take so long to see that Phil Fairs wasn't superman. He *was* brilliant, I'll give him that, and a very forceful personality, a great salesman, but…" She made a sour face. "He was also a very weak man in some ways, he had a lot of personal, you know, addictions. Liquor for one, and drugs."

"You said they both did drugs."

"I know, but with Rich it was recreational. He got into it because Phil and the crowd they hung around with all did drugs. Cocaine mostly. Cocaine was Phil's drug of choice—Rich did coke but he really liked grass and hash. Loved hash."

"And the gambling? You mentioned gambling. Did you mean horses, that kind of thing?"

"Horses, basketball, fights, baseball, football, anything. Anything at all. And they both gambled, a lot, and a lot of money, and I think…at the time I was worried that Rich had a problem with it, and now I think maybe I was right, but I know Phil had a problem with it. He was a little crazy where gambling was concerned, Mr. Whelan. Rich told me one time, after Phil had lost twenty-five thousand dollars on the Super Bowl, that Phil was obsessive about it because he viewed gambling as an extension of his business ability, of his…intellect."

"If he could win at gambling, beat the bookies, it proved how smart he was?"

"Yes. That's it exactly. He really thought he was a genius, Mr. Whelan. And when he found out he wasn't—" She spread her hands.

"Were you surprised when he killed himself?"

"I think you're always a little surprised by that, but I wasn't, you know, amazed. Toward the end Rich told me Phil hardly ever seemed to be thinking clearly, he seemed to have delusions about how he could turn it all around. Effortlessly. It was the drugs and the liquor, I'm sure. He wasn't all there anymore, and he killed himself. Maybe if he'd been sober it would have been different."

"Did you ever suspect that maybe his death wasn't suicide?"

She took the question in stride. "You mean, with all the seedy people he knew, did I ever suspect that one of them did it?" She smiled and nodded. "Sure. It was the first thing that came into my head. I was sure it was one of the people he owed money to—the gambling people, I mean, not the legitimate businesses or investors. They wouldn't do anything to him; how else would they get their money back?"

He thought of Victor Tabor. "Makes sense, but sometimes people are motivated by things other than logic."

"I told Rich what I thought, though, and he told me it couldn't be the gamblers."

"He say why?"

"Yes, he said the gamblers and even the drug dealers Phil knew were really small time."

"Twenty-five thousand doesn't sound like small time to me."

"Not to me, either, but Rich said it wasn't that big a deal. And as far as he knew, Phil didn't owe any of those people anything major. It was the business that was in trouble. They had a number of notes due and several of their ventures were really busts, and it all seemed to fall apart at once."

Whelan looked around and thought about what she'd told him. "How did your husband take the death of his partner?" he asked.

She gave him a frank look. "He didn't grieve and he wasn't happy. Toward the end they'd begun to argue about money and business decisions and Rich had started to assert himself, and

Phil just couldn't keep his end up. Rich said he'd seen it coming. I don't even think he was surprised, Mr. Whelan. And—" She stopped.

"What?"

"I don't know if it's fair. As you know, Rich and I aren't on the best of terms. But I'm certain that Rich viewed Phil's death as an opportunity to save his own fortune. That it was too bad that Phil was gone, but he now had a chance to turn it around."

"Which he did."

"Not right away, Mr. Whelan. He took a beating for quite a while, and he had virtually no credit."

"Did he declare bankruptcy?"

"Just to keep people off his back."

"What did turn it around for him, then?"

She gave him a look of wonder. "Who knows? His luck, Mr. Whelan. I told you about his luck. Nobody believes me, but that's what it was."

"Is it possible that there was money put aside, safe from creditors, that he was able to use to buoy up the business?"

"I don't see how, Mr. Whelan. Auditors were going over the company's books like ants at a picnic. He couldn't have hidden a thing from them."

"Cash, maybe?"

She gave him an amused look. "You mean in a safe deposit box or something like that? No, Mr. Whelan. It would have had to be a big box, with a lot of money in it, and I think I would have known about it, because there were times during that first few months after the company went under when Rich was walking on eggshells. I would have known if he was digging into a hidden stash. We needed money, Mr. Whelan, and all of mine was invested in that company. No, I would have known if he had money. You want to know how he got the money to continue in business, don't you? He just talked people into going along with him. Eventually he was able to dissociate himself from Phil Fairs and from the company and its troubles. If you want to know the truth, I think it's why he brought his brother into the company. Ron gave him an opportunity to go after other investors, establish new credit, and he had no connection whatsoever with High Pair because he was living in Arizona all those years."

"I don't know anything about the brother."

She shrugged. "Nothing to know. He owns a steak house on the North Side. He's like a little imitation Rich. But without the brains. He's conceited and thinks he's a lady killer and a wheeler-dealer, and he has no idea, really, no idea that Rich is the brains of the outfit. He's so young and he thinks he's such a hot number." She laughed and covered her eyes with her hand. "He's a joke. He wants to be Rich, that's what he wants. He even tried to make me once. He hit on me. His brother's wife, you believe that?"

"I've seen the elephant."

"Nothing should surprise me, right?"

"Doesn't sound like the greatest manifestation of brotherly love, though. How do they get along?"

"Rich tells Ron to do things and Ron jumps up in the air and, you know, clicks his heels. That's how they get along. Anyhow…it all worked. And now Rich is rich. And divorcing his wife, who intends to haul his ass into court and kick it." She punctuated her statement with a little nod and he smiled.

"I don't mean to pry into what was obviously a painful time for you, and I appreciate your frankness. So let me just ask this: what can you tell me about George Brister?"

"Not much. Mr. Whelan, he was just the hired help to me. I met him a couple of times. There was a party I went to at High Pair, and I met him there. He was drunk, which I gather was his normal state. He'd only been with the company for six months or so and they were already talking about canning him."

"Who was, exactly?"

"Rich, mostly."

"I was under the impression that Rich brought him in."

She frowned and shook her head. "Not what he told me. Said somebody referred Brister to them. Anyway, Rich couldn't stand him. He thought Brister was a bum. A 'slug' he called him. He had no use for run-down men like that in the first place.

You've seen him, Mr. Whelan, he's in perfect condition and expects everybody else to be."

"So why did they want to fire Brister?"

"He lost some records. Lost his entire briefcase, actually. In a bar someplace. Some of the records were in the computer and some were duplicates of things Rich and Phil had in their files, but they had to go to a number of their business associates to get copies of some of the things Brister had lost. Phil was furious—embarrassed, mostly—but Rich was nervous that if the guy could lose his own briefcase, he probably couldn't be trusted with much."

"Doesn't sound much like a guy who made off with enough money to bring down a company, does it?"

"No. I never really believed that business about him taking hundreds of thousands, you know? Phil said that. Rich didn't believe it. He believed Phil was taking money out of the company to feed his habits."

"And Brister wasn't smart enough?"

"Oh, he thought Brister took money. And a lot of it. But more like forty or fifty thousand. Enough to hurt the company but not enough to bring it down."

Whelan thought for a moment. "Did he strike you as the cunning type?"

"God, no. You could have knocked me over when I heard he'd taken off like that. But the most surprised person of all was Phil Fairs. Phil had gotten into the habit of browbeating that man, abusing him in front of the people in the office, and I think he was stunned to realize that there was this little tiny piece of George Brister that he hadn't anticipated."

"Sounds like there was a piece of George Brister that took everybody by surprise."

"Yes, that's true. Rich was floored. I remember him coming home and telling me that Brister had taken all this money and made it out of town. He just kept shaking his head and saying, 'I can't believe he had it in him. That fat slug.' He was more pissed off about a drunk swindling him than he was about the money. I know Rich, and I can tell you that much."

"I've seen George Brister's file, and the application. There's no record of anyone referring Brister to High Pair. And the initials on the application are Rich's."

She shrugged. "Maybe so, but probably just because Rich was the one responsible for hiring. He was the personnel officer. They both wore about a dozen hats in that company, Mr. Whelan. There were times when it would have cost them deals for somebody to know what a dinky little company they were. A couple of guys and some clerks and an accountant and...I don't know what else."

"And from what you're telling me, if a lot of money disappeared from the company, then it was Phil Fairs who took it—at least most of it. Is that right?"

She thought for a moment, then nodded. "Yes. And I hope I've convinced you I don't want to defend Rich or anything, but..."

"A good lawyer would say that by defending Rich, you're ultimately defending your own interests."

She nodded. "Right. A good lawyer probably would, but that wouldn't change the truth. And I'll tell you what, Mr. Whelan: you prove Rich took a lot of money out of that company and I'll give it back to whoever it belongs to after I stomp Rich in court."

There was an edge to her voice now and a luminous quality in the dark eyes, and he almost felt sorry for Rich Vosic, who had married far, far above his station in life and then compounded his mistake by underestimating her.

"I believe you will."

She sat back and gave him a satisfied half smile. "Anything else I can do for you?"

"Yes. Tell me, in your opinion, if your husband is capable of killing a man, or of ordering someone else to do it."

Her eyes widened and she shook her head slowly. "No. Oh, jeez, no. He couldn't do anything like that. He just...he's a sleaze, Mr. Whelan, but he doesn't have the stomach for anything like that. Why? What are you telling me? This is about Phil Fairs, isn't it?"

"You've told me a lot of things about Rich and his partner,

and it's obvious that there were some tense moments at the time in question, and I just wondered. It was just a question. Did you ever hear Rich mention Harry Palm?"

"No." She looked around the room and shook her head. "No, why? Is he one of your clients?"

"No. He's involved in some aspects of this, though. I just wondered if you knew him."

"No."

"Well, you've certainly given me a lot to think about. I'm not sure where it leaves me, though." He stood up and shook her hand. There was a vague disquiet in her face and he felt sorry for her. "So you think I should be talking to Janice Fairs, right?"

A little light came back into her eyes and she smiled. "Yes, I do. But remember—"

"I know, a Porsche and a nice suit."

"That won't be enough. Garlic, Mr. Whelan. Wear a clove of garlic around your neck. You know? Wards off evil spirits."

She smiled and looked surprisingly young, almost girlish, and Whelan laughed. He thanked her for the warning and she showed him to the door.

At the corner near his car a group of young locals interrupted what seemed to be a wonderfully Italianate conversation of loud speech and waving arms to look at him. There were five of them, all very tan, all wearing sleeveless T-shirts. They all had the same hair, hair that would not wave in the wind or catch in branches. They seemed amused by his shirt, leading Whelan to believe that his was probably the first *guayabera* they'd seen. You didn't get a lot of Mexicans passing through this neighborhood.

He got into the Jet, started it, listened to it die, pumped the accelerator, and tried it again. It started with the closest sound a car could make to moaning. As he pulled away he looked at the young Italians again. They were amused by his car, too; he couldn't blame them.

• • •

The expressway back into the Loop was packed, the city was in motion, people headed downtown and to the lakefront and the bars and parks. Cars filled with teenagers played bumper tag and chicken. Every kid in Chicago seemed to be in a car headed east, and they all seemed to be singing along to a car radio.

He punched a button on his own radio and heard the jovial baritone of Harry Caray, who didn't take over the radio mike till the fourth inning; he'd missed a third of the Cubs game. They were up six to one and threatening to sweep the Mets if someone didn't help them come to their senses. In first place and sweeping the Mets. He shook his head. It was getting out of hand.

He rolled down his window and decided it was time for a visit to Rush Street.

He parked on Pearson and walked back up to Rick's Roost. There was a mugginess to the air that he hadn't noticed in Melrose Park, and whatever breeze was coming in from the lake a couple of blocks away was sucked out of the air before it could make itself noticed. The air smelled of fast food and car exhaust, a hot night on Rush Street. He looked up at the moon—still a couple of days short of a full moon. Put a hot night together with a full moon and the city became the world's largest circus. Throw in a convention and you had an asylum without keepers.

A couple of conventioneers were arguing with a Pakistani cabdriver but for the most part the pharmacists hadn't brought their troops up for the main assault yet. There were no drunks break-dancing or attempting to fall in love. A quick look in through the window of Vosic's place told him the evening hadn't started yet in there, either, and he went on. He passed by the little hamburger place and saw her.

Pat sat hunched over the far corner of the counter, working on what appeared to be a crossword puzzle. She glanced up at exactly that moment, raised her eyebrows, smiled, and waved. The sudden eye contact caught him off guard and he was embarrassed. He raised one hand and gave her a half smile and wondered if he looked as obvious as he felt.

He started at the far end of the street and worked his way up: he hit Ye Hange Oute, the Fire Station, the Fox Hunt, the Firewater, and a couple of other taverns. He avoided the big ones, Mother's and Butch McGuire's, the meat markets frequented primarily by younger singles on the prowl, places where the people he was interested in would stand out and be out of place. He ordered a Coke or a coffee in each place, engaged the bartender in casual conversation, and then let a name drop— Rich Vosic, Ron Vosic, Frank Henley. All the bartenders knew the Vosics, both of them. A couple of the younger ones, eager to please or to seem streetwise, told him what great guys the Vosics were, what regular guys they were, not like other people with that kind of money. No one seemed to know anything about Henley—until Whelan made his way to the Fox Hunt.

The Fox Hunt was a bar you chose in order to avoid the rest of Rush Street, several blocks from the heart of the action. It was dark and cool and for the most part uninhabited—the TV had the Cubs game on and there were a pair of fortyish women watching the game. One of them looked him over as he sat down a few stools away. He nodded to her and she looked back at the TV set. The only other customer was a scholarly looking young guy in wire rims, scribbling feverishly into a spiral notebook and occasionally sipping from a glass of beer without looking at it.

The bartender watched the Cubs fill the bases and nodded and said something to the two women, whom he seemed to know. He looked around and saw Whelan, seemed startled, and came over quickly. "Sorry, guy, I didn't see you come in."

A professional, Whelan thought. The young ones don't care whether they make you wait or not. The bartender was big and going to fat, with red hair and a dense beard and a sunburned face. He grinned and shrugged. He looked like a happy Viking.

"It's all right. It's hard to notice the real world when this is happening." Whelan nodded toward the TV.

The bartender chuckled. "Sweeping the Mets at Shea. Yeah, who woulda thunk it?"

Whelan nodded. "My grandmother used to say the world

would come to an end when a lot of strange things started happening, so if the Cubs sweep, I think the world is going to hit an asteroid."

The bartender nodded. "Cold one?"

"Got any coffee?"

"Sure."

"Black," Whelan said.

The bartender brought him a white ceramic mug full of coffee. It was classic bar coffee, scalding and the color of bituminous coal; it tasted like old toast and you could stand a spoon in it.

"Good coffee," Whelan said.

"Might be a little old," the bartender conceded.

"Fresh coffee's for sissies."

The bartender grinned and looked out at the street. A pair of men with name tags were staring in through the window.

"You're in deep doo now, pal, the pharmacists have found your bar."

"Will they leave if I hold up a cross or something?" They watched and eventually the two pharmacists decided there wasn't enough action in the Fox Hunt and left.

"You dodged a bullet there."

The bartender wiped imaginary sweat from his forehead. "You ever tend bar for conventioneers?"

"No. I've been in a war and I was a police officer for the better part of a decade, but I've never had to face that kind of horror."

The bartender laughed again. "Well, it's nothing like those experiences, but you wouldn't believe what happens to grown men when you turn them loose, a thousand of 'em, with all their friends, in a city where nobody knows 'em. You wonder how they remember to put their pants on in the morning. We had a couple of guys in here the other night, just before closing. One guy, he's sitting there staring at his beer and he just blows lunch all over the bar and all over his shirt. He gets up, moves over one stool, sits down again, and takes a sip of his beer. And his friend doesn't even notice the barf on the bar."

"The worst part of it is, they won't remember most of the things they did here," Whelan said. He sipped his coffee and then put it down. "The Vosic brothers ever come in here?"

The smile died and the happy Viking wasn't so happy anymore. He shrugged and made a little half shake, half nod. "They come in once in a while, not often." He indicated the dark little bar. "This is not exactly their, uh, style. A little quiet for their taste, you know what I mean?"

"I don't really know them. I've just met them a couple of times. I'm trying to get a handle on them."

"You're still a cop," he said, nodding.

"No. I'm private. And this is actually…business."

"You ever been in their bar?"

"No. I know the place, but I haven't been in it yet."

"Well, you want to get an impression of those guys, spend a little time in their bar. You'll probably see them in action then."

"A couple of real high steppers, huh?"

"Yeah. High rollers, really neat guys. Well, you've met them, right?"

"Yeah. Can't say I really enjoyed the experience. Rich seems to think of himself as a mover and shaker."

The bartender nodded. "He's got a way…I don't know, he can come in here and buy the house a round and he seems like the nicest guy in the world. But he's got no interest in talking to any of the people he's buying a drink for. You know what I'm saying?"

"Yeah. He makes the gesture but the people don't really exist for him. He lives on a higher plane."

"That's it."

"What about the little brother?"

"'Little' is right. And he's got a complex about it, too. They don't like each other, those two. Nobody ever says it, but I see it. I've been in other bars when they came in, loud, obnoxious assholes that they are, and after they've had a few you can tell they can't stand each other. The young one really wants to be the honcho. And the older one treats him like a gofer."

Whelan thought for a moment. "Ever heard anything to

make you think the young one has any brains?"

The bartender shook his head and grinned. "Not one. Never seen or heard any evidence that would make you think there was a mind there. He's brain dead, that Ron. And he's a whore, that kid." He leaned over the bar and dropped his voice.

"He'll screw anything, anybody, and then he wants the world to know about it. He'll tell strangers who he's fucked."

"Neat guy. Ever hear any talk about how they got their money?"

The bartender gave him a warning look and Whelan nodded.

"Fair enough. I retract the question. But I've got another one: ever meet a friend or a hired hand of theirs named Henley?"

The bartender thought for a second and began to shake his big, shaggy head. Whelan added, "About your size, bald, a goatee, and a bad attitude," and the bartender's face changed.

"Oh, *him*. Hell, yes, I know him. I didn't know his name, though. He's a spooky sucker. We don't let him in here anymore. He picked a fight in here one night with a guy, a real young guy, I think they were arguing about politics or something, and this guy, this Henley, he really took this kid apart, and we couldn't get him off the kid. And you know what? He liked it. He was enjoying himself. So we threw him out, took about five of us, and Jay, he's the owner, he was here that night, and he told the guy not to come back. And this Henley, he tells Jay he's gonna be looking for him. So Jay tells him he'll get a peace bond on him and he'll get busted if he comes back."

"And has he?"

"No. I've seen him walking down the street but he hasn't come back here. I got the feeling that he didn't want things to get complicated, like he really didn't want to bring the law into it."

Whelan thought for a moment. "Ever see him with anybody?"

"No. He came in by himself." The bartender gave a sardonic laugh. "Who'd want to pal around with a spook like that?" Then he tilted his head to one side. "You looking for him? Is that it?"

"I hope not."

The bartender nodded. "Me, too. I hope you're not looking

for him. You want to stay away from him, mister. He'll hurt you if he gets a chance. Those other two are lightweights, but that guy isn't all there."

"Thanks. I'll have to keep that in mind."

"Hey, Bill, we're dying of thirst down here," one of the women said.

The bartender nodded to Whelan. "Duty calls."

Whelan stood up and dropped a five on the bar. "Later," he said and left the bar.

Outside it seemed hotter after the chilly air of the bar, and there was a lot more traffic. At the corner two men got out of their cars and examined the evidence of a fender bender as a half dozen motorists behind them leaned on their horns and filled the air with noise. There was a lot of foot traffic, large groups of well-dressed young guys and smaller groups of young women, and the pharmacists had landed in force.

They weren't getting in Rick's Roost, though, as the handsome, muscular young man at the door turned away a group of a half dozen middle-aged men, telling them that the Roost was too crowded.

"We're too crowded, fellas," he said, watching the cars go by. "Too crowded."

"It don't look so crowded in there now," one of them said. The bouncer shrugged. "We got a private party coming in. I can't let in any groups. Come back some other time."

The pharmacists turned away, grumbling, and Whelan walked up to the door. The kid didn't like the looks of Whelan, either, and was about to give him the same line when Whelan held up one hand.

"Save the speech. I'm here to see Rich."

"Oh. He's not here yet."

"I know that. His little toy car isn't in his parking space. But he'll be here and I don't think I'm gonna wait for him outside if it's all the same to you." And he stepped by the doorman before the kid could think of a comeback.

Inside, Rick's Roost was exactly what he would have expected—gaudy without being tasteful, showy without style, expensive without redeeming social value. There was too much light, framed photos of semidressed women hung on the walls, and the jukebox was up too loud. The back bar was all glass and chrome, the top shelf lined with softball and flag football trophies. In a prominent spot in the very center of the bar hung a team photo of the softball players, with Rich and Ron Vosic dead center. Whelan shouldered his way with some difficulty through several large groups of young men and took a stool at the far end of the bar. A couple of them glanced his way, looked him up and down, and seemed to be wondering what a forty-year-old guy who didn't wear tight shirts was doing in the Roost. They were big, clean shaven, corn-fed, and loud. One or two looked in the mirror as they talked, patting their perfect hair into further perfection, turning their heads one way and then another to see their own profiles. A few feet away a pair of slender, dark-haired guys were actually admiring the biceps of a big, beefy one who looked like somebody's tight end. He grinned, basking in their admiration, and demonstrated the types of lifts and curls he was doing in the gym.

At the far end there was a stage with three mikes, and to the left he could see the stairway that led up to the second floor.

The bartender came over, a clone of the one showing off his new muscles; he was wearing a Rick's Roost T-shirt with a big picture of a football on it.

I'm in jock heaven, Whelan thought.

The bartender nodded and raised his eyebrows. Apparently speech wasn't a requirement in these places. He nodded back and the bartender, forced into conversation, frowned.

"Can I help you," he said in a monotone.

Whelan ordered a ginger ale and asked pointedly if Rich were in, and the bartender immediately developed much sharper people skills. He grinned now, just a big, amiable Rush Street cowboy.

"The Bossman? Hey, it's early for him, you know? But he'll blow in here in a little bit."

The bartender poured a ginger ale from the soda gun, put a bar napkin on the bar in front of Whelan, and set the drink down. Whelan dropped a little pile of singles on the bar and the kid took two of them and brought back a quarter. Apparently ginger ale had become a delicacy; Whelan wondered how much a shot of quality bourbon would cost. A shot-and-beer drinker like Bauman could go broke in a place like this.

The bartender looked around the room with restless eyes and Whelan raised his hand.

"Yes, sir?"

"Got a question for you."

"Shoot."

"Friend of mine was telling me that Ron really runs the bar, not Rich, and I said no way. Who's right?"

The bartender gave a little snort. "Ron? Ron runs the bar?" He looked incredulous.

Whelan smiled. "I take it that's beyond the realm of possibility, huh?"

The kid opened his mouth to say something and then seemed to think better of it. He shrugged.

"Hey, Ron's a good dude. He's good people, they both are. It's just that, you know, Rich is a businessman, a *real* businessman, and Ron, old Ron is a party animal, he parties too hard to have time for much else. I, uh, I hear he's real good with computers and that. He's a smart dude, he's just not into running the bar."

Whelan looked satisfied. "Thanks. I know Rich, and I know if it's got his name on it, he's running it."

"Absolutely."

"But I couldn't tell this guy anything, he's one of those guys who's got all the answers."

The bartender nodded and Whelan hit him with the next one fast.

"What about Henley?"

The kid looked at him for a moment and then shook his head. "Henley? I...I don't know him."

"Sure you do. If you know Rich, you know Henley."

The kid refused to make eye contact. He looked around the room and then down at the bar, shaking his head. "No. Him, I don't know."

"How can you not know Frank?" Whelan laughed. "How can anybody not know Frank? It's impossible to miss him."

The kid backed up a couple of feet and leaned against the back bar, as though to put distance between them. He shrugged.

"Maybe you haven't been here long."

"No…I been here a year and a half. I was here when we opened. I just don't know this guy. Maybe I don't know him by his name."

"But you'd know him if you saw him, right? Big guy, bald, wears a goatee."

The kid shook his head. "No. That don't ring a bell."

"Okay, well…" Whelan took a sip of his ginger ale and the kid moved back up the bar and started emptying ashtrays that had nothing in them.

He finished the ginger ale and had another, and three cigarettes to go with them. Forty minutes in the enemy's camp had proved not dangerous but boring. It was the most obnoxious tavern he'd visited in years and he almost felt sorry for the people who came here to find their entire social lives.

Each time the door opened he wanted it to be Vosic, wanted to see Vosic's reaction, but there was no sign of the "bossman." No sign of little brother, either. He put his cigarettes back into his shirt pocket, left the bartender a single and change, and was about to leave when the door opened and Henley took over the room.

He stopped just inside, hitched up his pants, and took a long look around the room. He glanced at the bartender, ignored the kid's nod, and walked his rolling, swaggering walk to a corner stool. A pair of kids in knit shirts were arm wrestling right next to him and the one who was losing was leaning farther and farther back till he was almost touching Henley. The arm wrestler strained and twisted and rocked and finally had his back right up against the back of Henley's stool.

Henley slid off the stool and slammed the arm wrestler openhanded in the middle of his back. The arm wrestler lost his balance, lost his wrestling match, fell into the bar, and came up in a half crouch, fists cocked and face red.

Henley put his weight on his back foot and let his hands hang loose at his sides. The arm wrestler panted and stared and Henley gave him a little half smile and cocked his eyebrows. He made a little shrug as if to say, What's next? The kid rubbed his wrestling arm and Henley nodded.

"You were in my way."

The kid started to say something but Henley turned away and took his stool. He nodded to the bartender and turned his back on the bar. The kid came back toward Whelan, to the center tapper, and drew a beer without being told what kind.

Whelan leaned over the bar.

"Hey, young fella. That's Frank Henley. You know, the guy you never heard of." The kid looked at him briefly and then looked at the beer he was pouring. He looked embarrassed and miserable, and Whelan wondered what it was like to tend bar all night with Frank Henley in your crowd.

As he walked away the bartender called out to him.

"Uh, you want to leave a message for Rich or something?"

"Tell him I'll see him at lunch."

Whelan paused at the door, turned and saw, as he had known he would, that Henley was watching him. It was a predator's stare, made harder and colder by the eerie green color of the eyes. He held Henley's gaze for a moment and then had to look away.

Okay, he thought. So now we've been introduced.

He went by the hamburger place and saw that she was taking orders from a couple of girls. He walked past, got to the corner, stopped, thought about it for a few seconds, then walked back. She looked up as he opened the door and he wondered if she'd seen him go by. He wasn't sure, but he thought she colored slightly as he came in, and he found himself grinning. She smiled back and he wanted to laugh. A couple of adults, a couple of streetwise city folks, a man pushing forty and a woman close to it, and both of were overcome by fits of "Aw, shucks."

He walked to the back booth and slid into it and she came

over quickly.

"Hello, Paul."

"Hi, Pat. What's new?"

"Oh, not a whole lot. How about you?"

What's new? Oh, excellent, Whelan, way to put the moves on. Dazzle her with your rap, you smoothie, you.

He picked up a menu to disguise his sudden embarrassment and the thought struck him that this was probably exactly the way Bauman would try to pick up a woman.

He set the menu down and shrugged. "I'm putting on airs, Pat. I'm pretending to read the menu but I'm just a cheeseburger guy at heart. I'll have a cheeseburger and some fries—"

"And a chocolate malt, right?"

He smiled. "Yeah. Some of us fight adulthood tooth and nail."

She laughed and went back behind the counter and gave his order to the wild-haired little Greek. The Greek had three or four meals on at the same time and Whelan watched him flip a burger patty onto the grill and a double handful of fries into the fryer basket. He could probably put a dozen meals together simultaneously without making anybody wait. This was art, high art, an old and honored art, and Whelan never tired of watching a good short-order cook.

She brought back a glass of water and he lit up a cigarette. He was about to say something when she turned and went to the girls in the front booth. He watched her talk to them for a second and then she went back to the mixer, where his malt was churning away. He waited for her to come back and realized that he had absolutely no idea what to say next.

What comes next? What do I say now? He thought back to other women and no situation within memory seemed to match this one. A couple of women he'd dated had been people he met at weddings, there had been one who tended bar in a tavern he'd frequented for a while, two more whom he'd been introduced to by matchmaker friends. And there had been Liz, who had taken up the better part of his adult life, who had occupied center stage of his thoughts and plans and finally gone off to live in

Wisconsin and forget her past mistakes—one of which, in her opinion, had been an intermittent and at times very painful relationship with Mr. Paul Whelan. He wondered what he'd said to Liz the first time but he couldn't remember; after all, Liz had predated Vietnam in his life and had then outlasted it and his police career and a lot of other things.

Pat came back with his malt and he found himself shifting nervously in the booth.

"How about joining me for a cup of coffee?"

She looked quickly around the room and began to nod, and then the door opened and three young guys in yellow T-shirts came in, and immediately after them, a white-haired man with the newspaper folded over to the crossword puzzle.

He saw her wrinkle her nose in disappointment. She looked at him and shook her head.

"I don't think I can, Paul. It's been busy all night. Maybe in a little while."

He fumbled for words and then shrugged. "That's all right. We…we did this already anyhow, didn't we?"

She gave him a look, quick and surprised, and he smiled.

"We had a cup of coffee the other night. Maybe…we should move off square one. Maybe we could go out for a sandwich or a beer some night after you get off."

A half smile appeared and she nodded. "That would be nice. But I get off at midnight. Are you a night owl, Paul?"

"Sometimes. It doesn't bother me. Or we could do it another night. When you're not working."

She shot an anxious look at her new customers, then at the cook, who was looking over his shoulder at them.

"I'll be back."

"Right."

When she came back she had his burger and fries and a nervous look in her eyes.

"Here's your food." She set them down and looked at his table. "Can I get you anything else?"

"No, I'm okay." He nodded and then nodded again and suddenly realized that he was paralyzed, forty years old and paralyzed at the prospect of having to ask a woman out.

He sighed. "You know, I'm a little bit out of practice at...at asking a woman to go out, so..."

She smiled. "You already asked me out and I said yes. Now all you have to do is name the time. Or the time and place if you want to meet somewhere." She shrugged. "It's easy."

"Right. So let's go out." He was about to say "Tonight?" and caught himself, though he wasn't sure why. "How about tomorrow night?"

She raised her eyebrows. "Friday night? I happen to be off on Friday nights, and free tomorrow. Want to meet somewhere?"

"I can pick you up. I have what passes for a car."

"Fine. What time?"

"Let's be traditional. How about seven and we'll go out to eat somewhere."

"That'll be nice."

"You like Chinese food, right?"

"No, I love Chinese food."

"Okay."

She gave him a cryptic smile and then wrote down her address, on the 1300 block of Roscoe. He stared at it for a moment and then realized he probably looked like a rube. He stuffed it in a shirt pocket, she nodded to him, and then she was off taking care of other tables. He ate and watched the street, the brightly dressed groups of young women and cocky-looking young men and the staggering bands of conventioneers, and he liked it all.

All men are my brothers, he told himself. I have a date.

He looked around and caught her watching him and grinned, and she smiled and went on with her work. When he was finished he lost a moment worrying about how much of a tip you left a woman you were about to take out, then paid his bill at the ancient black register at the far end of the counter. She took his money, gave him his change and said, "See you tomorrow, Paul."

"Good night."

He sat on his porch and smoked and listened to the night noises of Uptown. Across the street somebody was playing his stereo too loud and on a porch down the block a group of blacks were working on a couple of six-packs, and in the distance he could hear sirens, a lot of them, and he knew that somewhere on this hot night something was burning in Uptown. Something was almost always burning in Uptown. He sipped at a dark Beck's and tried to get a line, the merest clue, on the shadowy figure of George Brister. He matched what he knew of the accountant with the face, the volcanic persona of the man called Henley, and shook his head.

Are you what I think you are, Henley? Did you do what I think you did?

Whelan went through what he'd been told of the personalities behind High Pair, and now he saw something quite different from what everyone else had seen—a couple of arrogant young men on top of the world, cutting deals and cutting corners and doing a fast dance and trying to pull off one more outlandish deal. For this they needed a dupe, a patsy, a fall guy, and they'd brought one in from the outside. And instead of a fall guy they got a predator, someone at least as smart as either of them. He visualized the scene witnesses had described to police—Phil Fairs setting fire to his own boat. A horrible way to go. Was that how a man despondent over gambling debts and bankruptcy killed himself? He tried to find the sense in that and couldn't. He could see something else, though—he could see a man torching his own boat and expecting to get off, and he could see someone else killing that man. *That* he could see. And the man he'd seen tonight, that man could kill. Whelan would have bet the rent on it.

He had another cigarette and finished his beer and tried to focus on this new woman in his life.

And then the car came by. Same car, same four men in it, watching the street, watching the people on the porches and stairs. They were drinking, and as they passed the yellow frame house across the street he heard laughter and saw a beer can fly through the air. It missed the main front window by inches, spattering beer across it.

Whelan told himself the cops could take care of it when the time came, that it wasn't his fight, that it was another man's trouble, but a part of him knew it wasn't true.

TWELVE

He killed part of the morning in the doughnut shop beneath the Wilson Avenue El station, shooting the breeze with an old man named Woodrow. It was ninety-four outside and the air-conditioning felt heaven-sent, and he believed he was the only man in this crowded, noisy, smoky little shop who had a date on this night. He bought Woodrow's coffee and threw in a doughnut, then bought breakfast for an old black man named Floyd who had given him information on the street more than once.

At the office there was mail, interesting mail—a brief letter from Ken Laflin, attorney-at-law and aspiring real estate mogul, informing Whelan that there was a need for his professional services and asking him to contact Laflin's office at his convenience. Whelan sat back in his chair and grinned. This was a wonderful turn of events; if Laflin needed him, then they could talk first about the money the lawyer still owed him from the last "service" Whelan had performed for him, and after that was paid up, they could talk about future services.

He stretched and yawned. The stifling little office didn't even seem hot at the moment. He had a date and it was a fine world. He looked at the other mail, a brochure from a roofer offering to put a new top on his building and a plain white business envelope with no return address. No postage, either. It had been hand delivered and dropped through his mail slot. He looked at it, turned it over, found nothing helpful on the back, and studied the handwriting—a woman's, a delicate but confident hand. What have we here? he asked himself and tore it open.

Inside was a short note and a check for twenty-five hundred dollars. Both bore the signature of Janice Fairs. The note was a marvel of brevity.

Dear Mr. Whelan:

Thanks in part to your efficiency, I will have no further need of your services. I want to thank you for your admirable work. I will not hesitate to recommend you in the future.

Enclosed, you will find my check. I assume this amount will cover all your expenses and make a final billing unnecessary.

Sincerely

Janice Fairs

He stared at the letter for several minutes, reread it, and looked at the check. He set them down on his desk and shook his head.

The last time I talked to this woman she was delighted with me, and now I'm terminated.

The letter was complimentary enough but there was no mistaking her intention: she didn't want to hear from him again, was even willing to pay through the nose to make a final billing superfluous. Counting the retainer she'd given him, the bonus, and this final check, Mrs. Fairs had paid him forty-five hundred dollars for less than a week's work.

He'd given her a name and she'd been happy; whatever the name did for her had also made Whelan's services no longer necessary. The name had given her something, a handle on things.

He made a quick call to her hotel and was told that Mrs. Fairs was not in but that he could leave a message. He said it wouldn't be necessary and hung up.

So she hadn't checked out yet. Whelan had a feeling that that meant she was sticking around for the duration. If Janice Fairs was going to hover around Rich Vosic's life, old Rich was in a world of trouble.

A while later the phone rang, and when he picked it up, Shelley's whiskey voice came through the wire.

"Well, up bright and early this morning, baby, aren't we?"

"You know what they say, Shel, if you want to get ahead…"

She laughed hoarsely. "Yeah, if you want to get ahead you have lunch in trendy places with hotshots. You had a call from a Mr. Rich Vosic."

"Lunch is canceled, I hope."

"Sorry, sailor. It's on. Only he wants you to meet him at the place. Jerome's." She lingered on the second syllable and chuckled. "So we have lunch at Jerome's these days, huh?"

"It's like the guy said in *The Godfather*, Shel—it's just business."

"Business, huh? Well, watch your purse around that one, baby. I know voices. Voices are my hobby, and that's a snake-oil salesman there. I bet I can tell you exactly what he looks like."

"I bet you can."

"I know what you look like, too, hon."

He laughed. "Okay, let's hear."

Without hesitation she said, "I'm guessing you're tall, and I'm sure you're on the thin side 'cause I know your eating habits…"

"But I love to eat."

"Yeah, but you eat on the run too often. Let's see, I think you have brown eyes."

He said nothing and she laughed into the phone. "Ha! You just told me I'm right. And I imagine you have a serious kind of face. I think you're probably nice looking 'cause there's been some women in your life, young ones, even, but you're no Paul Newman, they don't throw their panties at you or anything."

He laughed. "Okay, genius. What color is my hair?"

She hesitated. "I always kind of imagine you with brown hair, you know? But…I think you just told me your hair is, you know, different. Like maybe you're bald, but I don't think so. Or maybe you got silver fox hair, but…" She took what sounded like a long drag on a cigarette, made a sound like "mmmmmm," and then giggled, a surprising sound coming from Shelley, a young girl's laugh in a streetwise woman who was no longer young.

"I'm gonna say red! How close am I?"

"Close enough to be irritating, Shel."

She laughed with delight, and she was still laughing when he told her he'd talk to her later.

Jerome's was an upscale place, but more important, it was an open-air restaurant—of course it was, he would have bet lunch on it. On a ninety-degree day, Rich Vosic would choose an open-air restaurant, a place to be seen, to watch the street traffic, eye the women, have conversations loud enough to be heard by passersby. Whelan circled for ten minutes in a neighborhood whose streets had been laid out in the days when cars were a curiosity, narrow streets lined with maples and big houses and nary a parking space, and eventually settled for a spot three blocks from the restaurant. He walked up to Clark Street, then over to Arlington. He'd been to the restaurant before but would have found it in any case because Vosic's Lotus was parked in front of the hydrant just outside the restaurant. He went inside. It was dark within, icily cool, and there were shelves and shelves of homemade pastries for dessert. He wanted to sit across from them and stare, but when he gave Rich Vosic's name to the hostess he was shown to a table outside.

Years before, on a day like this, he'd been to Jerome's with Liz. They'd eaten inside, over her objections.

Vosic was at a table next to the wrought-iron railing that surrounded the outer dining area. He was perusing a menu and sipping from a tall iced tea. The hostess took Whelan halfway to Vosic's table and then seemed to linger, and Whelan realized that she was trying to catch Vosic's eye.

Eventually Vosic looked up, melted the hostess with an easy smile, and waved Whelan over to the table. He stood and extended his hand. "Hello, Paul. Hot enough for you?" He flashed teeth at Whelan.

"It'll do till something hotter comes along."

"This place all right?" Vosic asked.

"Sure."

He sat down and a dark-haired young man skated over to the table.

"Are you ready to order, Mr. Vos—"

"My name's Rich to you, Tony," Vosic said, waving a

chastising finger in the waiter's face.

"Okay, Rich," he said, obviously uncomfortable with the concept.

"You need a minute to order, Paul?"

"No." He scanned the menu quickly.

"Remember, I'm buying."

Whelan smiled behind his menu and then ordered an appetizer, a bowl of soup, sauteed scallops, and coffee.

Vosic blinked a couple of times, put on an awkward smile, and ordered a salad and a bottle of Heineken.

"No cocktail, Paul?"

"No, not for me. It's too early." And to himself he said, And I never, ever drink with assholes.

Lunch was what he had expected, an assault on his ears, a virtuoso performance by Rich Vosic. He made small talk, offered his views on politics, the cornerstone of which was a vision of Reagan as King Arthur, and gave an impromptu lecture on business, all of this delivered while Rich Vosic surveyed the young women at adjoining tables to assure himself that they were listening. It was impossible not to.

Whelan watched the young women strutting up and down Clark Street in summer dresses and sleeveless blouses and occasionally tuned Vosic in to see where he was in his lecture.

"…and I'm telling you, Paul, you can write your own ticket…they'll pay through the nose…you buy one with a garage on ground-level, it's like *gold*, Paul, there's no parking anywhere on the North Side…make your money back in a year, put it back in, watch it double, triple. I know, Paul, I *know*." He was gesturing to his chest with his salad fork. There was salad on it, and to a passerby it would have seemed that Rich was stabbing himself with a tomato.

Vosic seemed to notice Whelan's scallops, all but lost in a dense layer of cream sauce, and he launched into a brief sermon on fat and cholesterol, on fried foods and additives. He went on from there to various forms of cancer, and before Whelan knew what was happening Vosic was discussing diseases of the digestive tract and parasites.

Whelan started laughing and couldn't stop himself. Vosic paused with a forkful of healthy cucumber halfway to his mouth, tilted his head, and gave Whelan an amiable, slightly embarrassed smile, but his eyes were off in a different direction.

"Okay, Paul, what's the joke?" He grinned and shrugged. "Okay, I talk too much, right?"

"Well, I was just wondering if you're going to want to talk about leprosy next. Leprosy, I know. I did a research paper once in college."

Vosic bestowed a grin on him. They were buddies again.

"Okay, okay, I get a little carried away with health problems, diet and all that. I'm interested in it, and I've read up on it. You know, my old man and my uncle both died before the age of fifty—heart disease. They were both old school, you know? Fifty, sixty pounds overweight. So…" He shrugged, looked at the two blond women at the nearest table, and then shot Whelan a quick look of conspiracy.

"I picked this place for the scenery, Paul."

"Scenery's great. So are the scallops. What are we going to talk about next, Rich?"

Vosic pursed his lips, played with the label on his beer bottle, and made a little nod. "We're going to talk about this…I don't know what you'd call it, this investigation. Is that the right word, Paul?"

"It's a word."

"Okay, this investigation. About George Brister, supposedly."

"Why 'supposedly'?"

Vosic shrugged. "Oh, lots of reasons. You seem to be asking a lot of questions, a lot of questions that don't have anything to do with Brister."

"Like what? And how would you know what I ask people?"

"Oh, I hear things, Paul. I know what you ask Carmen, for one. And I know you've been in my place on Rush."

"Uh-huh."

"And I think you're going about things wrong. You're running around with no, you know, direction. You're asking a lot of questions about me and my business, and Brister and… this and that."

Whelan nodded; Vosic had stopped just short of saying "Henley." Or "Harry Palm." He could see that Vosic wanted him to say something, so he took a sip of his coffee, put it down, and continued eating. After a moment Vosic shook his head.

"And I hear other things, Paul. I hear your client—"

Whelan smiled. "You didn't *hear* about my client. You've had me watched."

Vosic's eyes opened wider and he seemed just slightly off balance.

"You've had me watched and you've had me followed."

Vosic regained some of his composure and nodded. "Okay, you saw my guy. You're a pro at this, he's not."

"It'd be hard to miss him. Subtlety is not one of his gifts."

"Well, maybe not. And it wasn't exactly my idea."

"Little brother, maybe?"

"Hey, I'm a businessman. I gotta take responsibility for what my people do, all right?" When Whelan said nothing, he went on. "That's Larry, Whelan, and he's all right. He's the most loyal sucker you'd ever want to meet. He'd step in front of a bus if I told him to. But, okay, you been following me around, I think, and I had you followed. Just to see what was going on. For no other reason."

"I really haven't been following you around, Vosic. I've just been listening to a lot of people who know you."

Vosic lowered his fork and his face darkened. "Yeah, I know who you been talking to. You been talking to Janice Fairs. Janice *Fairs*, for Chrissake." He shook his head and looked around the restaurant and then back at Whelan, and he was now into a new persona, the aggrieved businessman.

"So now what? Do we fight a duel, or what?"

Vosic gave him a pained expression. "Hey, I'm not the bad guy here, Paul, I didn't start this. I'm a reputable businessman with a reputation to uphold and interests to protect, and some guy comes sliding in and out of the shadows with a story about a guy from my past who wasn't real nice people, and I want to know why. I thought maybe some other outfit was trying to track Brister for something else he did; I believed your story. Then I…then I find out you're meeting with Janice Fairs. Janice Fairs is your client. There's no company trying to find Brister."

"Janice Fairs is someone I talked to in the course of—"

"Uh-uh, no, she came to see you, she comes all the way in from the suburbs to see you. That means she's the client."

"And what if she is?"

"What's she want with me? I got nothing to do with her. I don't want nothing to do with her, either." Whelan wondered if Vosic's grammar and pronunciation went south whenever he got angry or was just part of his regular-guy routine.

"She's interested in what Brister got away with."

Vosic studied Whelan with a little pout. He shook his head. "I'm not gonna buy it, Paul. I know what she thinks. She called me up one night, drunk and crying, and told me she thought I ripped her off. That's her angle. She thinks I have her money."

Whelan made a little shrug.

"Like she needs money, right? She's rolling in it, Paul. Her old man died and she was right back on top of the world. She's swimming in money. I got nothing she needs."

"Is that the point? If somebody takes something of mine, and I don't need it, does that make it all right?"

Vosic went red. It took him a moment to speak. "It ain't hers. None of it. It's mine."

"Maybe it's yours and Phil's."

Vosic looked at him openmouthed and then shook his head. "No. I made it all the way back by myself. I did it without any help from anybody. Phil Fairs didn't have what it takes. He couldn't handle it, Whelan, I told you that."

"Maybe he didn't kill himself. Maybe he planned to torch the boat and somebody decided to kill him."

It was further than he'd intended to go, but now that he had, he was pleased. Rich Vosic just stared at him.

Let's push, he thought. "Mrs. Fairs seems to think that if anyone killed anybody, it was you."

Vosic leaned forward. "No, Whelan, she don't think that.

She knows exactly what went down. She knows her husband punched his own ticket. She knows he went through all the money like it was never gonna end, and then he killed himself. He killed himself and left her with nothing. Insurance company wouldn't even pay on a suicide. He didn't leave her with a damn thing but the ring they took off his hand. But now she's got some money of her own and she's still singing the blues. You know why, Whelan?"

"Tell me."

"Maybe *she* should. She didn't tell you about her and me?"

Whelan made a little shrug with one hand'.

Vosic smiled. "No, she didn't. You didn't know about us. We had a little thing, Whelan. We had a little thing and it passed, it was one of those things. They don't last; the broads always think they're gonna last. Well, it didn't and she wants my balls, Whelan." He sat back in his seat and watched Whelan. "No, you didn't know that. The big detective and he doesn't know what's really going on. That's why Janice Fairs is after my ass, Whelan. 'Cause I dropped her."

Whelan finished his coffee. There was no card to play, so he waited.

"You see, Paul? There's no scam going on. And Brister?" He made a gesture of dismissal with his hand. "Who knows what hole he crawled into?" He smiled.

"Who's Henley?"

Vosic hesitated just long enough. "He's just a guy I've had some dealings with. He's got nothing to do with any of this other shit." He made the little wave of dismissal again.

Whelan shrugged. "I don't think so."

Vosic looked tired. He wiped his eyes with one hand. "What would it take to get you to drop this? Huh?"

"Well, now it doesn't seem that I should. I think you just told me there was something more."

Vosic glanced around, and when he spoke his voice was a hoarse whisper. "Maybe you need things broken down for you—simplified. Okay. You fuck with me, you keep digging around in this stuff, I'm gonna have the pleasure of seeing somebody beat you bloody. You think this is the minor leagues here, pal?"

"Yeah, I do." Whelan got up and stretched. "Thanks for lunch."

Vosic stood quickly and seemed to be making the effort to collect himself. "Hey, all right, Paul. I didn't mean that. I was just pissed off, I don't need all this aggravation from this woman…"

"It's okay, Rich. What's the point of being an asshole if you can't act like one."

For a second he thought Vosic would take a swing at him. They stood looking at each other till Vosic realized that people were staring. Whelan nodded to him and vaulted the iron railing. Standing on the sidewalk, he waved to Vosic.

Vosic pointed a finger at him. "Okay, smart guy…"

Whelan began to walk away. Then a thought struck him. He turned and smiled. "Hey, Rich? Your wife's gonna kick your ass in court. You're having a helluva month."

He turned his back and began the long walk to his car. He thought about Vosic's comment that Janice Fairs was driving all the way in from the suburbs and wondered how old Rich would feel if he knew Janice Fairs was staying in a hotel less than a half mile from Jerome's.

"Really great lunch," he said to himself.

He got in the car and drove over to the Harrison-Stratford Hotel. The hotel was a turn-of-the-century piece of elegance that faced the statue of Shakespeare in Lincoln Park. If you took a room with a window facing east you had a view of Mr. Shakespeare, flower beds, a fountain, and the zoo.

The hotel looked out on a pair of parallel streets, Lincoln Park West and Stockton Drive, the latter of which wound its tree-lined way through Lincoln Park and provided a bargain-basement tour of the conservatory, the zoo, and the Lincoln Park Lagoon. There was no parking on Park West so he tried Stockton and got lucky almost immediately, as a black Porsche pulled out in front of him.

He went across to the hotel, climbed the scarlet-carpeted

stairs, and crossed a lobby that should have been in the movies. A tall, serious-looking man gave Whelan's shirt a discreetly questioning look and then brought a smile up from his store of manners.

"I'm here to see Mrs. Janice Fairs. Can you ring her for me?"

"Mrs. Fairs hasn't returned from lunch, sir. Would you care to wait?"

Whelan looked around at the ornate lobby and decided a walk in the zoo was a better idea. "No, I'll come back later."

"Very good, sir."

He crossed the street, paused to stare at the wonderful seated Shakespeare, then went on to the zoo. The heat had gotten to the animals—the heat or the children, because almost all of the city's children were here today, brought here by day camp or summer camp or baby-sitter or parent, a horde of children making a wall of sound. The parents seemed irritable, the camp counselors close to violence, but the kids were making the best of the hot, airless day, as they always seemed to. Some of them were inner-city children and Whelan wondered how many of them realized that this hot, sticky trip to the zoo was the best they were going to get for a long time—maybe all they would get.

The lion was a lifeless pile of hair and fur, one paw hanging down over a rock. He stared off into space, oblivious to the flies that surrounded him or the humans who watched. A thin old man with white hair and a red face leaned against the iron railing and smiled at the lion. Whelan had been certain he'd see this man here. On cold days in winter and late fall you could find him inside the lion house, sitting on a bench and watching lions and leopards or simply nodding off. On such days, when the zoo saw no more than a dozen visitors at the end of a day, you saw the zoo's true regulars—this old man and a couple more like him, a retarded man in his forties who talked to anyone who would listen to him, a long-haired man in his twenties who always seemed to be reading, and at least a half dozen homeless. They huddled in the zoo buildings for warmth and seldom if ever panhandled, for they valued the shelter more than the prospect of a little pocket change. Once or twice he'd seen these shabby, lost men come out of the shadows and frighten people walking with small children and he'd been irritated at those people for their unreasoning fear of men who probably couldn't hurt you if they wanted to.

He tapped the old man on the shoulder.

"Whaddya know, pop?"

"Oh, not much, lad. How you been?"

"I get by. Crowded enough for you?"

The old man shrugged. "Oh, I don't mind 'em, the kids." He winked at Whelan. "Where I live there's just the old ones. We sit around on sofas and chairs in the lobby and see who can fall asleep first. I come home one night and there's six of 'em sittin' in the lounge there, and not a one of 'em's awake." He cackled and shook his head and Whelan laughed. "Anyhow, we're a lot better off, you and me, than this poor sonofabitch here." He indicated the lion with a nod of his head.

"Maybe not," Whelan said. "This one's not an African lion."

"You're right. He's from some forest in India."

"India's hot and crowded and full of flies, so he probably thinks Chicago's the promised land."

The old man laughed and looked up at Whelan. "You been to India?" His pale blue eyes sparkled at the prospect of an unusual conversation.

Whelan shook his head. "I don't travel much. Only time I was ever in a foreign country, people shot at me. I didn't like it."

The old man squinted in the bright sunlight. "Vietnam? You don't look old enough for Korea."

"Vietnam," Whelan said. "Another hot place."

They made small talk for a few minutes and he decided to try Janice Fairs again.

"Gotta run, buddy. Time to get back to work."

"See you around, lad."

"I'll come by next week sometime and we can talk lions again." The old man nodded and went back to staring at the overheated cat.

• • •

"Mrs. Fairs hasn't returned yet, sir," the tall, thin gentleman said before Whelan could ask for her.

"Okay, thanks." He went back outside and then decided to sit in the car where he could listen to some music. His car was stifling, the seat burned his back, and he knew he wouldn't be able to sit there long. He tuned in a jazz station and caught what seemed to be an R and B set, "Way Back Home," by the Crusaders, an old tune by Young-Holt Unlimited, a Booker T. number he didn't recognize, and something by Ronnie Laws. He was about to have a cigarette when he looked out at the hotel and saw Janice Fairs.

She stood in front of the hotel. She was smiling and listening to the conversation of her escort but he could tell by the way she looked around that she wasn't listening too hard. There was a confidence, a composure in her face that he hadn't seen, and he wondered what it had to do with the man she was with. The man chattered and ran a hand carefully across his blond hair and took his eyes off her only when a pair of younger women walked by. The gentleman was Ronald Vosic, and as Whelan watched, Mrs. Fairs said something to him and they went inside the hotel.

These people are some really interesting folks, Whelan said to himself.

They hadn't bothered to close the door behind them, and he stood outside the office for a moment to prepare himself for what he'd find. It didn't help.

He was aware first of the smell, a heavy, rank odor of sweat, and for a moment he thought the visitor might still be there. Two steps inside and he could see that the room was empty.

He crossed the room and sat on the edge of his desk and tried to imagine himself doing a more thorough job of trashing someone's office, but he couldn't. Aside from the desk itself, nothing was in its normal place—drawers lay upside down on the floor, spilling their shredded contents, and someone had put a judicious foot through one of them. That same person had emptied the wastebasket onto the floor, torn down the calendar and his two simple wall pictures, and ripped the phone apart. The receiver sat in one corner of the room while the earpiece peeked out from under a manila folder under the window. The intruder had reduced the contents of his Rolodex to a pile of scraps under the desk and turned the desk blotter into a twisted pretzel of green.

His desk chair had been smashed against the desk and the visitor had slashed the vinyl seats of his other chairs. Whelan studied the slash marks for a moment—long, loose wounds made with a large blade and an easy motion.

They hadn't touched his wall safe, but then he would have been surprised if they'd been able to do anything with it. His first purchase when he'd gone into the business, it was top of the line, purchased from a retired jeweler. If you wanted to know about safes, you talked to a jeweler.

He stared at the wreckage of his office and listened to the sounds of his quickened breathing and wondered if his face was as hot and red as it felt. Time to exert some control here, Whelan. He sighed and tried to assess the damage in terms of replacement problems and cost. The swivel chair would have to be replaced. The seats could be reupholstered, he could get a new calendar, new pictures for the walls, and he could buy new folders, blotters, and pens. The names on the Rolodex weren't all that important, many of them being former clients whom he wasn't likely to be talking to again. Most of the numbers he needed he kept in his head or had written down on a notepad next to his phone at home. He felt a moment of panic as he thought about his home. Maybe they were there right now.

He looked down at his telephone. Had to get a new phone, though. He nodded to himself. Yeah, a new phone, and I know exactly where I'm going to get one. He exhaled and told himself he was starting to feel better already.

It took more than an hour to put some kind of order back into the office, and it was still a wreck. Bare walls, a desk, a couple of badly damaged chairs, no phone.

There was no one else on his floor to ask; the nervous bookkeeper who had been the only other tenant on the second floor had finally given up his crepuscular existence in the building and gone on, perhaps to better quarters, perhaps to prison.

He stopped down on the first floor as people were getting ready to close up shop. The baby photographer hadn't noticed anyone unusual in the building but, as he put it, "This is Uptown. What's unusual up here?"

No one else had noticed anyone or anything, a fact that confirmed an old suspicion for Whelan: you could come in and torch the whole building, murder half its occupants, and knock out all the windows, and no one would notice. He left the building feeling tired and dirty.

He used the pay phone in the little greasy spoon down the street and called Janice Fairs, who, according to the switchboard operator, wasn't in. Then he went home.

They hadn't been to his home. The office had been intended as a warning, and they probably thought it would be enough. He opened all the windows and took a cold beer out of the refrigerator, then sat in the living room and listened to the street noises. He thought about the neat little office building with the blue awning and how ironic it was that such an impressive modern structure was filled with primitive types. There were a lot of men connected with Vosic Enterprises and he had the feeling they were all looking for a piece of Paul Whelan.

She had her hair up and was wearing a powder blue sundress and a small amount of makeup. She was smiling and there was a touch of red in her cheeks that made her look ten years younger.

"Hi," she said. She looked him up and down; he'd put on his one summer sport coat and shined his shoes, and he wondered if she had any idea of the lengths he'd gone to.

"You look nice," she said.

"Not as nice as you," he said honestly. "I feel like I'm robbing the cradle."

She laughed. "I love a man who can lie."

"You should meet the people I've been meeting lately."

She invited him in and puttered around in her bedroom for a few minutes and he studied the apartment. Small and neat with only a few pictures on the walls. In the dining room there were bookshelves from floor to ceiling but the bottom shelves were empty, and the table and chairs in the room seemed small for the amount of space. He decided she hadn't lived here long.

She came out of her bedroom putting a pin into the back of her hair. "Ready."

"Nice place. You just moved in, right?"

The question seemed to take her by surprise and he saw a frown flicker across her face. Then she smiled. "How did you know that?"

He laughed. "Easy, Pat. I'm not a weirdo. It's what I do for a living."

She looked around her place. "But…what is it that tells you I just moved in? It doesn't look dirty to you, does it?"

"No, no, not at all. It looks like you lived in a smaller place and now you're in a bigger place. You like pictures on the walls and books on the shelves but you've got unused space on your walls and shelves, and that usually means a person hasn't had a chance to buy new stuff. If you'd been here any time at all I think you'd have all those bookshelves filled."

She looked at the shelves, then at him, and raised her eyebrows. "Can you figure people out that fast, too?"

"No. Nobody can. People are special. Places, situations, those are fairly simple, because facts usually add up to only a couple of possible scenarios, but anything's possible with people." He got up from the chair. "Let's eat."

When he took her to the car it was his turn to be uncomfortable. He looked at the ungainly brown hulk of the Jet and told himself he'd get a new car some day. "Don't worry, it runs," he said.

"Hey, at least you have a car."

She slid into the front seat and he closed the door.

"We're going to Chinatown."

"The last time I was in Chinatown I was young."

He laughed. "It hasn't changed."

They drove through the great, gaudy gate of Chinatown and their noses were assaulted by the smells of three dozen restaurants all fighting for attention. There were street signs in Chinese characters and imported gift shops with carved ivory and ornate screens and big, ornate restaurants filled with Caucasians and small, barren cafeteria-style restaurants full of Chinese. Whelan promised himself he'd eat in one of them some day, probably during the day. If you visited Chinatown during the day you saw a different place, a Chinese community rather than a tourist area—Chinese men in conversation on the street corners, Chinese women doing their shopping, headless ducks hanging in the store windows, and Chinese shopkeepers weighing fish and whacking away at meat with huge cleavers.

They walked without touching through the crowded street and a night done up for Friday till they reached the far end of Wentworth and Lee's Canton.

They spent some time musing over the menu and making comments and in the end settled on shrimp in garlic and black bean sauce, Mongolian beef, and, at Whelan's suggestion, enough appetizers to feed a small village—eggrolls and crab Rangoon and *shu-mai*.

Once dinner was ordered he found himself curiously unable to get a conversation going. His thoughts went back to the violence of his wrecked office, to his conversation with Rich Vosic, to the volcanic man who called himself Henley, and, most of all, to the surprising sight of Janice Fairs entering her hotel with the younger Vosic. He was confused and preoccupied and it didn't seem to be the best night to take a new woman out to dinner.

He took out a cigarette and held it up. "Mind?"

"No. I smoke, too, remember?" She reached into her bag

and pulled out a pack of cigarettes. "You've gone quiet."

"Yeah. Sorry. Work is interfering. I have a…a problem with something I'm working on."

"Fine. Let's talk about work, then."

"No, this you don't want to hear about, believe me."

"Well…how about telling me what a private detective does. I assume it's not at all like television."

He laughed and told her she was right, and in a few moments he was firmly launched on a description of his work, his background, his family, his career as a police officer, and finally Vietnam. She watched him while he talked and it made him a little self-conscious, and he hoped he wasn't sounding pompous.

"You have intuition for this work? Instincts?"

"I guess so. People tend to open up with me. I've tried a lot of different techniques, but you have to go with the one that works best. In my case it's the most mundane approach possible—I get people talking and I listen, I listen carefully, and eventually, if they have something to tell, I pick it out. I'm not much good at the Sherlock Holmes-type thing, you know, scanning a room and noticing the most minute detail that's out of place and extracting the significance of that detail."

She was silent for a moment and then asked, "Was Vietnam a terrible experience for you?"

"Yeah. Yeah, it was. I just never expected in my lifetime to be in a situation where I was afraid almost constantly. It showed me a side of my nature that I didn't want to see. But other guys had it a lot worse. And a lot of them didn't come back."

"I've heard about…about the dreams some Vietnam vets have. Do you have those?"

"Not exactly. I came back pretty much intact, emotionally. But I was a medic, I pulled a lot of guys out of firefights, guys who were pretty horribly shot up. I still think about them a lot. And…and I pulled a couple of kids out who died later. I still see their faces. Those ones really bother me. See, I was older than almost everybody around me. I was twenty-two when I was drafted. A real smart guy. I'd already dropped out of college. A few months in Nam and I suddenly had a deep appreciation of college. I went back after I got out of the service. Anyhow, all the guys around me were just kids, it was incredible, they were all teenagers. Say what you want about the war and the morality of it, but the worst thing was that we fought it with teenagers, just conscripted kids, not grown men. We sent hundreds of thousands of eighteen-year-old boys overseas and nobody in authority even blinked."

He leaned back and realized that it was the closest to a sermon he'd come to in a long time, and he was embarrassed. Pat was smiling.

"I'm sorry."

"You shouldn't be. It's the most intelligent thing I've ever heard anyone say about that war. Everybody always wants to talk about our...responsibility or our role, everybody wants to deal with the politics of it or with the idea of morality. But this is an issue that puts it in a different light."

"Little boys," Whelan said. "That's all they were. A lot of proud, patriotic old men flexed their muscles and we sent over a half million little boys."

He felt uncomfortable and was relieved when the waiter came with a tray bearing the appetizers. When they had finished with the appetizers, the main courses came and conversation kept to a minimum.

When dinner was finished they went to a lounge at the edge of Chinatown and had a couple of drinks. She got him talking about his past, about Liz, and when he was finished he asked her about her life. He learned that she'd been married for twelve years, divorced for the last seven, that she'd had two years of college and then dropped out to support her husband while he got his degree, and that he had divorced her soon after graduation. Later she lost her job when her company relocated to Ohio. She became a waitress because there was nothing else available to her and she was still supporting her daughter. Her daughter's name was Maggie and she was going into her second year at Northern, and Pat had plans to become the city's oldest college student in the very near future. She talked about her daughter for a while and then he got her talking about her husband.

Eventually they both grew silent. Whelan wondered if the evening was shot. They'd spent an hour talking about the most painful and depressing events in their lives and had succeeded only in making each other uneasy. He thought about the trouble he was about to have in his life and of the way this case had caught him totally off guard, and he just wanted to be home with a cold beer and something mindless on the television.

He became aware of his own silence and laughed. "There's nobody who can make conversation like Paul Whelan. Want to talk about fatal illnesses now? Ax murders?"

She smiled. "You're sure it's not me?"

"Pretty sure."

"What did we do wrong?"

"We skipped the small talk, for one. It's one of the things you do with people you like. At least I do." He shrugged.

"That's nice to know. Well…" she said, making little lines in the sweat on her glass. "I'm not having such a bad time; I found out you're exactly who you appear to be, and that's reassuring. Besides—" She took a little sip at the melting ice in her drink. "—the night is young and there are all kinds of ways to fix it."

"Such as?"

She gave him a pointed look over the rim of her glass. "You could take me for a walk on the beach."

A walk on the beach, he thought. I'm in a time warp.

He couldn't sleep, and he wasn't sure he wanted to. He could still smell her perfume on him. He thought about her for a while, about how different his life could be with a woman in it. Then his thoughts turned to the trashing of his office and the people he'd become involved with and what might be in store for him.

He sat in his darkened living room and smoked and thought, and then he heard the car again. This time it stopped, and then he heard hoarse whispering and the sound of low laughter, and his heart began to beat faster. He got up and went to the window.

The beater was parked directly in front of Whelan's house

and they were already crossing the street. One was carrying what seemed to be a sort of wooden frame and another had a gasoline can, and at least one of them held a baseball bat.

He stood there, fascinated, watching the four men work in the front yard of the black man and gradually realized what they were doing. They were going to burn a cross.

The house was dark and the black man's car was nowhere to be seen. Maybe they weren't home. He saw the big one plunge the cross into the ground and then one of the young ones was dousing it with gasoline, and another one came forward and tossed a match. There was a soft whoosh and the cross was burning. He heard laughter.

What do you do now? he wondered. What do you do when four slugs come into your neighborhood, on your street, and burn a cross? He started to say something and stopped.

Time to make the call.

He was heading out to the kitchen phone and stopped himself. He could see his father, no street fighter, no tough guy, but a genuinely good man, and he knew what his father would have done—he would have said something. Somebody else could make the call.

Outside, the four men were having a party. Whelan went to the front hall, opened the door to the hall closet, thought about taking a baseball bat, and then decided on his father's ax. What the hell, he thought, why not make a good first impression.

He stepped out onto his porch with the ax on his shoulder and came quickly down the stairs. He looked at the four men, then at the darkened windows of his neighbors.

Somebody had better make the call.

At the foot of the stairs he picked up a couple of large rocks from what had been his mother's garden. He tossed one through Mrs. Cuehlo's window and the other through the window of Mr. Landis's place on his right, and the Uptown night was filled with the sounds of breaking glass.

He stepped out into the street. The four men turned at the sound and squinted across at him.

"Party's over, boys. Get off this man's property. I called the cops already."

The big one stepped into the street and moved toward him. He was not quite as tall as Whelan but a good thirty pounds heavier, maybe more if you counted his gut.

"This here is none of your business. We run this nigger out of one neighborhood already."

"Why don't you go back where you came from."

"Who the fuck are you?" The big man's eyes went to Whelan's ax.

"I'm the happy woodsman." He shifted the ax suddenly and the big man jumped and moved back. Whelan shot by him and moved to the burning cross. He whacked at it with the blunt end of the ax and it came loose. Another whack and it listed badly to one side. He hooked the ax head around the main pole and the cross came down.

"See? All gone."

One of the young ones made a move in his direction and he held the ax out where the kid could see it. The big one came closer.

"This is a white man's town, mister, and we're white men. I'm a white man, motherfucker." He slapped his chest and nodded.

"No," Whelan said. "I'm a white man. You're something else entirely."

The big man narrowed his eyes and Whelan waited for him to make his move. Behind him the old one pointed to Whelan.

"He'll stomp your ass good, boy."

"I don't think so."

"Take 'im, Butch. He ain't gonna use that ax."

Butch. This guy would have a name like Butch. His heart was pounding now and he was breathing through his mouth. He hefted the ax and waited. Across the street he could see people coming to their windows. Mr. Landis was out on his porch, inspecting his window, and he thought he could see Mrs. Cuehlo watching from a darkened living room.

The big man called Butch looked around him at his three companions, smiling and hitching up his pants; he pretended to look up the street to his right and Whelan got ready for the sucker punch that was coming from that side.

The big man brought his arm around in a roundhouse swing but Whelan was already side stepping and swinging the ax under the punch. The dull side of the axhead caught Butch square in the ribs and he went down gasping and holding his side.

"Oh, shit. Shit!" He rolled around on the black man's lawn and panted, then curled up into the fetal position.

Whelan pointed the ax at the young one closest to him. "See? See what you did? You told him I wouldn't use it and where did it get him? He's never gonna believe anything you say, pal."

"You got no call to hit him." The old one backed up but kept an accusing finger pointed at Whelan.

Whelan looked at him. "You old slimeball. If you had any kind of a life you wouldn't have time to worry about blacks or anybody else. That his car?"

"That's my car," the old man said, doubt creeping into his voice.

"Well, let's tune her up." In the distance he could hear the sirens, and now he could feel it all go out of him, the fear and the tension and his anger, and for a second he saw the face of the man called Henley and he was no longer worried how all this would turn out.

He walked across the street to the old man's beater and brought the axhead down on the windshield, and the old man screamed. A square gash appeared in the center of the window and white cracks radiated out from it. He swung the ax down, blade first, on the hood and the blade cut deeply into the metal. He stepped back and took a lowball hitter's swing at the front tire and it blew out with a noisy pop and a hiss.

The old man was screaming at him and the two teenagers were calling him names but keeping their distance. A pair of squad cars turned the corner off Lawrence and Whelan leaned against his ax and waved.

The cop cars pulled up a few feet away and Whelan was wondering if they would buy his story, and then one of the two kids clarified the issue by running. A lean young cop took off after him, grinning—a former track star, Whelan suspected. The cop caught the kid inside of thirty yards and when he came back he wasn't even breathing hard.

A gray-haired sergeant whose name plate said SHEA came over to Whelan.

"Did you make the call?"

"No. I think one of my neighbors did. I came out to stop them."

"What are you, a hero?"

"No. I just got a little pissed off. They were burning a cross over there."

"You got blacks living in that house?"

"Mixed couple."

The cop nodded. He looked over his shoulder at another officer, who was talking to Mr. Landis and Mrs. Cuehlo. The old man was making dramatic gestures at his broken window and Mrs. Cuehlo had lapsed into Italian, a sign that she was under great stress.

Across the street the lean young cop was questioning the old man and the two teenagers and Butch, who still hadn't made it up onto his feet. He left the four with his partner and approached the sergeant. The cop talking to Whelan's neighbors came over and joined the conversation.

"So what's their story, Bill?"

The lean cop shrugged. "They said they were just passing through and they saw this cross burning and they stopped to watch."

"Tourists, they are." Sergeant Shea folded his arms across his chest and nodded. His brogue seemed to be thickening with each sentence he spoke.

"Then this guy here came after them all with an ax," the lean cop said. "Hit the one guy in the ribs with it and then beat up on their car."

The sergeant pursed his lips and nodded. "Not bad. Not a bad story at all."

The other cop indicated Mr. Landis and Mrs. Cuehlo. "These people had their windows broken. They think it was those guys.

The old guy there, he says this car cruises this street every night and these guys yell out something about the people that live there. Something, you know, racial. And the old woman…she started talking in Italian, I think, but…she was saying…like, her cat's dead, or something." He made a little shake of his head and looked helpless.

"Somebody killed her cat a few months ago. She's never been the same. Could have been these guys," Whelan said helpfully.

The sergeant looked at the four men across the street, then up at the night sky. Then he began to laugh. He put his hand across his eyes and shook his head. "Is there anybody around here that isn't nuts?" He looked at Whelan. He pointed a finger at him and winked. "And I know you, lad. You're a rent-a-cop. You're also a friend of our beloved Albert Bauman. You were a police officer for a time, am I right?"

"That's right."

The sergeant looked around at the various personalities surrounding him and then studied the car. "That looks like the work of somebody with an ax." He raised a silver eyebrow at Whelan.

"No. It's just a beater. That's how it looked when they drove up."

"With no windshield? How could they drive it?"

"You can see through the hole, probably."

The sergeant looked amused. "And the slashed tire?"

"It was flat already."

"And they drove it here?"

"You never drove on a flat?"

The sergeant's face compressed into a smile and a set of wrinkles and then he nodded. "What I can't figure out is the broken windows. Why would they break the windows?"

"Vandalistic impulses. I don't know, maybe they wanted to call attention to themselves. They did set fire to the cross, you know. They wanted people to see it."

The sergeant nodded. The cop who had spoken to Mr. Landis spoke up. "That white-haired man wants to file charges about his window and the cross. He said they were lighting it when he came to his window."

The sergeant looked at Whelan. "And you, lad—will you testify in court?"

"Sure. That big guy there, he took a swing at me. For no reason." The lean one gave him an odd look and Whelan could see that this cop didn't like him.

"Oh, I'll bet. All right, boys, get their names and addresses and tell the old gentleman to get dressed. Book these four." He squinted at the home of the interracial couple, shook his head.

"I don't understand why people have to marry outside their own kind." He sighed and looked at his watch.

"You want a cup of coffee?" Whelan asked.

The sergeant looked at him and shrugged. "Why not?"

THIRTEEN

In the morning the charred wood of the cross was lying in the grass where it had been left and Whelan felt sorry for these people—nice thing to come home to.

He walked up Malden to Wilson, where the evidence of a hot Friday night in Uptown was everywhere. Broken beer and wine bottles lay in the street, and on the sidewalk at the corner of Malden and Wilson somebody had lost his shirt. There was blood on it and on the sidewalk a block or so up Wilson, and at the corner of Racine, right across the street from the fire-house, the street was littered with the glass-and-chrome aftermath of a car accident. The cars were still there—a candy-apple-red Mazda with its front pushed in and a rust-eaten Ford wagon with no plates. Bluish cracks spidered the windshields of both cars and there were large indentations from the drivers' heads.

There was a domestic argument in progress in front of the Wilson Men's Club Hotel, which now sported a new sign and, in keeping with the many advances of feminism, was calling itself the Wilson Club Hotel. A man and a woman of almost exactly the same size and build put their faces together and shouted at the top of their lungs, red faced and sweating. The man shot a quick look at Whelan as he passed.

Whelan went to the Subway Donut Shop on Broadway and had a quick cup of coffee and a doughnut. Woodrow came in and Whelan offered to buy him a cup of coffee, but Woody just held up a five and showed a mouthful of tobacco-stained teeth.

"My check come yesterday."

"Fine. Want to lend me a hundred bucks?"

Woody laughed and walked away, shaking his head.

Whelan watched the street traffic of a Saturday morning

in Uptown, watched the tired, sweaty men and women of the street and the people walking quickly by with shopping carts and laundry baskets. It was time to go to work.

He couldn't see the Lotus, and a pang of disappointment went through him, but the other cars parked in the lot told him that Vosic Enterprises worked Saturdays. He pulled in and parked next to the van.

The young security man smiled and nodded.

"You guys put in a lot of hours," Whelan said.

"Just till twelve on Saturdays."

Whelan nodded and held up the remains of his black desk phone. "Got something for the man," Whelan said. "Now he can't say I never gave him anything." The guard smiled and looked confused and Whelan made his way back to the executive offices.

Carmen was wearing powder blue today and looking like an Italian's idea of heaven. She glanced up but did not smile at him or speak. Her eyes moved to the phone in his hand but she just frowned slightly.

"Morning, Carmen. Where do you want me to put this?"

The frown deepened and darkened. "Put *what*? What is it?"

He looked at it. "It's a phone. It's a replacement."

"Replacement? Look, I don't know anything about any replacement phone, and Rich told me you have to talk to him before you set foot in this office again."

"Okay, that's fine. I don't really need to see anything this time. You pretty much gave me everything I needed last time. I am a little disappointed that Rich isn't here. But I'll see him later. I'll just put this phone down here." He set the black phone down on a desktop beside a sleek gray one, then bent down and took the gray phone's line out of the jack in the floor. He wrapped the wire around the gray phone and picked it up.

"So...just tell Rich I said 'hey.'"

"Wait a minute. What...where are you going with that phone?"

He gave her a little smile. "My office. He knows where it is. You have a nice day, now, hear?"

He turned and tucked the phone under his arm and left her staring openmouthed at him. Just outside the door the tall, thin workman was hooking a new monitor up to a computer in a small cubicle. Ten feet away and Whelan could smell him; it was the second time he had smelled this man. He stopped and watched the man work and eventually the workman realized that someone was watching him. He turned, saw Whelan, and straightened up.

The man had long arms and big hands, a massive jaw, and deep-set brown eyes under the heavy dome of his forehead, thick, dark hair, and dense brows. Raymond Massey in a work shirt. There were dark circles under the eyes and his skin had a greenish pallor to it. Raymond Massey with a hangover.

The man took a step forward and seemed to be having trouble deciding what to do with his hands. He jammed them into his side pockets, then brought them out again and put them on his hips: then he thrust them into his hip pockets and lifted his chin toward Whelan.

"You need something?" His lip curled a little. A bad smell and a worse attitude.

"You look a little bit like Lincoln. You know that?"

The man blinked and looked confused. Then he put on a smile. "I don't have no beard."

"Yeah. And he took a bath now and then."

It took the workman a second to realize that he was being insulted, and then he took a step forward.

"You got a problem?"

"Yeah, what you're doing to the air I'm breathing."

"Maybe somebody should kick your ass for you, mister."

"Yeah, and maybe I should just clock you upside your head with this state-of-the-art telephone. Come on, Slim."

The man gave him the time-honored stare of the tough guy who's trying to be patient.

"You did a pretty nice job on my office, there, Abe. You didn't set any records or anything, but you got my attention."

"I don't know what the fuck you're talking about." The man tried on a little smile.

Whelan took a step closer to him and the man shuffled his feet slightly. "You know my problem? My problem is I'm always talking to people in language they don't understand. Let me try again. You wrecked my office. You did it when I wasn't there. You made me angry. Come again sometime, when I'm there, and I'll pound pencils into your ears. Or take a whack at me now, and you'll be shitting this telephone for a week."

"You think you're some kinda badass."

"I think I'll embarrass you in front of your coworkers, that's what I think. And you think so, too." He gave the thin man a little wave and left.

He left the office area and patted the young guard on the shoulder. The guard looked questioningly at the phone but said nothing. After all, they were now friends.

He drove back to Uptown and parked around the corner from his office. A group of black men in their thirties stopped their conversation and watched him get out of the car. He nodded to them, several of them nodded back, and one said, "All right." He went up to his office and dropped off his spiffy new phone, then went back out for a cup of coffee. He headed up Broadway toward the Wilson Donut Shop under the El, picked up the paper, and walked slowly, reading the paper and trusting to the kindness of other pedestrians to avoid a collision. At the darkest point of the street, where the great steel bones of the El tracks made a tunnel of Broadway, something caught his attention.

Where there had been an import store carrying a thousand kinds of junk there was something else. The windows were covered with paper and there was a City of Chicago Building Permit in one of them, but the news was in the other window—a small, hand-lettered sign announced the coming of a new enterprise to Uptown: a restaurant.

COMING SOON TO THIS PLACE, the sign proclaimed. NEW GREEK RESTAURANT WITH FRESH, HOMEMAKE

FOODS, 100% AUTENTIC GREEK FOODS. RIGHT HERE, HOUSE OF ZEUS RESTAURANT.

The sign was good news to him, but two questions formed in his mind. First, what kind of Greek restaurant called itself House of Zeus? And second, what was there about this sign that seemed familiar? He shrugged and told himself to be thankful for any new restaurant.

He was reading the sports section when Vosic's call came an hour later.

"Whelan? Rich Vosic here."

"Rich? I've been waiting breathlessly for your call."

There was a pause, an incredulous pause.

"What are you, some kind of wiseass? You want to spend some time in the shithouse, or what? You come into my office and play head games with my secretary and rip off my phone—"

"Now wait a minute, Rich. It was a trade. I left you the one your guys destroyed and took one of yours. You're a businessman, Rich—what could be more fair?"

"My what? My *guys?* What is this, the movies? I don't have any 'guys,' Whelan."

"On the contrary, my friend, you have several. And a really interesting group they are, too. There's the tall, skinny one that smells like an onion and looks like Lincoln with constipation, and there's old Larry, the little dark-haired guy with one arm. And who knows what else you've got there in the cages in your basement. Anyhow, your professional staff trashed my office and busted up my phone. I wasn't here to receive guests, so I couldn't accord them the hospitality for which I am famous. But I thought I'd drop by and let you know how I felt, Rich."

"Yeah? Is that some kind of threat? You think I'm afraid of some busted-up ex-cop—"

"Oh, goodness, we've been digging, haven't we."

"Yeah, and it wasn't hard. I know all about you, pal."

"We're not pals anymore. You broke my phone." He heard a sigh and smiled into the phone.

"Look, Paul, there's a misunderstanding here——"

"Don't call me Paul anymore. I hate it when assholes call me Paul. Call me Mr. Whelan."

Another pause. Then a long, loud exhalation. "Okay, asshole."

"Good, Rich. Let's take off our costumes."

"You don't listen so good. That's what the real problem is here, that's the problem. I tried to get you to see you were fucking around with things you didn't understand, but you didn't want to hear about it. I warned you."

"A warning is a threat. I hate threats. I behave badly when I'm threatened. I steal phones."

"Ha ha, you're a comedian. You didn't like what happened to your office? Okay, how about this? Imagine that happening to your face, hard guy."

"You're not going to try it yourself, are you? You're gonna ask Mr. Henley to give it a whirl, right?"

There was a short pause, as though Vosic were rearming himself. "You know, Whelan, I can honestly say that whatever happens to you will be your own fucking smartass fault. One hundred percent. What happened to your office is your fault, and whatever happens to you is your fault."

Whelan laughed. "It takes maybe eight seconds to get you to admit that you're responsible for what these simians did to my office. All right, Rich, let's look at what we have here. I'm talking to your late partner's wife and looking at your old files and asking around about your less savory acquaintances, and you warn me off and then you trash my office—now, do you honestly think I'm gonna let go? You basically told me that just about every hunch I've had so far is on the money. And Rich, here's the real problem, from your perspective: you think I'm the only thing you have to worry about. That's true, isn't it, Rich?"

There was the slightest pause and then Vosic snorted into the phone. "Hey, go play head games with somebody else, Whelan, somebody stupid enough to listen."

"Okay, Rich, old buddy, but a word of advice: be careful who you talk to these days. You're surrounded."

"I'm *what*? Surrounded? What's that supposed to mean? That another wiseass joke?"

"No, not this time. You're surrounded. I can't think of a single person you can trust, except maybe Carmen, and I doubt she's gonna be much help." He listened for a moment to Vosic's silence and then hung up.

Whelan had a cigarette and looked out his window. Up the street he could see the El trains pulling in and out of the Lawrence Avenue Station. He blew smoke out into the dirty air and told himself that for everything there were consequences, and he could now await the consequences.

Rich, I think we're both in a little trouble.

Janice Fairs answered on the first ring, and when he identified himself her voice made ice on the phone.

"What is it that you want, Mr. Whelan? I believe we've concluded our business. I can't imagine what else we have to discuss."

"I guess we don't understand each other, Mrs. Fairs—"

"That doesn't surprise me at all," she interrupted. He heard her inhale smoke and blow it out and he could almost see the hard smile on her face.

"I just would have thought you'd remember what Fred Myers told you about me. I don't just drop everything because somebody sends me money. You get me involved in something and then you expect me to get out as soon as it gets interesting."

"I can't see how it is any concern of yours now, Mr. Whelan. It is no longer a business involvement for you, and it's certainly none of your affair personally."

"Whoops, there you're wrong. They made it personal. These are really lousy people, Mrs. Fairs. And not as sophisticated as I thought at first. They make threats, they follow me, and now they've done the unpardonable—they tore up my office and made it clear to me that if that wasn't message enough, they'd be happy to tear me up, too."

There was a long silence at the other end. She blew out smoke and said, "What? What are you talking about, Mr. Whelan?"

"Rich Vosic's people trashed my office, lady. They tore up every single piece of furniture, every item in or on my desk, everything on the walls, the shades on the windows. All of it. I came in and my office looked like a hobo camp. They even busted up my phone."

The same long silence and then a hissing sound, exasperation, and she said, "Shit." She made a short, tight little syllable out of it and it didn't sound as though she used it much, but there was sincerity in it, it came from the heart.

"Excuse me?" Whelan said.

"That...*moron*. He just makes me..." He could almost hear her scraping the edges of her brittle teeth together. "Mr. Whelan, I never intended for any of this to cause you trouble."

"That was a little naive, if you'll forgive my saying so. You go rooting around in somebody's life, you occasionally make someone angry, irrationally angry. And Rich Vosic does fancy himself a tough guy. This is not so out of character. These guys who spend too much time in the gym, they all think they're Muhammad Ali."

"I just never expected it to get to this."

"Don't worry about it."

"I will see that all your expenses are taken care of and that you are compensated appropriately. Mr. Whelan, I have to get back to you. Where are you calling from?"

"I'm at my office."

"Your office? I thought they...you said they ruined your phone..." She sounded confused.

"They did. I got a new one. I'm speaking to you on it. I just picked it up this morning—it used to be Vosic's."

"What?"

"I took it from his office. Don't be shocked. It was a fair trade—I left them the one they busted up."

There was a pause and then she laughed. It didn't come from anywhere deep, but it was a laugh, just the same.

"You really are an unusual man, Mr. Whelan. Aren't you afraid you've made more trouble for yourself?"

"Oh, I'm sure I've made more trouble for myself, but I didn't start it. They would have been a little pissed off at me anyhow, Mrs. Fairs, because I've been warned off and I've decided to pay absolutely no attention to them. Or you, for that matter—if you'll forgive my impertinence."

"I'm not sure I will. What can I do to make you understand that this doesn't involve you, Mr. Whelan?"

"Not a damn thing, as far as I can see. Because it does involve me. They made it involve me, Mrs. Fairs. They cemented our relationship. Now I'm officially involved. And you did, too, lady. You convinced me that there were two murders here that involved these people, and you and other people convinced me that there is no interest on the part of the police in my particular line of inquiry. So I'm here for the duration."

"You will cause me no end of irritation, Mr. Whelan." She paused and he could hear her sucking at the cigarette. Time to push.

"Sorry. I still have too many unanswered questions. And a couple of them are about you."

"I have no idea what you could possibly need to know about me, Mr. Whelan."

"I really want to know what you know now. And I want to know about Henley. And I want to know why you're out socializing with Ronald Vosic while his big brother is acting out movie fantasies about scaring people off." She said nothing and he was pleased with himself.

"I am finding you to be a very unpleasant man, Mr. Whelan." She sounded as though she was speaking through clenched teeth.

"I'm not surprised, Mrs. Fairs. All the other men you know seem to be assholes. No wonder you want to think I'm one, too. You have a nice day now, hear?" He held out the phone, and when he could hear the tinny sounds of protest coming from it, he hung up.

He fished out a cigarette and lit it and told himself he'd give a lot to be a fly on her wall right now. When he finished his cigarette he decided to be the next best thing.

He parked in almost exactly the same place and sat on a bench across from Mr. Shakespeare. A few yards away a pair of slender, young women had coated themselves with suntan lotion and little else. They looked to be in their early twenties, light years away from his life. He looked at them and then looked away. He had other opportunities available to him now, and it was up to him to see the value in them. The value in a woman his age, a nice woman who could keep up a decent conversation and liked to laugh and had kind eyes and a sense of humor and a nice figure. And, in all honesty, a woman who was quite a bit more of a find than he had any right to expect.

I'm forty years old and living on the fringe and I meet a nice woman about once every eleven years, he said to himself, and this is my one shot for the 1980s.

Janice Fairs emerged from the Harrison-Stratford Hotel and brought him back to the here and now. A valet dressed like a ringmaster fell all over himself trying to flag down a cab, but she spoke to him with a quick shake of her head and began to walk up Lincoln Park West. Whelan got up and followed her.

He kept east of her, walking along Stockton Drive parallel to her, with one tiny city block between them. There was a good deal of foot traffic on both sides of the street, and on Whelan's side the park seemed to be overrun with strollers and buggies and large families festooned with balloons. He threaded his way through all the zoo aficionados and tried to keep her in sight. It was hard to stay with her—she had fewer obstacles and she walked with the quick strides of someone on a schedule. Even when she went into a group of people he could pick her out from her stiff posture and speedy progress.

At the corner of Webster and Lincoln Park West, she stopped in front of Mel Markon's restaurant and looked around. She checked her watch, looked around again, and then fished inside her bag for a cigarette. She lit it and began puffing away in what Whelan thought must be a very uncharacteristic display of public nerves. He sat down on a bench a few yards from the corner and watched her, confident that she wouldn't notice him here if she was not looking for him.

A Checker cab pulled up in front of Markon's and the younger Vosic emerged.

Ronald Vosic straightened his beige summer jacket and ran one hand quickly over his hair. He reached for Janice Fairs's hands but one was cramped around her purse and the other held a cigarette. The look she gave him would have put anyone on notice that this was not a festive occasion.

Vosic said something breezy and got a short, harsh answer back from Janice Fairs. She blew smoke out and squinted up the street and talked without looking at him. He said something to her and she gave him a sudden, irritated glance, then put her face close to his and spoke to him with an urgency that Whelan could almost feel forty yards away.

Vosic took a step back and thrust both hands in his pockets. There was a slump to his shoulders and a subservient tilt to his head now. Whelan smiled. Body language speaks volumes.

Finally he saw Janice Fairs shrug. With a curt nod she indicated the restaurant behind them and went inside through the revolving door without waiting for Ron Vosic. Vosic looked around him as though considering a fast exit, then shook his head and went in after her.

Whelan decided that this couple was worth waiting for. He'd had hopes of catching a ball game, had even toyed with the idea of wandering over to the ballpark and buying a ticket from a scalper, just for the chance to cheer the returning Cubs, the victorious Cubs, the *first-place* Cubs. His Cubs. He smoked a couple of cigarettes and walked idly up and down the park, and then Janice Fairs and Ronald Vosic emerged from Mel Markon's. They parted quickly at the corner and Janice Fairs walked on to her hotel while Vosic walked west toward Clark Street. Whelan went back to his car and followed slowly. Vosic hailed a Flash cab at Clark and Dickens, and Whelan tailed it up Clark. He followed the cab until it stopped at the corner of Clark and Fullerton and let Vosic out. Vosic entered the Medinah Restaurant.

Maybe this guy's got a tapeworm, Whelan thought. He parked in a no-parking zone and went in after Vosic. He wasn't in the restaurant or at the small dark bar; he was in a phone booth. Whelan went back out, got into the Jet moments before a squad car pulled up behind him and started writing out tickets, and took off for the office. He expected a phone call. Perhaps lots of phone calls.

"Oh, you've got calls, all right. Baby, you've been popular." Shelley laughed into the phone.

"And from whom?"

"You had a call from the Witch of the North again, and you had one from Rich Vosic, and you had another one maybe twenty minutes ago from somebody that doesn't like you."

"These days that doesn't narrow it down much. He leave his name?"

"No. He said to tell you you were sticking your nose in places where it could get busted. And when I told him I was just the answering service he got all embarrassed and started apologizing." She laughed, a deep, resonant, barroom laugh. "You know what he said then? He said to forget about the message." She laughed again. "Like I could forget something like that, you know? Oh, Paul Whelan, you are the most interesting client we have."

Whelan laughed. It had to be Ronald Vosic. Every organization needed a loose cannon, and Ron was Rich's loose cannon. He thought for a moment—twenty minutes ago he had been watching Ron Vosic pump coins into a pay phone, so he was calling Whelan while Whelan sat perhaps fifteen feet away. He laughed again.

"Here's a thought for you, Shel. Imagine this guy calling me up with this message and getting Abraham."

Apparently this notion caught Shelley in her laughing spot. It was almost a minute before she could compose herself.

"I didn't tell you, baby, Abraham's wife is gonna have a baby. Abraham's gonna be a daddy and he's coming all undone. You think you had trouble talking to him before? Wait till you have a chance to talk to him now. He answered the phone in Hindi one day. Hindi, that's what they speak there. You believe that? Started talking to this guy in Hindi." She cackled happily to herself and then made an effort to get it under control.

"Listen, baby, can I ask you something? None of my business, of course, but…are you in deeper than you should be? Maybe this guy was no rocket scientist, but he sounded serious. Maybe you should take it seriously."

"If it's who I think it is, it's not that serious. There's one guy out there who really is somebody to step wide of, Shel, but if he wanted to talk to me he wouldn't leave the message with my service, and he probably wouldn't use the phone. He'd be here now. This other fella is a product of his time—too much TV when he was a kid and now he thinks he's Wild Bill Hickock. Well…I guess I'm never gonna be the popular guy I wanted to be."

"Aw, you're still my hero, Paul."

"Thanks, Shel. Talk to you later."

Phone threats from Ron Vosic and personally delivered ones from big brother Rich. I've got all these folks coming to look me up, all of them, and the guy they're really concerned about is big and bald and I haven't heard from him yet.

Whelan lit up a cigarette and filled the office with blue smoke.

He killed the afternoon watching baseball, enjoying the novelty of the Cubs appearing on the game of the week. The game was in the third inning when he got home and the Cubs were already leading three-zip. Dennis Eckersley was on the mound and it was his day—he was ahead of every hitter, missing the plate only when he felt like it, and the wind was blowing out and Cub hitters were lofting fly balls into it and watching them sail out toward Waveland Avenue. By the seventh inning four Cubs had homered and the Phillies were on their fifth pitcher, and the announcers seemed to think there would be a play-off at Wrigley Field this year.

He had dinner at Filipiniana, a little Filipino restaurant a couple of blocks from Wrigley Field. It was early and he was the only customer, but he knew the owner and her food and the lack of a crowd didn't worry him. He had *lumpiang shanghai*, crunchy little eggrolls filled with meat, the deluxe fried rice, which came with a half dozen large shrimp nesting on top, and an order of *pansit*, the national dish, stir-fried noodles with vegetables and various kinds of meat.

He finished his meal and had a cigarette and put together his game plan for the evening, which was quite simply to seek out some of the many people who seemed to want to talk to him. He left his money on the table, waved to the little Filipino woman, and went out. Bauman was waiting for him.

Bauman leaned against the gray Caprice and picked his teeth. He smiled and indicated the Filipino restaurant with a nod. "This place any good? Yeah, I guess it would be if you go there. You got good taste in restaurants, Whelan. I don't know shit about Filipino food, though."

Whelan shrugged. "It's a little bit of everything—Chinese and Spanish, it's got a couple different kinds of eggrolls, it's got noodle dishes like Thai food and stir-fry stuff like Chinese and Korean." Bauman studied the front of the restaurant with something like longing.

Whelan laughed. "Let me guess, you ate across the street, right?"

Bauman shrugged. The Royal Palace was across the street, a hamburger stand that defied description or categorization— it was big and white and brightly lit and stayed open all night, and the food was a cross between early greasy spoon and White Castle, little skinny fries and hamburgers of various sizes as well as hot dogs and Italian beef and Polish sausage. A visit to the Royal Palace in the middle of the night was a descent into the netherworld, Edward Hopper on PCP, one of Dante's circles crammed into a whitewashed stone box and dropped onto a Chicago street corner.

Whelan shook his head. "You should have come in and visited, since you went to the trouble of following me."

"I'm not following nobody. I saw your car around the corner, figured you were inside."

"I don't think so. Brown Oldsmobiles don't exactly scream for attention, and there are a half dozen places I could be in around here."

Bauman made a show of looking around the corner. "Liquor store, two saloons, two hamburger joints, and one little place run by foreigners; where would you look for Paul Whelan?"

"Good story. You stick to it, Bauman. Now, tell me what you want."

Bauman spread his arms. "Who says I want somethin'? Like I said, I saw the car, I decided to wait for you. Why, you *got* something I would want, Whelan?" He smiled and raised his eyebrows.

"If I found something, Bauman, I'd give it to anybody I thought might pay attention to it. Seems to me you've got a very short attention span. You've got no time for anybody but this mysterious black gentleman."

Bauman shrugged. "He ain't any mystery to me, Whelan. I know his name and where he eats and what kinda women he likes and what size shorts he's wearin'." Bauman sniffed and took out one of his skinny cigars, wet the end, lit it with a stick match, and shrugged. "Seen him lately?"

"Only the one time. I couldn't invite him back. He didn't leave a number where he could be reached."

"What, you need stuff written down? I thought you were psychic, Whelan. I thought maybe you read tea leaves or something. How do the Irish foretell the future, Whelan? You shake sheep bones in a cup and toss 'em on a table?" Bauman rocked back on his heels, obviously enjoying himself.

"We read the bumps on a potato. It's not an exact science yet, but we're simple people."

"What the hell, if I can't piss you off, Whelan, what fun are you?" He puffed on the cigar till a gray cloud hovered over him. Whelan studied the mottled face and saw a man going into a tailspin.

"You want to talk, Bauman, we can go someplace and get a cup of coffee."

Bauman took the cigar out of his mouth and frowned. "I

don't need a cup of coffee. Wouldn't mind a cocktail, though."

"What a surprise."

"Put a lid on it, Snoop."

"I give money to the bums, Bauman. You gonna be one of them? Okay, maybe you are. Let's go have a cocktail."

Bauman was a long time staring. Then he took a last pull at the cigar and tossed it. "Let's go."

"Where to? One of the saloons around here?"

Bauman looked as if he'd just stepped in something. "Around here? What, are you shitting me? The Cubs just played three hours ago and it's about eighty-eight, and every gin mill in this neighborhood is filled with drunks in Cubs hats lookin' for an excuse not to go home."

"So where are you taking me?"

Bauman gave him a sly smile. "You don't have no hot social engagements, do you?"

"No. You?"

"Fuck no, I ain't had one of them in about five years. Come on, we'll go someplace good."

"Someplace good" took them completely out of the neighborhood, all the way out to Belmont and Cicero. When Whelan saw the tall black transmitter of the WXRT radio station he knew where they were headed.

"We're going to the Bucket."

Bauman nodded and smiled without looking at him. "Figured you'd know the Bucket, Whelan. Guy like you, streetwise guy that likes taverns, you gotta know about the Bucket."

"The greatest tavern in a city of five thousand taverns."

Bauman nodded, turned onto Cicero, pulled over across from Joe Danno's dog-eared little tavern, and parked.

The place looked closed, as always, but Bauman just pulled the door open, yelled out, "Hello, Joe," and walked in. Whelan followed and waved to the short, white-haired man behind the bar.

Joe Danno looked at Bauman and nodded. "Hey, Al. How they treatin' you?" He squinted at Whelan through his thick glasses and blinked. He looked from Whelan to Bauman and back to Whelan again. "Hello, Paul. Couple of old cops, eh? I didn't know you two guys knew each other."

"It's not something I tell a lot of people, Joe," Whelan said. They took seats at the ancient, scarred bar and stared at the hundreds upon hundreds of open liquor bottles that lined the back bar, some of them showing labels of distillers out of business for thirty years. Here at the Bucket they had eternal life.

Without being asked, Joe poured Bauman a German draft and then a dark for Whelan. He looked at Bauman and raised his eyebrows. "The usual, Al? A little G & U?"

"Sure. Why not?"

Joe poured Bauman a shot of bourbon from a bottle in the first row. Bauman put money on the bar and pushed it toward Joe. "I'm buyin' tonight, Joe. Don't take this guy's money, all right?"

Joe walked away. "I'll run a tab."

Whelan looked around. The decor hadn't changed, would never change. Black walls and a yellowed ceiling, strings of Italian lights and five thousand liquor labels pasted to the back wall. At one end of the bar a sea turtle hung from the ceiling, and the wall near the kitchen still bore a marlin Joe claimed to have caught. A few feet away from Whelan's head a stuffed merganser dangled at the end of a piece of twine.

Bauman inhaled the shot and sucked down half his beer. A dark-haired woman in her fifties stuck her head out from the kitchen.

"Hello, fellas."

"Hey, Fena," Bauman said. Whelan waved. Bauman burped quietly and looked at Whelan.

"You want to split a pizza?"

"You just ate."

Bauman looked at Whelan as though he was speaking in an unknown language.

"This is the greatest pizza on earth. Come on, Whelan, loosen up. Hey, Fena. We'll split a small special."

Whelan shook his head. "You're a sick man, Bauman."

They drank in silence for a while and Whelan waited.

Bauman finished his beer and signaled to Joe for another round. When the drinks had been poured he looked at Whelan.

"So. Did he do one of his accents for you, Whelan?"

"Who?"

"Wardell Gibbs."

"I'm missing something here, Bauman." Bauman smiled. "Let me guess: Wardell Gibbs is the name of the black gentleman."

"That's right." Bauman took a sip of his beer and wiped his lips with his finger. "So did he? Do one of his, uh, voices?"

"He did an African accent. Nigerian, I think it was."

Bauman nodded approvingly. "He can do about eight of 'em. He can do that Nigerian bit, and Jamaican, and Haitian, he can pass as a black Puerto Rican. He's got some other ones, I hear. I don't remember 'em. And of course, he can slip into that 'down home.' He can talk like one of the brothers when he wants to."

Bauman stared at him for a while, a half smile on his face. The cheeks were already flushed from the first drink and there was a little more life in the gray eyes, but he seemed more relaxed.

"So you guys didn't exchange names, huh? I'm surprised you two didn't know each other. Sooner or later, Whelan, you meet everybody. How old would you say he was?"

"Late thirties."

"He's fifty-two. Know what I think, Snoopy? I think you had a meet with this gentleman. I think somebody clued you in that this guy was a business associate of the late Harry Palm and you decided to see if he had anything for you."

"I told you what happened. I was looking for anybody that had a problem with Harry Palm. Your friend came to see me. He told me to stop looking for him and I believe he threatened my well-being. I should fill out a report, right?"

"Right. That's exactly what you should do."

"What do you want from me, Bauman? I'm trying to find out what happened a couple years ago when a guy with a lot of money and a lot of reasons to go on living torched his own boat with him on it. We can go over this same ground a dozen more times if you like, Bauman, but my story will stay the same. The guy I'm interested in is a big white guy with no hair. I don't know if he had anything to do with Harry Palm becoming an obituary but I think he may have killed the man he worked for."

Bauman puffed at his cigar and shook his head. "I don't know, Whelan. You been straight with me in the past, so I got no real reason to think you'd lie to me, but…you got a tendency to make grandstand plays. You made the last one personal; maybe you're making this one personal."

"That other time, that was a mistake."

"A mistake in judgment, Shamus. Maybe you're making another one right now. Keeping a little bit back, just a little bit."

"No. I gave you what I had. You were just hoping for a little more. These guys probably don't have anything to do with one another…"

"Oh, I'm not saying they don't know each other. Here's what I think: I think the guy I'm lookin' for is the real deal. I think this black guy is the one that did old Harry Palm. I think your guy might be able to tell me something, but I think he's just a player. Maybe him and Wardell did some business together, who knows? But Wardell Gibbs is a special guy, Whelan."

Fena came in with the pizza, a thin-crust masterpiece on an aluminum plate, covered with razor-thin slices of mushrooms, peppers, onions, and pepperoni and then sprinkled with homemade sausage and anchovies. She set it down in front of them with a bottle of Joe's legendary hot sauce. Bauman had a piece in his hand before the plate hit the bar.

Whelan watched him for a moment. "Why is this guy special, Bauman?"

"He just is," Bauman said through a mouthful of pizza. "And he don't work with nobody 'cause he don't like nobody."

"Kind of like yourself, huh, Bauman?"

Bauman grinned. "I like you, Whelan. I like old Joe, here. I'm in love with his sister Fena, who makes the best thin-crust pizza I ever ate. Let's see…"

"You've exhausted your list."

Bauman shrugged. "Maybe." He gave Whelan an odd look. "I'm for sure not a good Sam like you, Whelan. I don't come runnin' out of my house with an ax when there's somethin' goin' down on my block." He winked. "Had some excitement there on Malden Street, huh? Couple apemen decided to burn a cross. Yeah, I know about it. I know everything, Whelan."

For a moment he suspected that Bauman had been there, had watched it all.

"Come on, Whelan. I can hear your wheels turning. I heard. That's all, I heard."

"The sergeant."

"Mike Shea. Yeah, me and Michaeleen, we go pretty far back." Bauman looked smug. He drained the rest of his beer and said "How 'bout a couple more, Joe?"

The old man carefully poured a couple of steins, waited till the thick head of foam settled a bit, then poured in a little more. Whelan had once seen Joe Danno pour a pousse-café, a legendary drink of six layers of liqueurs, six perfect, separate stripes of color in a pony glass, a drink that had to be served with perfect symmetry, without so much as the smallest drop of one layer of color mixing in with the next. The next day Whelan told a bartender acquaintance what he'd seen. The other bartender had simply shrugged and said "Gimme a break. Nobody makes them. I don't think anybody ever did."

"Joe Danno," Whelan said. The bartender thought about it, then nodded. "Maybe Joe Danno. Maybe."

Bauman looked at him. "You gonna eat any of this?"

"Yeah. It'll hurt her feelings if I don't."

He took a slice of pizza, put a couple of drops of Joe's pepper sauce on it, and bit in. Bauman took a sip of his beer and gave him a sidelong glance.

"So, Shamus. You got anything for old Bauman? Any little old thing at all?"

"Not a thing you don't have already. You've got more than I've got."

"No surprises there."

"So tell me why you've got such a hard-on for this guy, Bauman."

Bauman chewed his pizza and looked at the rows of old

bourbon bottles and cognacs and dark rums. "We go way back, me and Mr. Gibbs. I busted him twice when I was a uniform. He was Maceo James then, small-time thief is all he was. He's done it all since then, though. He'd have a sheet as long as the fucking Nile but he's smart. Hell on partners, though. Guys he does business with are either inside or they're dead."

"Harry Palm, for instance."

"Yeah. But old Harry wasn't a partner. He was tryin' to establish himself. Do a little dealin', make a little book. We even heard Harry was fencin' a little here and there. And you see, Mr. Gibbs, he thinks he's got some prior claim to all these, uh, business ventures."

"I'm still waiting to hear what makes this guy so special."

Bauman looked down at his thick, red hands and seemed to lose himself in his train of thought. "Whacked a guy I useta use. Just a wino, street people. Fucking guy was retarded. And old Wardell Gibbs took him out. Couple years ago, this was. He's been out there a long time. Long time."

"You don't think maybe you're doing what you say I'm doing? Rearranging the facts so they'll read the way you want them to?"

"No. And besides, this guy's dirt, Whelan. Any way you look at the facts, he's dirt."

"Yeah, he is, but you're still seeing what you want to see."

"Never said I was smart, Whelan." Bauman sipped at his beer.

"But if I hear something about this guy, he's yours."

"Anything, Whelan. If you hear anything, if you find even the smallest connection between what you're doin' and this guy, I want it."

"Okay." Whelan watched him for a moment. The only noise in the bar was the music coming from an old portable tape player behind the bar, Dave Brubeck.

"You ever get the crossbow guy? That one that shot the old guy on Lower Wacker?"

Bauman snorted and shook his head. "No, but I ain't through looking yet."

• • •

When they were finished, Bauman paid and they drove back to Whelan's car in a silence broken only by Bauman's occasional but heartfelt cursing at the foibles of other drivers. Bauman pulled up alongside the Jet, waved briefly when Whelan said he'd see him later, and then laid rubber pulling out onto Clark Street. Whelan knew Bauman would be driving to another bar.

He stared down the street after Bauman and wondered what this little encounter had really been all about. A little company for a Violent Crimes detective from Area Six, that was what it was all about.

He drove north on Clark, past the ballpark, where a cluster of people in Cubs hats were standing under the great orange sign. A couple of them still carried scorecards and one had a pennant. Five hours after the game and this bunch was still staggering through the neighborhood celebrating.

Mr. Ronald Vosic had tried to get in touch with him, and the only gentlemanly thing to do was to get in touch with Ron. He drove to the steakhouse on Irving that Susan Vosic had told him about and parked across the street. It was a small place, with a separate entrance for the lounge, but it had a big, bright sign with hundreds of bulbs and a fair share of neon and the sign said RON'S. Planes coming into O'Hare could see this sign.

I see more family resemblance the more I get to know these guys, Whelan thought.

It was dark inside, and cool, and the place smelled of grilled steaks and seafood. Some people were as predictable as the sunrise, and the younger Vosic was one of them. He was there, in a cream-colored suit, tanned and blow dried, greeting people and slapping backs and ordering drinks on the house in a loud voice. He was handsome and gregarious and looked like money, and the people ate it up as they came in for dinner. Ron Vosic laughed and made jokes and winked and grinned, and when he saw Whelan his smile died a horrible death.

Vosic looked around and then came forward. He was an inch or two shorter than Whelan but a lot younger, more muscular, another young guy obsessed with his own body. He lifted weights and worked out on ingenious devices and loved what he saw in the mirror, and right now he was scared shitless.

"What's up?" he said, and showed teeth. He smelled like the perfume counter at Field's.

"Paul Whelan returning your call. Something I can do for you?"

"What? What call was that? No, I think you're mixing me up with my brother."

"No. He threatened me over lunch. I figured the phone threat was yours. I put it all down to the contrast in styles. He's more of a wheeler-dealer, you're impulsive. So…what did you want to tell me?"

"Man, I don't even—"

"Let me help. I assume it's about Janice Fairs."

Vosic bit his lip and then decided to assert himself. "Look, man, nobody's trying to put the arm on you."

Whelan laughed. "Everybody named Vosic is trying to put the arm on me. You guys are gonna have to fight a duel over me."

Ron Vosic held up his hands, palms out. "Hey, whatever trouble you got between you and Rich is none of my business. That's got nothing to do with me. I don't work for Rich. I work for me. And I just wanted to, you know, get you to drop all this shit, stay out of Jan's face, you know?"

Whelan watched Vosic's eyes. "That's all?" Whelan asked.

Vosic's manner changed completely. He nodded and allowed himself a careful smile. "Hey, look, Paul—"

"Well, I'll let go of this when I feel like letting go. And right now I think I'm in better shape than the rest of you folks. Your brother is having a baby about me sticking my nose into High Pair's old business, and Janice Fairs is putting the squeeze on him, or about to, and you're on her like a leech, which puts you in the enemy camp. Your brother finds out about you and old 'Jan' and he'll have your balls."

Ronald Vosic's mouth worked and he nodded, but no sound came out. He put his hands on his hips and posed, then looked

Whelan up and down.

"You're gonna tell my big brother on me, huh? You know something, Whelan? Lemme tell you something. He don't scare me, my hotshot brother. He don't scare me and he don't impress me."

"His grammar's better than yours."

"Yeah? Maybe so. He was the schoolboy. I learned everything I know on the streets. I didn't learn nothing from him except what mistakes not to make. He's supposed to be so smart, how come he's the one in deep shit right now, huh?"

"I never said I thought he was smart, Ron. He overreacts, for one. Doesn't have any idea who he can trust, for another thing."

Ronald Vosic went slightly red and shrugged.

"And he's got neanderthals working for him. And then, of course, there's Henley." Whelan allowed himself a smile.

Vosic shrugged again and said, "Nothing to do with me," but didn't sound at all convinced.

"Oh yeah, he does. Mr. Henley's got something to do with all of us. Especially you, now that you've joined forces with Janice Fairs. How much did she tell you about Henley? Maybe nothing, right? You have no idea what her angle is, do you?"

Vosic crossed his arms across his chest and forced another smile. "I know about Henley. Big fucking deal. He ain't anything special, Whelan. He's just a big, loud asshole thinks he's hard. And he's a fucking user, he's a cokehead. Nothing to be impressed by, Whelan." He sucked air in through his teeth and then took out a cigarette.

Whelan watched him tap the cigarette against his black leather cigarette case, light it with a thin, very elegant lighter covered in the same black leather, and then exhale with the air of a man who's got it all covered.

"That's all, huh, Ronald? That's all you know? Then she hasn't told you shit, which tells me exactly the depth of your, ah, relationship. You have a nice night, now, hear?" And he left the restaurant without looking back. He was certain that he didn't need to look to know Ronald Vosic's facial expression.

• • •

He saw the van as soon as he made the turn off Lawrence and onto his block. It was Vosic's van and there were people in it and he had a fairly good idea which people they were. They were parked across from his house and they'd seen him already. He drove past the van and parked on the other side of the street, a couple of car lengths down from them, and then sat in his car and watched the van in his side mirror. After a few seconds the door on the driver's side opened and the tall, thin one emerged. The other man came around the front of the van and they both started walking down the street toward him. The tall one was carrying a tire iron and the little one had a pipe wrench, and from the way they strode manfully, shoulder to shoulder toward him he could see that they watched a lot of westerns.

He pulled back out of the parking spot, put the Jet into reverse, floored the gas pedal, and laid rubber for forty feet as he went up Malden backward and threw pure terror into his visitors. He saw them in his mirror, frozen there openmouthed, suddenly gone lead footed and confused and cowardly. At the last moment they dove for safety, one in each direction, and he blew on by them for another thirty feet or so before stopping the car. He pulled over, got out, and walked toward them.

The small one was already up on one knee but Abe Lincoln had apparently done himself injury. He was wedged up against a parked car and holding his right leg up close to his chest, the way a child clutches his skinned knee to himself. He made long gasping sounds.

The smaller man got to his feet and hefted the pipe wrench. He hit it against his leg and advanced, and from the corner of his eye Whelan could see the tall one starting to collect his parts. When the one-armed man was just ten feet away Whelan heard the scrape of metal on pavement and saw that the tall one was up on one knee. Whelan ran over toward him and threw a left into the man's rib cage that folded him over. Whelan pushed him against the car, kicked a leg out from under him, and watched him fall to the street. The man attempted to push himself up from the street and Whelan hit him in the gut again. The air went out of him and he went into the fetal position. He dropped the tire iron on the street.

The one-armed man froze, then raised the pipe wrench and came at Whelan. Whelan picked up the tire iron and swung it two handed just as the one-armed man brought the pipe wrench down. He caught the man a glancing blow to the shoulder as the wrench struck him. He took most of the blow on his forearm but the wrench caught the top of his ear. He heard himself howl and swung the tire iron again, and this time he felt the crunch as iron found bone. The one-armed man went down in the street in a sitting position, clutching his collarbone and gasping. Whelan staggered off, holding his head.

He made it to his stairs and sat down, clutching his head in both hands. A moment later he looked up, saw that his assailants were still on the street, and got to his feet and went inside. He locked the door behind him and threw the deadbolt, then went to the kitchen for ice. He wrapped half a dozen cubes in a dish towel and put it to his ear. It felt hot to the touch and there was already swelling. He sat at the kitchen table nursing his injury for ten minutes. When he went back to look out the window, the van was gone.

When the throbbing in his ear subsided, he called Janice Fairs and was told that there was no answer. He didn't bother to leave a message. He sat at his kitchen table for a long time, smoking cigarettes and putting ice to his ear and going over what he knew about the players in this little show. He believed he wouldn't have to worry about a visit from any of Vosic's people now. He could predict that these two would report back to the boss that they'd kicked Whelan's ass and left him lying in the street. But all these encounters with Vosic's underlings were just the preliminaries. Eventually he would have an opportunity to meet Mr. Henley. *That* would be the real thing.

He sighed and went to the bathroom to study the damage. His ear stuck out from the side of his head, discolored and swollen. I have Carmen Basilio's ear.

FOURTEEN

He came out onto his porch the next morning expecting at least a hint of a breeze and was hit by sheer, motionless heat. Nine-thirty on a Sunday morning and it was already miserable, and there would be no mercy in the afternoon. He walked south to the corner and then up Wilson. At Wilson and Racine the two wounded vehicles from Friday night's action were gone, replaced by one new car, a custom-painted Camaro with mag wheels and racing stripes. The front was pushed in like a bulldog's upper lip and you could see the engine. Hell, you could probably *take* the engine without anybody making much of a fuss. The car was half in the street, half on the sidewalk. A couple of feet away was the culprit, the actual cause of the accident—a lamp post that had refused to get out of the Camaro's way. Now it leaned slightly toward the street and wore some of the Camaro's yellow paint.

In front of Truman College there was a lively discussion under way among a group of street people; they were old and sun browned and all of them looked hot, and they'd be a lot hotter before the day was over. On days like this some of the local eateries charged money for a glass of ice water, to keep the street people out.

He bought a newspaper from the Walgreen's on the corner and had breakfast at the New Yankee Grill. He ordered sausage and eggs and hash browns and coffee, made small talk with Eva the waitress, and learned that she was planning a trip to Tennessee. He caught her noticing his ear, but she said nothing. She saw a lot worse at the counter every morning. She brought him his food and left him to his breakfast and newspaper.

Whelan took a quick look at the front page and decided not

to bother; a headline said there had been seventeen shootings over the weekend, six of them fatal. A steamy weekend in a crowded town where there were too many weapons and not enough money to cover up people's troubles. Seventeen shootings so far and no reason to believe Sunday would be any better.

He put the paper down, finished his breakfast, and had a cigarette with his second cup of coffee. At the far end of the counter a short, skinny man in a filthy T-shirt and a wool cap was staring at the change in his hand and trying to make it multiply itself. The man looked up at Eva, who waited silently for him to make his decision, then back down at his change. He made a little shrug of his shoulder and took a step backward.

Whelan raised his hand, caught Eva's eye, and tapped himself on the chest. She nodded and told the man he had enough money for something. He mumbled something to her and she went away, coming back with a cup of coffee and a danish. She set it down in front of him and, as an afterthought, set a glass of ice water in front of him. Then she winked at Whelan. By the time she came out to give him his bill, the old man had gulped down all the water.

She set the bill down beside Whelan's cup and refilled it.

"Here you go, Sugar."

"Don't be calling me those names or I'll get ideas."

She smiled. She was a small-boned girl with plain features and a slight ridge to her nose that said it had been broken, but she had long, honey-blond hair and wide, youthful blue eyes.

"If I didn't have an old man already, I'd let you get ideas. You're a nice old boy. You drink?"

"What? Do I drink? Well, a little…not much, though." She nodded, winked at him, and went away, and Whelan wondered if a man who drank was the major problem in Eva's life.

He left her three bucks and then paid his bill at the register, where the owner's fat little wife was staring, as always, at a small black-and-white TV.

He took a walk east, to the lake, and walked up to Montrose Beach and out onto the breakwater. At the end of the breakwater he sat down and smoked a cigarette. He wasn't alone; you were never entirely alone on the breakwater. A few feet away from him, a ma-and-pa fishing team had four lines in the water and their gear spread out behind them, blankets and brown bags of food and a radio and a thermos. At the very end of the breakwater a lone fisherman stared into the water as if he could will the fish onto his hook. Whelan had been out on the breakwaters all along the lakefront and the experience was always the same, no matter what the neighborhood—a quarter of a mile out on the lake, the city was massive and seemed to run on forever. There was silence, broken only by the harsh honking of the gulls and the wash of water against the steel and concrete side of the breakwater. He had always believed that fishermen in Chicago, at least the ones who came down to the lake, fished largely because they were able to leave the city here, to put time and space between them and the crowded, noisy places where they lived. Many of the fishermen were elderly, many were black, most of them had no money. He stared out at the boats, at the inviting isolation of the lighthouse, at the dark green water of the big lake, and thought about his case, which now seemed to be a jumble of contradictory facts with a hole at its center. He wanted to be finished with this case, with these people and their petty jostling for power and place.

For a moment he allowed himself to feel some sympathy for Vosic and his dead partner Fairs, both taken unawares by a personality of unimaginable complexity and formidable intelligence, a man able to con everyone around him and throw up defenses and disguises at will. What he was uncomfortable about was motive.

If this man who came and went and slipped back into the shadows was indeed George Brister, why was he back? If indeed he had ever left.

He thought about Henley again, the strange color of the eyes. Contacts. He wears *contacts*. And now Whelan remembered how Henley looked at him in the bar and thought he could see something else in the eyes, something more than hostility. A challenge. He was challenging me.

• • •

Eventually he made his way home. During the course of a hot, listless Sunday he made half a dozen attempts to contact Janice Fairs. Each time he was told that there was no answer.

He called his service on a hunch and sighed as Abraham Chacko's voice fluted across the lines.

"Hello, good morning, Paul Way-Lon Investigative Services."

He sighed. Almost five o'clock and Abraham was still telling people "good morning."

"Hello, Abraham."

Abraham made a little bark of excitement. "Oh, yes, Mr. Paul. I am recognizing your voice."

That's a first, Whelan thought. To Abraham he just said, "You are an excellent answering service person, Abraham. And please accept my congratulations on your impending fatherhood."

"Yes, yes, my wife, she is going to have a baby."

"That's usually how it works. You're a lucky man. Do I have any messages?"

"Yes, you have one message. He is Mr. Richard Vosic."

"Did he leave a number?"

"He said he will call you back, sir."

"Very good, Abraham."

There were four Richard Vosics listed in the phone book but only one of them lived on the Gold Coast. He called but got no answer. On a hunch he called Rick's Roost.

A man with a hoarse voice answered. "Rick's Roost."

"Is Rich there?"

"No. Haven't seen him today. He don't come in on Sundays, usually."

"Okay." As an afterthought he asked, "How about Henley?"

There was the slightest hesitation and then the curt response. "Don't know him."

"Big guy, bad attitude, shaved head, green eyes, goatee?"

"Can't help you."

Right, he thought, and he hung up.

• • •

Over the course of the next two hours he called Vosic's home number half a dozen more times but got no answer. It was almost seven o'clock and he decided to go out and eat. On an impulse he called Pat.

She answered on the fourth ring. "Hello?"

"Hello, Pat. This is Paul Whelan."

"Oh…hi." He listened for signals, for her state of mind, for anything. He heard silence on the phone, music in the background. George Benson, it sounded like.

"I, uh, I was just going to go out for a bite to eat and I thought I'd see if you've eaten yet."

There was a hesitation. "I'm…I'm eating right now, Paul."

"Oh. Sorry to interrupt. I'll just…" He couldn't think of anything to say and began to feel irritated that she wasn't saying anything to help him out. And then it struck him: she wasn't saying anything because she couldn't. She had company.

"I have wonderful timing. I'll give you a buzz sometime during the week."

Another hesitation and then, simply, "I hope so."

"I'll be talking to you. Enjoy your evening."

After he hung up he sat there and pondered the fact that another man was spending the evening in her home, and he wondered what that meant. At the very least it meant that the other man knew her better, was more involved with her, had some sort of established relationship with her.

So what did you expect? he asked himself.

Monday broke airless and humid and there was a thin, wet film on the stairs, the sidewalk, and his car, as though the city were sweating. The sun fought through a thin, gray screen of cloud and the air smelled of rain. On the car radio he learned that there had been eight more shootings over the weekend. The weekend had also been hard on the visiting pharmacists—four had been arrested on drunk and disorderly charges, one had driven a rented car into the wall of Wrigley Field, one was missing, and another had gone off the deep end after a night of drinking and was holed up in a Baptist Church, claiming sanctuary. All he would tell police and newsmen was that he was never going back to Pittsburgh.

Whelan called Vosic as soon as he arrived at the office, got Carmen, and was told that Rich wasn't in yet. He asked her to let Vosic know he'd called. She said she would and hung up without saying good-bye or anything else.

He went out and got a cup of coffee from the little greasy spoon down the street, and when he got back, his phone was ringing.

"Paul Whelan."

"Whelan? Rich Vosic. We gotta talk." He spoke fast and there was a tension in his voice that Whelan hadn't heard there before.

"You want to take a swing at me with a tire iron like your, uh, professional staff did?"

Vosic sighed. "All right. Maybe that was…things just got out of hand. It was a bonehead play all the way."

"Your first bonehead play was to hire those two primates. Sending them to see me was the logical conclusion. You're just lucky they didn't break into my house, Vosic. Then I'd have to do something perverse to your Lotus."

Vosic muttered something and said, "Look, I said I was sorry, all right?"

"No, you didn't. You said it got out of hand. You talk like an executive, Rich. Executives never say they're sorry. They talk about 'underestimating' and 'misjudging' and things getting 'out of hand.'"

"All right, all right. I'm sorry. You happy now?"

"My ear looks like it belongs on somebody else's head."

"Yeah, huh? Well…" He could almost hear Vosic smiling into the phone at this little victory.

"So you wanted to talk to me yesterday, huh?"

Vosic sighed again. "Yeah. I, uh…we might have a little problem."

"*We?* I like your style. You send two guys after me with a tire iron and a wrench and all of a sudden we're teammates."

"Ah…they were just supposed to, you know, put a scare into you. I told 'em you needed a little convincing to quit fucking around with me. And I *still* think so. But they weren't supposed to do any major damage, Whelan. I told you, it got out of hand. And what the hell, Whelan, you got your licks in, right? You banged 'em both up pretty good, from what I heard. So it's all over now, all right?"

"You sent these two mutants to do me some damage. It'll be over when I say it's over."

"Yeah? Well, I think there's more important shit coming down. We gotta talk."

"So you said."

"Look, I know you don't like me much, but maybe you'll come out of this with something. I don't know."

"Information, maybe?"

"Yeah. And maybe, ah, something else."

"I got paid already. But I'm not through. It's not how I do things. I still have some questions—now I've got more questions than I did before."

"Okay. You got questions, I got answers. I can answer some of your questions. Let's get together."

"Talk to me."

"Over the phone? Shit. No, I'm not saying any of this over the phone. No way."

"I can come by your office."

"No, no, not here. I'll come see you."

"When?"

"Later. I got some stuff to take care of. I'll be at your office—let's say four, four fifteen. We can go get a beer someplace and talk. You won't regret it. I'll lay it all out for you. You'll have the whole thing, Whelan."

"All right. I'll see you around four."

• • • •

He hung up and sipped at his coffee and shook his head. A man who drove a Lotus and lived like Diamond Jim Brady was coming to see him at his office in scenic Uptown.

He called Janice Fairs at her hotel again and was told that she was not in. The voice on the other end told him that Mrs. Fairs had left no messages.

He put down the phone and sat there for a while thinking. He envisioned the man pouring gasoline on the deck of the boat and wondered once again how Phil Fairs had been murdered.

The autopsy.

He made a call to the morgue and talked to a man who identified himself as Investigator Morris. The investigator was an older man and garrulous, a man who enjoyed his job and had been doing it for more than thirty years. He didn't remember the Fairs investigation but was happy to look it up.

"All right, sir. What did you want to know?"

"I'm interested in the autopsy findings."

"There was no autopsy. Wasn't necessary."

Whelan said nothing for a moment. "There was no autopsy?"

"No, sir. Next of kin identified the body, cause of death was obvious. No real need for an autopsy, sir."

He thought for a moment. "But it's my understanding that this man had been in the water for a long time."

"You can identify a body by what the deceased was wearing, by his personal effects, his jewelry, his watch, and so forth. You don't always have to perform an autopsy, sir. Sometimes these things aren't so complicated."

He'd called to learn something and found something else. A new scenario began to unfold for him and he was hardly listening as the old man regaled him with tales of the eerie things pulled out of the big lake. When he hung up he remained at his desk smoking. Now he needed to know about the name.

At the library he consulted the microfilm of the Chicago papers for the first weekend of August 1982 and learned nothing to confirm or refute his new theory, only that Philip Fairs had been buried after a one-day wake at Pinewoods Cemetery in Arlington Heights.

Then he used a pay phone in the library to call the cemetery, where a young woman informed him that there was no Fairs family plot, as such. Philip Fairs had apparently purchased three gravesites, one each for himself and his wife. The third was occupied by his mother.

"And what was his mother's full name? Can you tell me that?"

"Josephine Henley Fairs," the young woman said.

There was time to kill before his meeting with Rich Vosic. He had a hamburger and a cup of coffee from a small diner down the street from the library, then drove to the lakefront. Whelan cruised Lake Shore Drive for a while and eventually headed back to town.

It was beginning to cloud up, fast, and the weather report on the radio promised a summer storm, a big one. The air was getting denser, the humidity palpable, and it wasn't getting any cooler. He hardly noticed the traffic as he drove back, feeling a giddiness rising in him, a lightheadedness tempered by the knowledge that a man had been murdered and buried under another's name. For a moment he felt a rush of sympathy for the unsuspecting alcoholic who had been brought into town, set up, and killed here.

In his mind's eye he saw the beautiful blue boat in Belmont Harbor, a great, sleek wonder of a boat, a place where a man might live. A house without an address.

He parked around the corner from the office again and then looked around for the Lotus. Instead he saw the blue van that Vosic's two henchmen had been driving on Saturday night. He approached the van carefully, coming up behind it from the passenger side. There was no passenger, only a driver, and he would tell Whelan nothing, for he was dead.

He slipped inside the passenger side and felt Vosic's neck. The skin was clammy, going cold, but Rich Vosic had not been dead for long. His face was dark and puffy and the huge red hand marks on his throat nearly covered it. He climbed out of the van and made his way back to his office, then stopped a few feet from the building. No, you're in there, he thought. Lotus or no Lotus, it would be obvious why Vosic was parked here in the middle of Uptown.

He got back into his car and drove down to the lake, up Sheridan Road, and then up Clark Street and east on Belmont and parked in the lot of the yacht club. He got out of his car a few feet from where they'd found Harry Palm's, and now he understood who Harry Palm had been coming to see.

The wind was picking up and the gray mass of rain clouds had turned into a tightly coiled cluster of thunderheads. He could smell the rain. The dark green surface of the harbor churned and heavy waves slapped against the shore and sent thick spray high into the air. The few boats that had been out on a hot, muggy Monday afternoon were heading in to beat the storm.

There were several dinghies tied to the little pier off the end of the yacht club, reserved for members going out to their yachts. He hopped the cyclone fence and lowered himself into a dinghy, then rowed out against the wind and waves to the blue yacht known as *The Score*. He was sweating when he reached it.

He tied the boat up to the cable of the yacht and then climbed up the side. He allowed himself the luxury of inspecting the boat and found nothing that surprised him. It was a floating penthouse with living quarters that would sleep six people comfortably, though there was no evidence that anyone but the man who owned the boat slept there. One bunk was unmade. He found a small, well-stocked refrigerator and a pantry with full shelves. The boat had a radio and even a small, battery-powered television. Rich man's boat, with oak and maple paneling and furniture and gleaming brass fittings.

At the foot of the bed he found a full set of weights. There was liquor in a cabinet near the pantry, bourbon and vodka and one bottle in a leather pouch that looked like Cuban rum. He lifted it and felt no movement of liquor inside. He peeled the leather pouch down halfway and saw that the bottle was filled with white powder. He tipped it over and tasted it, and it was exactly what he expected.

There were no books on the boat. The man on this boat didn't read. He lifted his weights and drank and did a couple of lines a night and planned murder. He lived on the lake and felt he was outside the law, somehow beyond it.

He made a circuit of the deck. In front of the cabin there was a heavy blue tarp folded haphazardly on the deck. Whelan stared at it and saw the outline of what it covered. He felt the breath leave him. Reluctantly he pulled back one corner of the tarp and saw the frosted brown hair, the dead skin, the dark marks on the throat, the staring eyes. Janice Fairs had found what she was looking for.

Whelan looked again at the body and knew he should leave this boat, leave it now.

He went across the deck and leaned against the railing and watched the lake and the traffic on Lake Shore Drive. There were bikers speeding by on the bike paths and a couple of joggers trying to beat the rain, and out on the great green hook of land that created the harbor he could see a group of young Latin kids packing in a barbecue and running off to their cars. There were hundreds of people in the immediate vicinity and thousands more speeding by on the drive, but he knew he would be alone in the harbor in a few moments.

The dense clouds hung low overhead and made night seem imminent. A pair of young women rode by on ten-speeds and Whelan watched them for a moment. When they left his line of vision he looked back along the benches and saw the solid figure in white that had not been there a moment ago.

He followed me. Whelan felt the breath go out of him.

Fifty feet away Henley leaned against the cyclone fence surrounding the harbor and stared out at Whelan. He was smoking something dark and blowing smoke out against the wind. Whelan folded his arms across his chest and stared back.

Finally Henley tossed the cigar out into the water and moved back toward the yacht club. He emerged a moment later from a doorway and got into a dinghy, then rowed briskly out toward the yacht, as though the wind were no hindrance. He looked over his shoulder at Whelan every three or four strokes. Whelan watched him riding the waves and waited. There was nothing else to be done.

He watched as Henley tied the dinghy next to the one Whelan had used. Whelan looked around. A few feet away but up a short flight of steps was a fire ax. He'd never get there in time to get it out. Closer to hand at the foot of the stairway was a small wooden stool—not much, but better than nothing at all.

He heard the soft, firm footsteps coming up the side of the boat and realized that he was holding his breath. He let it all out and took out a cigarette. He bent down against the wall of the cabin, lit it, and inhaled just as the smooth head appeared over the side of the yacht.

The big man paused for a second, looked at Whelan, and smiled with his eyes. Then he vaulted his big body over the side rail and onto the deck. He put his hands on his hips and sniffed a couple of times, then brought out a handkerchief and held it to his nose, watching Whelan. Up close he looked bigger and quicker, his taste for violence almost palpable.

"Philip Fairs, I presume."

The big man nodded slowly and the smile took hold of his face. "That's right, friend. Philip Fairs. At your service."

Whelan puffed at his cigarette and took his time blowing out the smoke. It was important to seem as calm as possible now, keep him thinking.

"Got something for you, Mr. Fairs. And I think you have something for me."

Fairs blinked and hesitated, just for a second. "Oh? And what would you have for me?"

"Your partner was a talkative man. I have things for sale."

Fairs stared for a moment. "Like what? Gimme a for instance."

"You want to talk dollars first? You think this is free?"

"I figured you'd want to start talking dollars. I saw you come out, Whelan. Why else would you come see me alone?" Fairs wiped his nose again and sniffed. "Hay fever," he said, holding up the handkerchief.

"If I put as much shit up my nose as you do, I'd tell people it was hay fever."

Something hard came into the unearthly green eyes. Whelan shook his head. "I should have known about the contacts. A heavy, bald man like George Brister would have to do a lot more than change his eye color if he wanted to escape notice, but a man completely changing his appearance—shaving his head, growing a beard, changing the whole look—that guy would change his eye color."

Fairs took a step closer and then moved slightly to his left, cutting off the clearest escape route. He smiled.

"So you thought I was Brister, huh? Thought you were tailing George Brister. Brister was just a fat slob, no muscle on him. He was a physical wreck." Fairs rocked back on his heels and studied Whelan. "You're a smart boy, huh? Rich told me you were pretty clever, but old Rich was no Einstein. Well, maybe you are smart. I like smart people, I can always use smart people." He grinned and jabbed a thumb at his chest. "I'm smart, Whelan." He tucked his thumbs into his pants pockets. "So what's this gonna cost me?" He moved a half step closer and his eyes never left Whelan's.

Whelan took a puff at his cigarette, looked at it for a second as though something were wrong with it, and shook his head. "Thinking you were Brister, that wasn't the real problem. Thinking this was all about *money*, that was my mistake. It was never about money, was it?"

Fairs shrugged. "Fuck, no. Money's nothing, man. I've made and lost more money in one year than you'd make in your whole life. I had an idea and I fucking pulled it off. I changed my whole life. I dropped out of one life and started a new one, and nobody even caught on."

"Except your partner. Would have been a little too complicated, taking him out, too. Right?"

"Yeah, but that's not why. He was useful. I went underground, he got to keep the company. He took a real light fall, old Rich, and basically people figured he was a hard-luck guy with a crazy partner who killed himself and an accountant who played with the numbers till everything was gone. He was happy I was gone, don't kid yourself. He never cared much for being the two horse. And this way he could hang onto some of the money for me. And there was a lot of money, man."

"Why come back?"

"To prove I could. And to get a little of my bread."

"Why'd you start doing business with Harry Palm again?"

Fairs grinned and held out his hands. Then he held his finger to his nose and gave an exaggerated snort.

"Hey, I needed a little. A guy needs his recreation. He didn't know who the fuck I was. He didn't know anything about me. I never even used my real name when I made book with him before. I ran into him in a saloon on Rush one night. He didn't seem to know much, so I told him I just left town because of some people I owed. He understood that kind of problem, old Harry did." Fairs allowed himself a smile. "No reason why we couldn't do a little business, now that I was back—put a few bucks down on a ball game or a horse, buy a little blow."

"And when your wife came digging around to get something on Rich, Harry made you. He thought his ship had come in."

"Stupid fucker. He really was. He still wasn't sure what was going on. And her. Shit, she was the real thing I was leaving. That life."

"Married her for her money in the first place, didn't you? And then her old man got nasty."

"That old asshole. I should've taken him out when I left."

"What's it like to start a completely new life?"

"Beautiful. It's beautiful. It's the only complete freedom, the only pure freedom there is. I took off and got a boat and I been going from coast to coast, man. The Gulf, Mexico, Central America. Couple more days I think I'm gonna try South America. I can go where I want and do what I want, and the whole world thinks I'm dead."

"George Brister was a piece of luck, huh?"

Now Fairs moved closer and the smile fled. "Luck had nothing to do with it. I knew a loser when I saw one. If it wasn't him, it would have been somebody else. I had this planned for more than a year, before I even met Brister. I brought him in, set it all up, set him down right in the middle of it, and took him out again."

"Why not? He was disposable, right?"

"Yeah, that's right. He was." He was five feet away now, speaking through his teeth, and his face was flushed.

"How'd you get off the boat? No, let me try: you started the fire below deck, slid into the water, swam into the harbor..."

Fairs shook his head. "To the breakwater. I swam *out*." He smiled.

"And when the boat went up, every eye was on the fire. You had witnesses that saw you start it, saw it go up. And Brister was below, dead already."

The rain started and Whelan could see the drops streaming down Fairs's bald head.

"I still say a lot of it was luck. Brister's corpse was too far gone from the fire and the water to be recognized. You put your clothes on him and your wedding ring and counted on the coast guard pulling out a thing with no face. And you counted on your wife to identify the body as yours so they wouldn't have to look too closely at it. I talked to somebody at the morgue. It was just luck, Fairs. They don't have to do an autopsy if cause of death is obvious and the next of kin identifies the body."

"No, no luck. I planned it all out and pulled it off and every single step of it went perfect. I'm the smartest man you ever met in your life, Whelan."

"You're not nearly as smart as you think, Fairs. You're starting to screw up left and right. You made old Rich nervous. He probably wanted you out of his life, so you killed him in broad daylight."

"No, you made him nervous, Whelan, with your bullshit about Brister. I just had to clean it up."

"And then there's your wife. Came out here to see you,

did she? In her icy way, she probably scared the shit out of you, Fairs."

Fairs looked past Whelan to where the woman's corpse lay beneath the tarp. He raised his eyebrows. "Found her, huh? She put it together, came out here, and got in my face and thought she was going to get off this boat in one piece and go to the cops. What a broad."

"She didn't 'put it together,' Fairs. I think she had an idea all along. I think she was smarter than you."

Fairs stared at him and then he was moving quickly toward Whelan. Whelan flicked the cigarette into his eye, then reached around behind and got his hand on the wooden stool. Fairs covered his eye and took a step back but went right back on the offensive. He was bringing up a big left hook when the stool came down on the bare dome of his head. Even so, the punch landed, catching Whelan above the eye.

Whelan sagged back, felt his legs starting to go, and swung the stool again. This time he caught Fairs full in the face. He felt blood spray him and lurched back toward the cabin wall. Whelan sidestepped and looked around for something better to fight with.

Fairs staggered for a moment, put his hand to his nose, and glanced at his bloody fingers. Then he lowered his head and came straight ahead. He swung wildly, certain that he'd land one of those heavy hands, and Whelan backed off, swinging the stool. He stumbled over a coil of rope and started to go down, and the bigger man leapt toward him, making growling sounds as he came.

Whelan took a punch high on his cheekbone and fell onto the deck. He rolled as soon as his back struck wood and he felt Fairs's fingernails scoring his back. He jumped to his feet and ran to the far railing of the yacht, then looked back. Fairs was on his feet and running, and Whelan knew he couldn't stop him this time. He climbed over the railing and dove in.

He went down and felt a moment of panic as seaweed tugged at his legs. The water sucked one of his shoes off and he flailed and kicked to come up. Then he broke through the surface, took in a great lungful of air, and began churning to shore. It was raining heavily now and the rain dug up little spouts all around him. The harbor was a roiling mass of waves, and they slapped at him and tossed him and for a moment he thought he'd go under. The water smelled of spent gasoline and fish and tasted vile in his mouth, and his clothes weighed him down. When he chanced a look at the boat, Fairs was still there, leaning against the railing, blood staining his shirt. Twenty yards away he could see the green eyes following him.

He was ten yards from the little sandbar where they'd dug up Harry Palm when he heard the boat's big engines start up. His heart was near bursting. He could feel the rain pelting him and in the background he could hear Fairs screaming curses at him. He flailed wildly toward shore and then felt solid ground beneath his feet, stumbled up onto the sand, gasping, and collapsed there. He turned and saw *The Score* going out into the harbor in reverse and relief washed over him. Fairs was at the helm and as Whelan staggered to his feet, Fairs turned and held up one hand and gave him the finger. Whelan could still hear him shouting.

He climbed up over the cyclone fence and walked through the sheets of rain to a pay phone near the bridle path. He wasn't able to reach Bauman but the dispatcher said he'd send a patrol car and get word to Bauman.

Whelan hung up, walked slowly over to a bench, and sat down. He felt for his cigarettes and realized there wouldn't be much left of them. He pulled out the soaked pack, fingered around inside and felt the soggy, shredded cigarettes, and gave it up. A few minutes later a squad car arrived and pulled up onto the sidewalk. The two uniforms inside were just climbing out when the gray Caprice showed up.

The older of the two police officers looked at him, squinting through the rain. "You made the call?"

Whelan nodded. He pointed behind the officer, toward the gray Caprice. "I called him, too."

Bauman was prying his heavy body from the Caprice and he seemed to be mumbling, and the police officer laughed. "You called Bauman? What, you like to live dangerously? Don't you know he hates rain?"

Whelan sighed. "Okay, so none of us are having a good day."

The heavy rain drops made a slapping sound on his wet body and it was now coming down so heavily that it stung. He put his face in his hands and sighed, and when he looked up, Bauman was standing in front of him, trying to get a mustard-colored sport coat up over his head.

"I hate fucking rain," he said.

"It figures," Whelan answered.

"So what's this about, Whelan? What happened to you? Where's your shoe? You go chasing after the smelt, Whelan?"

"No. I was talking to the guy who killed Harry Palm. He didn't like me, so I had to get off his boat."

Bauman stared at him for what seemed like minutes. Then he looked out at the boats in the harbor. "That the one that was taking off when we drove up?"

"Right."

Bauman looked at Whelan for a moment and then looked away. "That the guy you been lookin' for?"

"Yeah."

Bauman half turned and squinted into the face of the wind and gave an irritated shake of his head.

"He ain't going nowheres in this shit. There's small-craft warnings out all over the lake. He'll be back, Whelan."

Whelan watched the dark, churning surface of the lake and shook his head. "No, I don't think so. He's on his way out. You want this one, Bauman, get on the horn and get harbor patrol or the coast guard."

"They won't come out in this," one of the uniforms said. "They're not stupid."

"Then we're not going to get the chance to talk to this fella," Whelan said. He held his arms around him and shivered in the wind.

As they watched the storm take on force, a long, elegant sailboat eighty yards offshore pitched over. On the far side of the harbor the waves took a pair of sailboats moored close to each other and smashed them against the concrete arms of the mooring. From around the long hook of the harbor a small motorboat came in and they could see the two people on board hunched down against the wind. They made for the nearest part of the harbor wall and tried to anchor as the waves slapped the little boat against the wall. One of the men fell over and seemed to be in danger of drowning till the other tossed him a life preserver.

"He goes straight out in this, Whelan, he's dead." Bauman punctuated his opinion with a nod.

"Yeah, I think so." Whelan said. "This time."

He looked up at the heavyset detective staring out over the lake. Bauman's knit shirt was soaked through now, his graying hair plastered down. He made a little shake of his head. He studied Whelan for a moment.

"You all right?"

"I'm fine."

"You don't look fine. You look like something big did the samba on you. Lookit your ear. Looks like fucking radar."

"Sit down and I'll give you what I have."

Bauman spun around, hands on his hips. "No, I ain't gonna sit down, Whelan, I don't sit in the fucking rain." He looked at the two uniformed officers.

"Bring him over to Six, arright? And drop by his house and let him get a dry shirt." He gestured toward Whelan's wet *guayabera*. "He's got about forty of them Mexican things. He ever has to leave the country, he's all set."

Whelan got to his feet and looked at Bauman's mustard-colored knit shirt.

"Don't go down to Mexico in that, Bauman. In Mexico they shoot things that color."

On Tuesday he gave himself the morning off. His ear was still not back to its original size, and his cheek was bruised and swollen from the fight with Fairs and there were long, red marks down his back from Fairs's nails.

He lay in bed for a long time, listening to music, then went out and walked down to Lawrence to get a paper from the box on the corner. He returned to his house and ran a large tub of very hot water, then climbed in with the paper and a cup of coffee.

The pharmacists were gone, finally, all of them. The drunk in the church had been talked out of his refuge and into returning to Pittsburgh. It was not clear why he had sought sanctuary or even whether there was still such a thing as sanctuary. The missing pharmacist was located in Lincoln Park, where he had apparently been locked in the Small Mammals House.

Most of the news, however, was about the storm that had struck Monday evening and taught the city that the lake still ran things on occasion. Winds upward of eighty miles per hour had taken out hundreds of windows, blown signs off businesses, and knocked people over in the streets, causing injury to many; the winds had uprooted trees and torn down fencing and the great gold cross atop Holy Name Cathedral had been pulled nearly off the spire. On the Kennedy a semi had been overturned by the sheer force of the storm and a driver with a few snorts in him claimed to have been forced by the winds into a utility pole. But the worst of the damage had occurred along the lakefront, and after reading about it for a few minutes Whelan decided it was worth a look.

He drove down Belmont to the lake and pulled into the parking lot of the yacht club. The harbor was already busy with boat owners and park district workers trying to undo what the storm had done, but they hadn't made a dent in it yet.

Leaning against the cyclone fence, Whelan counted fourteen boats either capsized or sunk. The stern of a big sailboat stuck ten feet out into the air, its bow imbedded in the soft harbor bottom. A few boats were simply lying in the water on their sides, and crews were working on these first, just to be able to say they'd achieved something. The harbor was strewn with bits of wreckage, large and small, and a little farther down toward Addison Whelan could see a spot where the storm had thrown two big yachts against one another, staving in their sides.

"Think this is bad? You should see Monroe Harbor. A lot more boats there."

Whelan turned to see a man in his sixties or seventies looking at him. The man nodded and Whelan smiled. "Haven't been down there yet."

"Worse than this, even. Lots more boats, lot of small ones, so there's lots more down in the water." There was a trace of a smile on the old man's face and his eyes, magnified by his glasses, were wide with wonder.

"I've never seen anything like this," Whelan said.

The smile took wings. "I have." The old man nodded. "I have. Only the boats were a lot bigger."

Whelan looked at him. "The war?"

"Pearl." The old man winked and nodded. "Pearl," he said again, the single syllable understandable to anyone who had been alive at the time.

"This must seem pretty minor to you, then."

"No. Always seems kinda sad to see a boat down in the water, no matter how big the boat is. Like a lot of people went to so much trouble, and something just wrecked it all. Like it wasn't such a big deal."

The man said nothing more, and Whelan could see he was staring out at the lake and seeing something far different. Whelan watched the lake and wondered when it would give back the body of Phil Fairs.

EPILOGUE

They found Fairs on Wednesday, washed up along the rocks between Montrose and Foster beaches. It was unclear whether he had drowned or died from his injuries, which appeared to be significant. This time there was no doubt; this time the body didn't have time to bloat and disintegrate in the warmest lake water of the year, and this time there was no one changing the clothing on the corpse before it went into the water.

This time they played it by the numbers—fingerprints and dental records proved beyond any doubt that the body was that of Philip Fairs.

A day later they found the body of Janice Fairs. She was still tightly wrapped in the tarp, so that her body was relatively undisturbed.

The storm had cooled the city off—for exactly twenty-four hours. The heat had returned, the wind was gone, and the whole town turned to tinder. He was bored and listless and found himself thinking more and more about the woman named Pat. He put off calling, and he recognized why. It would take an effort for him to start a relationship, to work at it, and he wasn't sure he could do it. And the knowledge that there was another man in her life, that Whelan might come in second in a two-horse race, made it complicated.

I'm too old for this.

He heard himself thinking and then heard himself answer, Jesus, Whelan, you're only forty.

• • •

He was walking up Broadway with a cup of coffee and a newspaper, heading toward the office to go through the motions of work. He had just passed under the El tracks and was crossing Leland, within a few yards of the place where his friend Artie Shears had been killed a year earlier.

When he was in the middle of the street, a car made a fast turn off Broadway and came to a tire-squealing stop a couple of feet from him. He froze and then spun around to say something to the driver.

Bauman leaned out the window on the driver's side. His round face was red and sweating and he was heaving with laughter.

"Why dontcha watch where you're going, there, Snoop? You wanta live to collect that pension?" Bauman chuckled and looked at Landini. The younger man sat in the passenger seat and looked with mild amusement at his partner, then regarded Whelan with a look Whelan couldn't decipher.

Bauman put a cigar into his mouth. Another motorist turned onto Leland and hit his horn. Bauman waved his arm irritably.

"So go around!" He stared at the driver as he passed, then looked back at Whelan. He tilted his big, square head to one side and made a show of examining Whelan's injuries. "Hey, most of your owies are gone. You see they found your buddy, Whelan?"

"Yeah. I saw."

"So how come you're not happy? That was a nice piece of work. Even Landini here thinks you're smart now. They're gonna give you the keys to the city."

"I doubt it."

Bauman's smile faded. "You don't look so good, Whelan."

"I'll live."

"You need some cheering up, huh? Okay." For a second he thought Bauman was going to say something friendly, and then he saw the gleam in the detective's eyes. "You're always telling me about restaurants. I got one for you. The new joint up the street here. Been there yet?"

"No. I passed by there a couple times but it wasn't open."

Bauman grinned. "It's open now. Nice place, Whelan. You'll

like it. I guarantee it."

"Come on, Bauman. How good can a Greek place be that calls itself House of Zeus?"

"Oh, it can be pretty special. Remember, you heard it here first, Shamus."

Whelan watched the gray Caprice drive off and he went up Broadway, then walked past Lawrence and his office to have a look at the new eatery.

It wasn't much to look at—a double storefront with a primitive sign overhead that simply said HOUSE OF ZEUS in large, uneven white letters against a sky blue background. The windows were littered with white letters proclaiming the presence of GREEK AND ALSO MIDDLE EASTERN FOOD and, in smaller letters, HAMBURGERS.

There was a primitive quality to the sign and the lettering in the window, a cave-painting quality to the awkward attempt to draw a Greek temple. Standing in front of the temple was either a Greek warrior or a cheerleader with a punk hairdo. Still, Whelan had seen his share of unprepossessing, even ugly restaurants that turned out to be little treasures of ethnic or down-home food, and he wasn't about to rule out the House of Zeus because it was homely.

The sign on the door said OPEN, and he did. A pair of black men sat in a booth along one wall and drank Cokes and shared a large basket of Greek fries. There were two dozen tables and half a dozen booths, and the walls and ceiling were painted a dark blue. There were fake swords and shields on the walls and imitation brass light fixtures attempting to look like candles, and there was a man standing behind a short, dark counter, and this man was grinning at Whelan.

"Hello, Detective," the man said, and Whelan looked at him. He stared at the man behind the counter, a dark, slender man with a great mop of thick black hair and a mouthful of gleaming white teeth, and as he stared, the man's body began to shake with laughter. He shut his eyes with mirth and laughed and nodded, and when he could speak again, he nodded again.

"Yes, yes, it's me. It is me, your old friend."

Whelan looked at him for a moment and then smiled. "Hello, Rashid."

"Hello, my friend." And Rashid began to giggle.

The kitchen door opened and another man came out, this one bigger and heavier than the first, a round-faced man whose longish dark hair billowed out from beneath his paper chef's hat.

Whelan stared at him and said, "And hello, Gus." Rashid's cousin Gholam smiled.

"Hello, Detective."

"Nice hat."

Gholam pointed to the hat. "Now I am the chef."

"Bah. He is for sure no chef, this one," Rashid said.

Gus snorted. "Who is the chef, then, you? Who is cooking the food?" He looked at Whelan and jabbed a thumb at himself. "I am the one cooking this food."

"What happened to California? You got tired of the sunshine and all the girls?"

Gholam turned slowly and looked at his cousin. There was manslaughter cooking here.

"Yes, ask this one what happen with California. Ask him, the poisoner."

Whelan smiled. "Did you actually poison somebody, Rashid?"

Rashid put his hands on his hips and shook his head slowly, an aggrieved Iranian. He looked up at Whelan and held out his hands. "I poisoned nobody. There was no poison, just... just unfortunate problem. Unfortunate problem, this was the whole thing."

"Old food, that was whole thing. I say 'Throw it away,' you say 'No, we can use him in something else, like the Chinese people.'"

Rashid gave Whelan an embarrassed look. "Recycling," he said. "In California, everything is recycled."

"We don't recycle our food much, Rashid. You, uh, run certain risks there." Whelan looked from one to the other and laughed. "So now you're back in town and you're Greek."

Rashid and Gholam looked at each other and burst out

laughing, a couple of Middle Eastern sharpies having a good day.

"Yes," Rashid said. "And now we're Greek."

"And what's on the menu this time?" Whelan asked.

Rashid wiggled his thick eyebrows and grinned. "Shalimar kebab, falafel, shish kebab, gyros, hamburger, cheeseburger, french fries, grilled cheese, pizza puffs." He grinned again.

"Onion rings?"

"Sure."

Whelan nodded. "That's the same menu. That's exactly the same menu as the A and W."

"Only now, it's Greek!" Rashid looked at his cousin and they laughed again.

"The streets are paved with gold, guys."

"Yes, yes, paved with gold," Gholam said.

And Rashid said, "You bet."

Whelan looked around at the bargain basement attempt at decoration and at the two con artists who had been run out of California for peddling salmonella and thought of a certain woman who might appreciate the House of Zeus, and decided it wasn't such a bad day after all.

"Okay, guys. Make me lunch."

DEATH IN UPTOWN

A killer terrorizes Chicago's diverse Uptown neighborhood. Private investigator Paul Whelan's specialty is tracking down missing persons, but when his good friend is found slain in an alley, Whelan is steered down a path of violence as he searches for answers.

His investigation is interrupted by the arrival of an attractive young woman, Jean Agee, who is on her own search for her missing brother. But as clues lead Whelan to believe the two cases may be connected, the body count rises quickly, and he finds himself racing to catch a killer before he strikes again.

THE MAXWELL STREET BLUES

Chicago private eye Paul Whelan is hired by an elderly jazz musician to find a missing street hustler named Sam Burwell. As Whelan delves into Burwell's past, the world of street vendors and corner musicians, he uncovers old enmities and love affairs, but his search for Burwell comes up empty. That is, until Burwell is found murdered.

Soon Whelan is swept up into a whirlwind of old feuds, dark pasts, unlikely romances...and a killer hiding in plain sight.

KILLER ON ARGYLE STREET

Chicago Private Investigator Paul Whelan takes the case when an elderly woman asks him to look into the disappearance of Tony Blanchard, a young man she'd taken in after his parents died. Instead, Whelan discovers a string of murders, all tied to a car-theft ring.

All the evidence suggests that Tony is dead as well, but Whelan keeps digging until he finds himself surrounded by a dangerous maze of silent witnesses, crooked cops, and people willing to kill to keep the truth from surfacing. When a friend from Whelan's past emerges—a friend Whelan thought long dead—his investigation takes a dangerous turn; one that brings him no closer to Tony, and a lot closer to his own demise.

THE RIVERVIEW MURDERS

Margaret O'Mara's brother disappeared thirty years earlier, so when his last known associate is found murdered, O'Mara hires Chicago PI Paul Whelan to investigate.

Whelan makes the rounds through seedy bar and dilapidated apartment buildings where he discovers connections to a long-gone Chicago amusement park where another murder took place forty years prior.

Soon, Whelan finds himself navigating his way through dark pasts, deep secrets, and a mystery that may cost him his life.